# LIMONCELLO YELLOW

(FRANKI AMATO MYSTERIES BOOK 1)

## TRACI ANDRIGHETTI

Limoncello
Press

LIMONCELLO YELLOW

by

TRACI ANDRIGHETTI

\*\*\*

*Grazie, Graham. The best is yet to come.*

*Grazie, Graham. The best is yet to come.*

# 1

"This place makes the Bates Motel look like a freakin' spa resort." My sarcastic quip wasn't intended for my partner, Officer Stan Stubbs. It was for me. Because I was shaking so badly from the cold and fear that I was afraid the gun in my holster would fire on its own. I longed for the cozy fire and protective embrace of my boyfriend that I'd felt as we'd exchanged Christmas presents just hours before.

"Folks, you need to go back to your rooms immediately," Stan announced to the crowd of curious motel guests.

The onlookers began to disperse, and the woman in room six moaned again. According to 911 dispatch, she had been in distress for at least half an hour.

I shivered and wondered what kind of psycho had harmed the woman.

Stan drew his gun. "Something about this doesn't feel like a regular domestic abuse situation. We need urgent backup, Franki."

I nodded and grabbed the radio from my belt. "I have a 10-39 at the Twilight Motel on Manor Road. Request backup."

Stan began his approach to room six.

I put the device away and drew my gun. I took my place on the opposite side of the door from Stan.

"I'm goin' in on the count of three." He used his dire tone to match the circumstances. "I need to get to the john, and quick like."

I gasped. "*Now*, Stan?"

Stan was my partner on the Austin PD. As a rookie on the force, I'd been paired with a seasoned veteran of the department. Even though we'd spent the past six months together, I'd learned little from Stan except that he had a "wifey" named Juanita who worshipped the ground he walked on, he valued his handgun collection more than he did his adult children, and he suffered from acute, chronic gastrointestinal distress. And despite his self-proclaimed "legendary instinct" for cracking cases, he was perpetually baffled by his stomach issues even though the culprit was clear—a steady diet of jelly donuts and chorizo-bean-and-cheese breakfast tacos that he washed down with a gallon or so of coffee and Gatorade because he was also chronically dehydrated from the diarrhea. Needless to say, he spent the better part of every shift visiting the nearest men's room.

Ignoring my concern, Stan grasped his gun with both hands and slammed his right shoulder into the door. It flew open, and he stormed into the room. "Police! Hands in the air!"

I rushed in behind him, my gun drawn, and the woman let out a hair-raising scream.

"What in the hell?" Stan shouted.

I followed his gaze to the bed, and a chill went through my body.

Stan snorted. "Why, it's just a couple goin' at it."

I blinked hard. *Was it my imagination playing tricks on me at 4:30 a.m., or was one member of that couple horribly familiar? As in, exchanging-gifts-by-a-cozy-fire familiar?*

"Vince?" My voice was barely above a whisper as I stared at my boyfriend of over two years.

He looked at me like a deer caught in the headlights. "Franki?"

Make that, like a cheating rat caught in the act.

Stan looked from Vince to me. "You two know each other?"

I nodded, unable to speak. The chill that I'd felt had turned to a dull aching pain, and all I wanted to do was run from the room and cry. But I couldn't because I was on duty.

"I'll let you take it from here." Stan rushed into the bathroom and slammed the door.

No sooner had he left than the woman leapt from the bed—all 6' 5" or so of her—wearing nothing but her outrage. "Zis invazion iz illegal in *Deutschland*."

"All right, Franki." Vince's tone was patronizing. "No crime has been committed, so why don't you put the gun down? Then we can all talk about this like rational adults."

*No crime? Rational adults?* The dull pain turned to red-hot anger. Before I could think it through, I shouted, "If you think for one minute that I'm going to sit down to chat with you and your German whore here—"

The furious *fräulein* kicked the gun from my hand, and I watched in what seemed like slow motion as it flew under the bed.

"Be careful, Franki," Vince warned. "She's here from Munich on a semi-pro wrestling tour."

"Oh, so *now* you're worried about my well-being?" I backed away from the German giantess. Now that I'd mentioned it, I was a little worried about me too. She was squatting down low with her hands raised, like she was going to make mincemeat of me.

"For you, ze 'tilt-a-whirl slam.'" She lunged for my waist.

From over her shoulder, I saw Vince leap from the bed to

tackle her. Without even so much as a glance over her shoulder, she laid him out cold with an elbow to the jaw.

"Ze 'discus elbow shmash,'" she explained, raising her chin and jutting out her King Kong-like chest.

It was clear that the crazed Kraut was a force to be reckoned with. Unfortunately for me, she was refusing to recognize that *I* was a force to be reckoned with too—a member of the *police* force. Before I knew what was happening, she had heaved all 5' 10" and 170 pounds of me over her right shoulder and begun to spin. Then she let go.

I landed on the floor with a thud and desperately tried to remember what the police academy had taught me to do in such situations. But the truth was that the trainers hadn't covered how to extricate oneself from a female German wrestler with a serious case of roid rage.

"*Und* now ze 'fist drop.'" She fell onto me while driving her fist into my belly.

I writhed on the ground in agony, gasping for breath. Then I saw the Munich Monster rise up from the floor like Godzilla from the sea. Clutching my stomach, I scrambled to my feet and did my best to mimic her sparring moves.

I dodged another lunge and glanced in the direction of the bathroom. "I really need you out here, Stan."

"Just another minute." I heard the toilet flush.

I had to reason with the raging wrestler. "Listen, Greta or Helga or whatever your name is—"

"*Mein* name is Petra. Petra ze Pretzelmaker." Her face contorted with rage as the veins bulged from her thick, manly neck. "It iz not *whore*."

"Well, whoever you are," I wheezed, "you're under arrest."

"*Nein. You* are under arrest. Prepare for ze 'body avalanche.'" She flew through the air, knocked me flat on my back, and pinned me beneath her hulking frame.

Trying to protect my stomach from another fist drop, I rolled over just as she introduced a "hair pull" move that jerked me backward into an upward facing dog position.

With my gaze locked on the ceiling, I frantically tried to visualize what a good cop would do in a situation she hadn't been trained for when her partner's in the bathroom and she'd already called for backup, but nothing was coming to me. In the meantime, Petra, as her wrestling named implied, was twisting me into a pretzel. I had to buy time until backup arrived, or she was going to turn me into *spaetzle*.

"Petra, you need to release me. In the U.S., assaulting a police officer is a felony offense. You could go to prison for a long time."

To my relief, she abruptly let go of my hair. But as I fell forward, she used her brawn to lift me into the air by my belt loops and sling me over her shoulder yet again. I heard the distinct sound of the seat of my uniform pants splitting.

*Wunderbar*, I thought as I remembered that I'd gone commando that day for lack of clean underwear.

"*Und* now I shpank."

"Don't you dare."

The full force of her giant paw came down on my bare behind.

I mentally swore at the backup team for taking so long to arrive, and I cursed my pants for splitting. I'd spent years avoiding my large butt, both visually and mentally. Since it was behind me, I'd never had to look at it or think about it. Ever. And that had been my strategy—until then.

I heard a wet smacking sound as her palm struck my bottom for the second time. My eyes filled with angry tears.

The toilet flushed again.

"I'm coming, Franki." Stan rushed from the bathroom,

fumbling with the buckle on his oversized pants. He drew his gun and aimed it at Petra. "Freeze! You're under arrest!"

Petra stopped in mid-spank, leaving my bare bottom directly under the glow of the only light in the dim room.

"Drop the officer, boy," Stan commanded.

To my chagrin, Petra promptly did as she was told, and I hit the floor with the full force of my weight on my right knee. I was almost positive that it was either dislocated or broken.

Stan waved the gun at Petra. "Now lie down on your belly real slow-like, son, and put your hands behind your back."

I rolled onto my back and clutched my knee. "She's the female, Stan. Vince is unconscious on the other side of the bed."

He sauntered over to Petra and squinted at her in the soft light. "Well I'll be damned."

After he cuffed the then astonishingly docile *Deutschländer* and pulled her to her feet, he whistled in amazement. "You're a real nutcracker, aren't ya?"

Despite my loathing for the woman, I rolled my eyes at Stan's remark. The guy had no filter.

I looked on angrily as he led the placid Petra out the door to the squad car, protecting her head with his right hand as he helped her into the backseat with the other.

From the corner of my eye, I noticed that Vince was regaining consciousness across the room. If I could have walked or even crawled to his side, I would've knocked him out again.

Vince sat up and rubbed his jaw where he'd been elbowed. "Are you okay, babe?"

I stared at him in disbelief. "You mean after finding you in bed with a woman who just tried to kill me? Yeah, Vince. Doin' great."

"I can explain..."

"That's classic." I turned my head to hide my tears. "Do us both a favor and shut your mouth."

Stan popped his head into the room. "Uh, Vince, can I talk to you outside for a minute?"

Vince nodded and followed Stan out the door. I couldn't hear what they were saying, but I would have sworn that I heard them chuckle. I watched furious as they solidified their male bonding moment over a handshake before Vince got into his car and drove away.

Stan reentered the room, and he nonchalantly pulled out his report pad and started to write.

I looked at him from my supine position on the floor. "Um, Stan? Do you think maybe you could help me up? Since I'm injured?"

"Huh? Oh sure. One sec." He finished writing his sentence and ambled over to me. He put his hands on his hips. "You looked pretty funny hanging upside down over Suzy Schwarzenegger's shoulder. Did you know your butt was showin'?"

"Yeah, thanks," I replied through clenched teeth. I was forever on the receiving end of his asinine comments.

"Sure, Franki. That's what partners are for."

I snorted. Since starting this job, Stan had been about as helpful to me as a ball and chain around my ankle and a noose around my neck. I had watched in frustration as the other rookies flourished under the watchful eyes of their respective partners while I had languished under the disinterested gaze of mine. And when I'd finally gotten up the nerve to privately request a new partner, I'd been publicly branded as a trouble-maker and earned the nickname "Finicky Franki," as though I were a petulant child or, even worse, a cat.

Stan helped me off the ground, and he let out a loud, greasy fart. "Hooo! That felt goooood."

I closed my eyes—and my nostrils—and promised myself that I would learn how to meditate.

"You know, I've really got to see somebody about my stomach," he said for what must have been the hundredth time since I had met him. "I think I might have some kind of problem, but I don't know why. Hell, I'm in the best shape of my life."

Stan patted his spare tire belly as he walked—and I hopped, unassisted—to the squad car.

As soon as he climbed into the seat, he emitted three resounding sausage-scented belches. "Ugh, this heartburn is a killer. I feel like Old Faithful's eruptin' in my gut. Hey, could you hand me my antacids? They're in the glove box."

By this time, I knew very well where he kept his antacids, anti-diarrheals, and anti-gas tablets, all of which I regularly replenished out of my own pocket unbeknownst to Stan. I opened the glove compartment and handed him the box of antacids. Then I rolled down my window for life-sustaining oxygen. He'd already left me to die a violent slamming death. I'd be damned if I was going to let him suffocate me too.

"You okay, Franki?"

"I'm fine."

"Well, you rolled down your window like you needed some air. You feelin' dizzy?"

*Oh indeed I am, but not because you let the Teutonic Titan spin me around the motel room for half a freakin' hour.* He had absolutely no concept that his bodily functions might present a problem for me, both in terms of my physical safety on calls and my ability to breathe.

We arrived at the station and took Petra to booking. After she was processed and taken to her cell, Stan turned to me for his customary end-of-the-shift lecture. "You know, you've really got to pay attention when you're out there on the street. This isn't the first time I've had to come to your rescue."

"Stan, I—"

"I mean, I'm not bragging or anything," he interrupted, "but

I'm the best of the best. If you can't learn from me, then I don't know if you're gonna make it on the force."

"Stan, you—"

"You know I have to write this in my report, Franki. You put me in real danger out there. I had no backup. I could've been killed."

That did it. Although I was mostly mad at Vince, Stan was about to find out what it was like when I lost *my* filter. And it's not like he didn't have it coming. "Let me get this straight. I put *you* in danger? Are you freakin' kidding me? You put *me* in danger when you left me alone with the *Deutsch* Destroyer. And this was hardly the first time. I mean, I'm always covering my ass while yours is parked on a toilet seat."

Stan smirked. "Well, you didn't do such a good job of covering your ass tonight, now did you?"

Why *did I have to mention my ass?* I'd practically handed it to him on a platter with that remark.

"And that's the problem." He gestured toward a window overlooking the street. "You can't protect yourself out there, and you can't be relied on to protect your partner from loonies like Schotsie the Sausagestuffer, either."

"Petra the Pretzelmaker."

"And if you really want to know something," he said in an offended tone, "it's inappropriate for you to discuss my bathroom habits."

*Me?* I'd had to endure play-by-play reenactments of the ins and outs of his bowels—make that the outs—on a daily basis since the first day of our partnership. But Stan was too self-absorbed to ever be able to realize that, much less admit it. Our conversation hadn't amounted to anything, just like my career. There was nothing more to say. Actually, there was *one* thing.

"I quit."

~

I SHOVED the crutch that the emergency room doctor had given me into the backseat of my 1965 cherry red Mustang convertible and winced as I climbed into the front seat. The pain in my sprained knee was intense, but it was nothing compared to the ache in my heart. I reached into my bag for my car keys but pulled out my phone instead. I glanced at the time on the display—seven thirty a.m. If I knew my workaholic best friend Veronica Maggio, she was already toiling away at her new detective agency. I debated waiting to call her until after I'd had some time to sleep on the painful events of the night shift, but I decided that I'd rest a whole lot easier knowing how she was going to react to my news. I scrolled through my contacts, tapped her name, and held my breath.

"Private Chicks, Incorporated." Veronica's phone voice was clipped and professional. "If you give us the time, we'll solve your crime. What can I help you with?"

I tried to pretend she was next door instead of five hundred lonely miles away in New Orleans. "Do you always answer the phone that way?"

"In this economic climate, you have to be aggressive. So I answer with my phone version of the thirty-second elevator pitch." Unlike me, Veronica was extremely practical and all business. Though, no one could tell that about her at first glance because she looked and acted a lot like Elle Woods in *Legally Blonde*—petite, blonde, perky and perfectly put together—only she had a cream Pomeranian named Hercules instead of a tan Chihuahua named Bruiser. Veronica was everything I wasn't, and that was putting it mildly.

"I guess that's a good idea," I said. "But I don't know about the 'If you give us the time' part. It makes it sound like it could take you a while to solve a case."

"It's an expression, Franki. It means that if you hire us, we'll solve your case."

"I suppose."

An awkward pause ensued.

"So?" Veronica prodded. "What's wrong?"

I did my utmost to feign surprise. "Why would you think something's wrong?"

"Because you're doing everything you can to avoid telling me why you called."

I straightened in my seat. "I called because I've decided to take you up on your offer to join your PI firm. I'm moving to New Orleans."

"Really? What about Vince? And your job?"

"Vince and I aren't together anymore." *There. I said it. And it had hurt.*

"Do you want to talk about it?"

Her tone had softened, prompting self-pity to prick at my eyelids. "Let's just say that I was in a committed relationship, but he wasn't."

"I'm sorry, Franki."

"Me too." I leaned my head against the headrest and wiped away tears with the back of my hand.

"But I hope you're not leaving your job because of Vince."

"He's got nothing to do with it." It was a fib, but if I had told her that I discovered Vince's betrayal thanks to a 911 call, she would've never believed that I was leaving the force because it was the right thing to do. "The hard truth is that I'm not cut out for the police force. I gave my two weeks' notice this morning."

"Are you kidding?" Her pitch rose with each syllable. "You're a born cop. I mean, you still need some experience and all, but you come from a Sicilian family, and you grew up in Houston. If you don't know crime, who does?"

"Verrrry funny. Need I remind you that you're half Sicilian too?" I asked, half-heartedly playing along.

"Yeah, but I'm also half Swedish, which tempers the Italian-ness considerably. You've got it on both sides, so you're screwed."

"You're a laugh a minute, you know that? I tell you what, let's leave ethnicity out of this," I said, as though I believed that were possible. Veronica and I had bonded as pre-law students at the University of Texas, and not over our criminology classes but over all things Italian—our Italian language courses, our fami-lies, endless bottles of Chianti and, of course, Gucci, Prada, Armani, and Dolce and Gabbana (in *Cosmopolitan* and *Vogue*, that is). "I might have the makings of a good cop, but that doesn't mean I belong on the police force."

"This doesn't have anything to do with your trusty partner, does it? What happened this time? Did the diarrhea king leave you high and dry again?"

"Something like that." I looked out the driver window and thought of Petra heaving me repeatedly into the air and rubbed my wounded knee. "But Stan's not really the issue. I need to get off the night shift and return to the world of the living. And I want a job that's a little more predictable. As a private investiga-tor, I'd have some say in the cases I take." *And the situations I find myself in.*

"Do you regret going to the police academy after UT?"

"You know I had no choice. I wanted to prove to my family that women could do more than make pasta and birth babies."

"I know," Veronica said. "But I still say that becoming a cop was taking rebellion to the extreme."

"It was the best way I could think of to show them that I was as tough and capable as any man. Besides," I said, eager to change the subject from my family, "you weren't happy as an attorney, and I knew that I wouldn't have been either, especially not as a criminal defense attorney. I want to catch criminals, not defend or prosecute them. If I work for you, I can still do that but in a less restrictive environment. I can be my own boss. You know, call my own shots and that sort of thing."

"I certainly understand wanting to be your own boss. But aren't you going to feel like you've proven your family right by leaving the force?"

"They'll probably see it that way. But I'm just going to have to figure out a way to prove them wrong."

"O-kay." She drew the word out, unconvinced. "As long as you're *sure* that you're leaving Austin for the right reasons, then I could really use your help down here."

"I'm sure, Veronica." I gripped the gear shift and gathered my resolve. "Austin was a great place to go to school, but now I need to move on. And with the New Year just two weeks away, it's the perfect time to start a new life."

"And just in time for Mardi Gras. *Laissez les bons temps rouler!*"

"*Oui, chère,*" I cheered in the Cajun custom—but with a *joie de vivre* that I definitely didn't feel.

## 2

———

S itting on the floor of my empty apartment, I stared at my cell phone. I wasn't waiting for Vince to call. I was avoiding calling my parents—for the past two weeks. Joe and Brenda Amato were as open to change as the Catholic Church, so the news of my breakup with Vince and the police force was going to hit them and my live-in Sicilian *nonna* like a divorce *and* an excommunication. As for the news that I was moving to New Orleans instead of home to Houston, they would view that as nothing short of my eternal damnation in hell. And based on what I knew about NOLA summers, that judgment might've been fairly accurate.

But since I was leaving in the morning, I sucked up my courage and sucked in a breath. Then I tapped their number and imagined that each ring was the toll of a death knell.

"Hello?" My mother's voice was so loud and shrill that Napoleon, my brindle cairn terrier who'd been sleeping in a corner, raised an ear.

"Hi, Mom."

"Francesca? Is that you?"

I rolled my eyes. "Yes, it's me. Your only daughter?"

"Well, I know *that*, dear."

*A conversation with Petra the Pretzelmaker would be easier.*

"Is everything all right, Francesca? It's a Wednesday."

"I know it's a Wednesday, Mom."

"You usually call on a Sunday, dear."

"Ah." I hadn't realized I was so predictable. "Listen, I'm calling because I have some things to tell you and Dad."

"Well, I hope they're good things. You know how your father worries about you. He just can't sleep at night if he thinks the slightest thing is wrong with his baby. And then he's absolutely *miserable* at the deli the next day. He acts like Anthony and me and the customers don't matter."

*I could make the case that he was right about my brother Anthony.* "Mom, can you just tell Dad to get on the line?"

"Of course, dear. All you had to do was ask." She slammed the phone down onto what was undoubtedly the kitchen counter. "Joe! Get on the other line. Francesca's calling from Austin." She picked up the receiver again. "Franki?"

"Still here, Mom." I sighed. "Dad knows where I live, by the way. I've been here for eleven years."

"Well, you know your father can't hear anymore. I told him to have his ears checked, but he won't listen to me. He's got that wax build up that older men get. One second, dear." She slammed down the phone again. "Joe!"

To my relief, I heard my father pick up another line.

"I'm here, Brenda." He'd used his irritated, this-had-better-be-good-news voice. "What's going on, Franki?"

"Hey, Dad. I was just calling to tell you guys about some things that are in the works." I'd added the spunky "in the works" line in a desperate attempt to put a preemptive, positive spin on my news.

"I hope everything's okay." His tone was unhopeful.

"Everything's fine," I lied through my teeth.

"Well, that's good because thanks to your brothers, I just don't know how much more bad news we can take around here." His tone had gone from unhopeful to downright unhappy. "It's looking like Michael's going to get laid off from the accounting firm, and Anthony's decided that the deli's not good enough for him anymore. He wants to go and manage a *bar*, of all things. Sometimes I don't know what's wrong with that boy. Amato's Deli is a solid business. I built it from the ground up, and I'm proud to go to work there every day with our family name on that sign. Besides, you don't just up and leave a good job on a whim in times like these, whether your family owns the place or not."

"Y-you're right, Dad." I leaned my back against the wall. "But anyway, my news is definitely good. I've got a new job as a PI at Veronica's agency and a new place to live...and I'm single again."

The other end of the line went silent for what seemed that eternal damnation in hell as we all searched for something to say.

My mom, who'd long suspected that I was solely to blame for the fact that I was pushing thirty and unmarried, cleared her throat in preparation to take the call to a dark place. "What did you do to Vince, Francesca?"

I decided to dispense with the pleasantries and make it painfully clear that I'd had nothing to do with *this* breakup, unlike a few others I could think of. "I caught him in bed with another woman, Mom."

"Now Francesca, are you *sure* it was Vince?" she asked with her characteristic talent for denial. "You know how quick you are to jump to conclusions."

I mentally replayed the scene of bursting into that motel room and seeing Vince's naked backside in bed with pair of long and not-so-feminine legs wrapped around his waist. "Yeah. I'm sure."

My dad, who'd never spoken to me of sex in his entire life and who'd taken great pains to feign sleep during unexpected sex scenes while watching TV with me, cleared his throat in preparation to shift the focus of the conversation. "You couldn't hack fighting crime with the protection of the law on your side in a nice college town like Austin, so now you're going to go it alone as a PI in a dangerous city like New Orleans. Is that what you're telling us, Franki?"

"Dad, I made it onto the force, so clearly I *can* hack it. I just don't like the rigid structure of police work. And you'll be glad to know that being a PI is actually safer than being a cop. Instead of going toe-to-toe with drug dealers, armed robbers, and murderers, I'll be investigating things like insurance fraud, infidelity, and missing persons cases."

"While you're out-a there looking for all-a those-a missing-a persons, maybe you find-a that husband you're missing," my nonna Carmela interjected.

I silently cursed my parents for having three phones in their house. "Hi, Nonna."

"Don't-a hi-a me. Now, I have-a no problem that you're gonna go to New Orleans. You know that your *nonnu*, God rest-a his soul, and I raised your *patri* and his-a four brothers there. There are still a lotta nice Sicilian boys in New Orleans, even for a *zitella* like-a you."

The back of my head hit the wall. My nonna had been calling me a zitella, the Italian word for "old maid," since I was sixteen. She'd also been telling me that she had one thing left to do before she could die—see to it that I was properly *sistemata*, or settled, and making lots of babies and home-cooked meals for my husband.

"I still have-a some good friends there with-a some sons," Nonna said. "They might-a be divorced once or twice, and they might-a have-a some kids. And maybe they don't have-a no job.

But remember, a zitella can't-a be choosy. I'll make-a some calls and get-a back-a to you."

I swallowed a lump the size of a calzone. "Thanks, Nonna. But I'd really rather meet men on my own."

My mother gave an unamused laugh. "Well, we can see where that's gotten you, dear."

"Franki, when is this move?" My dad had once again shifted the conversation away from men. "I can help you, if you'd like. I wouldn't mind going down to the French Quarter to check in with everyone at Central Grocery. That's where I got my start in the deli business, you know. Making muffulettas."

"Yeah, I know, Dad." As if I could've forgotten that Central Grocery's famous muffuletta sandwich was indirectly responsible for me and my two brothers' entire existence. "But that won't be necessary. I'm leaving tomorrow with only what I can put in my car. I got rid of most of my stuff because the apartment's fully furnished."

"*What?*" My mom and nonna shouted in unison.

"You gonna sleep in someone else's-a bed?" My nonna had genuine fear in her voice. "*Porta iella!*"

I'd heard her use this phrase, which was Italian for "It brings bad luck," at least twice a week throughout my childhood. To my nonna, practically every single action, if done improperly or in the wrong frame of mind, would either bring bad luck or invoke *malocchiu*, the dreaded "evil eye."

"And besides bad luck," my mother said, "it's just plain dirty, Francesca. You don't know anything about the people who slept in that bed before you. Some people don't bathe. And they might have had bedbugs. Or maybe—"

"Okay, well, thanks for the advice, everyone. I'd love to keep talking, but I've got packing to do before I leave tomorrow. *Ciao ciao!*"

I hung up without giving them a chance to respond—a technique I'd learned the first time I'd called home after moving away to go to college. Then I let out a long, slow exhale. To think I'd considered moving back home to Houston instead of New Orleans.

~

AFTER EIGHT HOURS OF DRIVING—FOR Napoleon, eight hours of dozing—we turned onto our new street in the Uptown neighborhood of New Orleans. We were greeted by a crowd of people, who had their backs to us. I heard a live brass band playing "When the Saints Go Marching In" and realized that the crowd was walking in procession in time with the music. The people in the back of the procession wore casual clothes. Some twirled parasols, others shook handkerchiefs. Those in the front, however, were dressed more elegantly and mostly in black.

"Oh, hell no. We're following a jazz funeral."

Napoleon's ears shot up as though he too understood that it wasn't an auspicious beginning to our new life.

As I inched down Maple Street, I caught glimpses of the horse-drawn hearse carrying a casket behind glass, and I watched as the funeral-goers danced joyously to the music. My father had once told me that the people in the front, the family and friends of the deceased, were called the "first line." Those in the back were called the "second line" because they weren't part of the funeral but instead were passersby following along and enjoying the music. Life was certainly different in New Orleans, and so was death.

I glanced at the street addresses on my left and saw that they were odd-numbered. I looked at the next address and discovered that we were close to 7445. "We're almost there, boy."

Napoleon cocked his head, no doubt wondering whether he

would ever crack the mysteries of human speech, and I gave his head an affectionate scratch.

A few minutes later, the funeral procession entered a large cemetery.

I looked to my left again and saw 7445, an old two-story house that had been converted into a fourplex.

And I shuddered in horror.

My new home was right smack across the street from that cemetery.

I was going to have to kill Veronica for not telling me about it. And after I did, I knew exactly where I would bury her. She was well aware that cemeteries—particularly creepy New Orleans ones with their assortment of tombs, sarcophagi, obelisks, gothic statues, and voodoo rituals—made my skin crawl.

The good news was that next to the cemetery was a tavern named Thibodeaux's, which it looked like I was going to need.

I parked on the street in front of the house. Before I could get out of the car, Veronica came out her front door, smiling and waving with Hercules in tow in a turquoise fuzzy sweater that matched hers perfectly. Despite her Sicilian father, Veronica looked Swedish like her ex-ballerina mother, with long blonde hair, cornflower blue eyes, and pale skin.

"Franki!" She squealed.

I climbed from the car and bent over—at the waist—to hug her. I'd forgotten how tiny she was, and I wondered for at least the hundredth time how her internal organs could function in such a small frame.

She looked at me and smiled. "How does it feel to be in New Orleans?"

I glanced over at the cemetery and then back at her. "At the moment, it feels fairly morbid."

"Oh, come on. You don't still have that weird cemetery issue, do you?"

"Yes, Veronica. And I can't believe you didn't tell me that there's one right across the street. Lots of people would find it disturbing to go to sleep at night with a cemetery in their front yard, especially a *New Orleans* cemetery."

Veronica shook her head in mock disgust as she grabbed a box from my back seat.

"Thank God there's a bar right next to it, in case I need to drink myself to death from despair."

She gave a sweet smile. "Well, if you do drink yourself to death, I wouldn't have to carry you very far for your burial."

I pointed my index and pinky fingers downward—the opposite of the University of Texas hook 'em horns gesture—like my nonna had taught me to ward off the threat of death, which Veronica had so carelessly cast upon me.

She rolled her eyes. "You still do that silly *scongiuri* gesture? God, Franki, you make me *so* glad my nonna stayed in Sicily. You're so superstitious."

"I do it just in case," I snapped. "I mean, you never know..."

Veronica walked to my new front door, which was next to hers, and pulled a key from the front pocket of her designer jeans. "Glenda—our landlady—told me to let you in. She'll come downstairs to meet you in a few minutes."

With the box balanced on her left hip, Veronica unlocked my front door and shoved it open with her shoulder. She turned to me and bowed. "Welcome to your humble abode."

Excited, I entered the apartment with Napoleon at my heels. As I surveyed the living room, a number of adjectives came to mind, but humble was *not* one of them.

The room was the home-decor equivalent of Amsterdam's Red Light District. The walls were covered in fuzzy, blood-red wallpaper with shiny gold *fleurs-de-lis*, and hanging from the ceiling was a baroque red-and-black crystal chandelier. The couch was a rococo chaise lounge in velvet zebra print, and next to it was a lilac velour armchair with gold fringe that matched the drapery to perfection. On the opposite wall there was a mahogany wood fireplace with a hearth covered in white candles of various sizes and shapes. In front of the fireplace, a bearskin rug replete with a bear head covered the hardwood floors. The only thing missing was the red fluorescent light in the living room window signaling my availability for prospective clients.

"Wow. So...this Glenda... Is she a prostitute?" It was a joke. Sort of.

"Former stripper, actually," Veronica said. "And she's really touchy about the difference, so don't use the word prostitute in front of her."

I gaped at my best friend. "You're serious?"

She blinked as though renting me an apartment from a former *stripper* across from a *cemetery* was normal. "You know, I was reading that the brothel look is really popular. I believe it's called 'bordello chic.'" She paced as she tried to reconcile her unusually conflicted sense of fashion. "But now that I think about it, Lenny Kravitz redecorated his house here in New Orleans, and designers call his style 'bordello modern.'"

"Something tells me that Lenny didn't decorate this place. And I wouldn't exactly call this 'bordello modern.' It's more like 'bordello seventies.'"

"Well, at least you won't have to add any touches of color."

"I'll say. Speaking of color, any idea of the backstory on this furniture?" I eyed the chaise lounge nervously. "I mean, I know it's used. But do you have any idea *where* it was used?"

Veronica shrugged. "Glenda's a collector. She's always going on some trip or other to buy antique furniture. You'll have to ask her where she got it."

I considered Glenda's potential sources and then immediately resolved to get a new couch. And a new bed.

"She also collects stripper costumes." Veronica took a seat on the lilac armchair.

"I guess you could say she's the Debbie Reynolds of the stripping world."

"How do you mean?" I was dying to hear the rationale behind that analogy.

"She collects stripper costumes like Debbie collected Hollywood costumes. She's got an Anna Nicole Smith, a Dita Von Teese, and a Gypsy Rose Lee. You know, Glenda was quite the local celebrity back in the sixties and seventies. She stripped for all the famous singers, actors, and politicians. She even danced for President John F. Kennedy. She made a fortune and invested it all in real estate, antiques, and strip memorabilia."

"What did you say her last name was?" I was determined to google her.

"O'Brien. But her stage name was Lorraine Lamour."

"Oh, solid choice." I was truly impressed.

"Do you want to go see the *boudoir*?"

"Okay. But promise me that it doesn't have a heart-shaped bed or a mirrored ceiling."

"Lord, no. I don't go in for the tacky look," a raspy voice said behind me.

I turned and saw standing in the doorway a short, wiry, sixty-something woman with a deeply lined face, platinum boob-length hair, and the longest false eyelashes I had ever seen. From the outfit she was wearing, I had no doubt whatsoever that it was Glenda. She was dressed in a sheer black robe with gold sequins, a ruffled leopard print corset with a matching ultra mini skirt, black satin stripper slippers with feathers, and a bright yellow boa. In her left hand, she held a Mae West-style cigarette holder, and in her right was a glass of champagne.

"You must be Miss Franki. I can see that you're Italian because you look like that actress from the 1960s, Claudia Cardinale. You've got her tits too." She sized up my chest as she took a drag from her cigarette. "My name's Glenda, but I also answer to Lorraine. Welcome to New Orleans, sugar."

"Thanks, uh, Miss Glenda." I threw in the *Miss* because I was uncertain of proper Southern stripper forms of address and whether I was supposed to throw in a *honey* or a *doll*. "It's a pleasure to meet you."

"Likewise, I'm sure." She inelegantly exhaled a puff of smoke. "I see that Miss Ronnie here has shown you the place. In case she didn't mention it, the laundry room is downstairs in the basement. And if you need more storage space, there's a walk-in closet down there you're free to use. I used to keep my costumes in it, but after the post-Katrina floods I moved them to the apartment upstairs."

"Veron—, I mean, Miss Ronnie, told me that you collect costumes."

"I still have every one I wore on stage, except one made of packing tape—they had to cut me out of that one, child." She laughed with a hacking sound typical of smoker's cough. "Anyway, I dropped a wad of strippin' tips on those costumes, so I've gotta look after my investment."

"Of course." I did my best to sound empathetic.

"Now. I don't mind your furry friend here as long as he doesn't poop and pee on my chaise lounge. I had to search all over Louisiana to find one in faux zebra."

I glanced at Napoleon, who was hiking his leg on Hercules, and nudged him with my foot. "Oh, he's house trained."

"Good. One last thing—The Visitor Policy. I don't allow my female tenants to have more than two male friends spend the night at one time. I've got a reputation to protect, and I don't want people to think I rent to whores."

"Certainly not," I said with conviction.

"Let me know if you have any questions."

I started to ask Glenda about the origin of the furniture and then decided to keep my mouth shut. "No, I think it's all painfu —, er, very clear for now."

"All right then, you ladies have a good evening. And when you're all settled in, Miss Franki, I'll take you over to Thibodeaux's for a Harvey Wallbanger. *Au revoir*."

I turned to Veronica. "What's a Harvey Wallbanger? Or is that a who?"

"It's some drink from the seventies."

"That's funny. I'd sort of taken her for a Fuzzy Navel or Slippery Nipple drinker."

She gave me a sideways look. "You know, Glenda's a little rough around the edges, but she's whip smart."

"An interesting choice of adjectives to describe her intelligence."

Veronica leaned over to pick up Hercules, who, despite his mighty name, had been having a tough time fending off Napoleon's skillful battle techniques. "So, what do you say, Franki?"

"I say that people think Austin is weird, but it's got nothing on NOLA."

"Are you ready to start work tomorrow?" She adjusted Hercules's sweater.

I took a seat on the chaise lounge. "After today, I'm ready for anything."

∼

MY PHONE RANG on the nightstand.

Thinking it was my mom or my nonna calling to make sure that I'd encased the mattress in plastic, which I had seriously considered doing, I rolled onto my side in the black French bordello-style bed and pulled the hot pink duvet over my ear.

But I could still hear Napoleon snoring beside me.

And my phone continued to ring.

I opened my eyes and glared at the hot pink canopy, Then I sat up and looked at the display.

*Vince.*

He'd called every day since I'd caught him in bed with the wrathful wrestler, but I never answered. I had also promptly deleted all of the messages he'd left for me without listening to a single one of them. Deep down I was thinking that if I just avoided him, I wouldn't really have to face the fact that it was over, that I was alone yet again. But I knew that the time had come to hear him out and then tell him in no uncertain terms that we were through. Otherwise, I was never really going to be able to reassemble the shattered pieces of my life—not to mention my pride—and move on.

I tapped *Answer.* "What do you want, Vince?"

"Franki, finally. Why haven't you returned any of my calls? I've missed you, babe."

"Oh, I'm sure you haven't missed me that much. You seem to be perfectly capable of finding other women to keep you company when I'm not around."

"Babe, listen. That...it was all a misunderstanding."

"*Really?* So, you're telling me that I didn't see the Munich Maniac's legs wrapped around your waist? Or, maybe I did, but she was just giving you private wrestling lessons? Is that it?"

"Look, the guys dragged me to one of those nude oil-wrestling joints—"

"Spare me the sordid details. I don't care anymore."

He sighed.

I punched a pillow.

Napoleon stopped snoring, but he didn't wake up.

"Okay, babe." Vince spoke with a note of surrender. "I admit it. I made a mistake. Haven't you ever made a mistake?"

"Yeah. I have. The day I decided to trust a cheat like you. And while we're on the subject of mistakes, did you happen to notice that Petra looked a lot like a Peter?"

"Damn it, Franki. Why are you being so harsh? Lots of couples deal with cheating, and they come through it stronger, babe."

I snorted a laugh. "First of all, stop calling me 'babe.' And second, don't try to make it sound like cheating is a normal part of a relationship. I don't have to accept womanizing, and I'm not going to."

"Yeah, because you're so damned perfect, aren't you? It's time to grow up and deal with reality instead of running away to New Orleans like a child."

I stiffened. "Wait. How did you know I left Austin? Have you been spying on me, or something?"

"I'm a lot of things, but I'm not a stalker, Franki. When you wouldn't answer my calls I got worried, so I called Nonna Carmela. She told me you'd moved."

*I'm sure she also told you to remind me that I wasn't getting any younger and that zitelle couldn't be choosers.* "Vince, please leave my family out of this. This is between you and me—at least it *was*. There's no you and me anymore. Not now, not ever."

"So, you're going to throw away everything we had over an indiscretion?"

"We're not talking about an *indiscretion*. It's a huge *betrayal*. And yes, I most certainly am." I was proud of myself for holding my ground, even though my legs would've been shaking had I been standing on actual ground. I had a history of looking the other way where men were concerned. But not this time.

"If that's what you want, you've got it. You won't hear from me again. But let me make something clear." His tone had turned lowdown, like him. "If you're waiting for Prince Charming or for a knight in shining armor, he ain't gonna come. Especially not at your age. So you'd best think about that long and hard, *principessa*, or you're gonna end up old and alone."

The call ended.

Vince had hung up.

I sat with the phone frozen to my ear. Not even a minute before I'd been so proud of myself, thinking that I'd come a long way from the insecure woman who would forgive a man practically anything. Then in ten seconds flat Vince had reduced me to a stubborn and naïve zitella with one foot in the grave—make that the cemetery across the street. And just like that all of my insecurities rushed back.

I nestled into my pillows and pulled the duvet to my chin. I certainly didn't think I was waiting for a fairy-tale guy, especially since I'd dated Vince. But the hard truth was that every relationship I'd ever been in had ended in disaster. And after spending roughly half my life dating unsuccessfully, it seemed like I might have some sort of problem. The question was, did I come to New Orleans to solve my problem? Or to run from it?

## 3

"What's that look for?" I glared at Napoleon, who'd lowered his ears at the sight of my first-day-on-the-job turtleneck and jeans.

He rose from the bearskin rug and hopped onto the chaise lounge.

"If you're suggesting I wear animal print like that tacky faux zebra, forget it."

He swallowed and rested his chin on his paws.

"Besides, a brown turtleneck is kind of an animal style."

Napoleon sighed and closed his eyes.

Anyone who thought I was crazy for talking to a dog hadn't met my cairn terrier. He had a way of communicating that was almost human.

I entered the kitchen, which was attached to the living room by a half-wall with a breakfast counter, and pulled a cold piece of pizza from the fridge. It was eight thirty a.m., which was the time Veronica and I had agreed we'd leave for the office.

Taking a seat at the kitchen table, I tried to quell my excitement and anxiety. Mostly, I couldn't wait to see the office building. Before establishing Private Chicks, Inc. two years before,

Veronica had settled a personal injury case fresh out of Tulane Law School that netted her a cool one point five million after taxes. Calling that payout her "ticket out of law," she paid off her student loans, maxed out her 401K, bought the Audi, and put a huge down payment on an old office building at 1200 Decatur Street. The thought of working in a French Quarter office with my best friend—as opposed to a smelly squad car with Stan—was exhilarating. But I was also nervous because I wasn't sure how I was going to handle the freedom of working as a PI after the rigid schedule and structure of police work.

*Would I actually get any work done? Or would I just sit at the nearby Café du Monde drinking chicory coffee and stuffing my face full of beignets?*

A knock at the front door interrupted a fantasy I was about to have that involved burning enough calories from all of my investigative legwork to eat a daily half-dozen or so of the pastries—with extra powdered sugar. But the split in my patrol pants weighed heavily on my mind—and my behind—because I was pretty sure I couldn't blame that on Petra.

I tossed the pizza in the fridge and opened the door to Veronica, who wore a pink-and-black Chanel suit with a vintage black Chanel handbag.

*Napoleon might've been right about my outfit.*

As if to confirm my suspicion, he sat up and wagged his tail when she entered the living room. The traitor.

She flashed her eyes. "I hope you're ready to get to work, because I just got a call from a new client. He's going to meet us at four o'clock."

"Who is he?""A financial advisor named Ryan Hunter. He's the primary suspect in the murder of his ex-girlfriend, Jessica Evans. She was found strangled to death at the LaMarca store she managed on Canal Street. The poor woman was only twenty-six."

"There's a LaMarca here? I love that store." I thought back to a trip to Italy I'd taken several years before and the fabulous black leather handbag I'd splurged on at the original LaMarca on Rome's chic Via Condotti. "You know, I think I heard something about the murder on the radio when I was coming into town."

"Yeah, it's been all over the local media for weeks. Come on. I'll tell you about it on the way to the office."

After assuring Napoleon that I would be back soon, I locked my apartment door and then got into Veronica's waiting white Audi convertible.

"So, here's what I know." Veronica started the engine of her car and then backed out of the driveway. "Keep in mind that I haven't seen the police report yet. But from what Ryan told me, and from what I've heard on the news, a salesgirl found Jessica's body when she came to work on the morning of December 13th. She said the back door was unlocked, and Jessica was lying on the floor in the middle of some racks of scarves. Nothing had been taken from the store."

"You said she was strangled, right?"

"Yeah, with a scarf."

"Was she killed that morning? Or the day before?"

Veronica took a left turn. "Sometime the night before. Apparently, she'd stayed late after the store closed. The police didn't release the information about the murder weapon being a scarf, by the way. Someone leaked that to the press. Anyway, Franki, this is big. If we can help clear this guy or even solve the case, we're golden. Private Chicks, Inc. will be a household name in NOLA."

"That would be amazing." I looked out the passenger window so that she wouldn't see my concern. Everything was happening so fast, and solving a high-profile murder in The Big Easy wouldn't be easy at all. I hoped I was up to the job.

~

VERONICA TURNED the Audi onto Decatur Street in the French Quarter and parked in front of a three-story, brown brick building with white doors, green shuttered windows, and a second-floor balcony—the kind that people threw bead necklaces off of during Mardi Gras. "Here we are. Your new headquarters."

The smell of marinara teased my nostrils as I exited the car and looked around. "I smell my nonna's kitchen, but I don't see Private Chicks."

She giggled. "It's on the top floor. I rent the first two floors to Nizza, an Italian restaurant and bar."

My jaw dropped—while salivating. It was classic Veronica—her mind was always so focused on work that she would forget to tell me some of the pertinent details of her life, no matter how momentous they might have been.

I followed her up three long, thigh-busting flights of stairs. By the time we got to the top, I felt certain that each flight would burn off a beignet.

"Our conference room." She gestured to an unmarked door. "And across the stairwell here is our office." She led me through an old detective movie-style door that had "Private Chicks" in black letters on frosted glass. "It used to be an apartment, so I turned the living room into the lobby, kept the kitchen and bathroom, and made the two bedrooms down the hall into offices."

"Nice." And it was, especially the old brick walls and the two overstuffed couches that faced one another in the center of the room. As soon as I got situated in my new digs, I was going to get situated on those couches.

She pulled her phone from her purse. "Oh, shoot. I need to make a call. Your office is the first door on the right down the hallway. Why don't you start getting set up?"

"Glad to." I was so excited to have my own office that I almost bounced down the hallway. And I spent the rest of the day organizing my desk and learning how to use Veronica's case management software for private investigators.

The lobby bell sounded at a quarter till four as someone entered the living room that served as our lobby. Thinking it was Ryan Hunter, I walked out to greet him. I was met by a young man with a thin, angular face and lanky frame. He looked no more than sixteen or seventeen. *He's clearly not Ryan—that is, unless Jessica Evans was into jailbait.*

Veronica walked into the lobby with her handbag and her laptop. "Franki Amato, this is David Savoie. David, Franki is our new investigator."

He extended a hand with long spindly fingers. "Nice to meet you, Miss Amato."

"Call me Franki. Please." I said the last word with a wince— David had a powerful handshake for such a skinny kid.

"Sure thing, Franki." He flashed a toothy smile.

Veronica perched on a couch. "David is our computer Boy Friday. He can do anything from programming to research. We have him fifteen to twenty hours per week, depending on his school load."

"Oh, you're in college?" I'd assumed he was barely in high school.

"Yeah, I go to Tulane. But I can see how you'd be confused. People think I'm *much* older than I really am." David straightened his posture. "I'm nineteen, but I can pass for twenty-three easy."

"I can see that," I lied.

Veronica and I shared a smile at his boyish confidence.

David slid out of his backpack and then his jacket, both of which he tossed onto a nearby desk. He looked like a boy who had grown two feet over the course of a summer, and he was so thin that I was tempted to order him a couple of large pizzas from Nizza.

His gaze went to the laptop on my desk, and he ran over to pick it up. "*Dude!* That's *your* computer? Awwwesoooome. Can I help you connect that to the printer, or anything?"

I watched anxiously as he turned my laptop over in his hands. I still owed the credit card company over two thousand dollars for that computer and would never be able to replace it. I snatched it from his grasp. "Thanks, but I took care of that this morning. Right now, Veronica and I are just waiting on a client—"

Our conversation was cut short as a tall, muscular man in his mid-to-late thirties entered the office.

*Speak of the devil. Wait. Is Ryan Hunter the devil?* I could sense a darkness about the guy, and it wasn't because he was under police suspicion. His ice blue eyes and cruel mouth spoke volumes about his character.

Veronica rose to greet him. "Ryan Hunter?"

"Yes. Are you Veronica Maggio?"

"I am, and this is my colleague, Franki Amato, and our IT consultant, David Savoie. Franki and I will be handling your case. Let's walk over to our conference room so we can talk in private."

Ryan furrowed his thick brow. "Sure."

I glanced at David before leaving the lobby. His exuberant chatter of moments before had given way to an uneasy silence. Even he seemed disturbed by Ryan Hunter's presence. I smiled at David and closed the office door behind me.

Veronica led us into a dark wood-paneled conference room. "Can I get you anything, Ryan? Coffee, water, a soda?"

I was reminded of the first time I'd met her—she'd shown up uninvited to a beer bash at my off-campus apartment with a liter of Pepsi, of all things.

Ryan settled into a brown leather chair. "Do you have any bourbon?"

"No, but we have Pepsi."

*What is her deal with Pepsi?*

Ryan frowned. "I'll skip the drink. I don't have much time anyway."

"Okay, then. Let's get started." Veronica took a seat and opened up her laptop, careful not to break one of her perfectly manicured pink nails. "We have some routine questions that we typically ask our clients. So if you'll just bear with us for a few minutes, we'd appreciate it."

Ryan snorted and stared at her.

Veronica seemed unfazed by his rudeness. "So, from what you told me over the phone, you're the main suspect in the murder of Jessica Evans. Is that correct?"

"I'm the *only* suspect in Jessica's murder."

I leaned forward. "Did you give the police an alibi for the time of the murder?"

He shot me a blank look. "No, because I don't have one."

I couldn't help but notice that he didn't offer any explanation of his whereabouts. "Do you know if the police have any other leads?"

He frowned. "Either they don't have any, or, if they do, they're not interested in investigating them. That's why I'm here."

"Okay. We'll look into that." Veronica typed a reminder on her laptop. But for now, let's talk about Jessica. How long had you been seeing her?"

"About six months." He twisted a paper clip he'd found on the table.

"Did you live together?"

"Yeah, for the last couple months or so. She moved into my place." He glanced out the window, clearly bored.

"Were the two of you close?" Veronica asked, almost hopefully."Yes and no."

I could see that she was getting nowhere fast, so I took over the questioning. "How would you describe your relationship?" "Jessica and I had our ups and downs. Like other couples."

"What do you mean by 'downs'?"

Ryan snapped the paper clip in half and tossed it onto the table. "We fought."

This guy wasn't going to give an inch, so I pressed the issue. "Can you tell us about the fights?"

He sat up in his chair and cast daggers at me. "What are you getting at, exactly?"It was clear to me that he had something to hide." I mean, was there anything about your relationship that would cause the police to suspect you?"

He snorted and leaned back into his chair. "Apparently."

"Were the fights verbal? Or did they get physical?" I was unfazed by his lack of cooperation.

He looked at me hard and said nothing.

"Look, Ryan," Veronica intervened, probably sensing that I was running out of patience for this guy. "We want to help you, but we can't do that if you don't tell us everything we need to know."

He let out a long sigh. "About a month ago, we had a fight. Things got out of hand, and Jessica called 911."

Veronica's eyes widened. "What did you fight about?"

"Money. Jessica was private about money. Well, about everything. I really didn't know anything about her aside from the fact that she worked at LaMarca. And she always had way too much money for someone who managed a retail store. So I asked her about it. She got defensive, and we started fighting." He picked up a pen from the table and started twirling it with his fingers.

"Was it a violent fight?"

"I threw her purse at her. She got pissed and lunged at me

with a bottle of wine. I bent her wrist until she dropped it, and then I hit her. She fell backward, grabbed her cell phone from her purse, and called the cops." He spoke as though describing scenes from a boring TV show.

"So, she was afraid of you," I said, trying only half-heartedly to conceal the contempt I was feeling for him. During my short time as a cop, I'd met enough domestic abusers to last a lifetime.

He laughed and put the pen back on the table. "Let me clarify something. Jessica wasn't afraid of anyone or anything, least of all me. She called 911 because she was a vindictive bitch."

I flinched at the phrase.

A muscle worked in Ryan's square jaw. "She actually had a smile on her face when she made that call."

Veronica cleared her throat. "I'm not sure I understand. Why would she be smiling?"

He paused for a moment and then gave an ironic smile. "It's simple. Jessica liked to see people suffer. She enjoyed watching people squirm. I'd pissed her off, so she was going to make me pay. That's just who she was."

"Then why were you still dating her?" I asked, despite the fact that I was starting to think Jessica and Ryan were made for one another.

"Because she was beautiful, and she was good in bed." His tone was matter of fact, as though those were the only criteria to judge a woman by.

*Just like a man.* "Well, if Jessica was like you say she was, then it's possible that she had enemies. Do you know of anyone who might've had a reason to kill her?"

"Look, I don't know if she had family or friends, much less enemies. Like I said, she was private. Secretive even."

Veronica looked at me and then nodded. "All right, Ryan. I think that's all we need for now. The first thing we'll do is find out where the police are in the investigation, then we'll start looking into Jessica's background to see if we can come up with other leads in the case. We'll also need to set a time to come by your place to look through Jessica's things for any clues."

He frowned. "I'd rather you didn't. I only recently got the damn police out of my house. And besides, she only had clothes and shoes and stuff. I'll box it all up and bring it to you next week. You can do whatever you want with it."

Veronica licked her lips. "Whatever works for you."

Ryan rose to his feet. "So when can I expect to hear from you?"

"We'll call at least twice a week to update you on the investigation and to ask any follow-up questions."

"I look forward to it." He nodded and walked out the door.

I let out a breath I hadn't realized I was holding. "Wow. That's an oddly enthusiastic comment from such a reluctant client."

"Yeah." Veronica pressed her index finger to her mouth. "What do you make of that guy? He's a real weirdo, right?"

I leaned back in my chair. "Well, judging from his defensive attitude and the nonchalant way he mentioned that he'd hit Jessica, I'd say he's a sociopath."

"We're going to have to do a full background check on this guy before we do anything else. If it turns out that he's a convicted felon or something, I'm not sure we want him as a client. I'll have David start on that." She closed her laptop.

"Good idea. I can call the detective in charge of the case."

Veronica burst out laughing. "You're joking, right? As an ex-cop, you of all people should know that the police don't work with private investigators."

I'd only worked as a beat cop in Austin, so I had no idea how detectives interacted with the public on a case. But I had seen a whole lot of *Murder, She Wrote* episodes where detectives were all too willing to discuss cases with Jessica Fletcher. Not the best example, but still. "You'd think the New Orleans PD would want to help us solve a high-profile murder case."

"No, they're afraid we'll crack the case before they do, which would make them look like fools—and on every news channel in Louisiana."

"Then how do we get police information?"

"Well, there are public records, which we can access like everyone else, but the police usually black out potentially compromising information on cases that are still under investigation. So, that means we either have to luck into a corrupt detective who's willing to trade information, or we use Benjamin."

"Who's Benjamin? An informant?"

Veronica reached into her handbag, pulled out a pink Chanel wallet, and extracted a crisp one-hundred-dollar bill with a flourish. "*This* is Benjamin. And sometimes I have to rely on a whole army of Benjamins to get the information I need from the police."

I smiled. "So, you *do* have an informant."

"Yeah, a police crime analyst who feels it's her duty to ensure that cases get solved—by any means necessary. Especially crimes against women."

"Perfect. Then this is a case she's sure to help with. Murdering a woman who also had the great fortune to manage a LaMarca is a double crime against women." It sounded like I was kidding, but I wasn't.

"Agreed." Veronica looked at the clock. "It's five already. We'd better leave, or traffic will be a nightmare. I'll drop you off at the apartment on my way to run errands."

"All right." But I wasn't particularly eager to go home because I had two big boxes in my kitchen that I was doing my best to avoid unpacking.

Veronica typed a message on her phone. "There. I texted

David and told him to do the background check on Ryan Hunter. Oh yeah, do you want to meet at Thibodeaux's at seven o'clock for a drink? I'll invite Glenda..."

I laughed. "Now there's someone I'd like to see a background check on."

~

AT SEVEN P.M. on the dot, I opened my front door to the grim reality of the cemetery across the street. I had quite the setup in New Orleans. My bordello-style apartment constantly reminded me that I wasn't having sex, and the cemetery constantly reminded me that I was going to die. I definitely needed that drink. I walked the thirty or so steps to Thibodeaux's Tavern and entered.

Veronica hadn't arrived yet, but Glenda was already at the bar contemplating three empty tequila shot glasses with a long *Breakfast at Tiffany's*-style cigarette holder in her hand. To complete her Audrey Hepburn look, she wore a black-sequined jumpsuit à la Cher and red platform stripper shoes à la Lady Gaga. She wasn't wearing a boa, probably because it would've covered the skin she was trying to expose.

I approached the bar, surprised by the sumptuous brown leather furnishings, the stainless steel-covered bar, and the warm glow of candlelight. "Hi, Glenda. *Heeeey*, this place is really sophisticated for a tavern."

"Did Miss Ronnie put you to work yet?"

*So much for the formalities.* I sat down on a barstool to her right. "Yeah, we got a big case today."

"You lookin' for a runaway, or what?"

I found it interesting that she would ask about a runaway. But then, she must have encountered quite a few of them in her line of work. "No, it's actually a murder case."

Glenda dragged off her unlit cigarette. "It's not that strangled girl, is it?" "Yes, it is." I was stunned by her insight.

She exhaled nonexistent smoke into my face. "I heard about that. She worked at Prada, right?"

For some reason, I waved away the smoke she didn't exhale. "No, better. LaMarca."

"Personally, I don't care for their designs. All that fabric they use on their evening dresses is frumpy and confining."

Of course, LaMarca had the most sought-after gowns in all of fashion. But compared to the clothing Glenda wore, their evening dresses—even ones that were strapless, backless, and slit to the pelvis—probably looked like pilgrim apparel to her.

An unkempt Sean Penn doppelganger approached me from behind the bar. "Can I get you something to drink?"

"Um—"

"Another tequila shot," Glenda interrupted.

"I'll have a glass of Prosecco, please."

Veronica slid onto the barstool next to me. "Make that two, Phillip."

I turned toward Veronica. "I didn't see you come in."

"That's because you two ladies were deep in conversation." She smirked. "What were you talking about?"

"We were talkin' about that girl who was strangled with the scarf, Miss Ronnie."

Veronica looked at me quizzically. I shook my head to indicate that I hadn't told Glenda any specifics.

"The case reminds me of a striptease I used to do when I was working at Madame Moiselle's in the Quarter."

"Oh?" I was instantly drawn in. There was something about Glenda that intrigued me.

"It was an artistic rendering of a woman's transformation from victimization to self-empowerment."

Her burst of intellectualism left me at a loss for words.

Veronica hadn't been kidding when she'd said Glenda was smart.

"I dressed entirely in sheer scarves. As I stripped away each one, it signified her metamorphosis. There was a top layer of black scarves, then underneath a layer of gray, beneath that a layer of white and then finally, a single pink scarf."

To my total astonishment—I was moved by her description. "That's really beautiful, Glenda."

Veronica leaned around me. "What did the pink scarf represent? The woman's soul?"

Glenda looked taken aback. "No. Her vagina."

"Ah." I was again speechless—but this time for a different reason.

Phillip the bartender returned with our drinks.

Veronica pressed a finger to her cheek. "So, the woman reclaimed her power by taking back her vagina from her victimizer?"

*Oh God.* I took several gulps of the drink that I was overjoyed to have at hand.

"Exactly." Glenda looked at her with renewed respect. "And after she took her vagina back, she did whatever the hell she wanted with it." She cackled and elbowed Veronica.

Taking "The Vagina Monologues" as my cue to leave, I stood up and chugged the remainder of my Prosecco. "Well, guys, I hate to drink and run, but I'd better head out. After all, I've got a case to start investigating tomorrow."

Veronica looked up at me. "I haven't had a chance to tell you this, Franki, but I feel so much better now that you're here. I know I can't go wrong with an ex-cop on my team."

Glenda tossed back another shot of tequila. "That's the first time I've ever heard that one."

"Thanks, Veronica." I shot Glenda a haughty look. "It's a nice change to work for someone who has so much confidence in my abilities. See you tomorrow."

I exited the bar into the crisp January night and got an instant chill—but not from the wintery weather. It struck me just how much was riding on this case. It wasn't only about my self-esteem, pride, and career. It was also about Veronica's professional reputation and the success of the business she'd worked so hard to establish, not to mention the family of the woman who'd been killed. And then there was the not-so-insignificant matter of Ryan Hunter, the sinister-seeming accused killer I'd be helping to potentially walk free.

With all of that sitting on my shoulders like a five-hundred-pound barbell, the thirty or so steps back to my apartment seemed like the longest walk of my life.

# 4

_____

The knocking at my front door grew insistent.

I hopped from my bedroom, pulling on the gray pants I'd bought on clearance at Target, and opened the door.

Veronica entered in a sleek brown Elie Tahari pantsuit with a cream-colored silk blouse. She looked like a gazelle, while I was the spitting image of a hippo.

"Morning." Her tone practically beamed sunshine. "How are you and Napoleon adjusting to your new surroundings?"

"Pretty well, especially Napoleon." I closed the door behind her as she entered the living room. "The bordello chic decor is really bringing out the animal in him. Last night when I came home from the bar, I found him lying on his back sound asleep on the zebra print chaise lounge with his legs splayed wide open."

"Men—of any species—have no shame." She followed me into my bedroom.

"I know, right?" I thought of Vince and his brazen attitude about his infidelity. I entered the adjoining bathroom to put on my makeup and was surprised by the scowling face looking back at me in the oval mirror of the knockoff red Louis XVI vanity. I forced myself to smile. I refused to waste anymore of my precious emotion on that cheat.

Veronica flopped onto the bed next to Napoleon. "Speaking of shame, we're going to church this morning."

My anger toward Vince was replaced by waves of Catholic guilt. I tried to remember the last time I'd been to church. I'd visited the Vatican on my trip to Rome three years ago, but they turned me away at the door for having bare shoulders, so I was pretty sure that didn't count. "Why in the hell would we do that?"

She sighed. "Relax, Franki. We're not going to mass."

I shot her a questioning look from the bathroom doorway, holding my liquid eyeliner brush like a weapon.

"Or confession," she said, interpreting my gaze. "We're going there to meet Betty Friedan."

I gasped, and my Catholic guilt morphed into feminist guilt for putting on my signature Sophia Loren-style cat eyeliner. "The founder of the National Organization for Women?"

"Gah, Franki. Calm down, will you?" Veronica was lying on her side with her head propped up by her arm, indifferent to my issues. "Betty Friedan is our informant's code name."

I was relieved that Betty was just an informant because that meant I could wear blush and lipstick too. "How was I supposed to know that? I mean, why doesn't she have a normal informant name like Deep Throat or Huggy Bear?"

"Because she's not Bob Woodward's Watergate source or a TV character from Starsky and Hutch. She's a feminist crime analyst from the New Orleans PD."

"So, we're going to a church to pay off a corrupt feminist employee of the police department." That seemed like an obvious violation of all that was holy. "What's the occasion?"

"She's going to give us the police report on the Evans murder and photos of the crime scene. I called her and asked for them after David texted me the results of Ryan Hunter's background check. His record is clean, by the way. That is, except for the assault charge on Jessica he told us about and a surprising number of moving violations."

I remembered how angry and aggressive he'd seemed yesterday. "I'm sure he's got a serious case of road rage. People like that are capable of anything."

"That's a big accusation coming from a woman who once intentionally ran her car into her ex-boyfriend's house."

I glared at her. "It wasn't his *house*. It was his *fence*. The little picket fence we'd painted white together when I was still stupid enough to think he was going to marry me. And I can't believe you would bring up Todd Rothman. College was years ago."

She blinked. "That was road rage, wasn't it?"

"No, it was relationship rage after he forgot to tell me he'd found a new girlfriend and was sleeping with her in the house that was supposed to be ours." I rubbed blush on my cheek so vigorously that it turned red on its own. "Besides, knocking down Todd's fence certainly doesn't make me like Ryan Hunter."

"Of course not." She rubbed Napoleon's belly, and he looked at her with love in his eyes. "I'm just trying to point out that road rage doesn't make someone a killer. So, until we find evidence to prove otherwise, we have to proceed on the assumption that Ryan is innocent, no matter how despicable he may be."

"I know, I know." It was so annoying when Veronica was right. I *had* all but convicted Ryan and was fully prepared to throw away the key. "But the jury's still out on that guy. And for the record, I've come a long way since Todd. Just look at how well I've handled Vince's cheating."

"I'm very proud of you for that."

Her admission took the angry wind out of my sails. "So where is this church?"

"On Rampart Street in the Quarter. It's the old Mortuary Chapel."

"A mortuary chapel, Veronica?" She knew how creeped out I was by cemeteries and churches, so I couldn't believe she would take me to a combination of the two. "Really?"

"Really. It's close to the police station where Betty works. And they haven't kept dead bodies there since the yellow fever epidemic of the 1800s, so you'll be fine. You'll like it too because it became an Italian immigrant church."

She'd intentionally used our heritage to persuade me. *Such an attorney.*

"Now let's go." Veronica gave Napoleon a final scratch and jumped off the bed. "I'll drive. You're kind of jumpy today."

"Okay, but we're going out the back door. There is no way in *inferno* that I'm passing by a cemetery on my way to a mortuary chapel."

~

VERONICA STOPPED the car in front of the chapel. "See? No gothic spires or gargoyles on the outside, and I promise there are no bodies inside."

I stared out the passenger window. "Why did you tell me this was called the Mortuary Chapel? The sign says Our Lady of Guadalupe Catholic Church."

"Because I know you, and if you'd read the historical plaque over there and learned that the original name had the word *mortuary* in it, you would've caused a scene. Possibly even in the church." She turned off the engine and put her keys into her brown Balenciaga bag.

*Good point.* I exited the car and walked over to the plaque eager to find out if there was anything else about the church she'd failed to mention. "Hey, this doesn't say anything about being an Italian immigrant church. But it does say that it's the official chapel of the New Orleans Police and Fire Departments. Is it really a good idea to meet Betty here?"

Veronica walked up behind me in her dainty Jimmy Choos. "It's the perfect place. No one in the police department would be surprised if an employee came here. Plus, with all these people around, no one would suspect a payoff was going down either."

"I hope you're right. You know my nonna would never live it down if I got busted in a church." My nonna was convinced that my lapsed Catholicism was a major impediment to my ability to attract a suitable husband. If I got excommunicated too, it would surely seal my fate as a lifelong zitella in her eyes.

Veronica looked at her phone, ignoring my concerns. "We're early. Betty might not be here yet. Let's go inside and wait."

"Why not?" I asked—not without a note of bitterness.

When I followed Veronica into the church, I noticed a line of people in front of a statue of a Roman centurion holding a cross and stepping on a bird that, on closer inspection, appeared to be a crow. He looked like one of the modern-day Italian men who hang around the Colosseum in Rome dressed in cheesy centurion and gladiator costumes to pose in pictures with tourists. I watched as each person who approached the statue rubbed its feet, murmured something, and then made the sign of the cross. A few people had deposited flowers at the base of the statue, but others had left slices of what looked like pound cake.

"Man, I wish people would leave me flowers and pound cake. Which saint is that anyhow? The patron saint of florists and bakers?"

"That's Saint Expedite," a strong masculine voice said behind me.

I turned to see an unorthodoxly attractive young priest with thick, wavy brown hair, sensual lips, and a ravishing smile. If he'd lived in Rome he would have been a candidate for the annual priest calendar, which, in my mind, was the bizarre and seemingly sacrilegious Italian equivalent of the fireman's calendar. Of course, I didn't think this priest was good looking or anything—it's just that he wasn't *anything* like the old priests I'd grown up around in Houston.

"I'm Father John." He clasped my hand in his.

The minute his skin touched mine, I itched. Ever since I was a young girl in Sunday school, I'd been allergic to the clergy. It was a psychosomatic reaction to the Catholic guilt I felt about my sporadic visits to church as a child, thanks to my parents' seven-day-per-week work schedule and the fact that my over excitable nonna couldn't be trusted with a car.

I withdrew my hand from his as though it had been burned by the fires of hell and blurted, "Bless me father for I have sinned."

He looked confused. "Did you come for confession?"

"Oh, no." I felt my face turning as red as communion wine. The phrase was the only thing I could remember ever saying to a priest. I forced nonchalance as I scratched a spot on my left elbow. "I'm good. I'm here with a friend. She needs to confess, though." It wasn't true, but it served her right for disappearing.

"Well, we can certainly help her with that." He flashed another gorgeous smile.

"Gr-great." I scratched my side. The icky combination of his handsomeness and his holiness really freaked me out. "I don't remember learning about Saint Expedite in Sunday school."

"You didn't learn about him in Sunday school because he's not officially recognized by the Catholic Church." He cast a doubtful look in Saint Expedite's direction. "But the Church occasionally tolerates the veneration of local saints."

I scanned the church for Veronica and mentally cursed her. Then I felt guilty for thinking profanity in a church. "What's he the patron saint of?"

"Anyone who's looking for a quick solution to a problem, who needs money, or wants to stop procrastinating."

*Me, me, and me.* The saint had gotten a lot more interesting. "So, why are those people leaving him pound cake? I mean, I can kind of understand the flowers, but cake?"

"Well, in recent years, Expedite has become the patron saint of people who need to win court cases. They leave him a slice of pound cake as an offering so that he'll be more inclined to help them stay out of jail or—"

"Hold on." A pang of guilt jabbed at my gut for cutting off a priest, but I had to get to the bottom of the cake thing. "They leave him pound cake so that he'll keep them out of the slammer?"

"It has its origins in voodoo. In New Orleans, voodoo and the Catholic Church are closely related. The fusion of the French and African cultures in Louisiana resulted in an association of the voodoo spirits with Christian saints. Some people call Saint Expedite the Voodoo Saint because he represents Baron Samedi, the voodoo loa of death."

I was shocked that a saint would be associated with voodoo. "The voodoo loa of death? What's that?"

"A loa is a voodoo deity. And Baron Samedi is a shady voodoo god who wears a top hat and tails. Voodoo legend has it that when people die, he digs their graves, greets their souls, and leads them to the underworld. He's also a sexual loa who loves to swear, smoke, drink rum, tell filthy jokes to the other spirits, and chase women." Father John winked.

*Awk-ward.* My cheeks were as hot as Hades as I scratched my neck and looked for Veronica from the corners of my eyes. "I still don't understand what Saint Expedite has to do with voodoo."

"It works like this: Followers of New Orleans' legendary voodoo queen Marie Laveau, who died in the late 1800s, visit her tomb in Saint Louis cemetery #1 to ask her for help with a problem. Since the cemetery is right behind the church on Basin Street, afterward they come into the church and leave a slice of pound cake for Saint Expedite so that he'll fast track, or *expedite*, the favors asked of Marie Laveau. It's really a fascinating mixture of religions."

"So, voodoo's a religion." I scratched my head. "I thought it was just like dark magic or something."

He smiled. "That's how pop culture has painted it, but it's centered around religious themes and a desire to do good in the world by channeling saints." He paused. "Hey, do you like James Bond?"

I slowly shook my head, wondering whether God approved of priests watching James Bond movies.

"No?" He sounded shocked. "Too bad, because Baron Samedi is a character in *Live and Let Die* with Roger Moore."

I spotted Veronica beckoning to me like a saving angel from near the altar. She stood next to what could only be described as the anti-Veronica—a young woman with short, dark hair tucked behind her ears, black rectangular glasses, a thin mouth, and no makeup. She resembled a real-life Velma from *Scooby Doo*.

*Betty*. I thanked heaven that I had finally found an avenue of escape. "Well, thank you for the information, Joh—, er, Father," I faltered. It was hard for me to think of a good-looking young guy as a priest. "I need to join my friend."

"Anytime. I hope you'll join us for mass this Sunday."

"Sure," I said, knowing there wasn't a chance in hell I'd show up. *Great, I just lied to a priest.*

I turned and hurried up the aisle to the altar, almost at a run. Then I turned right and walked to the end of the first pew where Veronica and Betty were sitting. I extended my hand. "You must be Betty."

She opted to pass on the handshake to take a moment to size me up. "Who are *you*?"

Veronica smiled. "Betty, this is Franki, my new partner I was telling you about. She's a super smart ex-cop."

"Right." Betty pulled a large manila envelope from a worn, brown leather bag and handed it to Veronica. "So anyway, here's the information you asked for. You won't find much in the report that hasn't already been leaked to the press, but the pictures should be useful."

Veronica, in turn, produced Betty's payoff, which she had disguised by placing it into a church-offering envelope. "Thank you so much. This is going to make a huge difference in our investigation."

"No problem, V." Betty stuffed the envelope into her briefcase. "I just hope you catch the sorry son of a bitch who committed this crime."

"You know, it might've been committed by a woman," I interjected, playing devil's advocate.

"The odds are against it." Betty spoke with a sneer. "Statistically speaking, this is likely an open-and-shut case of femicide—a man killing a woman just because she's a female—and we women need to come together to prevent this type of thing from happening." She stood and pushed up her glasses. "Let me know if you find the asshole who did this."

I watched her walk away, clutching her leather briefcase to her chest. "Wow, that Betty's a real charmer."

Veronica rose to her feet. "She takes crime very seriously. Now let's get going. I'm dying to look at the police report."

As we walked out of the church, I saw Father John waving goodbye to me. Instead of waving back, I tried to duck all 5' 10" of me behind Veronica's tiny frame. I must have looked like I was having a seizure.

The second we got into the car, Veronica tore open the envelope and studied a photo of Jessica at the crime scene. "Look at this."

It was a gruesome sight. Jessica was lying on her left side in the middle of four scarf racks that were situated in the shape of a square. Her face was directed toward the ceiling, and her eyes were open in a look of shock. She had been strangled with a black-and-white checked scarf with a bright yellow border.

Veronica, who owned a different scarf for every day of the year, was intently focused on the murder weapon. She pulled out the police report and quickly scanned the pages. "I knew it."

"What?"

"The scarf used to strangle Jessica isn't from LaMarca." Her eyes danced with excitement.

"How do you know?" "It's a cheap cotton-polyester blend. Everyone knows that LaMarca only sells silk scarves."

I didn't know that, but I did know that LaMarca's signature scarves were the most sought after in the fashion industry. "So, the killer brought a scarf to a store that's famous for selling scarves."

*But why?*

~

STANDING on Canal Street in front of Pontchartrain Bank, I leaned into the passenger window of Veronica's Audi. "I'll go straight to LaMarca after I get some cash. Anything in particular you want me to find out?"

Veronica lowered her sunglasses. "I trust your judgement. And if you have to buy something to keep up your cover as a customer, I'll reimburse up to fifty dollars, so hang on to the receipt."

I would. Because after my move to New Orleans, I was pretty sure that there wasn't enough room left on my credit cards to shop at the Dollar Tree, much less LaMarca. Thankfully, my parents had made a deposit to my account as a belated Christmas gift to help cover my moving expenses.

I entered the lobby and rummaged in my knockoff Gucci hobo bag for a pen. I filled out a withdrawal slip and got in line.

"Next," the teller called.

I approached the window. The teller, who couldn't have been more than 4' 10", looked remarkably like Tinker Bell sans bun and wings.

"May I help you?" Her accent was thick.

I glanced at her nameplate—Corinne Mercier—to confirm my suspicion that she was French. New Orleans was a popular city among French immigrants because of its historical ties to France. "I'd like to make a withdrawal, please." I slid my withdrawal slip toward her. "I haven't gotten my ATM card yet."

"Oh, *mademoiselle*, I am so sorry. Are you new to ze bank?" Her big blue eyes were rimmed with red like she'd been crying.

Guessing that she was having man trouble, I sympathized. "Yeah, I just moved here from Austin to take a job as a private investigator. Where are you from?"

"I come here from Toulouse to start a new life. My mother, she is *américaine*, but I was raised in France."

"I moved here to start a new life too. Besides getting a new job, I wanted to get away from my cheating ex-boyfriend."

"Ah. My boyfriend, Thierry, he cheat too. I come home yesterday, and I find him wis a woman." She struggled to enter my transaction into the computer as her eyes welled up with tears.

"I'm really sorry to hear that. The same thing happened to me. I'm Franki, by the way. You're Corinne, right?"

She nodded, wiping her nose with a tissue. "You too? Men! Zey are so...so...*volages*, *non*?" She blew her nose with a very un-Tinker Bell-like honk, and then handed me my money from the teller cash dispenser.

"Exactly." I put the money into my wallet. I had no idea what she'd just said, but I agreed with the tone of her voice one hundred percent. "All they think about is sex. You know, I really believe the old saying that a man thinks with his penis is true."

Corinne's big blue eyes got even bigger, and she fiddled with her pixie-style blonde hair.

I thought it was because I was coming on a little strong for a stranger and all, but then her eyes darted to something—or someone—over my shoulder. I turned and saw one of the most handsome men I'd ever seen in my life. He had dark brown hair, a chiseled jaw, and a sensuous mouth.

"Is this yours, miss?" He held up my birth control case—with a twinkle in his eye.

I must have dropped it when I was standing in line digging through my bag for the pen I'd used to fill out my withdrawal slip. My whole body burned from embarrassment. Not only had he probably heard my cutting remarks about men, but now he also knew I was having sex with at least one of them.

I realized that I'd been staring at him slack-jawed. I closed my mouth and swallowed hard. "Oh, gosh. Those? They belong to a friend. I'm just holding them for her." I laughed, and it sounded hollow. "While she's out of town."

I'd never been one to stop while I was ahead.

The corners of his mouth curled into a devious smile. "I'd better check the pharmacy label on the back to be sure. It says they were prescribed to—"

"Don't read that." I snatched the package from his hand. "You wouldn't want to violate the HIPAA Privacy Rule."

"Certainly not. My apologies." He gave a mock bow. "To your friend, of course."

Clearly, he enjoyed my unease.

I pretended to check the label. "They're hers, all right." I shoved the pills into my bag. "Thank you, Mr....?"

"Hartmann. Bradley Hartmann," he replied—not unlike James Bond. My Bond-loving priest friend would no doubt be impressed. "I'm the president of the bank." He reached out for a handshake. "Your name is Francesca, right?"

*So he* did *read the back of my birth control case. Just what my life needed—more men who delighted in humiliating me.* "Franki," I replied through the heat in my cheeks. "Franki Amato."

"I heard you tell Miss Mercier that you haven't received your ATM card yet. Why don't you let me look into that for you?" His devious smile turned dazzling.

To my dismay, my knees grew weak.

Corinne furrowed her brow. "*Mais non*, Mr. Hartmann. I will help Miss Amato."

"That's all right, Corinne." He placed a hand firmly at the small of my back. "I'll take care of Miss Amato."

The way his eyes were twinkling, I couldn't tell if he was flirting or mocking me.

"Call me Franki."

"I'd like that."

*Yep, definitely flirting.* And based on the way his thick-lashed blue eyes stared at me, I wasn't sure I minded.

I attempted a little flirt-back of my own, doing a spontaneous Veronica-style bat of my eyelashes that promptly dislodged my right contact lens.

"Are you okay?" he asked. "Your eye is tearing up."

"Oh, it's nothing." I tried to look composed as my lens sent little stabs of pain into my eye. "Just something in my contact."

He nodded. "Okay, good. Well then, I'll find out what's going on with your ATM card and give you a call."

"Great." The pain from my contact was shooting straight into my brain. I flashed him a Julia Roberts smile that probably ended up looking more like that of The Joker.

As I turned to leave the bank, I worried that Bradley might

be checking me out from behind. To cover my oversized back-side, I slung my bag behind me and walked serpentine-style toward the door, stopping and turning to one side every so often to feign admiration for a plastic plant or an employee-of-the-month plaque on the wall.

Ironically, however, when I got outside in the bright sunshine and popped my contact lens from my eye, things came more into focus. Bradley was more than likely being friendly to me to get me out of the bank. After all, there probably weren't too many bank presidents who would welcome clients who boomed about men, sex, and penises while leaving a trail of birth control behind them.

# 5

I walked the short distance down Canal Street from the bank to LaMarca, with its signature Italian white marble sign with the gold logo. Thanks to the police report, I had the name of the salesgirl who'd found Jessica Evans' body—Annabella Stevens. But I knew that if I introduced myself as a private investigator, she wouldn't give me the time of day.

A lot of people wouldn't talk to PIs because they weren't the police, which was ironic considering that a lot of people wouldn't talk to the police either. And, in all probability, LaMarca management had advised its employees not to discuss the crime with its customers. So, the plan was to find out whether Annabella was still working for LaMarca and, if she was, to approach her on the pretense of needing assistance with selecting a scarf for my mom. With any luck, I would glean some information about the crime.

I grasped the handle of LaMarca's tall glass door and discovered that my palms were sweating. This was my first real undercover assignment because rookie cops weren't allowed anywhere near detective work, and I was nervous. So, I did what any female PI would do as I entered the elegant store—I summoned Nancy Drew's cool-headed sleuthing techniques from the dark and murky depths of my adolescent reading memory.

Inside, I spotted the scarf department where Jessica's body had been found. Four, long, shoulder-height scarf racks were positioned in the shape of a square in the center of the room. On all four sides of the racks, there were glass cases displaying jewelry, wallets, and other accessories, and the walls were lined all the way to the ceiling with multiple rows of handbags of varying colors and shades. The ceiling itself was covered with ornate gold decorative elements like those of a Catholic Church. For a moment, I was breathless with emotion—not because I was at the scene of the crime, mind you, but because I was busy worshipping all those glorious LaMarca bags.

"May I help you?"

The blonde Amazonian salesgirl's booming voice startled me out of my fine leather-induced stupor. I glanced at her nametag. "No thanks, Svetlana. I'm just looking."

Without giving her a chance to respond, I scurried to the scarf racks. Nancy Drew would have never acted so nervous. I took a deep breath and tried to focus. I knew I should be looking for clues related to the crime, but I had no idea what those might be.

As I gazed at the beautiful silk scarves, the image of a vibrant young woman with shoulder-length blonde hair lying strangled popped into my mind. Again I wondered why the killer had strangled her with a scarf from another store when there were so many scarves right at his or her fingertips. Maybe Ryan Hunter or another male admirer had brought the scarf to Jessica as a gift and then used it to strangle her during an argument. Or the scarf could have belonged to a woman who'd removed it from her own neck to strangle Jessica.

*But was it mere happenstance that she'd been strangled with a cheap polyester scarf in a sea of expensive silk? Or was it some kind of message?*

"Can I help you with something?" a chipper voice asked from behind me.

I turned to see a chubby young girl with hazel bug eyes and Shirley Temple curls in a Lucille Ball red straight from the bottle. She wore a white, short-sleeved angora sweater, a black poodle skirt, and a pink scarf knotted around her neck, which was an astonishingly 1950s look for someone who worked in contemporary fashion. Her nametag read Annabella.

*It's her.*

"Yes, I'm trying to find a scarf for my mom, but I'm overwhelmed by all the options." My words sounded fake and stilted to my ear, but the 1950s pinup girl didn't seem to notice.

"Oh, I can totally help you with that. I just love scarves. What color did you have in mind?"

"Yellow." I waited to see her reaction. Even though Annabella had an airtight alibi—she was in the emergency room with a nasty case of the hives at the time of the murder—my instincts told me that she knew more about the situation than she had shared with the police.

Annabella's bulging eyes opened even wider for an instant, then she regained her composure. "What a lovely choice," she said stiffly. She beckoned me to follow her to another rack.

As she sifted expertly through scarves in hues of amber, gold, and yellow, I came up with a casual segue into the crime. "I'm so glad your scarf area is open. I wasn't sure it would be... after the murder."

"LaMarca is open three hundred sixty-five days per year." Annabella recited the hours like a slogan. Then she looked me in the eyes. "Actually," her voice had lowered, "we were open for business later that same day."

"Now that's customer service." It was the most innocuous

thing I could think of to say. I sensed that she was the gossipy type, so I decided to try winning her trust with flattery. "By the way, I *love* your look. You should be on TV, you know that? You have that glamorous quality about you."

Annabella blushed. "That's what I think, but Svetlana is always telling me I look dowdy."

"I can't believe that," I lied as I looked through the scarves. "So, um, did you know her? The woman who was strangled?"

"She was our manager," she whispered, her eyes darting from side to side to make sure no one was in earshot. "Her name was Jessica Evans." Annabella stopped searching through the scarves and draped her arm casually over one of the racks.

My compliments were taking effect—she was clearly in the mood to talk murder. "What was Jessica like? I mean, was she as stylish as you? I'm asking because I'm obsessed with true crime."

She leaned forward. "Well, she was drop dead gorgeous for one thing. A lot of people said she looked like a young Kim Basinger. And she only wore the latest styles—LaMarca, Hermes, Gucci, Chanel, Armani. You name the brand, she had it. And she *always* accessorized with a scarf."

"You don't say."

"Yeah, she said that a scarf gives your outfit that touch of class, unless it's a cheap one, of course."

One look at Annabella's scarf confirmed that she hadn't internalized that all-important accessory rule. But if Jessica had said that, what had it meant that she'd been strangled with a cheap scarf she would have detested? "Did she really say that? About cheap scarves, I mean?"

"Yeah."

I looked through the scarves. "Was she a good manager?"

"Well, she was cold as ice to her employees." Annabella's happy tone had turned huffy. "I mean, I know you're not supposed to speak ill of the dead. But for her, we were nobodies

—lower than nobodies. But that's the way it is in fashion, and she knew this business like the back of her hand. She actually got to intern at the original LaMarca store in Milan's Via Monte Napoleone fashion district. I don't know how she did it, either, because they never give internships to foreigners."

"How nice for her." I considered the connections Jessica must have had to land that kind of opportunity.

"I was hoping she would mentor me. You know, so I could work my way up? But she thought I was too unfashionable." Her double chin trembled with emotion from the perceived injustice of that last statement.

"Well, that's just *her* opinion." I wanted to reassure her even though I *did* think that the poodle skirt was killing her career chances. "I mean, you look like a 1950s version of Geri Halliwell —you know, Ginger Spice? So how in the *world* could you be unfashionable?"

"I know, right?" She sniffled. "But Jessica was nothing if not brutally honest. Besides, she always said that emotion had no place in the business world and that we should leave our feelings at home—along with our personal lives."

"Speaking of personal lives, the police think her boyfriend did it, right?" I pulled a hideous scarf from the rack and pretended to examine its bizarre horseshoe pattern.

"Yeeeeeah." Annabella's tone was doubtful as she plucked a stray yellow thread from her white sleeve. "But I'm not so sure."

"Why do you say that?" I watched as she twisted the thread around her fingers.

"Well, for starters, fashion is a cutthroat industry. If you've made it in this business, you've got enemies." She gave me an extra wide-eyed and knowing look.

"Gosh, I had no idea the business was like that," I fibbed as I put the ugly scarf back on its hanger. "Do you know if Jessica had any enemies?"

"Maaaaaybe," Annabella said, suddenly vague and evasive. Then she batted her eyelashes. "Oh, I guess I can tell *you*. You're not the police." She glanced from side to side again and even took a look behind her. "There was at least one guy who didn't like her. He came in here one night after we were closed. Jessica didn't know I was here because I'd left for the night, but I came back because I'd forgotten my purse. I went in through the back of the store, so I never saw him, but I heard him yelling at her."

"What did he say?" I turned to look at her, abandoning all attempts to seem like a scarf shopper.

"Well, I couldn't hear all of it, but I know he said she'd broken an agreement they had. And I think he warned her to stay away from New Orleans. He also said something about the London College of Fashion, and it almost sounded like Jessica had gone there. The weird thing is that Jessica never mentioned going to that school. It's not even on her company profile."

I shared her confusion. Leaving a prestigious institution like the London College of Fashion off your famous design house company profile was like intentionally not telling your doctor that you had cancer. It just didn't make sense. "Maybe you misunderstood."

"No." She broke the thread in half. "I'm positive the guy said she was a student. I mean, how could I mistake the London College of Fashion? Jimmy Choo went there."

"Of course." I said it as though I were an expert in Jimmy Choo's pedigree. "Did she say anything back to the guy?"

"Just that LaMarca had offered her amaaaaazing incentives on the condition that she manage the New Orleans store for a year. Sales were down, so they wanted a Louisiana native to try to turn it around. I heard her tell him that she wouldn't be in town for long, but he said he wanted her gone right away."

"Maybe it was an ex-boyfriend. You know how demanding men can be."

"I don't know."

I followed her bulging gaze as she glanced at someone who appeared to be a manager and then resumed the scarf search. "How long ago did this happen?"

"A few months ago, so I doubt there's any connection to her death. Hey, do you like any of these?" Annabella shoved four yellow scarves at me.

"That bright yellow one."

"Great. Should I put this aside for you while you continue shopping, ma'am?"

I could tell by her shift to a more professional tone that the gossip fest had ended. "No, I think that's it for today." I noted the two hundred forty-dollar price tag on the scarf with a sinking feeling. *Well, if I go without food this month, I might finally lose that twenty pounds.*

As Annabella bounced off to the register in her pink bobby socks and dingy white Keds, I pulled my wallet from my bag and accidentally upended my coin purse in the process.

"*Mannaggia.*" I muttered the Italian version of *damn* as my change spilled onto the gold carpet. I bent down to retrieve a quarter that had rolled underneath the base of the first scarf rack on the right, and I dislodged a small, hard object. It was a brownish-white bead the size of a hazelnut, and it was carved from ivory or some type of bone in the form of an eerie-looking skull. *Could it have something to do with Jessica's death?*

I checked to make sure no one was watching as I pocketed the bead and headed to the cash register.

∼

"A skull bead? That's freakin' awesome," David exclaimed as I pulled the bead from my pocket during an impromptu meeting in Veronica's office. He grabbed the bead with his long, skeletal fingers. "Hey, this looks exactly like one of those beads from Marie Laveau's House of Voodoo."

"Marie Laveau?" I took the bead. "The voodoo queen? Father John told me she was dead."

"She is." Veronica leaned back in her maraschino cherry-colored leather chair. "It's a voodoo store on Bourbon Street that uses her name."

David nodded. "Yeah, my buddy Alex has a bracelet made of those beads hanging from the rearview mirror of his Honda. He said he got them from there."

"Really?" Veronica sat forward. She had always been one to take an interest in jewelry, even of the voodoo variety. "Do you know what these beads signify?"

"Nah, you'd have to ask the kid who works at the store. I'd check it out though, cause that place is rad," David said in college speak. "They have voodoo dolls, chicken feet, gator heads, all kinds of potions. It's badass in there."

It sounded more beastly than badass. "Potions? For what?"

He shrugged. "Lots of stuff, like love potions and ones that'll help you score some cash. There's even one that'll help you beat the law, like in court."

I remembered the pound cake left for Saint Expedite. "There sure is a lot of voodoo that centers around winning court cases. I wonder if they make one that will help you *solve* a case."

"Speaking of solving cases," Veronica stood and removed a pale pink trench coat with a ruffled collar from the coat rack near her desk, "it's getting late, and tomorrow is Saturday. But there are a few things you and I will have to do this weekend, Franki. First, I need you to stop by Marie Laveau's sometime before Monday. If the murderer dropped the skull bead—and that's a big *if*—then we need to find out whether it came from that store."

"No problem." I kind of wanted to take a look at those love

potions David had mentioned while I was there. Not that I believed in that sort of thing, of course—at least, not completely. "Do you want me to call the police too?"

David stared at me, motionless.

Veronica blinked. "What for?"

"To tell them about the skull bead. If it does turn out to be connected to the Evans case, then it's evidence."

"We're not required to share evidence with the police." Veronica spoke slowly, like I was a child. "Just like they're not obligated to turn over any evidence to us."

"Oh, right. I know that." I did my best to sound like I'd simply forgotten that not-so-minor detail.

An awkward silence followed.

I rose and went to the door. "I'll go call the London College of Fashion to verify that Jessica was a student there."

"It's too late to call London now, so I'll take care of that first thing Monday morning." Veronica slipped on her coat. "Anyhow, the other thing you and I have to do tomorrow is scour local shops for that scarf. If we find out where it came from, we might be able to track down who bought it. Besides, all this talk of scarves and London has put me in the mood to do some shopping."

~

AT NINE P.M., I slid into a lavender-scented bubble bath in my pink-claw foot tub, and my phone rang. "Figures." I glanced at the display, which was face up on the toilet lid. "Aaaaand it's my parents."

I considered letting it go to voicemail but decided to answer. I would need a relaxing bath after a call from home. And maybe a bottle of Chianti. I took a deep breath and picked up.

"Hello?" I tried to conceal the anxiety in my voice.

"Francesca, I got-a you two." My nonna spoke with the cadence of someone who'd just crossed the finish line of a long, arduous marathon.

"Two what, Nonna?"

"Dates, Franki. Dates. *Mamma mia.*"

"Only two?" The question came out before I could fully think through the ramifications.

"It's-a hard work-a finding a date for a zitella who is-a twenty-nine years of age. Give-a me a break-a! Besides, you been around-a the block a time or two, *eh*? And you don't even go to church. *Dio mio!* I'm-a no Mother Theresa here. I don't work-a no miracles."

There was no point in arguing. Grandmothers in contemporary Sicily had modernized with the times, but those like my nonna, who had immigrated to the United States in the first half of the twentieth century, still mentally lived in Fascist Italy. We granddaughters could try to challenge their dictatorial rule, but we knew it was a futile and even risky endeavor. "So, who are these guys?"

"Bruno and Pio."

*Brown and Pius*, I translated. With names like those, they had to be the sons, grandsons, or nephews of her Sicilian friends. I just hoped that they didn't have the stereotypical Sicilian-American worldview, which necessarily precluded the best that modernity had to offer women—things like working outside the home, eating pre-made food, and wearing brightly colored clothing.

"Franki, are you still-a there?"

"Yes, Nonna." I tried to come up with a reason that would prevent me from going out with those guys. For lack of a better excuse, I opted for the truth. "Listen, I appreciate you trying to help me, but I don't feel comfortable going on blind dates."

There was a long, frustrated sigh on the other end of the

phone followed by silence—a sure sign that my nonna was summoning her inner matriarch in preparation for battle. And a Sicilian grandma was a formidable opponent, especially if she was your father's *mamma*. In that case, a girl couldn't rely on her dad for support because Sicilian mothers played their sons like finely tuned mandolins, and my dad was no exception.

"Francesca, you go on-a these dates, or I go to my grave-a."

In one savvy maneuver, my nonna had won the battle before it had begun. If I didn't go on the dates, she would tell my father that I was killing her. And my father, like a good Italian son, would tell me that I was being selfish for making my nonna so unhappy and guilt me into complying with her demands. There was nothing left to do but feign acquiescence, and then try to find an alternate method of escape.

"Okay, Nonna." I glanced at Napoleon, who'd entered the bathroom with one ear cocked to listen in. "What can you tell me about these guys?"

"Bruno, he is-a the son of-a my friend Santina. She's-a the one who hurt-a her back in that terrible car accident."

My ear pricked up like Napoleon's. "What car accident?"

"The one where Bruno was-a driving her to mass, and he run-a the red light."

I seized upon Bruno's less-than-ideal driving skills as an excuse to get out of the date. "He doesn't sound like a safe driver. I'm not sure that I should be going anywhere with him."

"Don't-a worry, Franki. He don't have-a the driver license no more. Besides, you gonna meet-a him at-a his house."

*Foiled again.* "I don't know this guy, so I'd rather meet him at a neutral place like a restaurant," I countered as I extended my hand and stroked the fur on Napoleon's head.

"No, because his *mamma* she gonna cook-a the dinner."

"Nonna, I'm too old to be chaperoned on a date by someone's mother."

"Franki, she's-a no gonna chaperone. Bruno live-a with his *mamma*."

*Of course he does—like all single Italian men.*

"And he is a nice-a boy because he take-a good care of his *mamma*." Her tone reflected her utmost respect. "And he don't have-a no kids."

My nonna was clearly trying to sell me on Bruno, which meant she was hiding something.

"How old is he, and what does he do for a living?" My voice was wary, and Napoleon's eye narrowed as though he were wary too.

"He is a thirty-nine, and he work-a for the New Orleans Saints-a for twenty years."

My nonna was well aware that as a Texas girl I was a *huge* football fan, and I was already envisioning a date that included box seats at the Superdome with catered Cajun food and a few Hurricanes thrown in. But I wondered if she knew that the Saints were a football team and not an association of Catholic martyrs. "What does he do for the Saints, exactly?"

"He manage a food-a stand at-a the stadium."

*So much for the box seats.* "What about Pio?"

"Pio, he is-a forty, and he is-a the nephew of Luisa, who is-a the cousin of my cousin, Agatina."

*A relative? This is an easy out.* "Nonna, I'm not going to date anyone I'm related to, no matter how old I get."

Napoleon must have felt comforted by my strong stance, because he closed his eyes and curled up on the bathroom rug.

"Franki, he don't have-a our blood. And his-a *famiglia* they own-a the funeral parlor in-a my town, Porto Empedocle."

*Of course they do, because that sort of thing makes my skin crawl.* "Does he live at home with his mother too?"

"No, he live at-a the YN-aCA."

"The YMCA, Nonna. And why does he live *there*?"

Napoleon reopened one eye, backing up my suspicion.

"He can't-a live with his *mamma* because he pay-a for her to live at-a the retirement home, and he also have-a to pay-a the alimonies to his ex-wife and kids."

"He's divorced, *and* he has kids?"

"*Sì*, five. But he has a good-a job, *eh* Franki?"

She threw the job part in, knowing full well that an invalid mother, an ex-wife, and five kids definitely qualified as baggage.

"Nonna, I don't mean to sound like a snob, but I'd rather not date a man who works at a funeral home. You know that sort of thing is disturbing to me."

Napoleon opened both eyes and raised his head. If he could've talked, he would've agreed with me.

"Franki, he work-a for the sanitation department."

*So did Tony Soprano. But if Pio lives at the Y, then I can rule out the Mafia. Well, maybe.* "I have an idea. Why don't you give me their phone numbers so I can call them?" I asked, knowing that I never would. It was a weak last-ditch attempt, but it was all I had.

"I already gave-a them your number. And your street address and your address for the emails too."

Nonna had covered her bases. Hers was no ordinary act of war—she'd declared a full-on state of emergency.

"I gave-a them-a Veronica's number too. It's-a better to be safe than-a sorry, *no*? And you've been-a sorry for a long-a time."

*Okay, that's it. Time to cut the call short, with or without my dating exit strategy.* "Nonna, I'll wait for Bruno and Pio to call. Give my love to Mom and Dad. *Ciao ciao!*"

I hung up and did what any self-respecting Italian-American girl would do following a crushing defeat from her nonna—I climbed from the bubble bath and headed straight for the kitchen where I opened the pantry door and grabbed a bottle of Chianti.

As I downed my first glass of the rich, red liquid, I wondered whether my dating prospects were so grim that I needed my grandmother to set me up with reckless mamma's boys who worked in concessions and divorced mobsters who lived at the Y. After all, I wasn't bad looking, and even though I'd gained a few pounds, I was trying to lose weight.

I poured myself another glass of wine and grabbed some fontina cheese from the refrigerator. Plus, I refused to believe that a single woman had to raise the white flag of dating surrender at the age of twenty-nine. To thwart the intentions of my nonna and her army of Sicilian suitors, I needed to find a guy and quick. And I couldn't lie about it because my nonna definitely had her sources.

I took a swig straight from the bottle and resolved to pay another visit to Pontchartrain Bank. If it was between Nonna's picks or Bradley, who may or may not have been flirting with me, I'd give the sexy bank manager a second chance—that is, unless he had a Sicilian mamma or nonna.

## 6

"Veronica, are you alive?" I crouched beneath her tiny front porch to avoid the pouring rain and knocked on her apartment door for the third time.

"Be right there!"

"Okay." I felt a tinge of apprehension. I'd been in New Orleans for almost a week and still hadn't seen the inside of Veronica's apartment. When we were in college, she had a Cinderella-style dorm room that had always made me uncomfortable. I could deal with the pink—even though I'd always been a purple girl myself—but her delicate princess furniture made me feel like Alice in Wonderland after she'd eaten the cake and grown to the size of a giantess.

Veronica threw open the door, and both she and Hercules were dressed in matching orange rain gear. "Sorry it took me so long. I could *not* get Hercules's galoshes on."

"No worries. Are you ready to go murder scarf shopping?"

"Yeah, I'm just going to run him outside for a sec. To do his business," she whispered and walked Hercules past me and out into the yard.

"I'll wait inside." As I turned to close her door behind me, I caught a glimpse of the living room and did a double take. Instead of the familiar princess furnishings, I saw chunky, animal print-upholstered furniture made of dark wood—the legs, arms, and backs of which had been carved to look like tiki idols. Adding to the bizarre décor were tropical curtains, lamps with fuzzy orange shades, lime green wall-to-wall shag carpeting and enough plants to simulate a rain forest. It looked like our landlady Glenda had bought out the contents of Elvis Presley's Jungle Room at Graceland on one of her antique-shopping trips.

Veronica returned with Hercules and removed her raincoat. "What do you think of my new couch?"

"Th-this is *your* furniture?"

"Yes." She beamed. "Do you like it?"

"Uh, it's wild." I took a seat in an armchair that had what looked like an angry island god perched atop its back.

"I know." Veronica kicked off her galoshes and freed Hercules from his teensy galoshes and itty-bitty raincoat, which looked a lot like a doggie straitjacket. "Franki, I think I've discovered something important about the Evans case."

"What?" My tone was hesitant. I was still trying to come to grips with her Polynesian Primitive style.

"Take a look at this." Veronica retrieved a crime scene photo from her lava rock coffee table and shoved it under my nose. "I don't know how I missed it before." She pointed to the photo, which featured the yellow-trimmed scarf that had apparently been used to strangle Jessica.

I scrutinized the edge of the scarf, which Veronica was jabbing at with a perfect pink nail. "I don't see anything."

"Here, use this." Veronica handed me a magnifying glass in the shape of a hibiscus flower.

As I looked through the lens, I saw something thin and white where she was pointing. "What is that?"

Her eyes glowed as bright as the lampshades. "It's a fine barb."

"Um, okay," I said sarcastically. "I guess you could call the scarf 'fine garb'—if you work at the Renaissance Fair."

Veronica rolled her eyes. "I said 'fine *barb*.' It's the piece of plastic used to attach a price tag to a garment."

I blinked. "You *would* know what that thing is called."

"Yeah, me and the millions of people who work in retail." She took the photo and magnifying glass from my hands.

"So, what do you think that fine barb thingy means?" I leaned over to stroke Hercules's fluffy fur.

She sat in the tiny armchair. "It means that the scarf was new."

"Why do you say that? Someone could have left it there without noticing."

"What kind of person leaves a fine barb on clothing and doesn't notice?"

"Beats me," I said, thinking of all the times I'd unknowingly walked around with stickers from the store still on my clothes, not to mention the occasions when I'd put on my underwear or even my T-shirt inside out. *Come to think of it, had I managed to put everything on the right way today?* I did a quick spot check and then returned my attention to the case. "But, so what if it was new?"

"I'm convinced that someone brought a brand-new scarf there on purpose." She crossed her arms with conviction.

"You mean, as a gift? But remember, Annabella said that Jessica hated cheap scarves. So why would someone bring her a scarf they knew she wouldn't like?" I smoothed Hercules's fur to see what he would look like without his Pomeranian poof.

"Maybe the person who brought it to her didn't know that. If it was a man—well, you know how clueless men can be about clothing."

"And if it was a woman, she would probably know that Jessica wouldn't like the scarf."

"Precisely."

Veronica seemed to understand everything perfectly. I, on the other hand, couldn't figure out how a gift-buying *faux pas* could solve a murder.

"So what do you make of it?" I leaned back and assessed Hercules. With his fur flattened, he looked a lot like a Jorge.

"If you're talking about Hercules's fur, I think it looks awful. But if you mean the scarf, I'm not sure yet. But something tells me that if we find out why someone gave her that particular scarf, we may have our answer."

"Well, the fact that the scarf was new should make it easier for us to track down."

Hercules struggled out of my arms and ran to Veronica.

"Correct." Veronica repoofed his fur and gave him a reassuring pat. "So, I've made a list of local stores and their addresses. We'll have to split up to cover more ground."

"Split up? That's no fun."

"Francesca Lucia Amato." Veronica shook her head. "A day of shopping is *always* fun."

∽

AFTER SPENDING several hours scouring boutiques in the Canal Street area, I decided that it was time to break for a late lunch. The rain had stopped, and it was shaping up to be a sunny and unseasonably warm day. Fortunately, Pontchartrain Bank was open from noon until six on Saturdays. So, I figured I'd stop by before grabbing a bite—to check on the status of my ATM card, of course.

I entered the lobby and scanned the room for Bradley. There was no sign of him, but I did see Corinne. She beckoned to me from her teller window, and she looked pale and despondent, like Tinker Bell without her pixie dust.

I approached her window. "Is everything okay?"

"Franki, you are a private investigator, *non*?"

"Yes. Why?"

Her eyes filled with tears. "Yesterday I come home from work, and my *petite Bijou*, she is missing."

I wasn't entirely sure who or what a *petite Bijou* was, so I hazarded a guess. "Is Bijou your pet?"

"*Oui*, she is my *chien—pardon*, my dog. She was a gift from Thierry." Corinne choked down a sob." She is just a puppy."

"What kind of dog is she?"

"She is a *bichon frise*." She reached for her handbag under the counter and pulled out her phone. She pulled up a picture of Bijou. He looked a lot like a white powder puff with black eyes and a black nose. "Franki, can you please help me find her? I pay whatever you want."

"Of course." I examined the picture. "How did the thief get into your house? Had any of the doors been tampered with? Or a window?"

"*Non*." She blew her nose with a honk. "I live in an *appartement* on ze fours floor."

"Was anything else taken?" I handed the phone back to her.

"Only *Bijou*." She wailed and covered her eyes.

"So, it sounds like someone went there just to steal her. Corinne, the last time I was here, you said that you and Thierry had broken up. Are the two of you back together?"

"*Non*. We are *fini*." She put her head in her hands.

"Do you think he could have taken Bijou?"

"It is possible." She raised her tear-stained face. "He still has ze key, and he is very angry wis me. But he loves *Bijou*, so I don't know if he would do zat to her."

"Does anyone else have a key? Like your parents or a friend?"

"No, but in ze *appartement* office, zey have a key."

I pulled a notepad and pen from my purse. "Where does Thierry live?"

"He stay wis a friend named Brady Reiff who lives near ze *Place d'Armes*. I don't know ze *adresse*."

"Where is the Place Darm?" I asked in my very best Texan-French.

"Ah, *pardon*. It is ze French name for Jackson Square, ze park by ze Mississippi River. You know, when Thierry live wis me, he take *Bijou* zere on Saturday afternoons for a walk."

"Then that will be the first place I look. I need you to text or email me the picture of Bijou and a few pictures of Thierry so that I know what he looks like." I wrote my contact information on a piece of paper for her.

"*Tout de suite*. But Franki, can I help you with somesing? You came to ze bank..."

"No, I just wanted to check on my ATM card." I tore the paper from my pad and handed it to her.

"Ah, *oui*. It came yesterday afternoon. I was going to call you, but Mr. Hartmann say he would do it. I get it for you. *Un moment*."

"*Non*," I shouted in French, not wanting to leave even the slightest bit of room for doubt. Nothing and no one was coming between me and a call from Bradley Hartmann.

Corinne blinked, confused.

"There's no time to lose. I have to get to work on your case right away," I gushed, trying to cover for my outburst. I shoved my notepad and pen into my purse and started to leave. "*Au revoir*."

"Wait."

I turned to look at Corinne.

"*Merci beaucoup*." Her big blue eyes were full of gratitude.

"*Prego*." I thanked her in Italian in keeping with the foreign language theme. "And don't worry, Bijou will be back before you know it."

As I turned and headed for the door, I again scoured the room for Bradley, using my peripheral vision so as not to seem too obvious. But there was no sign of him, which either meant that I was a bad investigator—entirely possible—or that he had the day off.

Outside I glanced at my watch and saw that it was two o'clock. Marie Laveau's was open until one thirty in the morning on Saturdays, so I had plenty of time to stake out Jackson Square before going to investigate the skull bead. But first I would need to let Veronica know that I'd taken a new case. I pulled my phone from my purse and dialed her number.

"Hey, Franki."

Veronica sounded extra upbeat, probably because she was shopping. "Any luck?"

"Well, I've found plenty of things for me, but I haven't found the scarf, if that's what you mean. What about you?"

I leaned against a lamppost. "No scarf, but I did get a case."

"How?"

"A bank teller I met named Corinne wants us to find her stolen dog. I know we're in the middle of the Evans investigation, but I'm thinking maybe her ex-boyfriend took the dog, so it should be a fairly simple case to solve."

"Way to go."

I breathed a sigh of relief. "So you don't mind?"

"Mind?" She giggled. "Private investigators work multiple cases all of the time. Besides, we could use a bank contact."

"What for?"

"At the moment, for the Evans case. Ryan Hunter seems to think that Jessica Evans had more money than she should. Your teller might be able to help us find out if someone was paying her."

"I'll keep that in mind. Corinne is really nice, so she might be willing to help us. Speaking of the Evans case, I'm going to Marie Laveau's later today. Right now I have to follow up on a lead about the dog."

She sighed with mock despair. "I guess I'll have to go it alone in the scarf search, then."

"You're a real trooper, Veronica." I'll call you later with an update." I closed the call and headed toward my car. I had parked at the office, which was just down the street from Jackson Square. But I needed to go home and get Napoleon. He and I were going undercover.

~

"We're on the clock now, Napoleon." I shot him a somber look as we walked along the sidewalk toward Jackson Square in the French Quarter. "And we're Texans, so we've got to go big or go home."

He turned and lifted a paw, confused.

I realized how my words of encouragement must've sounded. "I'm not talking about doing your business—or going back to the apartment. You dogs are so literal."

He resumed walking—his version of a shrug.

I scanned the area. I was fairly certain that Thierry wouldn't bring a stolen dog to the park, but it was as good a place as any to search. First I wanted to case the streets that bordered the square because they were more popular with pet-walking pedestrians than the park itself. Also, I had to keep Napoleon moving as I investigated the area because, as dogs go, he wasn't the ideal park companion. Either he didn't understand the concept of fetch, or he just plain didn't want to play the game. And like the French conqueror after whom he was named, Napoleon was territorial and made darn sure the other dogs knew it. On the plus side, he was the perfect cover for staking out a prospective dog thief.

We arrived at the heavy iron fence that enclosed Jackson Square, and I peered through the slats. It was fairly empty and really lovely with its brilliant pink and yellow flowers, perfectly manicured lawns, and gorgeous old oak trees. In the center there was an equestrian statue of General Andrew Jackson, commemorating the Battle of New Orleans. Overlooking the park was the Cathedral-Basilica of St. Louis King of France, the oldest Catholic cathedral in continual use in the United States, with its stunning gray and white spires.

Before entering the park, I led Napoleon across the street to Washington Artillery Park on the Mississippi River. A crowd had gathered at the small amphitheater near its replica Civil War cannon to watch a couple of boys tap dance, but there was no sign of Thierry or Bijou.

We walked back toward the Jackson Square Park entrance and turned left onto St. Peter Street, which ran along the park's west side and was home to the famous French Market with the yellow-gold archway. I stopped to window-shop at a cute little jewelry store called Ooh La La. After all, I had to look the part of a local on a Saturday afternoon stroll with her dog.

Next, we took a right onto Chartres Street, on the north side of the park. We were immediately thrust into the throng of tourists who had gathered to see the street musicians, mimes, and open-air artist colony. I enjoyed the work of street musicians and artists, but not the mimes. The appeal of painting oneself monochrome and silently pretending to do something like juggle or cry was lost on me. As I browsed the caricatures, portraits, and landscape paintings displayed on the iron fence that encircled the park, I did my best to ignore a pesky silver-colored mime who pretended to give me what I can only assume was a pretend flower.

After scouring the masses on Chartres, we turned right onto St. Ann Street. Napoleon pulled at the leash and growled at some tarot card readers who'd set up their little tables in front of the shops.

"Hey, Dog Whisperer." A genie wannabe with a hoop earring and a head scarf rose from his tiny card table. "How about you control your deranged mutt?"

I looked him in the blue-eyeshadowed eyes. "Let's go, Napoleon. I don't trust these sham fortune-tellers either."

A tarot reader in a top hat and tails scowled and stood in solidarity with the genie.

Before they could put a curse on us, or whatever tarot card readers did, I dragged Napoleon down the street to the gourmet and kitchen shop Creole Delicacies. I tucked him under my arm and popped inside to buy some pecan pralines—the riverfront streetcar box of twelve, to be precise. I didn't need the calories, but I considered sampling local specialties to be an essential part of my cover.

With pralines in hand—and in mouth—I decided it was time to stake out the park. We took a right onto Decatur Street and entered through the iron gates. We walked down the park's gravel-lined walkways, and I kept my eyes peeled for Thierry and the powder puff.

Napoleon kept his peeled for pigeons and squirrels.

We circled the park a few times, and I sat on a bench near the statue of Andrew Jackson. To pass the time, I pulled out my phone and snapped a few pictures of the statue and the St. Louis Cathedral. Then I reviewed the pictures that Corinne had sent of Bijou and Thierry. The photos of Thierry were blurred, so I wasn't sure if I would be able to identify him if he walked by dog-less. But the plan was to stay put for an hour or so, munching on pralines and watching joggers, people pushing baby strollers, and dog-walkers.

A small, fluffy white puppy appeared from behind a giant oak tree, and I dropped the last praline in the dirt. "*Mannaggia*."

Napoleon grabbed it before I could invoke the five-second rule.

With a sad sigh, I pulled out my phone and studied the photo of Bijou. As I looked from the photo to the dog, a big, strapping man with reddish hair emerged from behind the tree and scooped the tiny puppy into his powerful arms.

"Poo, poo, poo." He snuggled his ruddy red, freckled face into the little white ball of fur. "Poo, poo, poo."

I wasn't sure whether he was cooing or telling the dog to go, but either way it was embarrassing.

He turned the dog in his arms, and I spotted a tattoo on his right bicep. I looked again at the picture of Thierry. He seemed to have light brown hair, not red, and he wore a sweater, so it was impossible to tell whether he had a tattoo.

I dialed Corinne's number while the guy made smooching sounds at the dog. *Whoever this dude is, he sure loves that fluffball.*

"*Allo*, Franki?"

"Hey, Corinne." I spoke in a whisper. "I'm at the park at Jackson Square. There's a white puppy here that could be Bijou—"

"Really? What does it look like?"

"It's definitely a bichon frise, but the photos you sent of Thierry aren't very clear. And the guy who's here with the dog looks, well, Irish."

"Zat is him."

"What? Thierry is just Terry? I thought he was French." I glanced nervously at the guy, but he didn't seem to have heard me.

"No, he is Irish. His surname is O'Callaghan. Oh, Franki, it is him, *non*?"

"There's an easy way to find out. Does Thierry, er, Terry, have a tattoo on his right bicep?"

"*Oui.* It is a leprechaun. From *ze americain* cereal."

"Wait a second. Do you mean Lucky? The Lucky Charms leprechaun?"

"*Voilà.* You know him?"

"I know him well, Corinne." My tone had turned grim. Terry was kind of lame. An Irishman with a Lucky the Leprechaun tattoo was like an Italian with a tattoo of Super Mario. Pitiful. Notre Dame's Fighting Irish mascot would have made a way better stereotypical tattoo, especially for a big, muscular guy like the one romping around before me with the white powder puff.

"Franki, are you still zere?" She sounded panicked.

"Yes, sorry. I got distracted for a moment."

"Zis man, does he have ze lucky leprechaun?"

I turned, and the guy was walking the dog. His right arm was extended from holding the leash, so I had a clear shot of the tattoo.

*Lucky.*

I would know that leprechaun anywhere. "It's him, all right. Get down here right away."

## 7

"Corinne might look like Tinker Bell, but she definitely doesn't have her speed," I grumbled to myself. Twenty minutes had passed since I'd called and told her to come to Jackson Square. Terry wasn't going to stay at the park forever, and I didn't want to have to confront him over Bijou. After all, the guy was the size of The Jolly Green Giant.

I sent Corinne a text asking for an ETA. Then I looked up.

Terry and Bijou walked toward the exit.

"Dangit. I could die for what I'm about to do, and I'm not even getting paid for it." I sighed and chased down Corinne's giant ex, stepping in front of him. "Terry O'Callaghan? Stop where you are."

He lowered his eyelids but did as I instructed.

It occurred to me that if his whole body were green like his Lucky the Leprechaun tattoo, he would look a lot like The Incredible Hulk.

"Do I know you?" His voice was soft, but dangerous.

"No. I'm a private investigator, and I know that dog is stolen. So if you leave this park, I'm going to have to make a citizen's arrest."

He blinked. And then he began to cry like a baby—a large Irish baby. He sobbed and blubbered in a mix of English and Gaelic, calling Bijou his "wee *aingeal*" and "little *leanbh*," which I knew were terms of endearment from all the *Murder, She Wrote* episodes set in Ireland.

I took the leash from his boxing glove-sized hand, and I saw Corinne running toward us. Her face was drawn.

"Thierry! What is ze matter? Why you are crying?"

Terry's sobs turned to wails. And oddly enough, he sounded exactly like a howling dog.

Corinne wrapped her tiny Tinker Bell arms around his Hulk-like waist. "Zere, zere. Everysing is okay."

Open-mouthed, I wondered what I was witnessing. Then I left the odd duo to work out their differences.

I headed in the direction of the office to drop off Napoleon before going over to Bourbon Street to Marie Laveau's. Although I was hungry, I was going to skip dinner thanks to the pralines I'd eaten for lunch while staking out the park. Mardi Gras was just around the corner, and Veronica had told me that the average New Orleanian gained six pounds during the season, which meant I was sure to gain twelve. And frankly, I couldn't afford to gain any more weight because I was already bursting from my clothes, and I was in no position to buy a new wardrobe.

Trying to drive thoughts of food from my mind—a hard thing to do in the Quarter near dinnertime—I walked up Decatur Street toward Saint Ann. But after only about five minutes, I stopped dead. Right in front of me at an outdoor table at Market Café sat none other than Bradley Hartmann. This was my chance to work my date-getting magic. I'd always been pretty good at getting a guy—I just had trouble keeping one.

I stood up straight, sucked in my stomach, and sauntered past his table, but he didn't notice me because he was absorbed in *The Times-Picayune.* There were some empty tables near where Bradley sat, so I hurried to the hostess. In my haste, I bumped into a burly waitress with short, electric-blue hair, a sleeve tattoo, and triple-pierced eyebrows, causing her to drop a tray loaded with food.

"You just cost me a tip, lady." Her tone was as tough as her look.

"I'm so sorry." I bent down to help her pick up the dishes.

"Why don't you let me take care of this? I think you've done enough already."

I looked up from the pile of broken dishes and read her nametag—Charity. *Talk about a misnomer.* "Like I said, Charity, I'm sorry." I put another plate shard on the tray. "And I can take care of that tip."

"Like *I* said, lady, I got this." She shot me an aggressive look.

"Well, if you insist." I rose to my feet. "Listen, I'm really pressed for time, and I don't see your hostess. Would you mind if I seated myself?"

Her pierced brows twitched. "A member of the staff has to seat you. Restaurant policy."

"All right. Can you seat me then, please?"

She stared at me for a moment and clenched her teeth. "Let me get you a menu."

By then I was in such a hurry that I didn't want to wait. So I blew right past her and made a beeline for the banker. "Bradley!"

Apparently, he wasn't used to women shouting his name in restaurants, because he jumped and knocked over his beer, spilling gold liquid all over the bulk of his newspaper.

"I'm so sorry." I sounded like a broken record. "I didn't mean to startle you."

He gave an ironic smile as he rose to his feet. "I didn't want any more of that beer, anyway."

Charity, who had been standing with arms crossed by what was supposed to be my table, rolled her eyes and came over to help us clean up the spill with a towel. She wadded up the wet newspaper and pointed to a table far away. "Your menu is on the table *over there*."

"Thanks, Charity," I said none-too-appreciatively and willed her to leave. For reasons I couldn't fathom, she seemed adamant that I was going to sit at the table she'd selected for me, because she wouldn't budge. And I wasn't budging either.

Bradley, who couldn't help but notice the standoff between Charity and me, came to my rescue. "It's Franki, right?"

I nodded.

"Would you like to join me? I ordered a few minutes ago, so I'm sure there's still time to add your order." He winked at Charity to smooth things over.

"I would love to." I cast Charity a triumphant look. "But I'm not hungry," I lied, hoping he couldn't hear the growling—make that the roaring—of the mighty lion who had chosen that moment to take up residence in my stomach. "I was just going to have a glass of Pinot Grigio."

"So, just the wine?" Charity asked.

To my dismay, I remembered that I was still on the clock—and on a diet. "Make that a cup of coffee. Decaf."

She looked me up and down, as though weighing me with her eyes, and went to place my order.

Bradley turned to me. "You've really got a way with the staff, don't you?"

*Okay, so maybe he wasn't the best choice for a date.* I opted to change the subject to safer ground. "So, what have you been up to today?"

"Errands mostly. And Trixi and I took a walk along the river."

"Trixi?" I felt as though I'd just been kicked in the stomach by that ornery lion.

"Yes, she's my devoted companion." His eyes were twinkling.

"Oh." I was taken aback by my disappointment. After all, I wasn't really interested in the guy. I just needed a date to ward off my nonna.

Bradley looked under the table. "There's my girl."

I followed his gaze and saw a darling cairn terrier with wheaten fur lying at his feet. Of course, cairns were my favorite breed, but I hadn't exactly pegged Bradley as a cute little dog guy. It was definitely a point in his favor.

"She's adorable." I reached down to pet her.

Without raising her head, Trixi lifted one side of her mouth and flashed her teeth at me.

I recoiled in surprise. She wasn't as sweet as she looked. But then again, maybe she was timid and needed a little time to get to know to me. I acted as though nothing had happened with Bradley's beloved canine. "I have a cairn too. His name is Napoleon because he's small in size but big in personality."

"Cairns are great dogs, aren't they? I like them because they're spunky and independent. That's the way I like my women too." He shot me a wicked grin.

*Charming.* I shifted in my chair. The movement angered Trixi, who snapped at my shoe with the speed of a snake. I yanked my foot away. "You have to be careful with cairns, though."

"Yeah, but not with my Trixi." Bradley reached down to stroke her head. She rolled onto her back exposing her butterball belly. "She's an angel."

I glared under the table. *More like a con artist.* "She's something all right."

Charity the waitress returned and gave Bradley his sandwich, a po' boy filled with oysters that had been battered and deep-fried to a golden brown.

She placed the cup of decaf on the table. "Can I get you guys anything else?" Charity looked straight at me. "Like, for example, a meal instead of a cheap cup of coffee?"

I met her gaze with a hint of a glare. "Nope, we're doing great."

"Awesome." She slammed down a plastic tray with the bill and walked away.

Of course she'd left only one peppermint.

"This sandwich is huge." Bradley picked up half. "Would you like some?"

"No thanks." I devoured the po' boy with my eyes. "I couldn't even *think* of food right now," I fibbed, pouring four Splenda packets into my coffee in hopes of adding some density.

"Well, okay, then." He took a hearty bite.

I was starting to think that Bradley knew I was hungry and was rubbing it in. Trying to avoid watching him chew, I took a big, hungry sip of my decaf. It was much hotter than I'd realized, and it scalded my mouth. "Mmm," I moaned, tightening my lips to avoid spitting blistering hot coffee onto Bradley like an erupting volcano. I opened my mouth a crack to let some steam out. "Aawwhh."

"Are you all right?"

"Ow-huh." I forced the burning liquid down in one fiery gulp. "Iss juss so...goouh," I said, avoiding any contact been my tongue and the roof of my mouth.

"Oh, okay. Listen, I was planning on calling you—"

"You were?" I interrupted, forgetting about my scorched mouth—and my dignity.

He flashed a mischievous smile. "Your ATM card finally arrived."

"Right. My ATM card. That's what I thought you'd be calling about." I feigned an intense interest in stirring my coffee.

"I could mail it to you, if you'd like." He took another bite of po' boy.

"Oh no." I wanted to be sure I got that card in person. "What I mean is, I need it before that. I'll just drop by the bank and pick it up."

"Well, the bank's actually open until six today, so you could make it over there in time if you leave after you finish your coffee."

I detected a hint of teasing in his voice. Bradley seemed to think I was into him, which was utterly ridiculous. My interest was strictly business—family business. "It can wait until Monday. I mean, I have lots to do today."

He looked amused. "Anything fun on the agenda?"

"Well, after this I have to go to the voodoo store."

Bradley stopped in mid-bite. "Mind if I ask why?"

"For a case I'm investigating."

"That's right, Corinne said you were a PI. So tell me," he cocked an eyebrow, "which Charlie's Angel are you most like?"

Resentment boiled in my belly—or maybe it was the coffee. He was obviously insinuating that I was both a dilettante *and* a sex object, but I wasn't play-acting at my job. "Well, if you must know I…"

Bradley reached out and freed a strand of my hair that had gotten stuck on my lipgloss, his fingertips lightly grazing my check and my neck.

A shiver ran down my traitorous spine.

He leaned back and draped an arm over the chair next to him. "You were saying?"

"Um, what?" I didn't remember anything before those fingertips.

He flashed one of his fabulous smiles. "About your work?"

"Oh, yeah. That." I shot him an annoyed look. "Well, not just anyone can be a PI. It's a dangerous job. For instance, I just wrapped up a dicey missing dog case, and now I'm investigating a *murder*."

"Which one?"

"The Jessica Evans murder." I gave a solemn nod for effect.

He massaged his chin. "That was such a terrible thing. She was a client at the bank."

"She was?" I asked, surprised.

"Yeah, but I didn't know her very well. She only came in once a month, and she was pretty reserved."

"Really? Just once a month?"

"To make a deposit."

Charity barged up to the table. "Sorry to interrupt." She looked anything but regretful. "My shift actually ended at five, so I'm, uh, on my way out."

Bradley looked at his watch. "I didn't realize how late it was." He stood and pulled his wallet from his back pocket. "I've got a few more errands to run, so I'd better get going."

"Yeah, I'd better be on my way too. I've got to get over to the voodoo store." I shot a pointed look at Charity.

"Franki, I'd like to hear more about your work sometime." He handed Charity a twenty-dollar bill. "How about dinner?"

*A date! I'm saved!* my inner voice cheered. But I had to play it cool. "That would be wonderful."

Charity made a disgusted snort and left, no doubt intending to keep the change.

"Great. If you like Cajun food, we could go to one of Emeril Lagasse's restaurants."

"Perrrfect," I purred.

"I'll make reservations this week and call you."

As I stood up from the table, Trixi lunged at my feet. I stumbled and lurched forward into Bradley's arms.

Trixi, who was undoubtedly lying in wait for any misstep on my part, jerked her head down in the direction of my shoe as though prepared to strike again.

I gazed at Bradley, realizing with a shiver just how tall he was.

He gave a rakish grin, oblivious to Trixi's attack stance. "You didn't have to throw yourself at me, Amato. After all, I *did* just ask you out."

"You don't think I did that on purpose?" I was outraged, but I didn't dare move both because I liked being pressed against his muscular body and because I felt Trixi's hot breath on my foot. "I tripped over your d—"

"Shh." He placed a finger on my lips. "I was trying to get a rise out of you." His voice was husky. "You're really hot when you get worked up."

My eyes went into autopilot, closing in anticipation of a kiss. But, inexplicably, Bradley released me.

As he and the Trixinator turned to leave, I stood as straight and still as a statue. I was numb all over, and it wasn't from fear of his killer cairn.

～

AT SIX P.M. THE throng of partiers on Bourbon Street was already dense, and the sounds of blues and jazz blasted from the doorways of the bars. As I weaved my way through the crowd toward Marie Laveau's House of Voodoo, I was practically floating from the excitement of being asked out. In fact, I was so elated that I didn't even mind when a drunk girl wearing a pink boa, a black mini skirt, and a red-sequined halter top spilled strawberry daiquiri from her elongated plastic fleur-de-lis glass onto my arm. And I actually smiled when a shirtless and unshaven fifty-something-year-old man in a red-white-and-blue top hat looked at me and screamed the Mardi Gras cry, "Show me your tits!"

*Yes, life is good.*

I spotted the hand-painted black sign for Marie Laveau's at the corner of Bourbon and St. Ann and made my way through the crowd. I climbed the two small steps to the store and stopped short in the doorway, surveying the ghoulish scene. The place was jam-packed with candles, voodoo dolls, severed chicken feet, alligator heads, and a creepy altar to Marie Laveau, which had unidentified dead things on it and signs that said, "DO NOT PHOTOGRAPH" and "DO NOT TOUCH."

*Don't worry. I won't.*

"Can I help you?" A bored-looking cashier with a severe case of acne stifled a yawn.

"Yeah, do you have any beads like this one?" I pulled the skull bead from my purse and held it up for him.

"In the back next to the shrunken heads." He nodded in the direction of the next room as he picked at a cyst.

"Um, thanks." *I think.*

I walked to the back of the store. Despite the dim lighting, I could see that the smaller, secondary room was for the more serious voodoo practitioner. There were books on voodoo, talismans of various shapes and sizes, and supplies for creating altars and spell kits. As soon as I entered, my eyes were drawn to the "Speak No Evil Kit," which showed users how to drive coffin nails into a tongue to prevent someone from saying bad things about them. I shuddered but told myself that the tongue included with the kit couldn't be real.

"Did you come for a reading?" The deep James-Earl-Jones voice erupted from the semi-darkness.

And I almost erupted from the store.

The source was an older, heavy-set man with an oversized rockabilly pompadour. He sat behind a counter against the back wall of the room, next to a bizarre wooden statue of a seated woman.

I considered getting a reading to see what my future with

Bradley held, but I decided against it. Voodoo wasn't real—at least, I hoped it wasn't. I deposited the skull bead on the counter. "No, I was looking for beads like this one."

He glanced at the bead with bloodshot eyes. "It's from a Tibetan prayer *mala*. We sell them in necklaces and bracelets. They're right over there." He gestured toward the wall on his left, revealing a colorful tattoo of a decorative skull with his same rockabilly hairdo on his bicep.

"What's a *mala*?"

"It means 'garland,' but it refers to prayer beads. Buddhists use them like a rosary to keep track of time while they're meditating with mantras." His eyeballs darted left to look at the wooden statue.

"Oh. I thought this bead was for voodoo since it's made of bone and carved like a skull." *I mean, what else would anyone use a skull carved from bone for? Not decoration, surely.*

"Buddhists use skull beads made of bone or wood in prayer, and they often wear them around their wrists for protection and long life." He pulled a pack of Marlboro reds from his front pocket. "But devotees of Kurukulla, the Buddhist Goddess of witchcraft and enchantment, wear skull beads made from human and animal bone to—"

"Wait a second. This bead isn't made from a *human* bone, is it?"

"I couldn't tell ya." He shot a nervous look in the direction of the wooden statue.

Although I suspected that the guy was a little off, I pressed on. "So what does this Kookarulla do?"

"Kurukulla." He extracted a cigarette from the pack and laid it on the counter. "She's a young goddess who uses her nudity and voluptuousness to seduce and bewitch others to bring them under her control." The subject of sex must have reminded him to groom himself, because he pulled a comb from his back pocket and ran it through his greased-back hair. Then he tucked the cigarette behind his right ear and folded his hands on the counter.

"So, if you wear the beads, you could use them to try to make others do what you want?"

"That's right." He glanced at the statue. "Kurukulla's followers wear them to overpower spirits and humans who get in their way."

I thought about Saint Expedite, the pound cake, and even the potion. "Are these beads used to try to win court cases, by any chance?"

He nodded. "Yeah, we have a lot of customers who buy them for court."

"Dem beads don' madda none to Baron Kriminel," a deep female voice said from the darkness.

I jumped backward at least a foot. The wooden statue wasn't a statue at all—it was a real live woman with graying black dreadlocks, cappuccino-colored skin, and dark brown freckles on sunken cheeks. And she was shuffling toward me.

"He goin' ta git dem who profit from death." The nostrils of her wide, flat nose flared as she spoke.

"A-are y-you talking t-to me?" I stuttered. "I-I'm working a m-murder case, but I'm t-trying to *help*."

The woman's piercing amber eyes looked straight through me. "Ya not from 'round heuh,"

"N-no, I'm new to town." I hoped that my newness to NOLA would release me from the impending clutches of Baron Krim-inel, whoever he was.

"Baron Kriminel come from de grave to seek justice agains' de guilty."

"But I'm not guilty."

She raised a crooked, knobby finger. "Dat girl, she know what dat boy do."

*Wait. Who's 'dat girl'?* My mind was racing, but in my panicked state all I could think of was the old Marlo Thomas show I'd seen on Nick at Nite. *And 'dat boy'?* "I'm sorry, but I don't understand."

"I cain't tell ya what ya don' see, chile. But Odette see. She see." She had a faraway look in her eyes as she walked past me toward the door.

"Odette?" I watched her leave, more confused than ever.

She stopped and turned in the doorway, her mouth contorted with anger. "Dat boy, he done put a spell on her." Her faced softened. "Ya got a man. A good man. But ya goin' ta have ta work ta keep him."

*I've got a man? Is she talking about Bradley?* "What do you mean, work?" If she was talking about Bradley, then I wanted an answer.

"But don' let 'im take ya down ta de bayou. Ya bes' stay *far* from de bayou, chile, and everythang in it." She turned and shuffled out.

I stood gaping, trying to decipher her cryptic messages.

The aging rockabilly broke the silence. "That's Odette Malveaux. She's a *mambo*."

I turned to face him. "A what?"

"A voodoo priestess." He pulled the cigarette from behind his ear. "Some say she's a descendent of Marie Laveau, which is why she comes to the store from time to time. To keep an eye on things."

I swallowed my shock. "Do you know who she was talking about?"

"No, but if I were you, lady, I'd figure it out." He pointed the cigarette at me. "Baron Kriminel is an evil voodoo god. If he's after you, you're a goner. And it won't be pretty." He put the cigarette between his teeth and rushed from the room.

As I left the store and exited onto Bourbon Street, I realized that the excitement I'd felt when I first arrived was long gone. Instead, apprehension filled my chest. Because I was pretty sure Odette knew things about the Evans case and about Bradley too. Things that I couldn't see.

I headed down St. Ann Street in the direction of the office to get Napoleon, wondering what in the netherworld The Crescent City had in store for me.

---

## 8

**B**arking awoke me, and my eyes flew open. *Had Bradley's dog, Trixi, come to terminate me?*

From my prone position on the bed, I raised my head and realized that it was my new "Who Let the Dogs Out" ringtone. I'd changed it to something sure to wake me up, which had turned out to be an awful idea.

Collapsing face-down, I reached for my pillow so that I could put it over my head, but I couldn't find it. I reopened my eyes, peered over the side of the mattress, and saw it on the floor. Thankfully, the phone had gone silent, so I prepared to go back to sleep.

Less than a minute later, the barking started again.

*I needed a new ringtone.* I pulled myself into a sitting position, but my head spun so violently that I lay down. Whoever was calling could wait.

When the barking stopped, I wracked my aching brain to figure out what was wrong with me. *Was it a sinus headache? Or the flu?* Then I remembered. It was the quarter bottle or so of Limoncello that I'd tossed back on an empty stomach after my heebie jeebie-inducing encounter with Odette Malveaux.

The ringtone sounded a third time. Lying flat on my back, I felt for the evil device on the nightstand with my hand. When I finally found it, I picked it up and looked at the display with one eye—*Unknown.*

*Who would call so early on a Sunday?* Reluctantly, I tapped *Answer.*

"Hello?" There was so much phlegm in my throat that I sounded like Louis Armstrong.

"May I speak to Francesca Amato?" The male voice was high pitched—like Mike Tyson's but without the lisp.

"This is she." I used the flat tone I saved for telemarketers.

"Oh," the voice squeaked.

Silence ensued, and I wondered whether the line had dropped. "Are you still there?"

"Yeah. I thought you were your father."

Embarrassed, I cleared my throat. "Um, who is this?"

"Pio. Pio Principato." His tone was expectant, as though I would know his name.

"Oh, right." I mentally cursed my interfering nonna—in English and Italian—for giving out my phone number. "Listen, Pio, you've kind of caught me at a bad time."

"But your nonna said you'd be expecting my call."

I could tell that Pio and I were going to get along famously. "Well, yes, just not so early in the morning."

"But I was calling to invite you to mass at noon."

*Mass? On a first date?* "I'm afraid I can't. This is awfully short notice, and I have a lot to do today."

He snorted in frustration. "Well, how about tomorrow then?"

"I'm sorry," I said, even though I wasn't feeling the least bit apologetic in light of his rudeness, "but the truth is that I'm expecting a call from another man." *There. The proper thing to do was to tell him about Bradley and end the call. Honesty is the best policy, right?*

"Wow. I didn't know you were that kind of a woman."

Stunned by his presumptuousness, I had to ask for a clarification. "What kind of a woman is that, exactly?"

"A two-timer."

"A what?" I shouted. To hell with my aching head—my pride was more important.

"Well, apparently you date around."

*Who did this guy think he was?* I should have ended the call, but I was too mad to let it go. "In the first place, Pio, you and I are not dating. And second, I haven't even gone out with the other guy yet. All I said was that I was expecting his call. I hardly think that makes me a two-timer."

"I'm sorry, but this isn't going to work out."

*Un.Be.Lievable.* "You don't know how much I agree."

"This is goodbye, then, Francesca." His statement held a warning, as though he was giving me one last chance.

"Before you call another woman," I repressed the urge to yell, "try reading a dating manual." I tapped *End* really hard on my phone. Cell phones were convenient, but sometimes I missed being able to slam down a landline receiver.

I lay in bed, livid, wondering whether Marie Laveau's sold a potion or a spell that could make arrogant men like Pio vanish. Or better yet, one that could make Sicilian grandmothers stop meddling in their granddaughters' love lives. *No, not likely. Not even all the voodoo priestesses in Louisiana could conjure up a spell that powerful.*

Thanks to Pio's call, I was fully awake and far too angry to stay in bed. I got up and headed to the bathroom for some aspirin. And I almost stumbled over Napoleon, who was splayed out on his back on the floor against my pillow with one ear open and the other flopped over. He looked like he'd had a hard night too.

I stepped over him, grabbed three aspirin from the bathroom medicine cabinet, and headed for the kitchen where I found the telltale evidence that I'd tied one on the night before. On the counter, beside the empty bottle of Limoncello, sat a half-eaten jar of Nutella. *So much for skipping dinner to lose weight.*

I poured myself a glass of water and popped the aspirin. It hurt when I leaned my head back to take a drink, and my mouth was so dry it felt like I'd been eating spoonfuls of salt instead of the creamy chocolate-hazelnut spread.

As soon as the aspirin were down my throat, I collapsed into a Bordeaux-and-gold cushioned dining chair and tried to remember what, if anything, I needed to do that day—that is, besides tell my nonna to call off her Sicilian attack dogs.

My phone barked.

I sighed, steeled myself for another suitor call, headed back into the bedroom, and looked at my phone. *Unknown.* I didn't think Pio would call again after we'd ended things so badly, but just in case, I decided to give him one final piece of my mind.

"Hello?" I responded a little too testily.

"Franki Amato?" an equally testy male voice asked.

"Yes?" I tried to remember where I'd heard the angry voice before.

"Ryan Hunter."

*Did Mambo Odette put a curse on me? Because not even I could be this unlucky all on my own.* "I'm sorry, Ryan, I thought you were—"

"Listen to me." His tone was nasty, like him. "I don't have time to chit chat. I'd like to know why no one has called me with the biweekly update on my case that I was promised."

*Yeah, she put a curse on me all right.* I could envision the voodoo doll of me, tiny cell phone in hand, with pins jabbed into its head and stomach.

"Franki, are you there? I expect an answer."

"Yes, I'm here, Ryan." Despite my hangover haze, I remembered that we had accepted his case on Thursday afternoon, and it was Sunday. "We just took your case a few days ago, and I can assure you that Veronica is extremely organized when it comes to handling our workload. I'm sure she plans to call you tomorrow or the next day. During *business hours*." I added the last part to make the point that Veronica and I didn't need to be spending our free time on the likes of him.

"Look, I've already wasted fifteen minutes this morning trying to track down your contact information, which I don't appreciate. Luckily, I called your office and that kid Donny was there."

I sat on the edge of the bed. "David."

"David, Donny, whatever. The point is that I've already left two messages on your partner's cell this morning, but she hasn't bothered to call me back. Now, I have a meeting with my attorney first thing tomorrow. So if you've got any information, I need it. *Capish*?"

I stifled a gasp at his inappropriate use of Italian and somehow stopped myself from telling him off for being so rude *and* for calling me on the weekend. After all, Veronica was in charge of the human relations aspect of the business. And, whether I liked it or not, Ryan Hunter *was* paying us to investigate the Evans case. I took a deep breath and tried to recall everything we'd discovered.

"Okay then. We got the photos of the crime scene, and we have reason to believe that whoever killed Jessica intentionally brought an inexpensive scarf to LaMarca to strangle her with. The killer either wore it to the store or may have even brought it as a gift.

He laughed so hard his breath sounded like a storm in the receiver. "Well, that should clear me then, because I knew better than to give Jessica a cheap present."

His repulsive humor left me speechless. I stayed silent to let him know I had no comment.

"So, tell me, Franki," his tone was mocking, "how did you figure out that the killer brought the scarf there on purpose?"

"Because LaMarca is known for its silk scarf collection, but the killer didn't use a scarf from the store."

"Gee, you're a regular Miss Marple. What else you got?"

I flopped backward onto the mattress. The man was exhausting. "I went to LaMarca and spoke with the salesgirl who found Jessica's body. While I was there I found a bead made of bone and carved like a skull, near where Jessica's body was found and—"

"How do you know it's connected to the murder?" he interrupted. Again.

"I don't. Right now it's just a hunch."

"A hunch. Jesus Christ, my life is on the line here, and all you guys have are hunches?"

I rolled my head back and forth on the bed in silent protest, but the room began to tilt so I stopped. "No, that's not all we've got."

"Well then let's hear it, Franki. I don't have all damn day."

*Neither do I, and yet I'm spending my day off taking abuse from you.* "If you'll just let me speak I'll explain everything."

He stayed silent. Blissfully.

"Thank you. A man went to see Jessica at LaMarca one night after the store had closed, and from the sound of things she knew him, and they were arguing."

"Yeah, well, that's hardly surprising. Jessica had a talent for bringing out the worst in people."

His derogatory remarks about Jessica were getting on my already frayed nerves. "This guy was threatening her, Ryan. He said she'd broken some agreement they had and told her to leave New Orleans. Do you know anything about this?"

"So, you're asking me if I was that guy, right?" He snorted. "Why is it that every time I talk to you, I get the feeling that you're interrogating *me* instead of looking for the *real* killer?"

I bolted upright—and had to lay down again. "I just met you a few days ago. For all I know, you and Jessica had a fight one night at her workplace, and you told her to get out of your life or something."

"Well, that didn't happen because I've never even been to LaMarca."

"Okay, fine. But you need to understand that when I ask you a question, I'm not implicitly accusing you." *Although I certainly wouldn't put anything past you.* "I have to cover my bases to make sure I'm not following up on a dead end."

"Fair enough."

I sat up again, astonished. That was the first time Ryan Hunter and I had seen eye-to-eye on anything. "Apparently, this guy also mentioned the London College of Fashion during the argument. Do you know if Jessica attended this school or had friends there?"

"Like I told you the other day, I don't know anything about her past. She didn't talk about it, and I didn't ask."

"All right. Veronica is going to call—"

"Wait," he interrupted yet again. "I heard her mention London once."

Excitement coursed through my chest, and I rose and began to pace, albeit slowly. *A lead, finally.* "When?"

"On a phone call. A month or two ago."

"Do you know who she was talking to?"

"No, but she said a name. It sounded like a woman's name, but I couldn't say for sure. It was Eye-talian or something."

"Do you remember what it was?" I figured it was unlikely given his inability to recall the proper pronunciation of *Italian.*

"No, it was a weird name. All I know is that it ended in an *a.*"

*Well that narrows it down since pretty much all Italian women's names, including my own, end in the letter* a. "How did London come up in the conversation?"

"She said something like, 'You don't know what the hell you're talking about. You know I wasn't even in London when it happened.'"

"So, she was angry."

"Oh yeah. At the time, I thought she was having a fight with some Eye-talian girlfriend of hers from London."

I sighed. *Was it really so hard to say the* it *in* Italian? "Did she tell you anything about the call when she hung up?"

"No, she just stared at me. I don't think she even knew I was home. Then she started bitching at me about something." His tone had turned bitter. "I think I'd forgotten to take out the trash or pick my clothes up off the floor. Who the hell knows. I could never do anything right in her eyes..."

I sidestepped the toxic topic of his relationship with Jessica. "Okay, well, we're going to follow up on the London angle tomorrow, so I'll have Veronica call you in the afternoon with an update."

"Good, because I'm paying you for information. *Solid* information." He hung up, and he did it from a landline too because I could hear him slam down the receiver.

*The jerk.*

All that standing was getting to me, so I made my way to the chaise lounge to call Veronica. I tapped her number, closing my eyes as I waited for her to answer.

"Hello?" She sounded breathy.

"Uh, did I interrupt something?"

"Hercules and I are on our Sunday morning jog. What's up?"

Thanks to my hangover, I shuddered at the thought of bouncing up and down. "I just got a call from Ryan Hunter."

"What did he want?"

"His weekly update—and to harass me."

"Ugh. I'm sorry."

"No worries, but only because he told me something important. It's looking more and more like something went down in London that involved Jessica Evans. Any chance you can meet today?"

"Of course I can meet." Her cheerful tone megaphoned into my ear. "How about Thibodeaux's at noon? I could really use a mimosa. Oh, and some onion rings. *Mm.*"

The mention of alcohol and greasy onions made my stomach lurch. "Works for me. See you then."

I hung up and pondered the logistics of how I was going to make it from the chaise lounge to the bathtub.

The phone rang again, interrupting my planning.

Assuming it was Veronica calling back to change the time or something, I answered. "Hey."

"Franki, we've-a got a *problema.*"

A mental image of Odette plunging a pin into the backside of my voodoo doll flashed through my aching head. "What is it, Nonna?"

"I just-a got a call from-a Luisa, the cousin of my cousin, Agatina. Pio called her, and he told-a her you're a loose-a woman."

I sighed and spread out on the chaise lounge. In Sicilian-American circles, it was a cardinal sin for a woman to have questionable virtue, and in terms of gravity it was second only to the inability to make a good *ragù.* "Nonna, all I told Pio was that I couldn't go out with him because I have a date with another man. So—"

"A date? *Dio mio!* "

Her *my God* told me that the slight to my honor was old news.

"Who-a with-a? Bruno?"

"No, his name is Bradley. He's the president of Pontchartrain Bank here in New Orleans."

She let out a whistle like a sailor seeing a woman after six months at sea. "You did-a *good*."

I basked in her praise. "*Grazie*."

"Is-a he Italian?"

"He's not." I waited for the inevitable comment.

"Well, we can't have-a it all-a, can-a we Franki?" She was so happy she practically crowed. "Now-a when is-a this date?"

"Um..." I didn't want to admit that I didn't know, but I couldn't lie because she would call me immediately after the date—probably even during—to get the details. "I'm not exactly sure."

She gasped. "Not-a sure? You mean-a that you gave up a date with a fine-a man like-a Pio, and you don't even have-a no date with-a Bradley?"

*Fine man, my rear.* "Bradley said he would call me this week, and he will."

"Francesca Lucia Amato, you *never* turn-a down a date when you don't have-a no date."

"Have some faith, okay?"

"The only-a man I have-a the faith in, Franki, is-a the Pope."

When my nonna mentioned the Pope, it was time to end the call. "I've gotta run, Nonna. I'll call you right after the date. *Ciao ciao!*"

Next, I did what I should have done three phone calls earlier—I pressed the off button on my phone. Then I turned it back on because there was always the possibility that Bradley would call. Although, after talking to my nonna, I wasn't feeling all that hopeful. Maybe I really did "have-a no date." It wasn't like Bradley had set a time and place, or anything. The more I thought about my dating prospects, the better that mimosa Veronica mentioned was sounding. But not the onion rings.

I agreed with my nonna on one point, though—I shouldn't count on a date until I knew for certain that I had one. But I wasn't ready to believe that the Pope was the only man a girl could trust, at least not yet. And I couldn't afford to give in to defeat. Bradley Hartmann was going to call me whether I had to resort to Vulcan mind control, Jedi mind tricks, or even voodoo to make it happen.

## 9

"Jeez. It's like a giant lightsaber in the sky." I shielded my eyes from the noon sun that glared at me when I opened my front door. I recoiled into my apartment, rummaged in my purse, and pulled out my tortoise-shell sunglasses for the walk across the street to Thibodeaux's. After donning my shades to block the sunlight—and the equally harsh reality of the cemetery—I set off on the one hundred-foot trek. The street was deserted, so I stepped from the yard into the street.

A twelve-year-old kid on a bike appeared from out of nowhere and sped by not two inches in front of me.

I flailed my arms like a tipsy tightrope walker, landed squarely on my rear end, and, voluntarily, lay down in the grass to regroup.

"You're lucky I have extra cushioning, kid," I shouted from my supine position with a raised, clenched fist. If I could've stayed on my feet, it might've gotten ugly between him and me.

After a few minutes of contemplating the clouds, I stood, brushed the dead grass from my clothes, and walked my bruised behind to the bar. At the entrance, I paused to summon the strength needed to endure Veronica's ever-effervescent Sunday afternoon chatter. When I pushed open the door, I spotted her sitting at the bar with her back to me. She was sporting a Madonna ponytail á la The Blond Ambition Tour, a sunny yellow velour tracksuit, and matching yellow tennis shoes.

I slid onto the barstool next to her and caught a revolting whiff of fresh air and sunshine. "Hey."

She gave me the onceover. "What happened to *you*?"

"What do you mean?" I placed my bag on the bar.

"You look a little rough." She smirked and sipped mimosa from a straw. "Been rolling in the hay with anyone I know?"

I looked at her for a few seconds and realized that I must've had grass in my hair. "Give me a break, all right?" I finger-combed my long brown locks. "Within the past twelve hours, I've had run-ins with a voodoo priestess, Ryan Hunter, a Sicilian guy, a crazy kid on a bike, a bottle of Limoncello, and my nonna." I didn't mention the jar of Nutella because it just made me look pathetic.

"Oh wow, your nonna?" Veronica was unfazed by the mention of the voodoo priestess et al. "What did she want?"

"To alert me to the earth-shattering news that my womanly honor was besmirched after I jilted one of her saintly Sicilians." I started to remove my sunglasses but thought better of it. The dimly lit bar seemed excessively bright.

"Your womanly honor." Veronica belly-laughed and slapped the bar. "That's a good one."

The glare I shot her was not unlike that harsh sun.

Phillip the bartender approached. "What can I get ya?"

The thought of alcohol made me feel like crawling back to that spot in the grass to lie down. "A club soda with lime."

Phillip walked away, muttering to himself.

"So what did Ryan say about London?" Veronica fished a

piece of orange out of her mimosa with a toothpick. "I've been dying of curiosity ever since you called."

"He said that he came home one day and found Jessica on the phone with someone he thought was an Italian girlfriend. She was really angry and reminded the caller that she wasn't in London when something or other happened."

"When what happened?"

I gave her a look. "Don't you think I would've mentioned that if I knew?"

She shrugged and popped the orange into her mouth. "So, why does Ryan think she was talking to an Italian woman?"

Phillip passed me my drink, and I nodded my thanks. "Because she said an Italian woman's name."

"That doesn't mean anything. She could have just been gossiping about the woman or mentioning her for some reason."

"True." I nursed my club soda. My brain was in no mood to hypothesize about the case.

"Hey, Phillip," Veronica shouted into my ear. "Can I get an order of onion rings?"

"Sure thing, Ronnie."

"Sometimes, you just need a little greasy food in your diet, right Franki?"

I tilt-nodded, and my stomach also tilted at the mention of grease, but not just because of my hangover. My first impression of Phillip was that he looked a little greasy himself. And since the last time I was in the bar, I'd learned through the neighborhood grapevine that he was in an environmentally conscious grunge rock band that didn't believe in showering more than once a week, to save water. Unfortunately, Phillip also did double duty at Thibodeaux's as the cook.

Veronica leaned her arms on the bar. "Normally I'd say that Jessica's phone call was probably nothing. But it *is* interesting that London keeps coming up, and in such negative contexts. By the way, I'm going to call the London College of Fashion first thing in the morning. I hope they have some information for us, because as of right now, we've got nothing on Jessica's past."

"David hasn't been able to find anything?"

"Oh, he's found some things. Too many." She waved her drink toothpick.

Veronica might not have looked Italian, but her habit of talking with her hands gave her heritage away. "What do you mean 'too many'?"

"He googled 'Jessica Evans' and got over three hundred thousand hits, so I told him to not to bother checking the links. With his part-time schedule, it could take him weeks or even months to find one related to our Jessica Evans." She waved the toothpick close to my cheek.

Keeping a watchful eye on the wooden weapon, I asked, "Did he try narrowing down the search with any personal information, like her address?"

"Yeah, but that didn't turn up anything concrete either." She looked down at the bar. "At this point, we really don't have much to go on. We know Ryan doesn't have a clue about Jessica's personal life, and the only information on the police report was her Louisiana driver license number and birth date."

Surprised by the downturn in Veronica's chipper demeanor, I mustered up as much positivity as I could. "Well, that's good, right? Since we have her birth date, we can get her birth certificate and find out her parents' names. Annabella said that Jessica referred to herself as a Louisiana native when she was talking to the man at the store, so the certificate should be easy to find."

She shook her head. "No, it's not good. Louisiana doesn't have a public birth index like Texas. It's a closed record state, so only Jessica or her parents could request her birth certificate, not us."

"Oh. What about Facebook, Twitter, and Instagram? Or wait. I bet she had a LinkedIn page." I hoped that Veronica would perk up soon because being perky on her behalf was exhausting.

"Nope, not even a Pinterest page." Veronica gave a wild thrust of her toothpick.

I scooted my barstool a few inches away from her. "Maybe she's going by her middle name?"

"Could be. It's also possible that she was using an assumed name." She put the toothpick in its rightful place—on the counter.

"Yeah, I was thinking the same thing." I laid my aching head down on my purse. "So what do we do next?"

"We hope the London College of Fashion has some information for us. Because if they don't, we're at a standstill in this case."

Phillip slid a steaming basket of onion rings down the length of the bar.

I raised my head to avoid getting hit in the face and watched as the basket stopped in front of Veronica, who perked right up and clapped. "Nice sliding skills."

She cast an admiring glance at Phillip. "I know. Want one, Franki?"

"Nah." I eyed the basket with revulsion and suspicion.

"Now, tell me about this voodoo priestess." Veronica bit into an onion ring.

"First off, it was one of the craziest experiences of my life! Her name is Odette Malveaux and—"

"Odette Malveaux," a familiar chain-smoker voice exclaimed. "You into voodoo, Miss Franki?"

I turned to see Glenda in all her splendor. She wore what looked like a Kmart knockoff of J Lo's iconic jungle-green Versace dress—the one with the neckline that plunged several inches past the navel—only Glenda's plunged a good two inches lower, almost past something else.

I closed my jaw—with the help of my hand. "I can barely handle the mysticism of yoga, so no voodoo for me."

Glenda cackled as she took a seat beside me.

Veronica touched the sleeve of Glenda's dress. "What a stunning look."

*That's one way to describe it.*

"Thank you, sugar." Glenda crossed her legs and exposed six-inch-heeled stripper shoes with clear plastic, hollow bases that had writing on them. "So Miss Franki, how do you know Mambo Odette?"

"I met her at Marie Laveau's House of Voodoo last night." I tried to decipher the word on Glenda's shoes. "Do you know her?"

"Sure do. A long time ago, I consulted with her about a man I was seeing."

I lowered my sunglasses, intrigued. "Did you want to get even with him or something?"

"Get even? Real voodoo isn't about hexes and sacrifices and things. But that's a common misconception thanks to the way Hollywood has sensationalized it. Voodoo is about serving others, Miss Franki, especially the poor, the sick, and the lonely. And Odette is one of the finest priestesses in all of Louisiana when it comes to matters of the heart, I guarantee you that."

I wondered how in the world that terrifying woman could have become an expert on love.

"Besides, if I wanted to get even with a man, I wouldn't need any help. Know what I mean, jelly bean?"

I nodded. I had no doubt that Glenda could be a formidable foe. "Hey, before I forget, what do your shoes say?"

"*Tips.* There's a slot for inserting bills right below the word, see?" She spun around on her barstool and kicked a long, skinny leg out in front of her with the ease of a Rockette dancer so that I could examine her shoe, up close and personal.

"Why would clients put the tips in your shoe?"

"Because they're too damn drunk to reach the G-string." Glenda leaned over the counter and waved Phillip over with a dollar bill, like a customer in a strip club.

Veronica gave a tip of her head. "That's good business."

Phillip approached to take Glenda's drink order and flinched as he got a full-frontal of her in the dress. "The usual?"

"No, handsome, I'll take a mint julep with extra powdered sugar." She gave him a cougarish wink. "I'm feeling like a Southern belle today."

A hoop-skirted Glenda flashed through my mind. *Never happen. She'd suffocate in all that clothing.*

"You know, Miss Franki, I also consulted with Mambo Odette about a voodoo dance I used to do. It was inspired by Marie Laveau."

"Really?"

"I modeled the dress after Marie Laveau's own clothes."

Despite my better judgment, I wanted to know more. "Was it made of raffia and seashells like the voodoo priestess costumes I saw on sale for Mardi Gras the other day?"

"Hell no." Glenda wrinkled her mouth in disgust. "I wouldn't be caught dead in a cheap outfit like that."

Veronica shook her head. "Of course you wouldn't."

"It was a long muslin dress with a *tignon* that had seven knots pointing up like a crown."

Phillip appeared with the mint julep, blushing schoolboy style.

"Thank you, handsome." Glenda made eyes at him while licking the sugar from the entire rim of the glass.

My stomach tilted again. I had to get her to put her tongue back into her mouth. "What's a *tignon*?"

Veronica, who was the resident fashion expert of every culture and era, turned to me. "It's the type of headdress Marie Laveau wore." She turned to Glenda. "What color was the dress?"

"White to symbolize inner purity, and I had a boa around my neck."

I chewed my soda straw. "I knew women in New Orleans liked to wear boas during Mardi Gras, but I didn't realize that voodoo queens wore them too."

Glenda stared at me like I'd sprouted another head. "A boa *constrictor*. You know, a *snake*?"

"Oh, of course." My cheeks grew warm.

Veronica's brow creased. "What did the boa symbolize?"

"Well, in voodoo, the snake represents the practitioner's spiritual connection to the otherworld. So, when I wore the snake, it meant that if you connected with me, it'd be outta this world." Glenda laughed and slapped me on the back so hard that it felt like my brain rattled in my skull.

It was time to put me out of my increasing misery. "Hey, Phillip. How about a Bloody Mary?"

His face drooped as though he didn't want to return to our area.

*Go figure.* I turned to Glenda. "Was the snake real?"

"Of course the snake was real. But this wasn't no Tijuana donkey show, this was a *class act*." She slurped the last of her mint julep and let out a tremendous belch. "The snake was just a live accessory to cover my lady parts, no more no less."

I recoiled. "Wait, you wanted your, um, *lady parts* covered?"

She gaped at my lack of stripper sense. "Well of course, child, until the big reveal."

I considered asking how she got a live snake to cover her privates but decided to quit while I was ahead.

"Here you go." Phillip said placed the Bloody Mary in front of me, averting his eyes.

"Thanks. This should cover my tab." I shoved fifteen dollars under his chin so he could see it.

He took the money and scurried to safety.

Veronica blinked. "Are you leaving already, Franki? You just got your drink."

"I know. I'm going to finish it and head home."

"What are you going to do today?"

I stared at the glass. "This drink. This is all I'm going to do."

"Miss Franki's a real live wire, Miss Ronnie."

"Right?" Veronica's tone was as dry as my club soda.

I ignored them both and tossed back half my drink.

Glenda leaned forward to look at Veronica. "Whaddya say you and I celebrate our inner Southern belles by doing some corset shopping at Trashy Diva?"

Veronica beamed like her yellow tracksuit. "That's a terrific idea."

*And the perfect place for this mismatched duo.*

"Good. This one's on me, Miss Ronnie." She pulled some crumpled bills from her lacy black bra and dropped them on the bar. "I'll see you later, handsome." She shot a knowing look at Phillip and pulled a short red cigarette holder covered in cubic zirconias from her purse. Placing it between pursed lips, she exited the bar shaking her bony hips.

"See you tomorrow, Franki." Veronica waved and followed Glenda.

I finished my drink in one gulp and headed out. As soon as I got outside, I looked for cars and wayward biker kids before crossing the street. My only goal for the rest of the day was to make it to my bed without incident.

Midway to my apartment, my phone rang instead of barking. *Grazie a dio I changed that ringtone.* I looked at the display and saw the theme of the day—*Unknown*. *So much for making it home unscathed.*

I continued walking and debated whether to take the call or just go inside and hide. Then I reminded myself that it could've been Bradley and tapped *Answer*.

"Hello?" I used a sultry voice that was only mildly tinged with apprehension.

"Hey Franki, it's Bradley."

"Oh thank God," I exclaimed before I could stop myself.

"What did you say? The phone cut out for a second."

"Just 'hi.'" I uttered silent thanks to my cell phone for preventing me from making a fool of myself. I inserted my key into the lock and opened my front door.

"Listen, I was hoping to take you to dinner next weekend, but I have to leave town Thursday on business, and I won't be back until Sunday."

"Oh, I understand." I closed the door and tossed my purse in frustration on the chaise lounge. *Was he trying to back out of the date?*

"But if you're free on Tuesday night, I'd like to take you to a restaurant in the Quarter."

"Of course I'm free." *Smooth, Franki, real smooth.*

"Great. They serve classic New Orleans cuisine, things like gumbo, jambalaya, and red beans and rice. They even have my absolute favorite, the muffuletta."

*The muffuletta?* I stopped in my tracks and placed my hand on the wall. Then I drew it back. The fuzzy wallpaper freaked me out. "You're not Sicilian are you?"

"No, why?"

"Just checking." Relieved, I bent down to ruffle the fur on Napoleon's head. "That sounds wonderful, Bradley. I've been dying to eat some good Cajun food."

"Well, if you like Cajun food, they also have crawdads and even alligator for the more adventurous eaters."

I shot up arrowlike and gripped my spinning head. *Crawdads? Alligator? What was it Odette had said about the bayou?* I tried to keep my tone casual. "This place isn't on the bayou is it?"

"No, it's on Bourbon Street, but it's called Le Bayou." He paused. "Have you been there before?"

It was all coming back to me. Odette had told me in no uncertain terms not to let a man take me to the bayou. I was supposed to stay away from the bayou and everything in it, i.e., crawdads and alligators. *Should I suggest another restaurant?*

"Franki, is everything okay?"

I had to hide my fears about Odette's voodoo predictions or risk blowing the date. "Yes, absolutely. I guess my phone is acting up again. So, what time on Tuesday?"

"How about seven o'clock? I'll pick you up your place."

"I'll text you my address."

"Sounds great. I'm looking forward to it." There was a hint of devastatingly sexy in his voice.

"Me too." I tried to match his sexy tone, but it came out suspicious. "Bye, Bradley."

I hung up and went to my bedroom. As I crawled into bed I had a funny feeling in the pit of my stomach, and it wasn't from the Bloody Mary. I was probably overreacting about my encounter with Mambo Odette, but it *was* odd that right after she warned me about a man taking me to the bayou it seemed to be happening. On the other hand, Bradley wasn't taking me to an *actual* bayou. It was a restaurant in the French Quarter. And nothing and no one was going to prevent me from going. All I had to do was avoid the crawdads and the alligator, and everything would be fine.

*Wouldn't it?*

## 10

As I drove to work the next morning, I couldn't help but be in a good mood despite the disturbing developments around Odette Malveaux's predictions. My hangover was gone, the sun was shining, and I had a date with Bradley Hartmann. To celebrate, I'd put the top down on my Mustang and popped my "Beauty and the Beat" CD by The Go-Go's into the stereo. Nothing like '80s girl power pop to make you leave your voodoo cares behind.

I pulled up to the office and couldn't believe my luck—as if by magic, there was a parking space right in front. *This day is getting better and better.*

I parallel-parked, opened the car door, and started to get out, but I was knocked back into my seat by the appetizing aroma of marinara sauce from Nizza restaurant. *Yeah, it's going to be a great day.*

I bounded up the stairs to the office singing "Lust to Love" at the top of my lungs. In my mind, I had the same smooth and powerful voice as Belinda Carlisle, but in reality I sounded a lot like a female Neil Young—with a head cold.

I entered the office, and Veronica sashay-ran into the lobby, her forehead creased with worry.

Instead of alarm bells, I heard the barking from my ex-ring-tone. "What's the matter?"

"Didn't you hear that?" She exited the office and went to the stairs. "It sounded like a dog yelping in pain."

*Maybe I* had *heard barking.* I stood still and listened, but I couldn't hear a thing. Then it dawned on me—she was talking about my singing.

I went to the stairwell. "Hey, Veronica?"

She turned to look up at me from the bottom step.

I hated to lie to my best friend, but if she thought my voice sounded like an injured animal, there was no way I was claiming it. "I think that sound you were hearing was the squeaky brakes on a truck that went by."

"Are you sure?"

"Absolutely."

Veronica sighed and climbed the stairs. "Thank goodness."

"You're here early." I changed the subject even though my ego was still smarting from the indirect insult.

She reentered the lobby. "I couldn't sleep. I wanted to call London as soon as possible."

"And?" I followed her to her office.

She took a seat behind her desk. "There's no record of a Jessica Evans at the London College of Fashion."

I dropped into the armchair. "Well, like you said yesterday, she might've been using an assumed name. Maybe that's why the school has no record of her."

"Or she never went there at all. I mean, that salesgirl Annabella could've misunderstood what she overheard at the store that night."

"True, but I think we should check with the police."

Her brow went up. "What for?"

"Because, unlike us, they can get a court order to obtain Jessica's birth certificate. So, if she *was* using an assumed name, they might already know that. Why don't we ask your crime analyst friend for an update on the police's case?"

Veronica shook her head. "No, Betty puts her job on the line every time I ask her for help, so I only use her as an absolute last resort. For now, the best thing we can do is shift gears."

"How so?"

She opened her day planner. "We've got to get back out there and find the store that sold the killer the scarf."

"Sounds logical. Besides," I paused for effect, "I need to buy a new outfit for my date."

She gasped and leaned forward. "Your what?"

"My date." I hid a smile. "Jeez, Veronica, is it really so shocking that someone would ask me out?"

"I didn't mean it like that. It's just that I'm surprised you're going on a date so soon after Vince."

"Why?" I turned away so she wouldn't see me tear up. "It's not like I need time to get over that cheating bastard."

"Well, that's what I mean." Her tone had gone soft. "Are you sure you're ready to trust a man again?"

"Of course." Although, after thinking about it for a split second, I realized I wasn't sure at all.

"If that's the case, then I'm glad." She leaned back in her chair. "I'm just worried about you."

"Relax. Bradley isn't one of those deceptively sincere types I usually go for. He's a genuinely good guy. I can tell. The only thing we have to worry about is what I'm going to wear."

"Where are you going?"

"To Le Bayou restaurant." I sidestepped the probably insignificant matter of the warning I'd received from Mambo Odette about men taking me to the bayou. Veronica had no patience for my Sicilian-inspired superstitions, so she was sure to be annoyed by my voodoo misgivings, even though a healthy respect for the unknown was nothing to scoff at.

"You can always wear a basic LBD. It's perfect first-date material."

I hesitated. "I don't have one."

"What?" Her pitch neared a scream. "We're going to have to take care of that right now. I saw one at Ann Taylor the other day that would look amazing on you." She opened her laptop. "Let me see if I can find it on their website."

For Veronica, the little black dress was a simple, yet fabulous wardrobe item for any occasion. But for me, the LBD looked like what I would wear *underneath* my dress—a Spanx slip. I needed more coverage to feel at ease with a new man, not to mention the new roll that had appeared on my stomach since moving to New Orleans. But Veronica had an excellent eye for fashion, so if she knew of a dress that would be flattering on me, it was worth taking a look.

The lobby bell interrupted our style search.

Veronica was so immersed in online shopping that she didn't react, so I rose and went to the lobby.

Ryan Hunter held a large box and a woman's red crocodile handbag that must have been worth the GDP of a small country.

"Hello." My greeting was intentionally cool. I wanted to comment on his bag, but I didn't dare use sarcasm on this guy for fear of what he would do. "You know, Veronica was going to call you today with your report—"

"I'm not here about that."

His voice reminded me of the barking on my ex-ringtone. "Then what can I help you with?"

He placed the box on a nearby chair. "I found something in Jessica's things that might help my case."

Inexplicably, adrenaline surged in my chest. "Let me get Veronica."

I hurried to her office and poked my head inside. "It's Ryan."

Her eyes rose from the laptop.

"He's found something of Jessica's that he thinks may be important."

She stood and followed me into the lobby.

"Hi Ryan." Veronica's tone was professional, but distant. "Franki said you've found something?"

"Yeah, last night I packed up Jessica's stuff to bring it by today. I dropped one of the boxes as I was putting it into my trunk, and this handbag fell out. When I went to pick it up, I noticed the corner of a white envelope sticking out from between the interior lining of the purse and the exterior leather. Right here." He showed us an area of the bag where the stitching had given way.

Veronica's eyes widened. "What was in it?"

"This old letter." He pulled an envelope from inside his suit jacket and handed it to her. "It's postdated June 27, 1988."

She pulled the letter from the envelope and scanned the page.

My heart thumped so hard I was sure they could hear it. I had a gut feeling that the letter contained a key clue to Jessica's past. Plus, the whole idea of a secret letter made me feel like a sleuth in a mystery novel. "What does it say?"

"It's really short. I'll read it." She cleared her throat. "*Barbara, I got laid off from the refinery last week. I'll send you money for Angelica when I can. But like it or not I got a new wife and kid to take care of now. Sincerely, Bill.*"

"Wait." I looked over Veronica's shoulder. "Who are Bill and Barbara again?"

She examined the envelope. "Well, they have the same last name, Evangelista." She let the arm holding the envelope drop to her side and looked at me. "Are you thinking what I'm thinking?"

"I'm not thinking anything." My mind always went blank whenever people expected me to guess their thoughts.

Ryan shot me a contemptuous look. "Nice intuitive skills."

I pretended not to hear him. "Was Jessica maybe blackmailing these people?"

Veronica folded the letter. "I don't know, but now I'm convinced she was hiding something." She turned to Ryan. "Does any of this make any sense to you? Have you heard these names before?"

He shook his head. "No, never. Maybe this Angelica was one of Jessica's friends or a cousin or something."

The door burst open.

"Hey, party people." David entered the lobby and tossed his backpack on his workstation.

Veronica smacked the letter against her thigh. "David, one of these days we're literally going to die from fright."

He hung his head. "Uh, sorry."

I shot Veronica a drop-it look. There was no reason to embarrass the kid in front of a client. "Don't worry about it, David."

Ryan, true to arrogant form, didn't bother to acknowledge his presence.

Veronica looked at the clock by the door. "I hate to run, Ryan, but I need to call the London School of Fashion before they close to find out whether they have a record of an Angelica Evangelista. I called earlier this morning, and they had no record of Jessica."

"Well, isn't that interesting." Ryan rubbed his chin. "Okay, I'll bring up the other boxes from my car, and then I need to get to the office. But can I count on one of you to actually update me today on what you find out?"

"Of course." Veronica turned to me. "Franki, fill David in on everything and help him do an Internet search on Angelica Evangelista, okay?"

"Sure." I nodded a frosty farewell in Ryan's direction. "David, let's go use my computer."

"Right on."

I went to the hallway, and David followed. I didn't want to have to deal with Ryan when he returned with the remaining boxes, and I was sure David felt the same.

I entered my office and gestured to my desk. "You're the resident research guru. You take my chair. By the way, what time do you have class today?"

"Uh, I have Brazilian Dance at one." He took a seat and opened my laptop.

"Brazilian Dance? I thought you were a computer science major."

His gaze darted from mine to the floor. "Not a lot of girls, like, take comp sci courses."

"Got it." I smiled both at the thought of him taking classes to meet women and at the mental image of his long, lanky frame doing Brazilian dance moves.

His fingers flew over the keyboard, and he pressed the return key. "So, I just googled 'Angelica Evangelista' and got almost eight thousand hits. Let's add 'New Orleans' to narrow the search."

I walked behind him and looked at the screen. "Less than a hundred results. That's more doable."

We were interrupted by the clacking of Veronica's Manolo Blahniks, which were quickly approaching my office.

She burst into the room. "Incredible news. A student named Angelica Evangelista graduated from the London College of Fashion in 2008. Can you believe it?"

I looked at David and back at her. "Did you find out anything else?"

"Yes. Angelica got a bachelor's degree in Fashion Management."

I sat on the corner of my desk. "Which is exactly what Jessica Evans did for a living."

Veronica's eyes sparkled. "Exactly."

"Is that a four-year degree?"

"Yeah, why?"

I did a rapid calculation in my head. "Well, then the year would be about right, because Jessica was twenty-six, and that would make her around twenty-two years old when she graduated."

"Could Angelica be Jessica?" Veronica spoke as though she didn't dare believe it.

"I'm beginning to wonder that myself." I rose and returned to my position behind David. "Try searching 'Angelica Evangelista' and 'London.'"

Veronica joined me to see the search results.

"Whoa," David breathed.

Veronica and I didn't need to ask him why. The first link was a Wikipedia page entitled "Murder of Immacolata Di Salvo."

"What is this?" I said, stunned.

David clicked the link, and we all leaned in to read the screen.

*Immacolata Di Salvo, an American exchange student from New Orleans, Louisiana, was murdered on May 1, 2008. Di Salvo, aged twenty-two, was found dead in her dorm room in London, where she attended the London College of Fashion.*

I glanced through the rest of the article but didn't see the name Angelica Evangelista. "David, scroll down. I want to see how this Angelica person is connected to the murder."

He searched for "Angelica" and found her name in the middle of the page.

"There." I pointed to the cursor highlighting the name. "I'll read it aloud. *Angelica Evangelista, an American exchange student from New Orleans, Louisiana, and the flat mate of Di Salvo, found Di Salvo's body after returning home from a trip abroad at 3 a.m. There were no signs of forced entry in the dorm room, which led police to believe that Di Salvo knew her killer."*

"Oh. My. God." I sat on the desk.

Veronica stared at me in shock. "Could this be related to our case?"

"Dude," David exclaimed.

I started and almost fell to the floor. "What?"

"It mentions Stewart Preston. I totally remember hearing about this when I was a kid."

I couldn't help but repress a smile at the notion that David was anything but a kid in the present.

Veronica eyed the screen. "Who's Stewart Preston?"

"His family is rich. I'm talkin' uber rich. His father, Stewart Preston, III, owns, like, half of New Orleans."

"What does he do?"

"I never really knew. One second." David opened a new page and typed "Stewart Preston, III" into the search field. He found a Wikipedia page on Preston and scanned the contents. "Looks like he owns a bunch of textile companies."

I ran my finger down the long list of corporations owned by Preston and his associates. "Make that a textile empire."

Veronica squinted. "Franki, read the part in the murder article about Stewart Preston."

"Sure," I said as David switched back to the other screen. "It says, *'Stewart Preston, IV, an American exchange student from New Orleans, Louisiana, who was attending the London School of Economics, was charged with the sexual assault and murder of Di Salvo in August of 2009.'"*

David nodded. "Right. And he never went to jail either.

Everyone said it was because of his daddy's money and connections."

I leaned on the desk with my forearms. "It says, '*Preston was eventually acquitted and cleared of all charges in January of 2012.*' I wonder why."

Veronica frowned. "Does it say?"

"No, and it doesn't explain how Immacolata was killed either."

She sat on the opposite end of the desk. "David, look for a local article on the murder, maybe one from *The Times-Picayune*."

He returned to the main search results page.

She tapped her cheek. "It's certainly looking like Jessica Evans and Angelica Evangelista are one and the same person, but I wish there was something more concrete to link the two of them."

David pulled up a *Times-Picayune* article on the Di Salvo murder dated May 4, 2008. The opening line of the article reported, '*On May 1, 2008, Immacolata Di Salvo was found strangled to death in her dorm room at the London College of Fashion.*'

Veronica shot me a questioning look. "Strangled?"

My insides felt twisted, like they were being strangled. "Just like Jessica."

David pointed a bony finger at the second line of the article. "Yeah, and look at this part. '*The murder weapon was a scarf.*'"

"*Tombola,*" I whispered in Italian. Then I remembered that David didn't speak the language. "I mean, *Bingo.*"

## 11

"A scarf." I shook my head. "I can't believe it."

The three of us stared at the computer screen for a few minutes, dumbstruck.

David swallowed. "So, Angelica and Jessica were, like, the same girl."

Veronica looked like she'd just witnessed the strangulation, "It sure looks that way, doesn't it?"

"Yeah," I breathed. "This case is getting crazy, isn't it?"

David opened his eyes wide. "And dangerous too. Like, you guys could be dealing with a serial scarf strangler. If I were either one of you, man, I wouldn't even *think* of wearing a scarf while I was workin' this case."

Even though I wasn't wearing a scarf, my hand went to my throat. I started to protest but then opted to remain silent. The kid had a point.

Veronica walked to the front of my desk to face us. "Let's not jump to any conclusions, David. Even if these two cases are related," she paused to pace, "there's no guarantee that the same person committed both murders."

"I guess." David stared at his dirty white tennis shoes. He was clearly attached to the idea of a serial scarf strangler.

Veronica stopped and looked at him. "We need to actually prove that Jessica was really Angelica before we spend any time investigating the relationship between these two cases. Otherwise, we could make a critical mistake."

I exhaled a long breath. The plot was getting as thick as the marinara sauce I'd smelled earlier. "So, we need to track down Bill and Barbara Evangelista."

"Yeah, and Immacolata's family. Since Immacolata roomed with Angelica, then one of her relatives or friends must've seen a picture of Angelica at some point."

David's fingers flew over the keyboard. "Uh, here's an obituary for Immacolata Di Salvo. It mentions her family."

I scanned the text on the screen. "Here we go. It says, *'She is survived by her father, Rosario Di Salvo, her mother, Maria Di Salvo, and her sisters Concetta and Domenica.'* Wow, those are some serious Italian Catholic names."

"Huh?" David turned to look at me. "What do you mean?"

"Well, 'Immacolata' is Italian for 'Immaculate,' and the other family members' names mean 'rosary,' 'Mary,' 'conception,' and 'Sunday.' Oh, and the 'Salvo' part of their last name is the nick-name for 'Salvatore,' which means 'savior.'"

His head bounced in approval. "Wicked."

*Righteous, maybe, but not wicked.* "Religious-themed names are super common in Italy, especially in the South, so I'm guessing that the Di Salvos are fairly devout." I returned my gaze to the obituary.

Veronica was behind me again, trying to read over my shoulder. "Does the obituary list a funeral home?"

"Yeah, and it's in Slidell." I looked at David. "Where is that?"

"It's a suburb of New Orleans," His chest swelled with pride.

"It's, like, a forty-minute drive from here, but I can make it in twenty-five."

"That reminds me..." I turned to Veronica. "You never told us the cities that Bill and Barbara Evangelista were living in."

"Oh, right. Let me go get the envelope." She hurried from the room.

I leaned over David's shoulder. "See if you can find an address for the Di Salvos."

"Already got it. There's a Rosario Di Salvo in the white pages on St. Augustine Street. His phone number's listed. But I can't believe people still have landlines, man. That's sooooo last century."

Veronica clacked into the office with an envelope and stopped in front of my desk. "Barbara lived on East Queens Drive in Slidell, but Bill didn't write his return address. It was postmarked in Baton Rouge, though."

"Well, David just found a Slidell address for a Rosario Di Salvo. If it's the right person, then Angelica and Immacolata could've known each other before they went to college."

She put her hands on her hips. "Let's call the Di Salvos and see if we can find that out, shall we?"

"Sure." I looked at the screen to find the number.

She handed David the envelope. "While Franki and I are on this call, I need you to look up the property tax appraisal records for the parish that East Queens Drive is in and find out whether the Evangelistas own that house. Then get me anything you can on Barbara and Bill Evangelista."

He rose from my desk chair and stretched his long limbs. "Yes, ma'am."

Veronica shot him a scowl as she took his seat in front of my computer.

"Uh, I mean, *mademoiselle*." He scurried from the room to his workstation.

She smiled after him and then turned toward me. "Will you dial the number on speakerphone? I don't want to miss any details of the call."

"Okay." I pulled my desk phone closer toward us. "Do you want me to talk, or you?"

"You talk, but if they refuse to meet with us, I'll chime in and ask a few questions."

As I dialed the number, a knot the size of pizza dough formed in the pit of my stomach. It was one thing to chat up a gossipy salesgirl at LaMarca, but it was quite another to call a family whose loved one had been the victim of a brutal murder. I hoped the Di Salvos would be glad to know that someone was looking into their daughter's cold case. I tapped my fingers on the desk and waited through seven or so rings.

"Hello?" a female voice answered.

"Hi, Mrs. Di Salvo?"

"Yes, who's speaking?"

Even though she'd asked who I was, I could tell from her hollow tone that she didn't care about the answer—or anything, for that matter. "My name is Franki Amato, and I'm on the line with my partner, Veronica Maggio." I decided to sidestep the issue of Immacolata's case. "We're investigating a New Orleans murder that we'd like to talk to you about."

There was silence on the other end of the line. "But, we've already talked to the police."

"Oh. Uh..." I side-glanced at Veronica. "About your daughter Immacolata's case, right?"

"No, about Jennifer's murder, or whatever Angelica was calling herself."

Veronica and I exchanged a full-on look.

My heart pounded in my chest. "You mean, Jessica. Jessica Evans."

"Yes, that's it. What is this about?"

I sat speechless, replaying Maria Di Salvo's words in my mind, and Veronica tapped her chest to let me know that she would take over.

"Mrs. Di Salvo, this is Veronica. I know it must be tremendously painful for you to discuss your daughter, but my private investigation firm, Private Chicks, has been contracted by a local individual to investigate Angelica's murder. We're trying to determine whether her death is related to Immacolata's case. Would it be possible for us to meet with you this week?"

Another long silence ensued followed by muffled sobs. "You can come tomorrow morning at ten o'clock."

There was so much sadness in her voice that my eyes welled with tears. I couldn't imagine the nightmare that she and her family had been living.

"Thank you so much." Veronica leaned toward the screen to see the address. "Are you still at the St. Augustine Street address in the phone book?"

"Yes...see you tomorrow."

I hung up. "That was hard, especially when she started crying. She sounded so unhappy, almost haunted."

"I'm sure you know from your police work that when you're interacting with the family of a victim, it can take an emotional toll on you. Even if you solve the case, you can never undo what was done to their loved one. So, you have to try to keep your personal and professional life separate to the extent that you can. And if the case starts to get to you, then you need to do something to deal with the feelings of helplessness."

"Well, I know one thing I can do."

Veronica looked at me. "What's that?"

"Go out and find that scarf."

≈

As I WALKED toward Ann Taylor, I looked at my phone. *Six o'clock? No wonder I'm so hungry.* I'd spent the last seven hours scarf hunting at The Shops at Canal Place and hadn't thought once about lunch. I was pretty sure I'd never forgotten to eat a meal in my entire life, not even when I'd had a stomach virus. I had heard about people who "forgot to eat," but I always assumed that they had some sort of brain deficiency or damage from an accident or aneurism. But it looked like I'd just been going about the whole losing weight thing all wrong. Instead of dieting, I should've been doing some serious shopping. *Why hadn't I thought of that before?*

I arrived at the store and saw a ghastly pale, thin, and bald mannequin rocking the LBD that Veronica had picked out for me. I figured that what I lacked in terms of thinness, I could make up for with my olive skin and long hair. But after questioning the staff, I left Ann Taylor without buying the dress. I wasn't in the mood to dress shop after learning that no one in the store, or in the entire mall for that matter, had ever seen a black-and-white checked scarf with a yellow border. Plus, every time I thought of my conversation with Maria Di Salvo, I felt guilty about shopping for my date when I could've been working on a case that in all probability was related to the horrific murder of her daughter.

Scarf-less and LBD-less, I headed toward the mall exit and passed a jewelry kiosk displaying silver voodoo doll earrings. My mind flashed to Mambo Odette and her bizarre warning about the Evans case. *What was it she'd said?*

I thought for a moment, and it came to me—"Dat girl, she know what dat boy do." No matter how hard I tried, I couldn't understand who "dat boy" was. *Was it Ryan Hunter?* If so, I certainly didn't know anything about that guy or his past. I also didn't get why Odette had called me "dat girl" when she was talking directly to me. *Or was she?*

A light bulb went on in my head as if by voodoo—"dat girl" wasn't me, she was Jessica.

I rushed from the mall and speed-walked down Canal Street —I made it a policy never to run unless my life was in danger. It was less than a mile to Marie Laveau's House of Voodoo, and I wanted to get there fast to talk to Mambo Odette. As creepy and crazy as it seemed, there was a possibility that she knew something about the case. Although I certainly wasn't familiar with the inner workings of the New Orleans voodoo community, I had a sense that it was rooted in a system of informants and spies, much like the criminal underworld. It wasn't that I thought voodoo practitioners were crooks. I just knew that all underground movements—social, political, cultural, and religious—had historically relied on the covert exchange of information.

At Bourbon Street, I hooked a right and slowed my pace to weave through the thick crowd. Even on a Monday, the street was hopping. But I hardly noticed the revelers and the blaring jazz music because I was so focused on deciphering the riddle of Odette's message. *If Jessica was "dat girl," who was "dat boy"?*

My mind kept returning to Ryan. *Did Jessica know something he'd done?* His criminal record was clean, but that didn't mean anything. *Could he have been the one who strangled Immacolata?* It seemed unlikely that a strong-willed type like Jessica would have been living with him if he had. *Or...*

I stopped dead. *Had Jessica been covering for Stewart Preston?*

"Excuse me." I shoved my way through the last two hundred yards that separated me from Marie Laveau's and caused a guy to spill one of the two sixty-four-ounce plastic bottles of Miller Lite he was drinking. "Oops, sorry."

He stumbled and blinked.

*The guy didn't need to be drinking that much, anyway.* I hurried up the steps to the store and rushed inside, just in case he decided to come after me. Instead of the cashier with the acne, I saw an older woman who looked like she was dressed for a Sunday sermon.

"Hello." I gave a polite smile as I walked toward the back room.

"Mm." She frowned and looked down at me through her gray, horn-rimmed glasses.

I had to wonder why a woman like her would be working at a voodoo store, especially while wearing a pale pink church suit and a strand of pearls. *Was she keeping a watchful eye on the heathen world for her congregation?*

As I entered the dimly lit room, I saw the rockabilly sales clerk in his seat behind the counter. He was smoothing back his pompadour with a small black comb.

"Can I help you with somethin'?"

He seemed much more relaxed than when I was last there. "Yeah." I strained my eyes in the darkness for the wooden-statue woman. "I'm looking for Mambo Odette."

"She doesn't usually come in on a school night." He stood and began playing air upright bass and bouncing his head to the imaginary beat.

I tried to act like his rockabilly air concert was normal. "School night?"

"You know, a week day?" He pretend-strummed.

"So, she only works on weekends?"

"No, it's the other way around. She makes the long green during the week, then she comes in here on the weekends to hang out."

I might speak Italian, but rockabilly was Greek to me. "I'm sorry, the long what?"

He stopped air-strumming. "You know, baby. Bread, grain, money."

"Ah, gotcha." I opted to overlook the "baby" since it was part of his rockabilly culture. "So, being a voodoo priestess is a regular Monday-to-Friday job?"

"The weekend is when all the cheatin' and thuggin' goes down, you dig? So, Odette spends the work week helping the hapless victims."

"Oh. Then I'll come back another time."

"That's cool." He spun his nonexistent bass. "If you need anything else, just let me know. My name's Hep."

"Hip?"

He recoiled as though I were the least "with it" person he'd ever met. "No, darlin', 'Hep,' as in 'Hep Cat'?"

"Oh. Right." I smiled and returned to the main room. Hep was a different person when Mambo Odette wasn't around —*really* different.

As I headed for the door, the gleaming glass vials of potions near the cash register caught my eye. Although I was reluctant to endure the disdainful stare of The Church Lady, I decided to take a look. After all, I *had* kind of hoped to ask Odette about my date with Bradley after I'd discussed the Evans case with her. But since she wasn't around, it wouldn't hurt to see whether a love potion would counteract any voodoo hexes the Le Bayou restaurant had in store for me.

I browsed the assorted potions, wrestling with my ambiguous position on voodoo, superstition, and things of the like. I didn't want to believe in mysticism, but occasionally things happened in the world that made me wonder whether I was wrong. And sometimes, especially on a sad and frustrating day like the one I was experiencing, I needed to believe in magic.

In the end, I settled on the obvious choice—Love Potion #9. *A steal at only fourteen ninety-five*, I thought as I approached the cash register and placed the bottle on the counter.

The church-suited lady rang up the potion. "That'll be sixteen dollars and eighteen cents with tax."

I counted out the exact amount and handed it to her. I waited for her to tell me that there were better uses of my money, like tithing, but instead she grimaced at me as I placed the potion in my handbag and left the store.

As I walked in the direction of the office to get my car, I pulled out my phone and dialed Veronica's number.

"Hey, Franki. Any luck?"

"Nope. And I covered The Shops at Canal Street so thoroughly that I can even recite its motto—'32 names. 3 floors. 1 place.'"

"Impressive. So now that we've covered all the stores in the vicinity of the crime, we'll have to expand our search to the broader New Orleans area."

"I'm starting to feel like we're looking for a needle in a haystack."

"I know, but we have to keep looking." There was a firmness to her tone that left no room for discussion. "Now, tell me about the dress. Did Ann Taylor have it in your size?"

I hesitated for a moment. "I didn't get it."

"What? Why not? Your date is tomorrow night."

"I wasn't in the mood to dress shop."

Veronica sighed. "What did I tell you about keeping your personal and professional lives separate?"

"I know, I know."

"Then go back to Ann Taylor and buy that dress."

"Or what?" I was half kidding, half not.

"Or I'm going to have Glenda dress you for your date."

I got a mental image of me opening the door to Bradley in a black leather bustier, a gold lamé miniskirt, purple stripper shoes, and a green boa, with a long black cigarette holder in my left hand. "I'm on my way."

~

AT EIGHT FORTY-FIVE P.M., I strolled through Lenton's at Lakeside Shopping Center listening to the loudspeaker message announcing the mall closure in fifteen minutes and carrying the Ann Taylor LBD in a size twelve. The dress fit to perfection, which had done wonders for my mood. I'd even splurged on a pair of black pumps to celebrate the occasion.

Right before the exit, I spotted two large tables piled high with merchandise marked seventy-five percent off. Of course, I'd already maxed out my meager clothes allowance for the next four months with the purchases I'd made, but who could pass up the opportunity to buy clothing at a quarter of the price? It would've been financially irresponsible of me not to try to find *something* at those prices.

I sorted through the piles and saw the sleeve of what looked like a cute mulberry sweater tangled in a mass of clothes. I put my bags on the floor to unravel the knotted items. I set to work and caught sight of fabric with a black-and-white checked pattern in the mix. My heart raced as I worked to free the item from the other clothes.

It was a scarf—and it looked exactly like the one in the crime scene photo, except that it had a mauve border.

With scarf in hand, I picked up my bags and ran to a cash register. A heavyset woman with a nametag that read "Keisha" was busy putting anti-theft devices on a stack of cardigans. "Didya need help findin' somethin'?"

"Yes, I was wondering if this scarf came in any other colors." I placed it on the counter.

"One minute while I check." Keisha snapped another device onto a cardigan. She picked up a scan gun, scanned the barcode on the price tag, and looked at her cash register screen for what seemed like an eternity. She furrowed her brow. "Looks like it came in one other color."

By this time, my heart beat so fast that I thought I might faint. "Can you tell me which color?"

"Is says lye-moan-sell-low," she syllabified.

"What color is that?"

She shrugged. "Beats me. That's all it says."

"Do you mind if I look?"

She stepped to the side and splayed her arms. "Be my guest."

I rushed behind the counter to the screen. After scanning through a series of product names and lengthy codes comprised of letters and numbers, I saw it.

*Style: Limoncello.*

I threw my arms around Keisha. "It's yellow!"

She pulled away and took a step backward. "O-kaaay."

"Listen, Keisha, does Lenton's keep records of its sales?"

"Of course. But you'd have to talk to the store manager about that."

"Is the manager here now? It's important."

She looked at me for a moment, and her big brown eyes narrowed. "Hey, you're not a detective are you?"

"Yes, more or less." I hoped the slight exaggeration would convince her to help me.

"Is this a cheatin' husband case, or somethin'?"

"It's much more serious than that."

Her eyes bugged from their sockets. "*Murder?*"

I bit my lower lip.

She nodded. "The manager will be here tomorrow morning at nine thirty. Ask for Ed Orlansky."

## 12

"I'm just thrilled that you found the scarf store." Veronica threw her hands into the air as we sped down Interstate 10 East toward Slidell in her Audi the next morning.

"Me too." I watched to make sure she put her hands back on the steering wheel. Luckily, she did.

She veered into the left lane, cutting off a jacked-up pick-up truck with tractor-trailer tires in the process. "What time did you say we could call the manager?"

I looked over my left shoulder at the road-raging truck driver, who hit the gas and swerved into the middle lane. I shrunk into my seat, but not far enough to miss him saluting us with his middle finger as he roared around us. "Keisha told me he would be in at around nine thirty today."

Veronica glanced at the clock on the dashboard, oblivious to what had occurred. "That was ten minutes ago."

"I know. Let's give him another five minutes to get settled in."

"But we're going to be at the Di Salvo's house in fifteen minutes." She stared at me for way too long.

"All right. I'll call him." I straightened in the seat and pulled my phone from my purse. "You just watch where you're going. Eyes back on the road, missy."

She rolled said eyes. "You know I'm a trained racecar driver."

I gave her a look. "A few hours on the Ferrari racetrack in Italy doesn't make you Mario Andretti." I searched my phone contacts for the number for Ed Orlansky that Keisha had given me. "And honestly, when you get on the highway, you drive like you've had one too many skinny margaritas."

"Whatever you say, Nonna."

I ignored her, like my grandmother would do. "Now, what should I say to this guy?"

"Try to get us on his calendar for today or tomorrow, and don't tell him you're a PI if you can help it. Otherwise, he might not agree to meet us."

"Then how, exactly, are we going to convince him to spend hours and hours scrolling through electronic store receipts for all the people who bought that scarf once he finds out we're not with the police?"

"You leave that to me." She tossed her blonde mane.

"Gladly." I tapped the number and put the phone to my ear. Veronica ran a charm offensive that would rival that of even the savviest Washington political strategist. It was based on what I called the "bat-and-twirl effect," an irresistibly seductive combination of batting her eyelashes while twirling her dazzling golden locks around her fingers. The one and only time I'd tried it on a guy, he told me that I shouldn't tug on my hair because it made my eyes twitch.

"Is it ringing?"

I shook my head. "Voicemail."

"Hang up."

I pressed *End*. "Why?"

"He's the manager of a huge department store, so if you leave a message saying that you're investigating a local crime, he'll probably contact the police to verify that you work for them."

"And then he won't call me back when he finds out I'm not a police officer."

"Precisely."

"So, how do you want to handle this?"

"We know he's supposed to be at work today. I think we should drop in unannounced after we meet with the Di Salvos."

We both jumped at the unexpected sound of my new Booty-licious ringtone. It was better than the barking because it made me feel good about my curves, but it was still startling. On the display was the all-too-familiar *Unknown*.

"Maybe this is him." I tapped *Answer*. "Hello?"

"Yes, hello," a male voice exclaimed a little too animatedly. "Is this Francesca?"

I shook my head at Veronica. The caller was definitely not the Lenton's manager, because the only people who called me Francesca were my relatives or my prospective Sicilian dates. And this was no relative. "This is she."

"Fantastic. I'm Bruno Messina, and my mother, Santina, is friends with your nonna."

My heart sank, and I felt myself turning red. I glanced at Veronica and shrank in my seat. I wanted to get this call over with, but he sounded so excited that I actually felt kind of bad about intending to turn him down. "Yes, my nonna told me you'd be calling."

"Great. Listen, I'm calling to invite you to my house for dinner tonight."

*What is it with these guys asking me out on the day of the date?*

"My mamma is making her Sicilian specialty, *arancini*."

The thought of the deep-fried balls of rice, tomato sauce, meat, and cheese distracted me from the conversation, but I shook myself from my fried-food daydream and got back to the task at hand.

"Thanks for the invitation, Bruno, but I already have plans for this evening." Halfway hoping he'd think I was a loose woman like Pio had, I decided to clarify. "A date."

"Ah." His tone was less enthusiastic. Then he chuckled. "Well, we could meet after your date—for a nightcap."

*Seriously?* "That would be disrespectful to the man I'm going out with, don't you think?"

"Maybe he wouldn't have to know? After all, what we don't know doesn't hurt us, right Franki?" He chuckled again.

It was time to get down to the business of a brushoff by borrowing Pio's infamous line. "I'm sorry, but I just don't think this is going to work out."

"I see. Mamma will be so disappointed."

My eyes narrowed at the Catholic-guilt-inducing Mamma line. "I'm sorry about that. Goodbye, Bruno."

"Goodbye?"

The second I heard that uncertain "goodbye" I pressed *End* before he could bounce back with an exuberant "What about tomorrow morning?" Then I turned off my phone to be on the safe side.

Veronica raised an eyebrow. "One of Nonna's boys?"

"Yes, and hopefully the last." I sighed. "He just asked me out on a date for tonight at his house with his mother. I mean, how could my nonna think I would want to go out with a guy like that?"

"You know the mentality of our grandmothers." She turned into a neighborhood with small shotgun-style houses and covered porches. "Back in their day in Sicily, unmarried women our age had no expectations whatsoever of getting married. A warm body was more than *zitelle* like us could hope for."

"I know, I know. But what is it with men? I told this guy

about my date tonight, and he actually suggested that I go out with him afterward on the sly."

"That's his problem." She slowed to scan the street addresses.

"You think? If you ask me, cheating is fairly standard male behavior."

Veronica rolled the car to a stop in front of a modest-looking white house, pulled the keys from the ignition, and turned to face me. "You've had some bad luck with men, I agree. But you can't make a blanket generalization like that. Really, Franki, you need to start rethinking your attitude about men, or you could blow it with Bradley before you even get started."

"I'll see what I can do," I snapped, wondering what had gotten into Veronica. Normally when she was right, she was gentler about it.

"Good." She opened the car door. "Now that that's settled, we're here."

I got out of the car and followed her up the sidewalk, noting the particulars of the Di Salvo home. It was small, no more than fifteen hundred square feet, with cracked and peeling white paint. The yard was overgrown with weeds, and a few of the windows were broken. I wondered whether the general state of neglect of the house had anything to do with the tragic events the family had endured.

Veronica turned to me at the front door. "Ready?"

"I suppose so." But I wasn't at all sure I was emotionally prepared for the meeting.

She knocked and took a step back to wait.

After a few seconds, a chubby young woman in heavy Goth makeup opened the door. Her dyed black hair was boyishly short, and her bangs were long and brushed to one side, covering her right eye. She stood staring at us with her exposed left eye.

Veronica cleared her throat. "Hi. We have an appointment at ten with Maria Di Salvo?"

"I know." The young woman used her teeth to flick a silver stud in her tongue.

I looked at her, unsure of whether I should be grossed out, irritated, or empathetic in light of everything she'd been through. "Can we come in?"

She shrugged and turned to walk down the hallway, leaving the door wide open.

Veronica entered first, and I followed, closing the door behind me. The entryway consisted of a hallway lined with family photos, a large white ceramic cross, and a painting of the Virgin Mary. At the end of the hallway was a cluster of photographs of family members in their caskets. Many of my elderly Italian relatives had similar pictures in their homes, so I was familiar with the old-fashioned custom. But there was one photograph in particular that caught my attention. It was of a raven-haired young woman with fair skin and full red lips, who looked more like a sleeping Disney princess than a dead person. It had been taken more recently, and in an unusual twist, there was another individual in the picture—a young, rather homely woman standing beside the coffin. I was certain that the deceased was Immacolata. *But who was the woman standing next to her?*

I turned away from the photograph and saw the Goth girl glowering at me while slowly twisting her tongue stud with her hand.

She let go of the stud and led me into a small living room where Veronica was already seated on a floral-patterned couch encased in plastic.

As I took a seat beside my best friend, I noticed another cross on the wall behind the couch.

"Hang on." The girl disappeared down another hallway.

"I can't say I'm sorry she's gone," I whispered to Veronica. "She kind of gives me the creeps."

"It's just the all-black effect of her hair, makeup, and clothes."

"No, it's the all-black effect of her personality."

I scanned the room for any insights into the family, but aside from the cross, there wasn't much to see. The floor was covered in beige carpeting, and there were two dingy avocado-green armchairs facing the couch. One of the armchairs had a worn footstool in front with some knitting needles and yarn on it. Between the two armchairs was a small table with a lamp and what appeared to be an old photo of the Di Salvo family.

I rose and walked over to the photo to get a closer look. Then I heard the sound of footsteps approaching. I turned and saw a woman in her mid-fifties entering the living room in a worn housecoat and slippers. She had gray hair and a grayish tone to her skin, but it was clear from her high cheekbones and sensual lips that she had been beautiful in her youth.

She looked past Veronica and me, but not at anything in particular. "May I help you?"

"Yes." Veronica rose to her feet. "I'm Veronica Maggio, and this is my partner, Franki Amato."

Maria Di Salvo gave no sign that she recognized our names.

Veronica gestured to me. "We're the private investigators who called you about the Angelica Evangelista case?"

"Oh, yes."

I extended my hand. "Nice to meet you, Mrs. Di Salvo."

She grasped it limply. "Call me Maria."

Veronica and I took our seats on the couch. The noise was so loud when we sat on the plastic that I almost didn't hear Veronica ask, "Was that your daughter who greeted us at the door?"

"Yes, that's Domenica." She let out a sigh as she took a seat in the armchair with the footstool.

Veronica glanced at me, willing me not to comment. "And you have another daughter, right?"

"I have two. The twins, Concetta and Immacolata."

Concetta must've been the woman in the photo who was standing next to Immacolata's casket. "Immacolata had a twin sister?"

"Yes, they're fraternal twins. Concetta wanted to be here today, but she couldn't leave the convent."

"She's a nun?" I don't know why, but I was surprised.

"After Imma's death, Concetta felt she had a calling to become a nun. She wanted to help others to honor Imma's memory."

Veronica gave a sweet smile. "What a selfless, loving gesture."

"Yes, I'm very proud of all my daughters. But I'm especially proud of what Concetta has become, especially after the agony of losing her twin."

"Which high school does Domenica attend?" I resisted the urge to ask why she wasn't at school today.

"Slidell High. She's working toward her diploma and studying cosmetology at the same time."

Veronica licked her lips. "Can you tell us about Imma? We'd like to know more about her life in London."

"You mean, you want to know who murdered her," Domenica interjected from the hallway.

Maria gave a tired sigh. "Domenica..."

"It was that sick son-of-a-bitch Stewart Preston." Domenica was insensitive to the embarrassment, not to mention the pain, she was causing her mother.

"Domenica, please."

Undaunted, she entered the room. "And the bastard killed Angelica too, because she knew he strangled Imma."

Veronica and I exchanged a look.

"That's enough now." Maria's firmness was surprising given her obvious state of depression. "I'd like to speak to these ladies alone."

I looked at Veronica, and then watched Domenica storm out.

Maria turned to us. "I'm sorry about that." She looked down at her lap for a moment. "She's really been through a lot."

It made me feel awful that she felt she had to explain. "We understand."

"First her sister, then her father…"

Veronica's brow shot up. "Her father?"

"Rosario passed away a few days after Stewart Preston was acquitted of Imma's murder." Maria wiped a tear with her index finger. "It was his heart."

I was stunned to hear of the loss of her husband. "I'm so sorry."

"He never really recovered from Imma's death." She suppressed a sob. "None of us did, but Rosario took it especially hard because he felt he should've been there to protect her."

I thought of my own dad and how he would've felt if anything had happened to me. "Fathers are especially protective of their daughters."

"Yes, and he was so upset when Imma started hanging out with Stewart." She pulled a handkerchief from the pocket of her housecoat. "He told her to stay away from him, but she didn't listen."

Veronica leaned forward. "Why did he tell her to stay away from him? Did he know him?"

"No, but he knew of him." She twisted the handkerchief with her hands. "Stewart is the son of a very wealthy New Orleans family. He was always in *The Times-Picayune* society pages with a new woman on his arm. He'd also been in the news after being arrested for several DWI's and possession of the drug Ecstasy."

I was confused. "So, did Imma meet him in New Orleans or London?"

"They met during London Fashion Week in 2007, the year before Imma died. There are fabric tradeshows in London at the same time as fashion week, and Stewart was there representing the family textile business. Imma never missed the fabric shows because she was majoring in fashion textiles. One thing led to another and then..."

Veronica pressed her temple. "Um, we've read about Immacolata's case in the papers, and we've also seen reports of the trial. Do you believe Stewart is responsible for her death?"

"Yes." Her tone was harsh, and she jerked the handkerchief. "They went to a party, and he took her back to her dorm. There were witnesses who testified that they saw him go upstairs with her to her room."

"So there was no chance that she met someone else later that night after he left?" I asked.

"In our opinion, no. But the jury didn't see it that way." Anger had crept into her voice. "They acquitted him due to a lack of evidence."

"What about Angelica? She testified at the trial, right?"

She stiffened. "She did, but she insisted that she didn't know anything."

Veronica and I exchanged a look.

Maria wiped her eyes. "At the time, I believed her. But later, she changed, and then Rosario wasn't so sure anymore. He thought she knew something, but I just thought she felt guilty for not being able to help at the trial."

The change in Angelica could be important. "How did she change?"

"Well, we'd known her since she was a child." She shifted in her seat as she put the handkerchief back into her pocket. "She practically grew up in our house because her mother, Barbara, worked long hours as a seamstress. Angelica's father ran off when she was small. So, we were like her family. But after the trial, she was different. She avoided us, and we eventually lost contact with her."

She could've avoided them to escape the painful memories, but her behavior was curious. "Did you know she'd changed her name to Jessica Evans?"

"Not until the police came and questioned us. We didn't even know she was back in New Orleans. We just assumed she'd gone to work in the fashion industry in some big city somewhere."

"What about her mother?" Veronica asked. "Did you keep in touch with her?"

"She died a week before Imma's death. Breast cancer. In fact, Angelica was returning to London from Barbara's funeral here in Slidell the night Imma was murdered."

*So much tragedy.* "An article we read indicated that Angelica returned from a trip abroad at three a.m. the morning of the murder. What was the official time of Imma's death?"

Her gaze lowered to her lap. "Around one a.m."

I wondered whether Angelica had actually witnessed the murder. "Do you think it's possible that she returned earlier than she reported?"

Maria looked surprised. "Rosario asked that same question, but the police were able to verify the time she arrived with flight records and the taxi service that took her back to the dorm."

Veronica scooted forward on the couch, causing the plastic to crackle. "Do you have any pictures of Angelica?"

Maria hesitated. "Well, we have the twins' high school yearbooks."

"Could we see one, the most recent?"

"Give me a minute." She rose from the chair and shuffled

down the hall.

"Did you get the feeling she was hiding something?" I whispered.

"Yeah."

"I wonder what it could be? I mean, we just asked to see some pictures."

Veronica opened her mouth to reply but stopped.

Domenica and Maria were arguing in a back room.

I strained to listen but couldn't make out a word.

A few minutes later, Maria returned to the living room, flushed. She handed a yearbook to Veronica. "Here you are. Angelica would've been a senior that year, the same as the twins."

Veronica flipped through the pages as I looked on. First she went to the Ds to the class pictures of Concetta and Immacolata. The difference in appearance between the twins was striking. Imma was an exotic beauty with almond-shaped eyes, full lips and high cheekbones, but Concetta was plain with a round face, close-set eyes, and a pencil-thin mouth.

She turned the page to the Es and stopped. It wasn't hard to locate Angelica's picture—not only because she was a dead ringer for Jessica Evans—but also because there was a word scrawled across it in red ink—*puttana*, the Italian word for "whore." Whoever had written the insult had gone over it several times with the pen, tearing the photo.

An uncomfortable silence ensued.

Maria rose from her seat and walked into the adjoining kitchen. "I have another picture of her."

She returned with a brown billfold and opened it to reveal a small, black-and-white photo. "There, that's her." She pointed to a young blonde in a sundress standing beside Immacolata and Concetta. "It was taken at a family barbecue."

Even though Maria suspected Angelica of having information about Imma's death, she carried her picture in her wallet. I realized that instead of losing one daughter the night Imma was strangled, Maria Di Salvo had actually lost two.

"Barbara made that dress for her," she said softly. "She hated it."

I remembered Angelica's penchant for expensive designer clothes. "Why? Because it was homemade?"

"Most of her clothes were homemade, or they were purchased at yard sales. And they were a constant reminder to her that she was poor. She always used to say that she was going to do whatever she had to do to make money when she grew up so that she could buy herself expensive clothes."

I offered a wan smile. "And she did."

"But that's not why she hated the dress."

Veronica looked up. "Oh?"

"She hated it because it was yellow."

My gut gave a little kick. "Yellow?"

"Yes, when she was a little girl, her mother told her that yellow was her father Bill's favorite color. You see, Barbara still loved Bill even though he'd run out on her and Angelica. I know because Barbara used to tell me that Bill would come home to them one day, and when he did, she wanted them to look nice for him. So she made Jessica wear yellow, and often." Maria looked at her lap and grimaced. "But as the years passed and it became obvious that Bill wasn't coming back, Angelica began to despise yellow. She wore it to make her mother happy, but she always said it was the color of cowards."

*Yellow is the color of cowards.* My mind began to race like a black-and-white checked flag had been waved in front of it—or the black-and-white checked scarf with the Limoncello yellow border that was wrapped around Angelica's neck in that horrible crime scene photo.

*Had the killer known of Angelica's hatred for the color yellow?*

## 13

"What's Orlansky doing back there?" I knocked the back of my head against the wall of the Lenton's waiting room. "Sleeping, or something?"

Veronica shifted in her seat. "Calm down, Franki. I'm sure he'll meet with us soon."

"You said that thirty minutes ago." I leaned forward in my chair. "Seriously, he had better hurry. Otherwise, I won't have time to get ready for my date. And if that happens, you'll have another murder to investigate."

"You know," she rummaged in her red Fendi bag, "I just can't stop thinking about Domenica's reaction to our visit."

I crossed my arms. "I still say we should've questioned her."

"No, we need to talk to her alone to avoid the mother-daughter dynamic." She opened a compact. "That way we can find out if she meant the things she said, or if she was just trying to get a rise out of her mother."

"I'm not sure I want to be alone with The Dark One. There was something about the way the girl looked at me that made my skin crawl."

"She *is* awfully angry." Veronica powdered her nose. "I'm

going to have David do a background check on all of them. If this business about Jessica hating the color yellow is relevant to the case, then every member of the Di Salvo family is a potential suspect."

I looked at my phone. "It's six o'damn clock." I leapt from my seat and paced the room, and I ran right into a stick-thin fifty-something administrative assistant as she walked through the doorway. "I'm so sorry."

She straightened and pushed up her glasses. "Mr. Orlansky will see you now."

Veronica and I looked at one another before following the woman as she tottered on scuffed beige heels down a long hallway and stopped without a word beside an office doorway marked "Ed Orlansky."

I followed Veronica into a small, windowless room decorated in varying shades of brown. The balding middle-aged man behind the desk was also wearing brown from head to toe, including the cigar in his mouth. I looked at the cigar to see whether it was lit.

His eyes met mine. "Don't worry, I don't smoke this thing." His voice was gruff like his demeanor. "I just like to chew on it."

My stomach lurched at the thought of swallowing tobacco cud. "Oh. Sure."

He rose and pulled up his pants, which sagged below his protruding belly.

"Which one of you ladies is Veronica?"

"That's me." Veronica extended her hand. "Thank you for agreeing to see us about the Jessica Evans case."

"Happy to be of service." He shook her hand and stared into her eyes. "Did you say that you and Miss—"

"Amato," I interjected. "But please call me Franki."

He nodded. "Franki. Are you with the New Orleans PD?"

"Actually," Veronica grasped a lock of her hair and gave it a twirl, "I own a private investigation firm called Private Chicks, Inc." She batted her long eyelashes.

"We don't normally give information to private investigators..." The cigar went limp between his lips.

Veronica's bat-and-twirl offensive was taking effect.

He drew in his breath, as though shaking off a spell. "But, given the seriousness of this case, I suppose I could help you ladies out."

"That's wonderful, Mr. Orlansky." Veronica clapped and leaned closer to his desk.

"Please, call me Ed." He flashed a mouthful of yellow teeth. "Why don't you take a seat?"

I sat in one of the two chairs in front of his desk. I had a date to get ready for, so it was time to get to it. "Were you able to look up the sales information for the Limoncello scarf?"

He started as though he'd forgotten the reason for our visit. "Oh, yes. Well, the scarf belongs to an exclusive Lenton's line that's only sold in this store. And based on our inventory records, we received five in yellow and five in mauve."

Veronica batted and twirled. "Can you tell us who you sold the five yellow scarves to?"

He paused, mesmerized by her charms. "We have an electronic record of all purchases. But those would only tell you who bought the scarf if the customer used a credit card or check to pay."

I glanced at the time on my phone. "Is there any way to find out the identity of a customer who paid with cash?" Ed hesitated, as though debating something, and licked his dry lips. "You could get an image of the customer from the computer."

"Computer?" I met Veronica's baby blues straight on.

"Yeah, we have a camera on every cash register in the store, and the video from the cameras is stored on a computer hard drive. So we can search the electronic receipt files for the ID number of the scarf, and then check the computer video file for the day and time the scarf was sold."

I nodded to encourage him. "Would it be possible to check the video file for all the Limoncello scarves purchased with cash? We'd like to see those first."

"It depends. If the scarf was sold more than thirty days ago, then the video would be backed up to DVD and stored at our headquarters in Baton Rouge."

"You could get the DVD from Baton Rouge, though, right?"

"Well yes, my secretary could have them mail us a copy. But I'm not sure we have the resources to go through all that video right now. We're understaffed at the moment, and that kind of thing could take hours."

Veronica batted and twirled away. "I could help you go through it."

"In that case," he lit up like a cigar, "I'm sure we could work something out."

"Oh, Ed, you're the best." Veronica gave a sensual hair flip.

He blushed. "Thank you, but it's going to take time." He paused to ogle Veronica. "We'll probably be working late for quite a few nights."

Veronica gave another sexy hair flip. "I'm available."

"All righty then." I shot to my feet. "We sure appreciate it, Ed. We'll check in with you in a day or two to see how the research is coming, but right now we're late for another appointment." I headed for the door and gestured to Veronica to follow suit.

"Yes, thank you, Ed." She sprung from her seat and gave a little wave. "I'll call you."

"I'm looking forward to it." He breathed the words as though exhaling smoke.

We rushed from his office, and I turned to Veronica. "You have mad skills."

"Who, me?" She batted her eyelashes and twirled a lock.

"And while we're on the subject of your skills," I looked at the time, "I'm gonna need you to kick that racecar driver thing into high gear. My date with Bradley is in forty-five minutes."

~

"*Madonna santa*," I whispered as Veronica and I pulled up to the fourplex exactly forty-five minutes later thanks to the evening traffic.

She squeezed the steering wheel. "Holy mother of God, indeed."

Not only was Bradley waiting in the driveway in his black BMW, but Glenda was leaning into his driver-side window in one of her lingerie loungewear ensembles—a black teddy and a fuchsia fur-lined robe with matching high-heeled slippers. She wasn't holding her customary cigarette lighter. Instead, she had a bottle of champagne in one hand and two long-stemmed champagne flutes in the other. And she was clearly in the mood to entertain.

Veronica nudged me from my stone state. "You get into the house and get your LBD on ASAP. I'll have Bradley help me walk Hercules and Napoleon around the neighborhood. That'll give you some time to get ready and get Glenda out of the picture. She won't be able to walk the dogs in those heels."

I spun in the seat. "Are you kidding? That woman has been performing in six-inch platform stripper shoes since the age of sixteen. Not only could she walk the neighborhood in those heels, she could run a marathon and then compete in the freakin' high jump."

She chewed her lower lip. "Don't worry. I'll think of something."

"You do that." I threw open the car door and mad-dashed to my front door.

I wasted precious seconds fumbling with the lock, and then I pushed open the door and started to run toward my bedroom. Unfortunately, Napoleon was waiting to greet me on the other side of the door, so I took an impromptu leap to avoid stepping on him. My foot caught the tooth of the bear head on the bearskin rug, and I careened onto the floor, landing on both knees. I jumped up, limped to the bathroom, and threw off my clothes only to discover that both of my knees were bleeding.

"*Mannaggia*," I cursed, rubbing an antibiotic on my wounds. I had about twenty minutes to get ready to avoid making us miss our dinner reservation at Le Bayou. There was no time to wash and dry my hair. Instead, I took a speed-of-light shower.

I started to apply my make-up and heard Veronica and Bradley returning with the dogs. To my dismay, I also heard Glenda's unmistakable smoker's-cough laugh. I willed Veronica to keep her in line, but I knew there was no use. Glenda was a force of nature, and she was more powerful and unpredictable than a hurricane.

My hands shook as I did my eyeliner. When I stood back from the mirror, I saw that my signature Sophia Loren-style cat eye looked more like that of Cleopatra. There was no time to fix it. "It's okay, Franki," I said to my horrified reflection, "Cleopatra was one of the greatest seductresses in history."

I hurried to my closet, pulled my dress off the hanger, and stepped into it. I wrestled with the zipper and slipped on my black slingbacks. I didn't stop to look in the mirror again for fear of what might look back at me.

When I entered the living room, I saw the second most horrifying spectacle of the day—Glenda had propped one of her skinny white spider-veined legs on the chaise lounge and was doing her best to look sexy while extracting a card from her fuchsia garter belt.

"Here you go, sugar," she said to a grinning Bradley as

Veronica looked on in a mix of astonishment and admiration. "My business card."

"Thank you, Miss Glenda." He took the business card and raised her hand to his lips.

"If you ever need anything, darlin', and I *do* mean *anything*, you just call Miss Glenda."

The only thing I could think of to do was clear my throat. But thanks to my mold allergy, I sounded like a cat hacking up a hefty fur ball. The noise startled the unlikely trio, who turned to look at me.

"Oh." Veronica put her hand to her mouth and rushed to the kitchen.

Glenda raised an eyebrow and tossed back an entire glass of champagne.

I felt what must have been a trickle of blood run down my right knee. *So much for my grand entrance.*

Bradley had a gleam in his eyes. "Jaclyn Smith with an Italian twist."

"What?" I didn't have a clue what he was talking about.

"That's which Charlie's Angel you are."

"Thanks." Of course, I would have preferred to be Farrah, but at least he hadn't compared me to Bosley.

He shoved his hands into his pockets. "But..."

*But what? Is it the blood? Or did I cough up some phlegm?* I felt around my mouth to check.

"Did you get my message?"

"No," I said, confused, as Veronica knelt and dabbed at my knee with a paper towel. "What message?" Then I remembered —I'd turned off my phone after Bruno called, and I hadn't turned it back on.

"There's been a change of plans. A client of the bank, Craig Burns, is having a crawdad boil, so I thought you might like to do that instead."

"Oh." I tried to think of anything I could change into that was both cute *and* clean.

Glenda, seizing upon the momentary lapse in conversation, sidled up to Bradley. "The crawdad boil reminds me of a strip-tease I used to do—"

"You know what?" I practically shouted over her as I walked toward the door. "If it's all right with you, Bradley, I'll just go like this."

I simply could not allow her to subject him to one of her stripping stories, especially one that involved shellfish and boiling water.

"As you wish." Bradley smiled as he followed me from the apartment. "With you in that dress, I'll be the envy of every guy at the party."

I smiled up at him. Despite his obsession with Charlie's Angels, Bradley Hartmann was growing on me.

～

"HERE WE ARE." Bradley eased the BMW to a stop in front of a stately Victorian home.

I admired the long white columns that lined the exterior. "What a gorgeous house."

"Yeah, Craig owns a major construction company here in New Orleans, so he's done quite well for himself."

I sighed as I stared at the serene-looking body of water directly across the street.

"It must be wonderful to sit on that veranda and gaze at the river."

"The river?" He turned to look at me. "You mean, Bayou St. John?"

My head spun like Linda Blair's in *The Exorcist*. "Bayou?"

"Yes." He frowned. "Is something wrong?"

"No, no." I couldn't tell him about Mambo Odette's warning, or he'd think I was a flake. "I just thought I knew my bodies of water better than that."

"Well, if you're interested in bodies of water, Craig would be only too happy to tell you all about the history of this bayou. He's always going on about how this particular stretch in front of his house is where Marie Laveau used to practice some of her voodoo rituals."

"What? Right here?" I looked back at the bayou. Upon second examination, that water was definitely murky.

"So local legend would have it." He opened his car door. "One sec, I'll help you out of the car."

"Thanks." I smiled and turned to scrutinize the bayou. *Why did Marie Laveau choose this spot for her rituals?*

He helped me out of the car and pulled me close. "Are you sure you're okay, Franki?"

"I'm terrific." I smiled and returned his sexy gaze. *To hell with superstition.*

We walked up the driveway and entered the backyard through an iron gate. Twenty or so people stood around two long tables in the center of the yard. Each was covered in newspaper and had piles of crawfish that had been boiled with corn on the cob, large chunks of onion, and potato and spice bags full of Cajun seasonings. On the opposite side of the yard was an outdoor bar manned by a bartender.

Bradley took me by the hand. "Let's head over to the bar. Then I'll introduce you to some of the guests."

We stepped off the concrete walkway into the grass, and my three-inch heels sunk into the soft earth. I sighed and walked on the balls of my feet like I'd seen high-heeled Italian women in Rome do on the cobblestone streets. I imagined that I was taking the graceful strides of a runway model, but I suspected that I actually looked more like I was plodding along on a Stairmaster.

We reached the bar, and an elegant blonde with aristocratic features turned and looked at Bradley. "Why, look what the cat dragged in." She threw her arms around him and kissed him on the cheek.

Bradley stiffened as he returned the woman's embrace. "I didn't realize you were in town, Sheilah."

"Oh, you know how dull Boston society is during the winter months, darling." She pulled from the embrace but made no move to back away. "But then again, you haven't been home in so long. Maybe you've forgotten."

*Darling? Home?* I stepped closer to Bradley to make it clear that we were together.

Sheilah turned to look at me and frowned. "Who's this?"

"This is Franki Amato." Bradley gazed at the ground. "She just moved here from Austin."

I couldn't help but notice that he hadn't introduced me as his date, nor had he mentioned precisely who the woman was. I didn't need to be a PI to know they had a history.

The bartender looked at Bradley. "What can I get you, sir?"

"A white wine and a Sam Adams." Bradley pulled out some bills to tip him.

Sheilah looked me up and down. "What an interesting outfit to wear to a crawdad boil."

I looked at her white Capri pants. "You know what they say. It's better to be overdressed than underdressed."

She scowled and opened her mouth but closed it when Bradley approached with my wine.

"Franki," he handed me the glass, "why don't we go find a quiet table somewhere?"

It was clear that he wanted to keep me from Sheilah, and I intended to find out why.

"Brad the Bad," a male voice boomed behind me.

I started, and my heels sank deep into the dirt. I lurched backward, spilling wine on my chest.

"Damsel in distress!" The man grabbed me from behind, wrapping his arms around my breasts as I fell into his soft belly.

"Let me help you, Franki." Bradley took the glass from my hand and placed it on the bar.

Sheilah snorted. "That's what happens when you wear high heels to a backyard party."

I shot her a look of death. Whoever this woman was, she was no friend of mine.

"I'll hold 'er steady, Brad," the man said, "and you yank her feet from the dirt."

"Oh, I can manage." I tried to extract my heels, but Bradley knelt and helped me step from my shoes. I cringed as I remembered that I hadn't had time to do my toes.

Bradley pulled my shoes one by one from the earth. "Franki, meet Craig."

"You ready to suck some mudbug heads, Franki?" Craig released me from his clutches.

"I'm sorry, what?" I was certain that I'd misunderstood him.

Craig grinned. "That's what we call crawdads in these parts."

"I think I knew that." I took my shoes from Bradley.

Sheilah smirked. "Craig, Franki's new to New Orleans. She probably doesn't know about the local traditions."

"Actually, I know about sucking crawdad—I mean, mudbug —heads. I've just never done it, but I've been dying to," I fibbed and slipped my shoes back on. As much as I wanted to keep them off, I didn't dare give Society Sheilah the opportunity to point out that my unpedigreed feet were unpedicured.

"Let's show her how to eat a mudbug, Brad." Craig led me by the arm to the nearest table and picked up a tiny crawdad with his huge hand. "You grab the little guy by the torso, see, and you yank off his tail. Then you peel off the shell and eat the meat.

Right after that, you suck the head to get the fatty brains and the juice. It's dee-licious."

"Sounds, uh, great."

"Here, try it." He peeled the tail and handed me the meat with his bare hands.

I hesitated before taking it, and then, not wanting to look like a germaphobe, popped the meat into my mouth. "It's good."

He handed me the crawdad head. "Okay now, pucker up and suck."

Reluctantly, I placed my lips around the crawdad head, and as Craig, Bradley and the ever-present Sheilah looked on, I inhaled sharply.

Bradley gave a half smile. "What do you think?"

"It *is* delicious," I said, surprised. "I really like the spicy flavor."

"I told you she'd like 'em." Craig chuckled. "I know a mudbug sucker when I see one." He gave my back a hearty slap.

I jerked forward but managed to maintain my balance and smile, even though I was unsure whether to be flattered or upset by the remark, especially after I saw Sheilah smirk.

Bradley reached for a stack of dishes. "I'll make us a couple of plates."

I felt a serious need for alcohol. "Okay. I'm going to get another glass of wine. Can I get you anything?"

"Sure, I'll take another beer."

"Be right back." I smiled and trudged to the bar.

The bartender looked up from a glass he was drying with a towel. "What can I get you?"

"A glass of Pinot Grigio and a Sam Adams, please." I licked my lips, which were tingling from the spicy Cajun seasoning. I needed to touch up my lip gloss after sucking that crawdad head. I rummaged in the bottom of my bag and felt the cylindrical-shaped object. But it wasn't lip gloss that I'd found. It was the bottle of Love Potion #9.

"Here's the Sam Adams." The bartender placed the beer on the bar. "I need to run into the house to get another bottle of Pinot."

"No problem." I stared at Bradley's open beer and grasped the potion in my hand. *Should I?*

Sheilah's flirtatious laugh cut across the yard.

I turned and saw her sitting next to Bradley at a patio table, practically in his lap. *I must.*

Glancing from side to side, I opened the potion. No one was looking, so I poured the contents into his beer and slipped the empty vial into my bag. *I mean, it's probably just water, right?*

I approached the table, annoyed to see Sheilah and Bradley huddled together in conversation. I slammed the beer onto the table, and they jumped like two necking teens who'd been caught by the cops.

"I've got to go get my wine." I locked my gaze onto Bradley's like a laser. "Don't forget about me while I'm gone."

I ball-footed it back to the bar. I couldn't leave those two alone for a minute.

The bartender extracted the cork from the Pinot Grigio. He poured a glassful and handed it to me.

"Thanks." I pulled a dollar from my wallet and put it in his tip jar.

He looked at me wide-eyed. "Sure."

I wasn't sure why he would look so surprised by a dollar tip, but I assumed that most people didn't tip at backyard parties.

I turned and headed toward the table. My feet ached from the high heels and from walking on the balls of my feet. And my mouth was strangely numb. I wondered what kind of spices were in Cajun seasoning and decided to lay off the mudbug heads and stick to the tails.

Given Bradley and Sheilah's suspicious behavior, I snuck up behind them to do a little eavesdropping.

Bradley sipped his beer and muttered something to Sheilah.

"Now, darling," she gave him a playful shove, "is that any way to talk to your wife?"

*Wife?* The glass slipped from my hand and shattered on the tiled patio.

Bradley spun around and gave a start, and Sheilah spit out the sip of wine she'd just taken.

Not one for discretion, Craig shot up from a nearby table. "Ho-ly smokes, Franki. Your lips are all fat."

"Bwhat?" I touched my lips. They felt unusually full, which would've been great if it weren't for the speech impediment.

Everyone at the party went silent and gawked.

Bradley turned to Craig. "She's having an allergic reaction. I need to get her to the hospital."

"Let's give her some Benadryl first so her throat doesn't close up," Craig said not-so-soothingly. "I've got some in the bathroom next to the kitchen."

Taking me by the arm, Bradley rushed me into the house with Craig close behind.

I wanted to confront him about Sheilah's stunning revelation, but my tongue had gone numb.

He led me to a small room off the kitchen. "There's the bathroom."

I entered first and switched on the light. As Craig searched a cabinet for the Benadryl, I looked into the mirror. But instead of my regular semi-full lips, I saw inflated pillow lips—almost twice the size of Angelina Jolie's.

## 14

"They're still pretty big." Veronica stood in front of my desk, scrutinizing my lips. " But you can't seriously think this is voodoo."

"Mambo Odette told me to stay away from the bayou. I didn't, and look what happened." I pointed to my mouth. "I ended up on a date with a married man. And to punish me, some loa puffed me up like a blowfish."

She rolled her eyes. "Like I said, I'm sorry about Bradley. But really, you're as superstitious as your nonna. Deep down, you know this whole lip thing has nothing to do with voodoo. It's a coincidence."

"Here's what I know." I snapped the cover of my laptop shut. "I've been eating shrimp from the Gulf of Mexico all my life, and I've never had a problem. I suck the head of one lousy mudbug, or crawdad, or whatever they call the stupid things down here, and my lips plump up like Ball Park Franks."

"So what? Crawfish are more closely related to lobster than shrimp. Just because you can eat one doesn't mean you can eat the other."

"I don't need a lecture in marine biology to know what's

going on here, Veronica. Don't you see? Mambo Odette has some kind of psychic voodoo power. She knew that the bayou and I wouldn't mix. So now I need to find her and ask her about Bradley."

Veronica furrowed her brow. "Why? You're not thinking about seeing him again, are you?"

"Certainly not." I leaned back in my chair and crossed my arms. "It's just that Odette told me he was a 'good man,' and now I want to know why she would say that if she knew he was married."

"Maybe she didn't know."

"Oh, she knows, Veronica. She knows." I gave a grave nod. "In fact, I think we should consult with her on the Evans case."

She shook her head. "Not a chance."

"Odette's omniscient, and my lips are the proof." I puckered the evidence.

The main door of the office slammed, and Veronica jumped and threw up her hands. "David's here."

Footsteps bounded up the hallway, and David popped his head into my office. "G'day, la—" He dropped the faux Australian accent and recoiled like a turtle pulling its head back into its shell. "Whoa, Franki. Did you get into a throw down or somethin'?"

"Yeah, with an overzealous crawfish."

He shot Veronica a questioning look.

"Don't ask," she said under her breath.

"That's cool." He looked at the floor.

Veronica turned to face him. "I'm about to call Ryan Hunter with a case update. Were you able to find out anything about Bill or Barbara Evangelista?"

"Oh." He stood up straight and pulled back his shoulders to assume his professional stance. "So, I couldn't find any record of the Evangelistas owning the house in Slidell, but I did find an obituary for Barbara. The problem is that it doesn't tell us anything we don't already know."

I sighed away my lip frustration and decided to get to work. "What about Bill? Did you find anything on him?"

"Nope, not yet." He stared to my left to avoid my lips.

"Keep digging. And don't forget about his wife and child. They could factor into this case too."

Veronica nodded. "And while you're working on that, I need you to run background checks on the Di Salvos—Maria, Concetta, and Domenica."

I shivered at the mention of Domenica's name, and my phone began to vibrate like it was scared of her too. I looked at the display and saw the number of my parents' deli. "Sorry guys. I need to take this."

Veronica and David filed out of my office, and I answered the phone in speakerphone mode. "Hello?"

"Francesca?" my mother asked shrilly, as though she were unsure whether she was speaking to me or to some random woman who sounded exactly like me and had my same phone number.

"Yes, Mom, it's me. Is something wrong?"

"Why would something be wrong, dear?"

I was already irritated with the call. "Because you normally call me from home."

"Well, your date with Bradley is a special occasion."

I put my face in my hands. This wasn't going to go well.

"Your nonna and I are calling to find out how it went."

"*Nonna*? What's she doing at the deli?" My nonna *never* left the house, not even for mandatory hurricane evacuations.

"Well, your father and I made her promise not to call you to ask about your date until we came home tonight. She refused to keep that promise, dear, so your father made her come to work with us."

Embarrassment paralyzed my brain. "Wait. Dad's in on this call too?"

"Yes, dear, we've all been talking about it this morning. Rosalie Artusi, Larry from the drycleaner's, Mr. Giangiulio from the bakery, Marjorie—"

"Mom," I interrupted through clenched teeth, "I've asked you a thousand times not to discuss my personal life with the customers."

"But you know we've always thought of our customers as family, Francesca, so it wouldn't be right not to share good news about our children. Besides, everyone has been worried about your problem with long-term relationships."

I focused on resisting the overwhelming urge to curl up in the fetal position under my desk. Then I inhaled. "Mom, about that good news…"

"Yes?"

"The date didn't go perfectly."

She slammed the phone receiver onto the counter. "Joe! The date was a disaster."

I gasped. "Mom."

My dad groaned. "Not again, Brenda."

"*Mom!*"

"Yes, dear?"

"I didn't say it was a disaster."

"Well, then what happened, Francesca?"

"Bradley took me to a party, but after we got there my lips began to swell because—"

The phone slammed to the counter again. "Her lips swelled during the date."

"Oh, Lord," a customer half-shouted. "Franki's got herpes."

"Lip swelling's also a sign of hand, foot, and mouth disease," another bellowed.

I cringed as I listened to the customers, who continued to theorize about the source of my unfortunate lip mishap.

My mother returned to the phone. "Francesca, was it herpes? Or foot and mouth? Or something even more terrible?"

I mentally counted to ten. "Mom, I don't have a disease. I went to the hospital, and the doctor said it was an allergic reaction to crawfish."

Down went the receiver. "She's allergic to crawfish, Rosalie." My mother wailed, as though my chances of ever finding another man were now even further diminished in light of my new shellfish affliction. "What are we going to do?"

I put my head on the desk and heard what sounded like the phone hitting the floor followed by a scuffle.

"It's-a not-a the crawfish-a, Franki. It's-a Bradley." Nonna's doom-and-gloom voice boomed through the speaker. "I told-a you that you should-a go out-a with only Italian boys, but don't-a you worry. I find-a you a nice Sicilian."

*Oh, sweet* Gesù, *no.* I had to discourage a second round of the Sicilian Dating Game. "Nonna, it's not possible to be allergic to a person. And besides, I don't have time to go out with anyone right now. After all, I've got a killer to track down."

"If-a you got-a the time to find a killer, you got-a the time to find a husband."

The line went dead.

In a shocking tactical maneuver, my *nonna* had hung up on *me*.

～

To keep my mind off the whole Bradley affair—or rather, marriage—I buried myself in work. After spending several hours sifting through British and American websites for details about the Di Salvo murder trial, I pondered a disturbing picture of Stewart Preston. It was taken on the steps of the courthouse after he'd been acquitted for murder. He sneered with his fist raised in a sign of victory. Everything about the guy oozed sleaze, from his distasteful gesture to the gold chain link necklace and dark chunky watchband he'd selected to accessorize his designer suit. And that was how he looked and behaved after his attorneys had undoubtedly worked overtime to get him to clean up his image.

The image of an arrogant Stewart did nothing to calm my already upset stomach. I pulled the seventh or eighth Tums tablet from the roll in my desk drawer and put it between my back-to-normal lips.

*What is* wrong *with me?* I pressed my hand to my burning belly. Of course, my heartburn could've had something to do with the four slices of sausage and garlic pizza I'd eaten for lunch at Nizza. It also might've been caused by the threat of a renewed surge of Sicilian suitors looming on the horizon. But the most likely culprit was the fact that I'd fallen yet again for a cheater, and a married one to boot.

The lobby bell interrupted my personal pity party.

I rose from my desk and headed down the hallway.

A young, dark-haired woman stood in the middle of the lobby with her hand on a large crucifix hanging from her neck. She wore sensible black shoes and a plain white cotton shirt with a full, ankle-length gray skirt, which accentuated her thick waist and chubby thighs. "May I help you?"

"Yes." Her voice was soft, soothing. "I'm here about the Jessica Evans case. I'm Concetta Di Salvo."

I realized that I recognized her from the photos I'd seen at her mother's house.

"I'm Franki Amato. My partner, Veronica Maggio, and I spoke with your mother and sister yesterday."

She grasped my hand rather than shaking it. "That's why I'm here. May I sit down?"

"Of course. Let me show you to our conference room, and then I'll have Veronica join us."

"That would be nice." She gave a pleasant smile. "Thank you."

After I'd settled her at our conference table with a glass of water, I closed the door and ran from the room to Veronica's office. And I understood why she hadn't responded to the bell.

She stared at her computer with her hot pink headphones on, which could only mean one thing—she was communing with the goddesses—The Spice Girls.

I waved my arms SOS style in front of her desk. "Concetta Di Salvo is here."

"She is?" Her lips went into yikes-mode as she rose to her feet. "But I haven't prepared any questions for her yet."

"We'll have to wing it." I waited for her to gather her laptop and pushed her toward the conference room.

We entered, and I let Veronica take the lead.

"Thank you for the unexpected visit, Concetta."

She squeezed a rosary. "I loved Angie like a sister, so I want to help with the investigation in any way I can."

She had a calming presence about her. *No wonder she'd become a nun.*

Veronica opened her laptop. "Your mother told us that Angelica was like one of the family."

"Oh, absolutely. In fact, Imma, Angie, and I used to joke that we were actually triplets."

I glanced at the rosary. "But your mom also said that your family lost touch with Angelica after Imma died."

"Yeah. Things were never the same after we lost Imma." She took a sip of her water. "My whole family was in mourning, of course, and then there was the emotion and stress of the investigation and later the trial. After it was all finally over, we never heard from Angie again. But I'm sure she felt uncomfortable after everything that happened."

"Why do you say that?"

"Well, because my family was in ruins, for one thing. We weren't the same big happy family that Angie had known before." She paused and looked at her rosary. "You see, Imma was the beautiful, extroverted one. And she had so much energy and enthusiasm for life. Without her we all just...fell apart. But I also think Angie cut off contact with us because she felt bad that she didn't help us at the trial."

Veronica furrowed her brow. "Your mother told us she testified."

"Well, she took the stand, but she said she didn't know anything about Stewart or his relationship with Imma."

I pursed my lips. "And you didn't believe her."

"I wanted to." Her eyes were earnest, like her tone. "It's just that Imma died so *violently*. I felt that Angie must have noticed something, like some sort of abusive behavior. And..."

I leaned in. "What?"

"Well, I'm sure Imma told me that Angie had been the one to introduce her to Stewart when they met at London Fashion Week."

Veronica straightened in her chair. "So Angie knew Stewart before Imma did?"

"Yes, I'm positive that Imma said Angie had met Stewart at Mardi Gras before she and Imma ever went to the London College of Fashion. I remember because she said that Stewart had pulled Angie from the crowd onto his float in the Krewe de Eros parade."

My eyes went wide. "He had his own parade float?"

Concetta nodded. "Yes, he's very active in Mardi Gras."

Veronica typed a note on her laptop. "Why do you think Angie would have lied in court about knowing him?"

"I don't know. Maybe because she was scared?"

I glanced at Veronica. "Of what? Stewart?"

Concetta harrumphed. "Angie wasn't the type to be intimidated by anyone. If anything, she was worried about her reputation. She was very driven to succeed. In fact, Imma said that as soon as Angie got to London, she would only associate with people who could help her career in some way."

*That certainly jives with the way Ryan and Annabella described her.*

Veronica resumed typing. "Did you see Angie again after the trial?"

"No, never." She sighed. "The last we knew she was in London. We had no idea that she'd come back to New Orleans, and we certainly didn't know she'd changed her name."

Veronica tapped a finger to her cheek. "Do you have any idea why she would've used the name Jessica Evans?"

Concetta looked at her hands. "The name specifically? No. But my guess is that she wanted to disassociate herself from Imma's murder."

I scratched my head. "Why would she want to do that? Do you think she had something to do with your sister's murder?"

"No, not at all." Concetta's eyes filled with tears. "Angie could never have killed Imma. I'm sure of that."

Not wanting to upset her further, I changed the subject. "You joined the convent after the trial, right?"

"No, I entered aspirancy about six months after Imma died, before the trial. God called me to service after I lost her." Her voice was soft, distant. "It's funny, when Imma was thousands of miles away in London, I still felt like she was with me. But then when she was really gone...well...let's just say that I could never have gone back to the life I led before."

I felt terrible for her, and I hoped that her decision to become a nun was truly the right one, and not a choice made solely based on her loss.

Veronica placed a hand on Concetta's back. "I've always heard that the bond between twins is so powerful."

"It is," she whispered. Then she cleared her throat. "And I'm sure my mother told you about my father."

I nodded. "Yes, we were so sorry to learn of his passing, especially under the circumstances."

Concetta's lips tightened, and she touched the crucifix at her neck. "Imma's death killed my father. And it killed my mother too, even though she's physically still with us. The person she used to be died a long time ago."

I thought of her Goth sister. "What about Domenica? How has all of this affected her?"

She inhaled. "Domenica was only thirteen when Imma died. Then she lost her father—and her mother, for all intents and purposes. She's had an awful time coping."

Veronica closed her laptop. "That's certainly understandable."

"Yes, and even though I haven't always agreed with the way she's handled her grief, I know she still has faith in God, so she'll be all right."

I wondered whether she was referring to Domenica's dark look and demeanor. "What haven't you agreed with?"

"Well, her dropping out of school, mainly. But I also disapprove of her Goth makeup and clothes."

"So, she became a Goth after Imma's death?"

"Yes, I think she felt isolated, but she also wanted to be left alone. The Goth persona was like a mask for her to hide behind."

Veronica's lips thinned. "I'm sure it's just a phase."

"I think so too."

I wasn't so sure I agreed with them, but I knew I shouldn't press the issue. "What about Stewart Preston? Did you or anyone in your family ever have any interaction with him before Imma died?"

"No. My family doesn't have much money, so we weren't able to visit Imma in London while she was seeing Stewart."

"And she never came back to New Orleans with him after they began seeing each other?"

Concetta looked at her rosary. "Like I said, we didn't have the money. The annual tuition at the London College of Fashion was around sixteen thousand dollars, not including the cost of living. So Imma took out student and private loans, got scholarships, and worked to pay her way through school. My parents helped as much as they could, but I can tell you for sure that she had *nothing* left over for an international plane flight."

My mind wandered to Angelica's flight home for her mother's funeral. *If Imma couldn't afford a plane ticket with her parents' assistance, then how had Angelica managed to pay for one?* "Do you know anything about Angie's finances during school?"

She shrugged. "In the beginning, she had a harder time paying for school than Imma did because she didn't have any help from her parents. But then she came into some money at the end of her senior year."

Veronica's chin lowered. "You mean, when her mother died."

Concetta reached for her crucifix. "Yes, but she didn't inherit any money from her mother, if that's what you mean. Angie always said that she and her mom lived paycheck to paycheck. She also told me that her father had stopped sending child support when she was only two or three."

I sat up, intrigued. "Then, where do you think the money came from?"

"We never knew, but my mother thought it must have been an advance from a company. You know, like a signing bonus."

"Do you know whether it was a large sum of money?"

"I have no idea. I just know that around the time of the investigation, money no longer seemed to be an issue. Plus, she started wearing the occasional piece of pricey jewelry or an expensive blouse. She would tell people that these things had belonged to her mother, but I knew better."

Veronica and I exchanged a look.

"Let's go back to Stewart," Veronica said. "Did you talk to him during the investigation or at the trial?"

"Definitely not." Her hand went to her crucifix. "The police warned us that if we had any contact with him, we could jeopardize the case. And of course, our attorneys wouldn't let us speak to him during the trial, either." The corners of her mouth tightened. "But he wouldn't have talked to us anyway, even if we'd tried. In fact, he never so much as looked at any of us at the trial. Not even after he was acquitted."

Veronica licked her lips. "Are you convinced that he's guilty of Imma's murder?"

Concetta looked her in the eyes. "I am, yes."

I leaned forward. "And what about Angie's murder?"

"What about it?" she asked, surprised.

"Well, you know that Imma and Angie were murdered the same way, right?"

Concetta winced. "Yes, they were both strangled."

I met and held her teary gaze. "With scarves."

She nodded, seemingly unable to speak.

"So, do you think it's possible that Stewart had anything to do with Angie's murder?"

"I couldn't possibly speculate on something like that." She spoke as though winded. "It wouldn't be right."

Veronica put a hand on her shoulder. "Of course not."

Concetta placed her rosary on the table. "I pray for Stewart every day, and I've forgiven him for what he did to Imma. I hope that one day he confesses his sin and asks the Lord for forgiveness, but I don't think he will."

I would've expected a nun to hold out hope that a sinner would repent.

"Why do you say that?"

"Well, if what I've seen in the society pages is true, then it seems unlikely. He was known around New Orleans to be a partying playboy when he met Imma, and it appears he still is."

Veronica opened her laptop.

"Plus..." Concetta pressed her lips together. "I doubt he would seek counsel from the Church since I've heard he practices voodoo."

My brow shot up. "Voodoo?"

I barely heard her when she replied, "Of course, that could just be a rumor." I was too preoccupied with thoughts of the skull bead I'd found at the murder scene.

## 15

"Can you believe the bomb Concetta dropped?" I asked after I'd watched her exit the building from the conference room window. "Stewart was involved in *voodoo*."

"She also said that might not be true." Veronica picked up her laptop and headed out the door to her office.

I followed close on her heels. "But even *you* have to admit that the skull bead I found takes on a whole new meaning in light of this news."

"It *is* intriguing." She spoke over her shoulder as we walked down the hall. "But we need proof of Stewart's association with voodoo. And then we have to connect that bead to him, which could be next to impossible considering that this town is full of people who buy that stuff."

"That's where Odette Malveaux comes in. If Stewart *does* practice voodoo, then she might know him. That would explain how she knew about this case."

"Talk to Odette." Veronica entered her office and took a seat behind the desk. "But take whatever she says with a grain of salt."

"Sure." I leaned casually against the doorjamb, even though I was cheering inside. "Apparently, she only goes to Marie Laveau's on weekends, but I'd be willing to go there on my day off if it meant getting a lead on this case." *And asking her about Bradley.* "But first I'll do some research on Stewart to see if I can find anything connecting him to voodoo."

Veronica gave a dismissive wave. "Enough of this voodoo nonsense. What did you think about the revelation that Jessica came into money right around the time of Imma's murder?"

I took a seat in front of her desk. "Honestly, it made me wonder if someone was paying her off."

"I thought the same thing." She tapped a pen on her chin.

"I mean, even Ryan Hunter said Jessica had a suspiciously large amount of money, which is odd for a woman who, by all accounts, didn't inherit anything from her mother and should've been strapped with student loan debt."

"Good point." Veronica leaned back in her chair and propped a resplendent pair of beige and gold Louis Vuitton pumps on her desk.

"So, I have this theory." I held up my hands. "Suppose Concetta was right, and Jessica *did* know something about Imma and Stewart's relationship, or maybe even about—"

"Imma's murder," she interrupted with a flourish of her pen.

"Precisely."

"Then Stewart could have been paying her to keep quiet."

I nodded and crossed my arms. "That would also explain Jessica's reluctance to testify at the trial. Of course, it's pure supposition at this point, but this could be the link between the cases that we've been looking for."

"True." Veronica pressed the pen to her lips.

"That reminds me. Have you looked at the picture of Stewart at the courthouse after his acquittal?"

"I have. And judging from his demeanor, I wouldn't put bribery past him."

The mention of bribery jogged my memory. "Oh my gosh. I just remembered something."

"What?"

"That day I ran into Bradley at Market Café, he told me that Jessica came to the bank to make a deposit every month. Do you think it could've been a payoff?"

"Well, it might've been her paycheck. But we definitely need to look into that."

"I'll text Corinne and ask if she'll help." I pulled my phone from the pocket of my jacket. "After all, I did find her dog."

"Great idea. I also think it's time we paid Stewart Preston a visit."

"I doubt he'd talk to us." I typed a message to Corinne. "I mean, it's not like he's going to want to associate himself with Jessica's murder, especially not after he was lucky enough to get off for Immacolata's."

"Oh, I know he won't talk to us. We'll have to go undercover."

I placed my phone on her desk. "What do you have in mind?"

"Well, what do we know about Stewart?" Veronica had a mischievous gleam in her eyes.

I shifted in my chair. I'd seen that look before, and it always spelled trouble—for me. "Besides the fact that he's an acquitted murderer, you mean?"

She cocked her head. "Yes, Franki. Besides that."

"He loves Mardi Gras and women?"

Veronica picked up my phone. "Right. The Mardi Gras parades have started, but according to this year's schedule, the Krewe de Eros parade isn't until a week from tomorrow. So, we'll have to go with women." She gave me the once-over.

"Oh no." I jumped to my feet in alarm. "*You're* the bat-and-twirl girl. And I already went undercover at LaMarca, so it's your turn."

"If Immacolata is any indication, Stewart has a weakness for busty, dark-haired Italian girls. That would be you." She nodded in the direction of my breasts.

I shot her a look. It really was true that blondes had more fun, mainly because they left all the crap to us brunettes. "All right." I sighed and flopped into my chair. "What do I have to do?"

She grinned, triumphant. "First we have to contact Stewart. I've been doing some searching, but I can't find a phone number or email address for him. His parents are listed in the phone book, though, so we'll start with them."

"Do you just want me to pretend to be interested in him, or something?"

"If you get one of his parents on the phone, yes. But if by some chance Stewart actually answers, then tell him you're an old friend of Jessica's and that you need to talk to him, urgently."

I again leapt from my seat. "Are you crazy? If he *did* have anything to do with Jessica's murder that'll make him think I want to blackmail him. You could get me strangled."

"You'll be fine." She leaned back and crossed her legs. "Besides, you know we're going to have to play hardball to get a guy like Stewart's attention. If you just pretend to be some floozy who wants to sleep with him, he'll figure out that you're a fraud the minute you ask a question about Jessica. This way, he'll know you're looking for information about her from the start."

"Yeah, and he'll be suspicious of me from the start, too." I rubbed my neck. "Maybe he'll even bring a scarf to our meeting."

"We can worry about the meeting later. Right now, all you have to do is call him. I've already signed you up for a Google Voice number to conceal your identity."

"Veronica, a guy with Stewart's financial means could find out the identity of the most protected person in the federal witness protection program. He's not going to have any trouble figuring out who owns a Google phone number."

She leaned forward. "There's a chance a master hacker could trace it, but it would take some time because I registered the number from a public computer. And besides, I used an old email address that can only be traced to me."

"I see that you've been thinking about this." I glared at her as I returned to my seat. "Have you picked out a fake name for me too?"

She repressed a smile. "I have."

"What is it?"

"Gina Mazzucco."

"That sounds like one of the freakin' Pink Ladies." Veronica had always gotten to play Sandy in our college dorm *Grease* sing-alongs, while I'd been forced to play Rizzo. I had the sneaking suspicion that she was rubbing that in yet again.

"I know." She chuckled and dialed a number on my phone and then shoved it into my hand. "Here you go, Rizzo—I mean, Gina."

Suspicion confirmed. I scowled at her and gripped the device.

"Preston residence," an older woman's velvety voice replied on speakerphone.

Nerves pricked at my belly. "Uh, hi. May I speak to Stewart, please?"

"The third or the fourth?" she drawled.

"Pardon?"

The woman gave a sigh that sounded more like a huff. "Are you looking for my son or his father?"

"Oh." My face grew warm. "Your son."

"He lives in New York."

Even though Stewart's mom clearly wasn't in the vicinity, she was pretty darn intimidating. "Um, would you mind giving me his number?"

"Yes, I would mind." Her tone had turned to steel. "Who *is* this?"

"Gina Mazzucco." I glared at Veronica. "I'm an old friend."

"Stewart has asked me not to give out his private number. Good day."

"Wait—"

She hung up, and it was definitely a landline receiver because the sound punched my ears. "Nice manners."

Veronica shrugged. "She *did* say 'Good day.'"

I sigh-huffed like Stewart's mother. "What now?"

She drummed her manicured fingernails on her desk. "We'll try again tomorrow. Maybe someone else will answer."

"And if not?"

"Then we'll just have to wait and pay a visit to the Krewe de Eros parade."

"Do you really think Stewart will come home for Mardi Gras? He might want to steer clear now that Jessica has turned up dead."

"Franki," she gave a knowing tilt to her head, "it's one of the biggest parties in the world, and one of the few where women flash their breasts unprompted."

I folded my arms across my chest to send her a don't-look-at-me message. "You're right. A scumbag like Stewart won't be able to resist a powerful combination like that, not even under the threat of a murder investigation."

～

I LOOKED at my phone—eight p.m.—and shoved it back into my bag. I'd been waiting for Odette Malveaux for two hours, but I was determined to stay at Marie Laveau's until it closed. I'd been unable to find any link between Stewart Preston and voodoo on the Internet, so Mambo Odette was my best chance to establish a connection.

I walked to the store entrance and looked out at the bawdy crowd on Bourbon Street. Then I turned and leaned against the cashier counter. Thankfully, the kid with the acne was back, so I didn't have to endure the disapproving gaze of The Church Lady.

To kill time, I glanced around the room at the merchandise, starting with the vials of potion right next to me on the counter. Heartburn crept up my throat. *So much for Love Potion #9.*

My gaze moved to the necklaces on the other side of the cash register. I inspected the various charms, and a woman shoved her way into the store, thrusting me into the cash register.

I turned to say something and stopped dead.

*Mambo Odette.*

With her graying black dreadlocks hidden by a crisp white *tignon* and matching dress, she seemed more approachable than the last time I'd seen her, despite the fact that she'd shoved me. So, I summoned up the courage to walk over to her. She was grabbing handfuls of chicken feet from a bin and throwing them into a burlap sack.

I was so stressed that my heart did a voodoo dance. "I don't know if you remember me, but you gave me some advice when I was here a few days ago."

Mambo Odette didn't respond. She kept her head down as she continued to put chicken feet into the sack.

Nevertheless, I was undeterred. "I'm investigating the murder of Jessica Evans, and I'd like to ask you a few questions. I'm willing to pay you for your time."

She moved from the chicken feet to the alligator teeth without a word.

I decided on the direct approach. "Do you know anything about Jessica Evans?"

"I know she didn' make no offerin' ta Baron Samedi."

I jumped but tried to act cool. "Offering?"

"He don' have ta dig de grave fo' Baron Kriminel if he don' wan' ta. But ya got to give 'im rum soaked in twenty-one hot peppas an' Pall Mall cigarettes."

"I-I'm sorry?" I got distracted by the mention of grave digging.

Mambo Odette didn't reply. She sifted through the alligator teeth as though looking for a specific one.

*Looks like I need to try another tack.* "Can you tell me anything else about Jessica?"

Again no response. Instead, she counted the items in her bag.

*Okay, I'll take that as a* no. "What about Stewart Preston, IV?"

"Don' know 'im. But Erzulie D'en Tort do. And she goin' ta deal wit 'im."

I wondered whether this Erzulie was associated with Jessica or Imma. "Who?"

She moved to another bin full of some shriveled items.

I shrunk from the bin in case they were body parts or heads. "Can you tell me if Stewart Preston practices voodoo?"

Mambo Odette stopped sifting and looked me in the eyes. "I tol' ya, chile, I don' know him."

I took a step back before I pressed on. "Can you tell me anything else about this case?"

She looked down. "Watch out fo' dem who take magic."

"Take magic? Do you mean drugs or something?"

Without a word, she began selecting dried up items from the bin, sniffing them, and placing them into her bag.

The conversation was going nowhere, and I was starting to

think I'd been wrong about consulting Mambo Odette. So, I shifted the focus to Bradley.

"You told me to stay away from the bayou—"

"And ya didn' do it," she interrupted.

I was struck yet again by the scope of her knowledge. "No, and now I've found out that the man I'm crazy about, the one you said was a 'good man,' is married."

"Thangs ain't always the way they seem, chile." Odette turned to a small display of gris-gris bags that promised everything from love to prosperity to the bearer. She selected a red bag and untied the yarn at the top. Then she rummaged around in the pocket of her white cotton dress and pulled out a dried root. She put it into the bag, retied the yarn, and pressed it into my palm. "Ya need ta go *home*."

I wasn't sure what I was supposed to do with the gris-gris bag, but there was no point in asking. I pulled a twenty-dollar bill from my wallet and handed it to her. She slipped it into her pocket and returned to selecting items for her sack.

I went to the kid at the cash register to pay for the gris-gris bag. "So, do you know who Erzulie Dentor is?"

"*D'en Tort*. It's French for 'of the wrongs.'" He rung up the gris gris bag. "She's a voodoo loa who protects women and children and takes revenge on people who do bad things to them." He scratched his neck. "Five dollars and forty cents."

"You've been a big help." I handed him the exact change, deposited the gris-gris bag in my purse, and exited the store.

And I wondered whether Erzulie of The Wrongs should've been protecting me.

~

ON THE DRIVE HOME, I tried to crack Odette Malveaux's enigmatic words. I had to figure out what she'd meant when she said that Erzulie was after Stewart. Based on Erzulie's role in the voodoo world, it seemed like Mambo Odette was implying that Stewart had harmed a woman. *But if so, who? Imma? Jessica too?* I also needed to know if she was trying to tell me that Stewart wasn't involved in voodoo when she said that she didn't know him. As for the crazy warning about people who take magic, if she was referring to drugs, then it was possible that she was talking about Stewart.

Of course, I knew it seemed insane to put so much stock in the bizarre ramblings of a voodoo queen, but New Orleans was like nowhere else in the world. If something was going down in The Big Easy, the voodoo world knew about it before anyone else. It was just a matter of figuring out how to speak their language.

The worst part of all was that I was out twenty bucks plus the five for the gris-gris bag, and I hadn't found out a thing about Bradley. I couldn't imagine what Odette had meant when she'd said that things weren't always the way they seemed, because it was painfully clear to me that Sheilah was Bradley's wife. It was also glaringly apparent that he hadn't tried to call me, maybe because he'd figured out that I'd overheard what Sheilah had said.

I pulled up to my house and walked to my front door, debating whether to text Bradley and confront him about Sheilah. I inserted the key into the front door lock and froze.

Someone was at my back.

My police academy training kicked in—literally. I gave a few swift kicks to the genitals and a mighty karate chop on the back of the neck, and the perpetrator was in the grass, rolling in pain.

As soon as I had a chance to look at his face, my body went cold. "Bradley!" I knelt. "I didn't realize it was you."

"Yeah." The word sounded like a grimace looked. "I got that."

"I'm so sorry," I said, although a swift kick to the groin seemed appropriate for a cheater like him. "Can you stand up?"

"Just...give me a minute." He rolled onto his back and inhaled sharply.

I waited at his side with a heavy feeling in my stomach. The heartburn was gone, but I had a lead weight in my gut. Seeing Bradley again made me realize how much I didn't want him to be married.

After a few minutes, he stood and brushed himself off. Then he bent over, still favoring his privates, to retrieve the dozen yellow roses he'd brought me. "I shouldn't have come up behind you like that, Franki. I'm sorry."

"You're right, you shouldn't have." My tone was more hostile than accusatory. "What are you doing here, anyway?"

He scrutinized my face and handed me the bouquet. "I came in hopes of giving you the goodnight kiss I wanted to give you last night."

I lowered my gaze. Bradley had no idea that I'd overheard him and Sheilah. Telling him to get lost was going to be so much harder than I'd thought.

"Franki." His voice was soft, sinuous, seductive.

I looked up, and his fingers slid to the nape of my neck and wove into my hair. His other hand pressed the base of my back. He pulled me close, and his lips covered mine. He kissed me gently at first, and for a second I went rag doll. When he parted my lips with his tongue and kissed me more deeply, energy—not to mention heat—spread through my limbs.

As I wrapped my arms tightly around his neck, I wondered whether the magic between us was the work of Love Potion #9, the gris-gris bag, or something more primal than voodoo. Then Bradley pressed his body hard against mine, and I decided that I really didn't give a damn what it was.

When he released me, I gazed into his beautiful blue eyes. And I gave him a right hook to the cheek.

Without so much as a glance back, I entered my apartment and closed the door. *Serves him right for kissing me when he's married.*

## 16

"Thank you for meeting me at seven a.m., Corinne."

She took a seat in front of my desk. "You have been so kind to me and Bijou. I am happy to do it."

I wasn't happy. I hadn't slept a wink after punching Bradley, and my insomnia had nothing to do with the fact that he'd pounded on my door for twenty minutes demanding to know what was going on. It was because I'd wanted so badly to open the door and throw myself into his arms, even though I knew he was a cheating rat. "So, how *is* the little powder puff?"

"She is growing so fast. She look more like a little pillow now." Corinne laughed, and then her face grew serious. "By ze way, I did not receive ze bill for your services."

I shook my head. "I can't accept your money, especially not now that you've agreed to help us with the Evans case."

She hesitated. "*Bien.* If you insist."

"I do." Catholic guilt panged my chest. "But are you sure you want to do this? I mean, you could lose your job for giving us client information."

She blinked her big blue eyes. "I did not know Jessica, but I sink it is so awful ze way she died. If I can help find who killed her, zen it is wors ze risk."

"That's incredibly generous of you." I double-clicked the Evans file on my laptop. "And just so you know, I'm going to do everything in my power to make sure that no one finds out you helped with the case."

She smiled. "What do you need for me to do?"

I glanced at the file notes. "Well, we know that Jessica came to the bank to make monthly deposits. We need to find out whether she was depositing her paycheck from LaMarca. And if not, we'd like to know who the deposits were from."

She shrugged her shoulders. "Zat is easy to discover."

"I'm not so sure." I closed my laptop. "I'm assuming that she made the monthly deposits in cash."

"Why do you say zat?"

"Because we have reason to believe that the deposits were a payoff."

Corinne crinkled her Tinker Bell nose in confusion. "What is zis 'payoff'?"

"A bribe."

"Ah." She nodded. "Well, I don't remember her bringing cash. I sink she always deposit a check, but I will find out." She looked at her watch. "I must go. I have to be at ze bank before eight."

"Okay. Thanks." I rose to see her out. "And remember, if you change your mind about helping, I'll understand."

"I know." She grasped the doorknob and turned to face me. "But I will not change my mind."

After she left, I thanked my lucky stars that I'd met a nice woman like Corinne.

My thoughts turned to Bradley, but I was no longer thinking about the night before. Instead, I wondered how he'd react if he found out that I'd asked one of his employees to provide me with confidential bank information. But whatever. It served him right.

~

AT TEN A.M., I rose from my desk to stretch and glimpsed something yellow outside the window.

Across the street from our building stood a plump, sixty-something woman in a yellow sack dress with a white scarf tied over coiffed silver hair. She looked like a giant lemon with bright pink lipstick.

The she-lemon glanced from side to side through huge white Jackie O-style sunglasses, as though she were afraid she was being followed. She lowered her shades, looked up, and made eye contact with me. She dipped her head, shielded her face, and hurried toward the entrance to our building.

"Looks like we have a reluctant visitor," I called to Veronica as I walked into the hallway. I entered the lobby.

The woman's white-scarfed head emerged from the other side of the door. "Pardon the intrusion," she said in a Southern drawl. "Are you with Private Chicks, Incorporated?"

"Yes ma'am," I said in Southern kind.

The rest of her body entered. "Well, hiii. My name is Twyyyla. Twyla Upton." She extended a hand with yellow-lacquered fingernails. "I'm the wife of *the* Harold Upton?"

I shook her chubby, bejeweled hand. I had no idea who "*the* Harold Upton" was, but I could tell by the exquisite rings she wore that he was a wealthy man. "I'm Franki Amato."

Veronica clicked into the lobby. "Mrs. Upton, I'm Veronica Maggio. What a pleasure to meet you."

"Likewise."

Veronica turned to me. "Mrs. Upton is something of a local

celebrity here in New Orleans because of her fabulous rose garden."

Mrs. Upton removed her sunglasses and untied her scarf. "I have eighty-nine species of hybrid teas, miniatures, climbing roses, and floribundas. And please call me Twyla."

"Wow," was all I could think of to say. I wondered whether she'd tried to conceal her identity when entering our office to protect her rose-gardener reputation.

Veronica gestured toward the door. "Why don't we chat in our private conference room across the hall?"

"That would be luuuvely." Twyla smiled and followed Veronica out. "I *do* love to chat."

We sat at the table, and Twyla sniffled. She retrieved a lace handkerchief, also lemon yellow, from her vintage white beaded handbag and dabbed her eyes. "It may surprise you young ladies to know that I'm not here on a social call."

I feigned surprise. "No?"

"I was out shopping, and I saw your sign out front. I came in because I simply have nowhere else to turn." Her sniffles turned into sobs. She reached into her bag and pulled out a glass vial, which she placed in front of me on the table.

Panic leapt into my chest. *Was it Love Potion #9? Was she here to expose me for dosing Bradley?*

She looked me in the eye. "Those are my smelling salts. I'm prone to fainting spells."

"Good to know." Relieved I hadn't been outed, I accepted the responsibility of reviving her from a future faint.

She gave a sniffle. "I'm here because my Harry has been working late for the past several weeks, which is very unlike him. In the forty-eight years we've been married, why, he's never missed a dinner at home. That is," she dabbed her eyes, "until recently."

"I see." Veronica opened her laptop. "Have you asked him why he's been working late?"

"Y-es," she said—in two syllables. She gave a dismissive wave. "He says he's working on a big legal project. He's a highly respected patent attorney, you know."

I smiled. "Well, if he's an attorney, it wouldn't be unusual for him to work late, right?"

"It is unusual because my Harry doesn't work. That's what his employees are for."

The smile slipped from my face. As an employee myself, I resented that. "So, what do you think he's doing?"

"Oooh!" Her tear-stained eyes squinted with anger. "He's in the clutches of a brazen hussy."

Veronica began typing. "Is this a woman you know?"

"Oh, yes." Her drawn-on eyebrows furrowed. "Her name is Patsy Harrington, and we've been rivals since our debutante ball in 1963."

"Rivals?" I loved cotillion catfight stories.

"I met my Harry at that ball. Patsy had her eye on him because he was the most eligible bachelor in New Orleans, so she purposefully spilled punch on my dress. But that didn't matter one whit to Harry. He danced with me the whole night, and Patsy has been after him ever since. She's not one to be outdone."

I was skeptical. "That's a long time to chase after a man. Are you sure about this?"

"I'm sure." She wiped away a tear. "Even after all these years, my Harry is still a catch. And that Jezebel Patsy is shameless. She'll go to any lengths to get him."

Veronica looked up from her laptop. "So, how can we help you?"

"I need for you girls to follow Harry and get pictures of him with Patsy so that I can confront them." She raised her chin, and with it her pride. "He's going to be working late tomorrow and Saturday night."

Veronica put a finger to her cheek. "We have a big case right now, but it sounds like we could take care of this in an evening or two. What do you think, Franki? Are you willing to work some overtime?"

Twyla looked at me and turned up the sniffling, sobbing, and dabbing a notch.

I didn't mind giving up a weekend if it meant catching a cheater in the act. I, of all people, knew the pain and self-doubt that came with betrayal, and it infuriated me to think that a husband would cheat on his wife. Especially if that husband had been dating me. "I'm game."

"Maaahvelous!" Twyla turned off the tears as quickly as she'd turned them on. She reached into her purse and pulled out an envelope that she handed to Veronica. "Here is a recent picture of Harry, his business card, the make, model, and license plate of his car, and my contact information."

Twyla was well prepared for a woman who'd happened upon our office by chance.

Veronica examined the picture and passed it to me.

Her "catch" of a husband looked exactly like Alfred Hitchcock with a Hitler mustache and a bad toupee. *If Patsy's been chasing this guy for fifty years, she's either blind or senile. Or both.*

Veronica rose. "We'll be in touch Sunday morning with a report."

"Thank you, ladies." Twyla tied her scarf around her hair. "When this dreadful mess is all over, I *do* hope you'll stop by for some tea in the rose garden. In the springtime, of course."

Veronica beamed. "We'd love to."

Slipping on her Jackie-O glasses, she wiggled her chubby fingers at us. "Toodle-loo."

She slunk out the door.

~

VERONICA LEANED over the steering wheel of the Audi and squinted at the students exiting the Slidell School of Beauty. "They must be coming out for lunch or a break."

I sunk low in the passenger seat. "It's not going to be easy to deal with the Babe of Blackness so soon after that sunnily clad Southern belle, Twyla Upton."

"I'm sure you'll manage."

"Don't be too sure of that." I glanced out the window. To my dismay, I spotted Domenica smoking a cigarette with some other students. I pointed in her direction. "There she is. At the picnic table."

Veronica lifted her Chanel sunglasses. "Where?"

"How can you miss her? She's the only one wearing all black."

"I see her now." She placed her sunglasses into her handbag. "It was hard to make her out with that black SUV behind her."

I snorted. "So, how do you want to handle this?"

"We'll go over there and tell her we'd like to talk to her."

"In front of the other students?" I asked, surprised. "Do you think she'll agree to that?"

"She won't let the presence of the students stop her. If she's got something to say, she'll say it."

I remembered the no-holds-barred comments Domenica had made in front of her mother. "You're probably right about that." I opened the passenger-side door. "Let's get this over with."

We walked across the campus, and Domenica shot up from the picnic table, her face dark with fury—and a lot of Goth makeup. She threw her cigarette to the ground, stubbing it out with her foot, and strode toward us.

Veronica forced a smile. "Hello, Domenica."

"What are you doing here?" She looked from Veronica to me. "Why are you harassing me at school?"

I was already over her attitude. "Looks like you're on a smoke break to me."

Veronica shot me a silence-it look. "We'd like to ask you a few questions. This will only take a few minutes."

"My mother and I already told you everything we know." She flipped her bangs. "Stewart killed Imma and got away with it. Then he obviously killed Angelica too. End of story."

I struggled to control my temper. "That's what we wanted to talk to you about. Is there somewhere we can sit down?"

Domenica stared at me blankly, refusing to make a suggestion.

"Okay then." I abandoned all attempts to hide my frustration. "Let's just do this right here. I'll start. Why are you so sure Stewart killed Angelica?"

Domenica took a step toward me and raised her chin in defiance. "Who the hell else would have done it?"

"I don't know. But she could've had other enemies. From what we've been told, she was a difficult person to deal with."

"That's for *damn* sure." She flicked her tongue piercing. "But do you really think anyone else hated her enough to kill her?"

"Domenica," Veronica said in a soothing tone, "that's what we want to find out. But we need your help."

She shook her head. "The only person who had a reason to kill Angelica was Stewart."

"But why? He'd already been acquitted of your sister's murder, so what did he stand to gain by going out and killing someone else?"

"You're the PIs." She curled her lips. "Why don't you two go figure that out and leave me alone?"

I rolled my eyes. "Come on. If you know something, you need to tell us. Do it for your sister."

She assumed her hostile, sociopathic stare. "Here's what I think happened. Stewart got sick of paying her to keep her mouth shut, so he told her he wasn't going to do it anymore. She threatened to go to the cops, and he strangled her—with a scarf, just like he did my sister."

Veronica met her gaze. "Why do you think he was paying her?"

"Well, someone certainly was. All of a sudden she started buying fancy clothes and jewelry and stuff, and she didn't have a job. Even my dad thought Stewart was paying her off."

I licked my lips. "Did your dad have any proof?"

"He didn't need any. It was painfully obvious."

Veronica shifted her handbag. "Okay, but what do you think Angelica knew about Stewart? According to your mother and Concetta—"

"Wait," she interrupted, stunned. "You talked to Concetta?"

"Yes."

"Well, that's interesting, because my Mom and I haven't seen her for months."

Despite her acidic disposition, I felt kind of sorry for Domenica. One by one, her family members had all abandoned her, and some had apparently done so of their own volition.

"I'm sorry to hear that," Veronica said. "But as I was saying, Angelica testified that she didn't know anything about Stewart or his relationship with Imma, so I'm not sure whether she really did have any evidence against him."

She crossed her arms. "That's hilarious, because Angelica made it her number one priority to know other people's business. That's how she got ahead in life. So I'm sure she was keeping an eye on Stewart, if for no other reason than his connections."

I pursed my lips. "In the fashion industry, you mean."

"Yeah, what else? I'm sure you've heard all about Jessica's

ambition by now. It was legendary." She turned to look at the other students, some of whom were returning inside the school. "Are we done here? Because I've gotta get back to class."

Veronica touched her arm. "Just a few more questions."

She pulled back. "Like what?"

"Your sister told us that you became a Goth after Imma's death."

"Oh, God. Of course my sister, the saintly nun, would bring that up."

I shrugged. "She's worried about you."

"Only because she thinks I belong to a Satanic cult." She crossed her arms. "But black clothes, makeup, and death rock don't make me a devil worshipper."

"True," I said, although I had my doubts, particularly in light of what appeared to be the points of a pentagram tattoo protruding from the low-cut neckline of her black cotton shirt. "So, what you're saying is that Goth is basically a fashion statement for you."

"No, I'm not saying that. For me, Goth is a way of life. But having a fascination with death doesn't make me a disciple of Satan."

"O-kaaay." I was unsure what to make of the "fascination with death" revelation.

"I'm glad we're clear on that." She looked behind her and saw that the other students had gone inside. "Now I've *really* got to go."

I took a step toward her. "One more question. Were you close to Angelica, like Imma and Concetta were?"

"Let's see, Angelica always told me I was fat and ugly when I was a kid, and she betrayed my sister's memory for money. So, what do you think?"

Veronica exhaled. "It sounds like you didn't like her very much."

"Honestly, lady, I hated the bitch, and I'm not the least bit sorry she's dead." Domenica stormed toward the school.

I waited until she was out of earshot and turned to Veronica. "So, do you still think she's just going through a phase?"

She didn't reply, and she didn't need to. Like me, she was wondering whether Domenica could've killed Jessica.

I was also wondering how long our list of suspects would grow.

## 17

"Concetta left an interesting message while we were out." Veronica stood in her office with the phone to her ear and her hand on her hip.

"What did she say?" I returned the growing Evans case file to its place on her desk.

She hung up. "She remembered something she'd forgotten to tell us. She's coming in."

"I wonder if it's about her psycho sister."

"No clue." She glanced at the time on the phone display. "But she'll be here any minute."

"Intriguing. Any other messages?"

"Mr. Orlansky's assistant." Veronica took a seat at her desk. "Apparently, three of the five scarves were purchased with cash. They have the video file for one of the scarf purchases, but they had to request the DVD for the other two from Baton Rouge. Mr. Orlansky wants to go through the first file with me tonight."

"Looks like someone's in a hurry to watch videos with you." I sat down on the edge of her desk and shot her a knowing grin.

Veronica's smile was wry as she turned on her laptop. "Maybe I should bring some popcorn and Raisinettes."

"That should keep his hands and mouth busy. For a while, anyhow."

"Cute, Franki." She looked at her agenda. "Right now I've got a scheduling problem to work out."

"What do you mean?"

"Well, we've got the Upton stakeout tomorrow and probably even Saturday night. So, if the DVD for the other two purchases arrives in the next day or two, we won't be able to look at it until Sunday at the earliest. And I can't let the Upton case jeopardize the Evans investigation."

"Do both of us need to do the stakeout?"

"It's my company policy to have backup in a situation like that. It's one thing to go undercover to talk to a sales girl at LaMarca, but it's another thing altogether to try to entrap a man committing a crime. For all we know, Harry Upton could be dangerous."

"I'm sure Mr. Orlansky would be only too willing to work some really late nights with you." I winked, but I hoped she wouldn't ask me to go with her. Although I'd been doing my best to keep my chin up in the workplace, I was really down about Bradley. All I wanted to do was go home and curl up in my bed.

"I don't want to be there alone with him after the store closes." She chewed her lip for a moment. "Maybe David could go through the tape with him?"

As much as it pained me, I had to give her my honest two cents. "Veronica, you know as well as I do that Mr. Orlansky isn't going to work late with the likes of David."

"You're right. So..."

*Here it comes.*

"Any chance you could go with me after the stakeout? If it comes to that, of course."

"Yeah." I looked at the floor. "I don't have any plans for the weekend."

"How are you feeling about the whole Bradley situation?"

"Bummed." I sighed. "But my main worry right now is my nonna. She's been too quiet after hanging up on me."

"You think she's up to something?"

"Of course she is." I gesticulated Veronica style. "She's busy scaring up some more Sicilian suitors. And based on the ones I've encountered so far, Harry Upton *is* a 'catch' by comparison. So is Ed Orlansky, for that matter."

The lobby bell sounded.

Veronica rose. "That must be Concetta."

I followed her into the waiting area, where Concetta stood looking uncertain. She was dressed almost exactly as she had been the day before, in the same sensible shoes and white shirt, only her ankle-length skirt was a muted brown instead of gray.

"I hope I'm not interrupting." Her close-set eyes had a worried look about them, and she was fingering the cross at her neck.

Veronica patted her arm. "No, not at all."

"Oh, good. This case is so personal to me. I'd really rather not talk about it over the phone."

"I understand." Veronica gestured to the door. "Why don't we go over to our conference room?"

Concetta shook her head. "This won't take long. I remembered something about Angie and Stewart, but I'm not sure it's important."

Veronica retrieved a pad of paper and pen from David's desk. "We appreciate all the information you can provide."

She tugged at the crucifix. "Well, not too long after Imma's murder, the police called and told us we could come and get Imma's things. So, my father and I flew to London a few weeks later, um, under the radar, so to speak."

I flopped onto a couch. "Under the radar?"

"We didn't tell Angie we were coming." She sounded

remorseful. "My father didn't want to give her time to prepare for our visit."

Veronica's head snapped up from her notepad. "Why not? Did he think Angelica had something to do with Imma's death?"

"It's not that he believed Angie killed her, but he *did* think she knew something about her murder. And after I told him what I'd seen, he was convinced of it."

My curiosity was more than piqued. "What did you see?"

"Well, I went into Angie and Imma's room first, while my father was downstairs talking to the dorm manager. The manager had given me a key so that I could get in. When I walked into the room, Angie was there with Stewart."

I was shocked that Stewart would be bold enough to return to the scene of the crime when he was under suspicion for the murder. "Really?"

"Yeah, and I could tell that they'd been deep in conversation." Her eyes opened wide. "In fact, when Angie saw me, she jumped up and started babbling, as though she felt nervous. Or guilty."

Veronica scribbled a note. "Did you hear anything they said?"

"Nothing."

I scooted forward on the sofa, eager to hear more. "And what did they say to you?"

"Stewart never said a word. He lowered his head and then walked past me and left. But Angie said the usual things. You know, like 'What a surprise!' and 'Why didn't you tell me you were coming?'"

I noticed that Concetta was gripping the crucifix so tightly her knuckles were white. "Did you ask her what Stewart was doing there?"

"Of course." She jerked her necklace. "But she never answered because my father walked in."

Veronica looked up from the pad. "And you didn't tell him what was going on."

"Not until we got back to New Orleans." She looked at the floor.

I massaged my neck. "Did you ask Angelica again later what Stewart was doing there?"

"I never got a chance to. She refused to speak to me after that trip."

"So," I said, confused, "why didn't you tell your father that Stewart had been there?"

She looked at Veronica and me. "My father was a stereotypical, hot-blooded Italian male. I was afraid that if I'd told him what I'd just witnessed, he would have done something awful. To Angie or Stewart or both. I'd already lost my sister, and my mother was ill...I couldn't lose my father too."

"Of course not," Veronica soothed.

Concetta's eyes filled with tears, and she studied Veronica's face as though searching for something. "But I lost him anyway."

Veronica placed her hand on Concetta's back. "I think we have all the information we need. Can I get you a glass of water? Or maybe some chamomile tea?"

She shook her head as though coming out of a stupor. "I need to get back to the church." She headed for the door. "I'll let you know if I remember anything else."

After she left, I turned to Veronica. "What do you make of that?"

"I think it confirms what we already suspect—that Jessica and Stewart had some sort of illicit relationship."

"It also confirms that Stewart is every bit as arrogant as he looks in that picture of him after he'd been acquitted."

"That reminds me," Veronica tapped her pen on the pad, "have you tried calling his parents again?"

"No. I'll do that now."

I went to my office and dialed the Preston number. I waited for a couple of rings.

"Preston's rezidens," a husky female voice responded.

"Mrs. Preston?" I wasn't sure whether it was her, but I thought whoever it was might be drunk. Or Hungarian.

"No, I maid."

"Oh, hello. May I please speak to Stewart Preston, IV?"

"He not here."

"Okay, well—"

"Who zis?" she interrupted. "Zsuzsanna?"

I hesitated, unsure how to respond.

"Vat you vant?"

I couldn't tell whether she was being harsh or just foreign. "Um, his cell phone number?"

"I say you before," she whispered, "I sink he bad man. But, you vant number, I give. You vait."

"Thank you." I was shocked at my unexpected success. I grabbed a scrap of paper on my desk—a receipt for tampons, gelato, and wine—and prepared to jot down the number.

The maid returned to the phone and recited Stewart's contact information.

I repeated it to her.

"Good. You no call again."

I shook my head, marveling at the less-than-stellar phone manners of the Preston household.

My message tone sounded. It was my dad reminding me to check the oil on my car. I rolled my eyes. And I got another text. My heart skipped when I saw that it was from Bradley.

*In back-to-back meetings. But we need to talk. Call you later, B.*

Veronica entered my office. "Did you call the Prestons?"

I jumped as though I'd been caught cheating on a test. "You're not going to believe this, but I actually got his cell number."

"Have you called him?"

"I was just about to." I fired off an angry one-word reply in Italian to Bradley. Even though he didn't speak the language, I was certain he'd know what it meant.

"Let's put it on speaker." Veronica pulled up a chair.

"Sure." I typed Stewart's number on the keypad and tapped *Call.*

The phone rang three times and went to voicemail. There was no recorded message, only a beep.

"Hello, Stewart. My name is Gina Mazzucco." I shot Veronica a nasty look as she flashed a wicked smile. "I'm calling about an urgent matter regarding Angelica Evangelista. Please call me back at your earliest convenience." I recited my number and hung up.

Veronica crossed her arms. "Now we sit back and let him stew."

"I hope he takes the bait."

My phone vibrated.

Veronica and I exchanged a look.

With my heart pounding, I read the display. "Oh. It's my parents. They know better than to call me while I'm at work."

"You should take it. It could be important."

"I suppose." I tapped *Answer.* "Hello?"

"Francesca?" My mother's voice was unusually shrill. "This is your mother."

"Mom, I'm in a meeting, so I don't have much time. What's up?"

"Well, your father says he texted you about your car, and you replied '*vaffanculo.*' We're just wondering what in the heck is going on down there."

I swallowed—hard. I'd told my *dad* to go screw himself, albeit in slightly more scathing terms, instead of *Bradley.* The only thing to do was take the easy way out. "Mom, like I said, I can't talk now."

"Now Francesca, your father is waiting for an explanation."

"Tell him I meant to send that message to Bradley, okay?"

"I don't think that's going to make him feel any better, dear. You know we didn't raise you to use language like that. Not in Italian or English."

"Mom, I've *got* to go." I hung up and dropped the phone on my desk, as though it had scalded my hand.

Veronica raised an eyebrow.

"Don't ask." I massaged my temples. That text message wasn't going to help the already tense situation with my parents. On the positive side, I figured it would put a stop to the annoying car reminders from my dad.

∾

"You got a minute?" David's usually bright eyes were dark.

Veronica had warned me that he was lovesick for a girl in his Brazilian dance class who only had eyes for the Samba instructor. "I was about to head home for the day, but I've always got time for you." I threw that last part in to try to lift his spirits. "What's up?"

"I've got to get to the library to study for an exam, but Veronica's on the phone. Can I fill you in on my research real fast?"

"Absolutely. What've you got?"

He sat in front of my desk and leaned over with his elbows on his knees and his hands clasped in front of him. "Not much." He looked even more defeated than he had moments before. "I ran the background checks on the Di Salvos, and they're all clean."

"Even the Diva of Darkness?" I was kind of expecting some

sort of run-in with the law to surface—a public menace charge, at the very least.

"Yeah, her too." He looked down at his hands.

"What about Bill Evangelista?"

David sighed. "Nothing. It's like the dude dropped off the face of the earth."

"That's so odd. You know, I just keep wondering whether he or his family could be connected to this case in some way."

"You mean, like his daughter, right?"

I nodded.

"Yeah, she definitely could've been jealous of Jessica, and maybe she wanted to eliminate the competition, you know? Women are ruthless like that." His face turned as red as an apple, and he held up a spindly fingered hand. "But not you or Veronica, or anything."

I smiled. "I knew what you meant. Anything else you want to talk to me about?"

He opened his mouth, but Veronica burst into the room. "Come to my office. Quick."

David and I followed the order.

Veronica's face was somber. "I just got off the phone with Betty at the police station. Domenica Di Salvo has been arrested."

David and I looked at each other, stunned.

"For Jessica's murder," I breathed. "I *knew* it."

"Not for Jessica's murder." She frowned. "For grave dancing."

David yelled "Holy crap!" as I shouted, "Say what?"

"According to Betty, Domenica was arrested two hours ago, at around four forty-five . Apparently, she belongs to a group that dances on graves, and they've been charged with defacing a tombstone."

I closed my shocked mouth. "I *told* you that girl was creepy.

What normal person would *ever* want to hang out in a cemetery, much less freakin' dance a jig there?"

David's head bobbed. "I know, right?"

"And where, exactly, have they been doing this?" I held up a hand. "No, don't tell me. Let me guess—where Marie Laveau is buried."

Veronica cocked her head. "Wrong. In Slidell. In the cemetery where *Immacolata* is buried."

I stared at her, speechless. "No. Way."

"Yes way. From what I've been told, it's the only place they've been doing this. And that's not even all there is to the story."

I wasn't sure how much more of the story I could take.

"The police are also investigating whether this group had any involvement in the murder of a man named Henry Withers." Veronica placed her hands flat on her desk. "He was the cemetery's caretaker, and he was hacked to death with an ax in the cemetery last Halloween night."

David stood openmouthed as I gasped and collapsed into a chair. I'd been suspicious of Domenica and her deviant demeanor, but I hadn't expected a hacking murder.

She reached for her day planner. "So, we're going to have to pay Domenica yet another visit."

I ran my fingers through my hair. "How are we going to do that if she's in jail? You know her mother isn't going to have the money to bail her out."

"I'm a criminal attorney, Franki. I have a right to speak with my client."

"Veronica, you're not seriously thinking of representing her, are you?"

"Definitely not." She raised her chin like my nonna. "But that'll be our little secret, now won't it?"

## 18

I t seemed perfectly normal that I would be at an Elvis Presley concert. But something in the back of my mind told me that The King wasn't singing "Burning Love" to me in person. It was the sexy, black leather-clad Elvis from the '68 Comeback Special, not the sparkly cape-wearing, bell-bottomed Vegas version, and I was pretty sure he hadn't gotten back in shape since he was dead.

Then it hit me—I'd been listening to my "Burning Love" ringtone in my sleep. *I really need to get an old-school alarm.*

I opened my eyes and shrunk from the daylight. Elvis was singing below me, so I peered over the edge of the chaise lounge where I'd spent the night. Nothing could have prepared me for what I saw. On the floor next to my phone were a bag of potato chips, a tub of sour cream and chive dip, a container of Ben & Jerry's Dublin Mudslide, a box of chocolate-covered cherries, and a bottle of red wine, all of which were empty. I whispered a silent prayer that Napoleon had eaten all the food while I'd been sleeping, because it was clear that I'd been the one to drink the wine. But given that he was sitting beside the empty containers with his plastic food bowl in his mouth, the chances of that were slim.

I rooted out my phone from underneath the potato chip bag and saw that Corinne was calling—at seven a.m. "Hello?"

"*Bonjour*. It is Corinne. Is zis Franki?"

I couldn't blame her for not recognizing me. I sounded like my mouth was full of gravel. Or chips. "Yes, hi. It's me."

"I have some information for you." Her tone was hushed. "But I am at ze bank, so I must hurry before ze osers come to work."

I flopped onto my back. "Is it about Jessica's monthly deposits?"

"*Oui*. Ze deposits she make each mons were checks."

"Her LaMarca paychecks?" I held my breath in anticipation.

"*Non*, for her paychecks she have ze direct deposit." Zese checks were from a life insurance company."

I exhaled. They weren't payoffs from the Prestons, after all. "A life insurance company? Is there any way to tell who the policy holder was?

"*Non*, but ze policy is from an oil company in Baton Rouge."

"Really?" That was weird. "How big were the checks?"

"Zey were small. One hundred dollars."

It was looking like the bank lead was a bust. "I guess the policy was from a relative or family friend. It's obviously not a bribe."

"Wait, Franki. I save ze best for last."

Hope filled my chest. "What?"

"Jessica receive other PPD deposits, besides her paycheck."

"What do you mean by 'PPD deposits'?"

Napoleon put his food bowl down and gave a high-pitched bark.

I put my finger over my lips as though he could understand.

"Ah, 'PPD' is an SEC code, so it tell ze bank ze transaction type. A code of PPD means 'Prearranged Payment and Deposit.' It is a repeat deposit, like for a paycheck or pension or somesing."

"How much were these deposits for?" I switched the phone to my left ear so that I could pet Napoleon with my right hand to keep him from barking.

"Ten sousand dollars."

I sat straight up on the chaise lounge. "Ten *thousand* dollars?"

"*Oui.*"

"How often did she receive them?" I was reeling from the amount of those deposits.

"Every mons."

It looked like I'd hit pay dirt—as, apparently, had Jessica. "Is there any way to tell who these direct deposits were from?"

"Ze registry shows zey are from ze Vautier Group."

"Could you spell that?" I ran and grabbed a pen from the kitchen counter. For me, French might as well have been Sanskrit. Using the box of chocolate-covered cherries as a note pad, I jotted down what she said. "Do you have any idea what this company does?"

"*Non*, I never hear of it."

"Corinne, this is very important. Can you tell me how long Jessica has been receiving these deposits?"

"Since she open ze account with us in 2012. I do not know if she receive ze money before zat."

*If only she'd been with the same bank since Immacolata's murder.* "Did you see any other activity in her account that looked unusual?"

"*Non*, zat is all."

"Well, if these payments are what I think they are, this could be a *huge* break in the case. I can't thank you enough for your help."

"It is my pleasure. But now I must go. *Au revoir.*"

"*Ciao*, Corinne."

I hung up and saw the second awful sight of the day—Bradley had called the night before. And I needed to talk to him —to tell him to stop calling me, of course.

I flopped onto the chaise lounge in a funk. I'd fallen asleep early because of the wine, which I'd only drunk because I'd been disturbed by Domenica, a.k.a. the Dame of Demise, and her deathly antics. That girl was getting on my last nerve. Or maybe I should say she was dancing on it. And I had to be ready in half an hour to go to the police station with Veronica to question her.

I sent a text to David asking him to find out the names of the owners and board of directors of The Vautier Group. Then I walked and fed a testy Napoleon before heading to my closet to pick out something attorney-like.

$\sim$

THE SLIDELL CITY JAIL came into view, and my stomach tensed. I didn't relish the idea of going into a police station on false pretenses. "So, what am I supposed to do when we get inside?"

Veronica turned into the parking lot. "I'm going to introduce you as my paralegal. That way, the police will direct all the questions to me."

"That's good." I glanced at her smart gray suit and raspberry silk blouse. In comparison, the Forever 21 black blazer and leopard-print dress I'd thrown together made me look more like I was ready for a night of fist pumping at the Jersey Shore than a day of representing incarcerated clients.

She maneuvered the Audi into a parking space right next to an old pink Toyota that was covered with Barbie parts.

I was mesmerized by the dismembered dolls. "I wonder if

the driver of that car is in the slammer. If so, it's got to be for Barbiecide."

"Killing Barbies isn't a crime, but bad taste in car décor should be." She put her sunglasses into her bag. "We'd better get going. Domenica will go before a judge first thing this morning, and we have to talk to her before that happens."

"Why?" I reached for my purse. "Aren't we allowed to talk to her after that?"

"No, the judge is going to ask her who's representing her. So we need to meet with her before she names her attorney or before the court appoints one to her. Otherwise, it'll be too late for me to pose as her legal counsel."

"Burning Love" blared from my purse. "Why didn't I change that thing?" I muttered as I pulled out my phone. "It's Bradley."

"Are you going to answer?"

The tension in my stomach crawled to my chest. "I have to talk to him sooner or later."

"Okay, but try to be cool."

I nodded and tapped *Answer*. "H-hello?"

"Franki, it's Bradley."

"Oh?" I feigned a surprise that I regretted. In the smartphone era, it was obvious who was calling.

"I'm sorry to call you so early, but I've got back-to-back meetings again today, and I wanted to catch you before they got underway. Do you have a minute?"

"I suppose." This time I feigned an indifference I didn't feel. Even after finding out about his wife, my mind couldn't help replaying the kiss-to-end-all-kisses.

"I tried to call you last night, but I guess you were out?"

"Uh-huh." I *had been* out, just not the kind of out he was thinking.

"Listen, I've been thinking about what happened the other

night, and I realized that I came on a little strong with that kiss. So I want to apologize if I was, uh, forward."

I bit my lip. If only it were as simple as a kiss.

"Anyway, I know it's short notice, but I have two tickets to the opening of *Jersey Boys* tonight. I was hoping you'd do me the honor of going with me. I promise I'll behave like a gentleman."

There were no words to express how much I did *not* want to turn down a date with Bradley, especially when he was being surprisingly sweet and respectful—and when I was already wearing the perfect Jersey-style outfit for the occasion. But after everything I'd been through with Todd and Vince, I couldn't go from being cheated on to being a cheater. I didn't want to hurt another woman, not even Sheilah. I had to draw the line firmly in the sand—or maybe quicksand because I felt like I was sinking. "I'm sorry, Bradley, but I don't date married men."

There was a deafening silence on the other end of the line followed by what sounded like a sharp intake of breath.

"I was planning on talking to you about that after we—"

"So it's true?" I interrupted.

He paused. "I can explain..."

That was exactly what Vince had said. Tears filled my eyes and anger surged in my stomach. "I don't need your explanation, Bradley. It's all quite clear, thank you very much."

"Franki, it's complicated..."

I gave a bitter laugh. "Another tried and true cliché."

He let out a long sigh. "Will you please hear me out?"

"No, because there's nothing more to say except that I don't ever want to see you again." I ended the call and then stared at the phone before throwing it into my purse.

Veronica looked at me. "This guy really got to you, didn't he?"

I nodded.

"I'll take you home." She pulled her keys from her purse.

"No." I placed my hand on her arm to prevent her from starting the ignition. "I came here this morning to do a job, and I'm going to do it."

"I know, but I can handle this one on my own."

I shook my head. "I can't keep getting sidelined by unfaithful men. The plan was to start over in New Orleans, and that's what I'm going to do. Life is just going to be a little different than I thought."

She cocked an eyebrow. "How so?"

"Well," I opened my car door, "instead of getting a guy, I'm going to get...cats."

Veronica smirked. "I think Napoleon will fiercely object to you becoming a cat lady."

"True." I glanced at the Barbie car. "Maybe I'll start a dismembered doll collection."

~

"THIS IS TAKING WAY TOO LONG," I said for at least the tenth time since we'd entered the jail. After going through a rigorous security screening and a meticulous administrative process complete with a semi-interrogation about the purpose of our visit and a stack of paperwork almost as high as my Jessica Simpson heels, we'd finally been taken to a small room to wait for Domenica.

Veronica didn't look up from her notepad. "Welcome to the life of a criminal attorney. It shouldn't be much longer now."

"I hope not. I can actually feel myself rotting away in this jail."

"It's not like you're locked up in a cell. Besides, be glad you're not at the police department in New Orleans. This place is a palace in comparison."

"Well, it's better than I expected." I surveyed the room. Everything about the Slidell jail was surprisingly clean and well kept, from the mowed lawn out front to the sparkling tile floors inside. It looked nothing like the seedy pictures of the New Orleans jailhouse that I'd seen in the tabloids following the much-publicized arrests of Nicholas Cage and Russell Brand.

The door opened, and Veronica stood. Domenica entered followed by a tall brunette police officer with a Miss America smile. Instead of her customary basic black, the Darling of the Dead was outfitted entirely in tangerine courtesy of the Slidell PD.

"I'll be back for her in fifteen or so." The officer flashed her pearly whites and closed the door behind her.

"To what do I owe the pleasure?" Domenica spoke in a bored monotone as she took a seat at the table.

I bared my teeth. "We're here to ask you some follow-up questions. You know, in light of your recent arrest?"

"Is this even legal? I mean, I'm in *jail*. So how is it, exactly, that the two of you can just cruise in here and interrogate me?"

Veronica folded her hands. "I'm a criminal defense attorney."

Domenica scrutinized her for a moment. "So, are you here to defend me, or something?"

She looked at the table. "No, I'm not." Then she looked Domenica in the eyes. "But I've been informed of the charges against you, so I can provide you with free legal advice in exchange for your answers to a few questions."

Domenica looked from Veronica to me. "You people are incredible." A silence ensued that included several pensive flicks of her tongue piercing. "So, what is it you're so desperate to ask me?"

I draped my arm on the table. "For starters, we'd like to know if you had anything to do with the murder of the cemetery caretaker."

Her eyes cast daggers—or tongue spikes. "I had nothing to do with that, understand? I've never even seen that guy before."

"But you admit that you were a frequent visitor to the Slidell cemetery, right?"

"Sure."

I smirked. She acted as though hanging out in cemeteries was as natural as hanging out at the mall.

Veronica stared at Domenica. "You know, I actually don't believe that you had anything to do with Henry Withers' death, but I may be in the minority on that count. So if you know something, even if it's just secondhand gossip, then I'd advise you to tell the police with your attorney present."

Domenica returned her stare but remained silent.

"Because if you don't," Veronica said, undaunted, "there's a strong chance based on your Goth appearance, your defiant attitude, and this grave-defacing charge that you'll go down with your friends for first degree murder, a charge that carries the death penalty in the state of Louisiana."

"That's profiling."

I leaned forward. "Is it? Or is it just reality? Because I'm an ex-cop, so I can tell you from experience that the police will be a *whole* lot more inclined to believe that someone like you murdered a cemetery caretaker than someone like my partner here."

She shot me a look of pure hate. Then she studied her hands and began picking the black nail polish off one of her fingernails.

Veronica crossed her arms. "Now, why don't you tell us about this grave dancing business?"

"What about it?"

I snort-laughed and shook my head. "You *do* understand that most people find the notion of dancing on a grave to be bizarre?"

"That's their problem."

Veronica sighed. "Can you tell us why you do it?"

"It's not a big deal, all right?" Domenica's devil-may-care demeanor had turned defensive. "My friends and I think death is cool. It's a part of life, you know? So we dance on graves to celebrate it."

I shuddered. I could think of *plenty* of ways to celebrate life, and none of them included cemeteries.

She smoothed her black bangs over her eye. "And it's not like we're doing anything bad."

Veronica held up a finger "But you *did* do something illegal. The arresting officer said that you spray-painted a word on a gravestone, but he wasn't sure if it was foreign or just misspelled."

I remembered the insult Domenica had scrawled on Jessica's yearbook picture. "What did you write?"

She hesitated. "*Vendicata.*"

I straightened in my chair. "The Italian word?"

She nodded and looked at her nails.

Veronica and I exchanged a look. *Vendicata* meant *avenged*, and the *a* ending indicated that the avenged person was a woman.

I instantly thought of Immacolata. "Whose tombstone did you write this on?"

"Imma's," she said, deadpan.

Veronica and I stared at each other, trying to process the revelation.

I cleared my throat. "Can you explain what you meant when you used the word?"

"I think it's self-explanatory."

"Actually, it's not. Here's why—It doesn't indicate who did the avenging."

The door opened, and the brunette officer flashed another pageant-winning smile. "It's time to go."

Domenica stood, and a smirk formed at the corners of her mouth. "Well, I guess that's what you two hotshot PIs have been hired to find out, now isn't it?"

As I watched her leave, I pondered the ramifications of her use of the word *vendicata*. And I wondered whether someone with such a positive view of death would find it easy to take a human life.

## 19

"You're off the hook, Franki." Veronica stood in my office doorway.

I looked up from my mid-afternoon bag of beignets, consumed by Catholic guilt for whatever I'd done wrong. "For..." I inhaled a mouthful—make that a throat full—of powdered sugar and coughed. "...what?"

"I just got off the phone with Ed Orlansky, and he agreed to let me screen the video this afternoon."

"Huh?" Powdered sugar puffed from my mouth. "And miss a chance to work late with you tonight?"

"I told him about the stakeout and said that if I couldn't come within the next hour, I was going to have to cancel."

"That explains it." I turned back to my beignets. Like a good Italian-American girl, I'd decided to drown my dating sorrows in dough products.

"I also talked to Ryan."

I yawned. That guy made me tired. "What did the charming Mr. Hunter have to say?"

She smiled like a cat who'd caught a canary *and* a cockatoo. "He's pleased with our progress."

"*Pleased?*"

Her smile turned Cheshire. "Apparently, the police hadn't figured out the *vendicata* clue."

"I *told* you Italian was a useful language." I felt vindicated. During our sophomore year, I'd persuaded her not to switch from Italian to Swedish when she was in the throes of a burst of Nordic pride. "But how did Ryan know what the police had or hadn't found?"

"Simple. His attorney went to the police station after Domenica was arrested and demanded to know what was going on."

"Smart move." I nodded and noticed I had powdered sugar on my chest. I was going to have to switch to something less messy, like raw cookie dough.

"He also found out that the police questioned Stewart Preston." She crossed her arms. "Two days ago."

I steepled my powdered fingers. "So he's probably in town and hasn't returned my call, which means I'm going to have to get insistent."

"Or even demanding."

"While you're at Lenton's today, I'll go through *The Times-Picayune* society pages and make a list of the restaurants and bars where he's been spotted in the past. That way, if he doesn't return my call, we can try to track him down at one of his favorite hangouts."

"That's a great idea." Her lips thinned. "Stewart Preston is no match for two Private Chicks."

The slamming of the lobby door announced the arrival of David.

I grinned at Veronica, who massaged her forehead.

"Ladies." David bowed and entered my office. "May I?"

"You may." I wondered whether I should've been concerned about his uncharacteristic formality.

He bounded into my office and plopped into a chair. "Prepare to be amazed." He pulled his laptop from his backpack with a flourish. "I had some time to kill between classes this morning, so I did some research on corporate affiliations." He paused for dramatic effect. "Turns out that The Vautier Group is the parent company of Preston Textiles, Inc."

"So the Prestons *were* paying Jessica." I pounded my fist on my desk. Then I looked at Veronica, anticipating one of her voice-of-reason-style responses.

"Now hold on, Franki," she said, not disappointing me. "I know it looks suspicious, but Jessica *was* in the fashion business, as is Preston Textiles. There's always the possibility that they were paying her for a legitimate service."

"But Preston Textiles wasn't paying her. The Vautier Group was."

Veronica turned to David. "What does The Vautier Group do?"

"Uh, basically, they just buy and control other companies through majority stock ownership. And by the way, Stewart Preston, III, is on the current board."

"Well," she met my gaze, "it's certainly beginning to look like those deposits could've been payoffs."

"Which would explain the weird conversation Concetta witnessed between Stewart and Jessica *and* the extravagant purchases Jessica started making right after Immacolata's death."

She chewed a pinky nail. "We've got to find Stewart ASAP."

"Don't worry. As soon as you leave, I'll start calling him. Every hour if I have to."

David cleared his throat. "Um, before you go, I've got some more information."

Veronica lowered her hand. "What is it?

"So, I've been going through the Google hits for 'Bill Evangelista' and 'William Evangelista,' and I found one that says a guy named Bill Evangelista died in a car accident in Gulfport, Mississippi in 1989."

"That's close to here, right?" I asked.

"Yeah, a little over an hour away." He broke into a boyish grin. "My buddies and I went there for spring break last year because it's got some freakin' *awesome* beaches. Even though it *is* an oil town."

I thought of the life insurance payments Jessica had been receiving from the oil company.

Veronica looked at me. "Sounds like our Bill Evangelista. The age of the daughter would also be about right, since Bill referred to her as a baby in his letter."

"Dude—" David looked up from his lashes. "I mean, mademoiselle—it's totally him."

I leaned forward. "What makes you so sure?"

"Because the obituary I found said his daughter was named Jessica. And she and her mother, Wanda, died in the accident too."

~

VERONICA SLOWED the Audi's speed to ensure that we were following Harry Upton's blue Mercedes at a safe distance.

I looked out the passenger window at the gorgeous nineteenth-century architecture of the historic New Orleans neighborhood of Uptown and sighed.

"What is it?"

"I spent all day calling Stewart Preston, and I haven't heard a peep out of him. Not even a text telling me to go to hell. I feel like the chances of questioning him are getting slimmer by the minute."

"Give it a little more time. I think he'll call, either out of concern or just plain curiosity."

"Maybe." I turned toward her. "Anyway, you haven't told me what happened at Lenton's today."

"It must have slipped my mind."

"I take it you didn't find anything?"

Veronica shook her head. "The scarf buyer was an African-American male."

I flashed a lascivious smile. "How was Ed?"

"He wasn't there. He's got the devil's grip."

"Do I even want to know what that is?"

She smirked. "It's a disease that causes severe chest pain that lasts for up to a week."

I had to goad her a little. "Are you sure he wasn't just overexcited about spending the day with you?"

Veronica stared eagle-eyed out the windshield. "Harry just pulled into Pascal's Manale."

"Hey, I read about this restaurant today."

She slowed the car to a stop outside the parking lot. "It's kind of a New Orleans tradition. Everyone eats here sooner or later."

"Including Stewart Preston. According to *The Times-Picayune*, he comes here fairly often."

"Really?" Veronica gave a well-what-do-you know frown. "That would be amazing if we saw him here too."

"Yeah, well, don't get your hopes up." I watched Harry park in the back of the lot. "Coincidences like that only happen in books."

She pulled into the lot and parked in the row in front of Harry's car, and we slouched in our seats.

I peered over the dashboard and watched Harry open his car door and struggle beneath the weight of his Hitchcockian belly before exiting. He buttoned his over-sized sport coat, patted his toupee, and smoothed his mustache with his index finger and thumb. Then, he gave a little skip and a hop and set off for the restaurant entrance.

I gasped, outraged. "Did you see that? He's so jazzed about his affair that he did a little dance."

"Oh, that reminds me." Veronica rummaged in her pink Prada handbag. "Twyla emailed me a picture of Patsy." She handed me her phone.

I flinched when I saw the photo of the alleged cotillion coquette. Patsy had the white beehive hairdo and sharp features of the late Texas Governor Ann Richards, but the teeth of Alvin the Chipmunk.

"She won't be hard to spot in a crowd." I gave the phone to Veronica. "So, what do we do now?"

"We need to go inside. If we wait out here, we run the risk of Harry and his date leaving the restaurant separately. Then we'd miss the photo op."

"We're not going to let that happen." I leapt from the car, slung my hobo bag over my shoulder, and assumed a vigilante posture. "Let's do this."

I entered the restaurant followed by Veronica and did a double take. The place teemed with men in full-on cowboy gear, from cowboy hats and neckerchiefs to chaps and boots.

I leaned over to Veronica. "The newspaper said this was an Italian restaurant, but based on the clientele, it looks more like a Wild West saloon. Minus the showgirls."

Veronica tightened the belt of her Burberry trench coat.

We made our way through the crowded lobby, avoiding any spurs, to the empty hostess stand.

While we waited for someone to arrive, a lonesome-looking cowpoke with a toothpick between his teeth tried to take a gander down the front of my dress. I narrowed my eyes like Clint Eastwood in a spaghetti western. "Giddy on, little doggie."

The toothpick fell from his lips. Then he adjusted his hat and moseyed away.

A harried-looking hostess rushed up to us. She had a partially untucked shirt and a run in her stocking, and I wondered whether an overzealous broncobuster had tried to lasso and hogtie her. "I hope you're not waiting for a table."

Veronica peered at the waitlist. "Actually, we are."

"Well, then," she said in a grim tone, "you're looking at a two-hour wait."

I counted ten total cowhands in the waiting area. "It doesn't look like that many people are waiting."

The harassed hostess gripped the edges of the stand, bowed her head, and took a deep breath before looking me straight in the eye. "There aren't. But the good folks who decided to organize a cowboy convention in New Orleans thought our famous barbecued shrimp were cooked on a grill instead of a stovetop. So, the cowboys have all sent their orders back to the kitchen and are threatening to quote 'rustle up a passel of wood and cook the dad-gum shrimps in the dad-blamed parking lot.' As you might imagine, it's going to take us a while to settle what the cowboys are describing as 'this here sitchiation.'"

I sensing that it wasn't the time to insist. "You know, I think we'll just head on over to the bar."

I led Veronica to an oyster-shucking area. "I don't know about you, but I think we need to leave before these crazy cattlemen decide to brawl or stampede or something."

"I agree, but we have to figure out a way to get a few pictures of Harry first."

I thought for a moment. "I know. I'll pretend like I'm one of those people who go around taking courtesy pictures of the guests."

"That's perfect. What do you need me to do?"

"Help me find Harry at the O.K. Corral here."

"On it." She took off, weaving through the tables.

I followed close on her heels and got an idea of what it must've been like to have been a pioneering woman in the Old West. The lewd whistling, suggestive winking, and flat-out leering—a girl could get used to that.

I spotted Harry at a table in the back corner of the restaurant. His back was to me, and he was blocking my view of his date.

I grabbed Veronica's arm. "There he is."

"Okay, give me your purse."

I pulled out my phone and handed the bag to Veronica. "Here goes nothing."

I walked to the table where I was shocked to discover that Harry's date wasn't Patsy at all but rather an attractive forty-something brunette in a white Chanel suit with black trim.

*How* does *he do it?* I approached the double-crossing duo. "Good evening."

Harry jumped in his seat, and the brunette hung her head.

"How would you two like a picture as a memento of your dinner at Pascal's Manale?"

The bashful brunette looked at Harry.

His cheeks puffed like Alfred Hitchcock's. "Oh, no. No. That won't be necessary."

"Don't be silly." I gave Harry a not-so-playful shove. "This'll just take a sec."

He shielded his face with his hand. "We'd really prefer not to have our picture taken."

"Nonsense." My teeth were clenched as I placed my hand on Harry's back and pushed him toward the brunette. "Now you two lean in and say *cheat*. Wait, did I say *cheat*? Oopsy, I meant *cheese*."

"Please leave us alone." Harry waved his arm and knocked

his wallet, which he had placed beside his silverware, onto the ground. He leaned down to retrieve the wallet.

"Franki!"

I turned and saw Veronica pointing at a manager-type who stormed in my direction. I had to take the picture, and fast.

I spun around, aimed, and snapped. When I pulled the phone away from my eyes, a red-faced, toupee-less Harry with little pieces of pink tape on his head made a grasping motion toward my chest.

"Whoa, there, partner." *Was Harry trying to take a swing at me?*

He grabbed at me again, and I looked down and saw it—his toupee was caught on the top button of my blazer. *Eww.* I struggled to remove the rebellious rug from my button.

The manager-type arrived at the table. "What's going on here?"

"She...my...we..." Harry sputtered.

"I'm helping this gentleman with his toupee." As proof, I slapped the offending item on Harry's hairless head. "There. That toupee tape ought to stick now, sir." I turned and hightailed it outta there faster 'n a polecat in a perfume shop, followed by Veronica.

Outside, we jumped in the car and peeled out of the parking lot.

Veronica glanced in the rearview mirror. "I wonder who that woman was with Harry."

"Who knows. A 'catch' like that could get any woman in the city."

~

"WHAT THE...?" I stared out the window of Veronica's Audi.

In our yard stood a five-foot-five body builder with gel-styled hair and a thick gold chain with a huge cross and a *cornicello*, a twisted horn-shaped charm for warding off the evil eye. Even in the dim porch light, I could see the Italian pride-themed tattoos on his bulging biceps and the orange glow of his spray tan.

Veronica gripped the steering wheel. "Do you know that guy?"

I squinted to get a better look. Although I had no idea who he was, I didn't have to look beneath his wife beater to know that he'd spent far too much time at the gym. "No, but he looks like he would have been a shoo-in for the cast of *Jerseylicious*."

The steroid stud's eyes caught mine. He puffed out his chest like a toad expanding its throat and revealed a mouthful of teeth as florescent white as his velour track pants. Then he bent over to pick up something.

"Get down." I ducked into my seat. "He's got a gun."

"Actually, it looks like a small guitar."

I peered out the window and saw the offending instrument —a mandolin.

"*Mamma mia*," I wailed, sinking into my seat. "I'm about to get a Sicilian serenade—Jersey style."

No sooner had I spoken the words than I heard my nonna's favorite song, *E vui durmiti ancora*," which meant *"And you're still sleeping."*

Veronica looked thoughtful. "Say what you want about your nonna, but I really admire her determination."

I didn't bother to comment. I sat in my seat waiting for my ripped Romeo to finish his serenade and leave.

"Well?" Veronica nudged me. "Aren't you going to get out of the car?"

"No." I crossed my arms like a stubborn child.

"Come on, Franki. You've got to deal with this."

I turned to face her. "Or what? He'll wake the dead across the street with all that romantic racket?"

Veronica rolled her eyes. "So you can ask him to leave."

"Good point." I started to get out of the car, but then a disturbing thought occurred to me. "Oh no."

"What?"

"I'm wearing leopard print."

Veronica blinked. "So?"

"He's from New Jersey. They go *crazy* for leopard print there."

Veronica shook her head. "That's stereotyping, Franki."

"Can you not *see* him, Veronica?" I gestured toward my serenader. "He's pretty much a walking stereotype, I'd say."

"Well, at least he's not singing 'O Sole Mio.'"

"Ain't that the truth."

Veronica and I exited the car and started up the sidewalk, and Glenda flung open her front door. She was wearing what looked like Borat's mankini in shocking pink underneath a sheer baby doll robe. Of course, because it was cold out, she'd put on matching faux fur leg warmers over her high-heeled slippers. To keep her calves warm, naturally.

"Loooord almighty," Glenda breathed as she gave the buff bodybuilder a once-over that would make a seasoned gigolo blush. "What *do* we have here?"

I shot her a wry look. "We have what's known in New Jersey as a juicehead."

Glenda took a drag off her foot-long pink cigarette holder and blew an alarming smoke signal—a perfectly formed heart-shaped smoke ring. "Well in that case, sugar, I'd like to take a long, slow drink of that nectar."

My stomach churned. I had to put a stop to the serenade-slash-stripper circus, and *pronto*. I turned to the strapping Sicilian. "Stop singing."

He ceased, mid-word, and stared at me.

I walked up to him and looked down (I was a good seven-to-eight inches taller than him in my heels). "Listen, uh..."

"Guido."

*Seriously?* "I'm sorry, Guido, but you went to all this trouble for nothing. I'm not interested in dating right now. Or in men, for that matter."

"Yo, if you're into chicks," his lips spread into a leer, "I'm down wit' that."

My lips went Mr. Grinch. "How incredibly generous of you."

Glenda took another drag off her cigarette. "Speaking of men..."

I turned and followed her gaze toward the street. Bradley had just walked out of Thibodeaux's. My stomach dropped. I didn't want to see him. Well, I did, but I didn't.

Bradley crossed the street. He narrowed his eyes as he walked up the sidewalk. "Evening ladies." He nodded stiffly at Guido.

I feigned a look of surprise. "I thought you'd be at *Jersey Boys* —with your wife."

Guido jutted out his lower lip. "That's a great show, bro."

I turned and shot Guido a piercing look, and his chest deflated like a popped balloon.

Bradley put his hands in his pockets. "I guess I deserved that." His brow rose. "Am I interrupting something?"

Glenda sidled up to Bradley like a stripper to a pole. "Miss Franki's getting a serenade from a juicehead. Isn't it delicious?"

Bradley's lips tightened into a line. "I see."

I moved to stand beside Guido, who reinflated his chest, and an uncomfortable silence descended upon the yard.

Bradley sought my gaze. "I guess that's my cue to leave."

I wanted to ask him to stay, but I couldn't.

He turned and headed for his car.

Glenda dragged off her cigarette. "A crying shame, sugar."

"Stay strong, Franki." Veronica slipped her arm around my shoulders as I stared after him.

"I'm trying. But this time it's really hard."

She gave me a squeeze. "You're a tough girl, though."

I nodded and heard the reprise of the mandolin. I spun around to give Guido a piece of my mind and stopped, horrified.

He was no longer serenading me—he was serenading Glenda. And she was doing what she did best—a striptease.

I saw the first faux fur leg warmer fly, and I fled to the sanctuary of my bordello, er, house.

## 20

The morning sunshine streamed into the CC's Community Coffee House on Royal Street. The bright, warm room and smell of coffee made me kind of glad that I'd had to wake up early to get my laptop from the office. After the events of the previous night, I'd intended to wallow in self-pity in my house—actually, in my bed—all day. But an early Saturday trip to the French Quarter had turned out to be what I'd needed to lift my spirits.

"What can I get you?" a teenaged cashier with charming braids and freckles asked.

"A double soy latte to go."

"Anything else?"

"Now that you mention it, I could use a little something to eat." I rested a hand on my bloated belly. *How could something so empty feel so big?* "I'll take a lemon pastry."

"The iced lemon pound cake or the lemon square?"

"Both. And make that three of each."

She placed the pastries into a bag and rang up my order. I swiped my credit card through the reader, dropped fifty cents into the tip jar, and headed toward the coffee bar.

While I waited, I looked around the rectangular-shaped room at all the people enjoying a lazy morning reading newspapers, studying, and surfing the Internet on their laptops. An older man at the table closest to me edited what looked like a play or a screenplay with a red pen, and I was reminded of some of the cool movies that had been filmed in New Orleans—*A Streetcar Named Desire*, *Interview with a Vampire*, *The Curious Case of Benjamin Button*, and the all-time classic *Big Momma's House 2*.

I admired the architectural features of the old building, starting with elliptical transom window over the entrance. My gaze lowered to the glass pane of the door below.

And I jumped.

Concetta peered inside wearing a scowl that clashed with her nun's habit.

I wondered what she was doing in the area, and then I remembered that there was a Catholic Center up the street. I held out hope that she wasn't looking for me. Maybe she was mad because she hadn't had her morning coffee.

Her eyes zeroed in on me like a heat seeking missile.

*No such luck.*

She shoved open the door and marched to me. "I heard you and Veronica paid Domenica a visit in jail yesterday."

I shifted in my purple Ugg boots. Gone was the charitable nun—she'd been replaced by an overprotective big sister. "Yes, that's right."

She leaned close. "Do you mind telling me what that little charade was all about?"

"It wasn't all a charade, Concetta." I guiltily watched the cross on her necklace swing from side to side rather than look her in the eyes. "Veronica *did* give her some legal advice."

She put her hands on her hips and snorted in disbelief. "You call telling her to be frank with her attorney 'legal advice'?"

"Listen, I can understand why you're upset, but Domenica

needed to hear what Veronica had to say." I glanced around to make sure that no one was watching me argue with a nun. "She's not exactly forthcoming, you know."

She rolled her eyes. "Well *of course* she doesn't feel like talking, much less being interrogated after losing half her family. Tell me, just *how* do you expect a teenager in her situation to behave?"

"I don't know. But I certainly *don't* expect her to dance on graves and deface her own sister's tombstone, and especially not in a cemetery where an unsolved murder took place."

Concetta's face contorted in anger, and her right eyelid twitched. "I told you and your partner before—I don't approve of Domenica's Goth look. But that's all it is, *a look*. My sister is *not* a Satanist, if that's what you're insinuating. And she's definitely not a *murderer*."

From the corner of my eye, I saw the cashier conferring with a pasty-faced twenty-year-old guy who appeared to be the manager. They were whispering and casting concerned looks in our direction.

"We're disturbing the customers. I think it would be best if we continued this conversation with Veronica at our office."

"That won't be necessary. But you guys gave Domenica advice, so let me give you some—If you really want to solve this case, you'll leave my sister alone and start interrogating Stewart Preston. Unlike her, he's a known voodoo practitioner *and* a killer." She spun on her heels and left the store.

"Double soy latte," the barista shouted.

Ignoring my coffee call, I reflected on what had happened with Concetta. I was frustrated by her inability to understand that we had to re-question Domenica after her unexpected arrest. But I did think she'd been right about one thing—If Veronica and I were ever going to solve this case, Stewart Preston was the key.

I walked over to the counter to get my latte and resolved to step up my phone call assault on Stewart, right after I called Veronica about my run-in with the nun.

~

I PULLED in front of my house twenty minutes later and scanned the yard for Sicilians before getting out of the car. I hadn't heard a word from my nonna since the serenade, so the Sicilian coast was by no means clear. As soon as I was certain the area was suitor-free, I grabbed my bag of lemon goodies and bounded up the sidewalk to my apartment. It was my first lazy Saturday morning in ages, and I was determined to enjoy it—boyfriend or no boyfriend.

I opened the door expecting to find Napoleon waiting for me to take him on a walk, but he was nowhere to be seen. Dogs were supposed to greet their masters when they came home, but Napoleon occasionally opted to continue napping because his life was so exhausting and all. No matter—it meant that I could get right to the important business of the morning—eating and shopping online. In between calls to Stewart Preston, of course.

After grabbing a plate from the kitchen, I headed to the living room and sat cross-legged on the chaise lounge. I opened my laptop, placed it in front of me, and laid out my pastry picnic. I picked up a slice of the pound cake and was preparing to take my first delicious bite when I heard a whimper coming from the floor below. Napoleon was staring at me, begging.

"You know sugar isn't good for you. Go lie down."

Napoleon knew the phrase "go lie down" as well as he knew the words "bath" and "treat," but he chose to ignore me and whimpered again.

I looked him in the eyes. "Trust me, boy. I'm doing you a favor."

He stared at me with the intensity of a hypnotist, willing me to give him the pound cake.

I sighed and put down the pastry. "Come on." I went into the kitchen to get him a dog treat. I took a biscuit from a box in the pantry and held it to his mouth. "Here you go. Now scram."

He took the treat with his teeth and ran to the living room to eat it, presumably so that he could punish me by leaving crumbs on the bearskin rug.

I flopped onto the chaise lounge and picked up the pound cake.

Someone knocked on my front door.

I bowed my head. "Who is it?"

"Veronica. Open up."

I rose and opened the door to find Veronica dressed in a faux shearling coat, jeans, and boots. "Howdy, partner," I drawled in Texan. "Are you on your way to the cowboy convention?"

"Don't be silly." She blew past me into the room. "The whole cowboy incident reminded that I hadn't worn this outfit in a while."

I closed the door and returned yet again to the chaise lounge, doing an eye roll on the way.

"Anyway, I got your message about Concetta." She spotted my mini banquet and squealed. "Yummy. Thanks for getting me some too."

My heart was as heavy as the pastry bag. I wasn't going to admit that all six of those lemony treats were for me. "No problem."

Veronica bit into the slice of pound cake that I'd been trying to eat for the past ten minutes. "So, you don't think Concetta was following you, do you? I mean, from what you told me, it sounds like she just happened to see you as you were going into CC's."

"That's what I think too." I snatched a piece of the cake for myself. "I guess I was just taken aback by how angry she was."

"Well, I can see how she'd think we were targeting Domenica, so it's really not surprising that she would get upset. Nuns are people too, you know."

"I suppose so." Although, based on my Sunday school experiences, I was half convinced that nuns were actually a special race of super humans who had x-ray vision that they used exclusively for the purpose of seeing right through those with guilty consciences.

"I wouldn't worry about it." Veronica waved what was left of her pound cake. "She's such a nice person. She'll probably call you to apologize."

"Maybe." But I wasn't so sure about that. Concetta had seemed pretty darned mad.

She finished the last of her pound cake. "So, are you ready for round two of the Harry Upton stakeout tonight?"

I watched with a growing sense of panic as she moved on to a lemon square, and I seized one for myself. "As long as we don't have to go back to the rodeo restaurant."

"Definitely wear a dress again in case we have to follow him into someplace nice."

"Ugh, I don't want to be in a dress while we're looking at video at Lenton's. I'd rather be in my comfy jeans."

"We're not going to Lenton's."

"Why not? Is Ed still in the grip of the devil?"

She shrugged and took a bite of lemon square. "I don't know, but his assistant called me this morning and said that the DVD of the other two purchases hasn't arrived yet."

"That doesn't sound promising."

"Don't worry. It should be here in a day or so. She said it was sent via FedEx." Veronica looked at her phone. "Oh, crap. I have a mani-pedi in thirty minutes. I've got to go."

I looked at the plate and was relieved to see that I still had one of each of the pastries left.

Veronica grabbed the last piece of pound cake to go.

"Well, I'll see you later." I rushed her from the apartment before she could do any more damage to my dessert, er, breakfast. Then I locked the door behind her.

Alone with one lousy lemon square, I picked up my laptop and clicked my Internet browser. On a whim, I pulled up *The Times-Picayune* picture of Stewart Preston waving on the courthouse steps. There was something about the photograph that wasn't right, but I couldn't figure out what it was.

I studied the image for a few more minutes. As my eyes roved the picture, it hit me—There was no clasp on Stewart's watchband. I stared at the watch trying to determine whether it was the slip-on kind, and then I decided that it wasn't a watch at all. But to be sure, I needed a high-resolution version of the photo. I scrolled to the bottom of the page and clicked "Times-Picayune Store." After a quick search, I discovered that the picture wasn't readily available, so I filled out a web-form request for a copy.

If the watch was actually a bracelet, it could blow the Evans case wide open.

~

BRADLEY LICKED MY FACE, and I turned over on my left side with a giggle.

*Wait. That doesn't sound right.*

I sat up with a start. Napoleon stood on his hind legs with his front paws perched on the chaise lounge, his tongue lolling from his mouth. I put my hand on my right cheek and touched something wet and sticky. Dog saliva mixed with lemon square.

*Nice.*

I looked at my phone to check the time. *Three o'clock?* I

must've crashed and burned from my caffeine-sugar high, which meant that it had been a successful lazy Saturday, after all.

There was also a voice mail from my parents' number. It had to be my nonna wanting to find out the results of her serenade scheme. I gave silent thanks to the universe for allowing me to miss that call. I tapped the message and steeled myself for what was to come.

"Franki, I talk-a to Guido, and a wow-a." My nonna had never sounded so happy. "He tell-a me that-a you two had a date last-a night. And he say that-a you're gonna have another one again-a tonight. I *told-a* him that-a song would do the trick-a. Now, he did-a say that you were *a lot older* than-a he thought-a you was gonna be, but that-a was because-a I tell-a him that-a you were twenty-one and not-a twenty-nine." A smack ensued. "Ha!"

I imagined her slapping the kitchen table in a fit of self-induced hilarity and paused the message.

*What is she talking about? Guido and I did* not *have a date last night. And just where did he get off saying that I looked "a lot older" than he'd anticipated? I could pass for twenty-one or so.*

A disturbing realization dawned on me—He was talking about Glenda. *Guido thought I was Glenda.*

I lay back on the chaise lounge slightly nauseated, and it wasn't because of the pastries and coffee. I toyed with notion of deleting the rest of the message—I wasn't sure I wanted to hear anymore. *Who knows what Guido had told my nonna about what he and Glenda did on their date?*

Then I remembered something I was always hearing on TV or wherever—Knowledge is power. And power was something I needed to take on my nonna.

I tapped the play arrow.

"So make-a sure you don't-a tell-a him your real age. Remember, a zitella like-a you—"

I tapped the trash can.

For a moment, I wondered whether I should tell my nonna the truth about what had happened. But I realized that I must've been delusional from low blood sugar. Because if Guido was dating Glenda and thought she was me, then I was finally off the hook. No more nonna in my love life. I just had to hope—or, rather, pray—that Guido wasn't the type to kiss and tell. The mere thought of the stories he could divulge made me cringe.

My phone vibrated.

I looked at the display and sat up with a jolt.

*Stewart Preston.*

My hand shook as I tapped *Answer.* "Hello?"

"Who the hell *are* you," he practically growled, "and why have you been calling me and my family?"

Stewart was ready to play hardball, so I needed to stay cool. "Like I said in my messages, I'm an old high school friend of Angelica Evangelista."

"What's that got to do with me?" His voice was thick with suspicion.

"I need to talk to you about her murder."

"You must not have heard my last question," he said in a slow, threatening tone. "I repeat, what's that got to do with me?"

"Well, I know you and Angelica go way back—"

Stewart cut me off with a loud, raucous laugh. "Darlin', Angelica goes way back with a lot of men."

The conversation was harder than I'd expected, so I spoke to him in the only language he seemed to know. "First of all, don't call me 'darling.' And second, I know your father's company was bribing Angelica to keep her quiet, and I can prove it."

A stony silence followed on the other end of the line.

Fueled by a surge of confidence, I summoned my inner TV detective. "So if you know what's good for you, you'll meet me tomorrow night."

"Where?"

I gulped down my surprise at his blasé reaction. "The Carousel Bar and Lounge at five o'clock. Don't be late." I ended the call.

My palms were sweating, and I was breathing hard. I'd tracked down the elusive Stewart Preston, but there was a voice inside my head reminding me of the obvious. All indications were that he was a cruel, callous killer—and I'd just put myself squarely into his murderous hands.

## 21

"You're bringing a *gun* to the Carousel Bar when I meet Stewart Preston?" I turned in the driver seat of my Mustang.

"Just as a security measure." Veronica kept her binoculars trained on Harry Upton's office building on the Garden District's swanky St. Charles Avenue.

I didn't even know she *had* a gun. And while I was confident in my own ability to handle a firearm, thanks to my police training, I had less faith in Veronica. "But I'm meeting him in a public place in broad daylight."

"Franki, you and I both know that Stewart Preston could be dangerous."

I swallowed hard and glanced across the street as Harry emerged, pants drooping well below his massive belly, from the rotating glass doors of his office building.

"Heeere's Harry!" Veronica sounded like Jack Nicholson's character in *The Shining*. "Precisely at six, just like last night."

"He's nothing if not punctual."

Harry stopped and pulled up his pants, and a gust of wind

blew his toupee into an upright position on his head. Seemingly unfazed, he tamped down the unruly rug and climbed into his Mercedes.

"Jeez." I started the engine. "You'd think a guy with all that dough would have a better hair piece."

"I know. It's amazing what men are able to get away with in terms of their appearance."

I pulled onto southbound St. Charles, staying a few cars back from Harry's Mercedes. I followed him for about a mile and a half, trying to focus on his car and not on the spectacular multi-million-dollar mansions that lined the avenue.

"So, what kind of gun do you have?" I asked, more out of concern than curiosity. Guns weren't one size fits all, particularly when you had tiny hands like Veronica.

"A Smith & Wesson."

"A LadySmith?"

"No, it's the nine-millimeter Pink Breast Cancer Awareness model."

"Interesting marketing choice."

Veronica leaned forward. "His turn signal is on. It looks like he's turning onto Seventh Street."

"On it." I slowed down and turned onto Seventh just in time to see Harry turning onto Prytania Street. I followed suit, careful to hang back.

He drove a few hundred yards and pulled to a stop in front of a stunning pink two-story Greek Revival mansion with a columned porch and wrought iron balcony. The house was shrouded in privacy hedges and majestic oaks and magnolias. I pulled to the curb, and Veronica and I slouched in our seats.

Harry carried out his now familiar car-exiting routine—battling his belly to get out of his seat, tamping down his toupee, buttoning his sport coat, and smoothing his Hitleresque mustache.

Veronica pulled her camera from its bag. "Okay, now drive slowly by the house. I'll get shots of him with whoever comes to the door."

I straightened in my seat, pulled away from the curb, and drove at a crawl. When I reached the mansion, an elegant brunette opened the front door. It only took me a second to recognize her. "That's the woman from last night."

"It sure is." Veronica was slouched in her seat, snapping pictures.

As we drove past, the brunette glanced at my car. She ushered Harry into the house and closed the door.

I hit the gas. "I think she saw us, but I'm not sure."

"Let's hope she didn't." Veronica straightened in her seat.

"It doesn't matter because we've got what we need. Let's go back to the office so we can download the pictures and send them to Twyla."

"What?" Veronica looked at me. "We can't leave now. We still need more pictures."

"Why?" I braked at a stop sign. "Twyla hired us to take pictures of Harry with Patsy so that she could use them to confront him. Now we just need to show her proof that he's spent the last two evenings with another woman. It's up to her to decide whether she still wants to confront him or have us find out the brunette's identity first."

"But the pictures we have don't prove that Harry is actually cheating on Twyla." We need to try to get some photos of Harry and the brunette in a compromising position."

I turned to look at her. "How do you propose we do that?"

"Easy. We could snap some photos through one of the windows."

"But what if they're on the second floor?"

"Well, in that case, we might be out of luck."

I tapped her arm. "I know. We could climb ones of those trees."

Veronica crossed her arms. "I don't know, Franki. We're in dresses and high heels."

"So? Charlie's Angels wore dresses and heels all the time." The reference reminded me of Bradley, and my gut gave a pang.

"No. One of us could fall out of a tree and get hurt."

"C'mon, Veronica. Where's your sense of investigative duty?" I appealed to her scrupulous, workaholic side. "This guy is cheating on his wife of forty-eight years. We've got to prove it and nail him."

She scrutinized my face. "Do you think you might be taking this case a little personally, Franki?"

I feigned a look of disbelief, both for her benefit and my own. "What are you talking about?"

"I can't help but think that your zeal to nail Harry, as you put it, might have something to do with Bradley."

"Don't be ridiculous." My voice was a telltale octave too high. "This case is purely business."

She shrugged. "If you say so. Anyway, for now let's just plan on doing a quick round of the house to see if they're in one of the rooms on the main floor."

"Sure." I turned onto Sixth Street and shivered. It bordered Lafayette Cemetery No. 1, the oldest and creepiest city-owned cemetery in New Orleans. I parked the car in front of the cemetery and stuffed the car keys into my bra for safekeeping.

Veronica grabbed her camera from the floor. "So, how do you suggest we do this?"

"Because the backyard is fenced, we're going to have to approach the house from the side. And we need to do this fast in case the brunette did see us. If she called the police, we could get arrested for trespassing."

She nodded.

We exited the car and set off down the street. When we reached the house, we dashed into the yard and peeped in the windows—the living room, family room, den, parlor, and study.

I couldn't believe the luxury. "What does a single family *do* with all these living spaces?"

"Shh!" Veronica looked into the kitchen and adjoining dining room. "Empty," she whispered. "They must be upstairs. Let's get going."

"No," I whisper-shouted. "We've come this far. We've got to get some pictures."

"Franki, we can't climb these trees. I can't take the chance of one of us getting injured."

Unwilling to accept defeat, I scanned the side of the house and saw a metal trellis. "But I can."

I rushed to the ladder-like structure, kicked off my beige pumps, and climbed the twenty-or-so feet to the second floor.

"Get down," Veronica whisper-shouted. "That thing can't possibly hold your weight."

"Just what are you trying to say, Veronica?" I scowled down at her.

She scowled back. "It's made of flimsy pressboard."

Ignoring her warning, I climbed until I reached a window. I peered over the windowsill into a spacious office and spotted Harry and the brunette sitting close on a sofa. She was curled up with her arm stretched out behind him on the back of the couch, and they were looking at what appeared to be a photo album.

"I see them." I realized that I had no way to photograph them. "I need the camera."

"I'm not climbing up that thing," Veronica whisper-protested. "It'll break."

"Fine," I whisper-huffed. "I'll come down."

I lowered myself slightly more than halfway. Gripping the trellis with one hand, I leaned and extended my arm.

Veronica rose on her tiptoes. "I can't reach you."

"One sec." I took a step down and leaned a little farther.

The top half of the trellis cracked and pulled from the wall.

I heard Veronica gasp and fabric tear as I fell. I landed rear-end first on an immaculately groomed shrub as the trellis smacked loudly against the side of the house, like a rubber band that had been stretched too far and then released.

Veronica ran to the shrub. "Are you okay?"

"I think so." I checked my limbs to make sure they were all intact.

Veronica gasped again. "The brunette just looked out the window. We've got to get out of here."

I tried to move, but my bottom was stuck in the shrub. "Pull me out."

She grabbed my hand and tugged with all her petite might. While she pulled, I leveraged myself on a branch with my other hand and broke free of the stubborn bush. I rolled onto my stomach, hopped down, and grabbed my pumps.

The front door opened.

Veronica and I exchanged a look of panic before hoofing it down the street. We reached the cemetery, and I ripped the car keys from my bra. Then we jumped into the Mustang and burned rubber.

⁓

Veronica patted her camera as I drove back to the office. "I wonder how Twyla is going to react to these photographs. After all, she's expecting to see Patsy, not a beautiful young brunette."

"Give me...a sec." I gasped between breaths. A few minutes

had elapsed since we'd left the brunette's mansion, and I still hadn't recovered from the two-hundred-yard sprint to my car.

"Maybe we should deliver them to her in person. She *is* prone to fainting spells, and I'd hate for something bad to happen."

"Me too," I wheezed.

"Okay, then it's settled. We'll bring them to her tomorrow."

I slowed to a stop at the intersection of Governor Nicholls and Bourbon. It was a residential district, so the streets were quiet. I looked both ways and did a double take.

Bradley walked down the street with a masked young woman in a Mardi Gras queen costume—make that a teeny bikini with a few sequins and feathers.

I recovered the full force of my lungs. "Is that Bradley with that hot blonde?"

Veronica looked out the passenger window. "Didn't you say his wife was a blonde?"

"Yeah, but that's not her. She doesn't have waist-length hair."

"Well, it's impossible to tell who that man is. He's walking away from us, and it's dark."

"Oh, it's not impossible." I speed-turned onto Bourbon.

"What are you going to do?" Her tone was panicked. "Run them down?"

"No. We're going to follow them."

"But there's a barricade up ahead. You can't drive through there."

I pulled into a rare Bourbon Street parking space and shut off the ignition. "That's why we're going to follow them on foot."

Veronica put her hand on my arm. "Franki, this is *not* a good idea. If it *is* Bradley, what are you going to do?"

"I'm not going to do anything," I said, although I wasn't sure I was being entirely honest. "I just need to know if it's him or not."

"You might want to look at your dress first. It's torn."

"Veronica." I threw my hands in the air. "This is hardly the time to worry about a little rip in my dress."

Before she could reply, I blew out of the car and rushed down Bourbon. I could still see the man and the blonde a couple of intersections ahead. I had to catch up to them before they passed the barricade at St. Ann Street that separated the homes from the bar district. My high heels were slowing me down, but there was no way I was taking them off. It was one thing to run barefoot down a residential street in the wealthy Garden District, but it was quite another to do it on Bourbon.

I arrived at the intersection and spotted the guy and the blonde near the barricade. He turned to her and said something that made her laugh. The minute I saw his profile, I recognized the outline of Bradley's Roman nose and strong jaw.

Veronica caught up to me. "Well?"

"It's Bradley, all right." I was so angry that I was sure flames shot from my eyes. "He's already found a new woman to cheat on his wife with."

"Okay. Now that you know it's him, let's go back to the car."

I clenched my teeth. "Not before I get a better look at that blonde."

I ran to St. Ann and pushed my way through the partiers, keeping my eyes glued to the back of Bradley's head.

"Franki, wait," Veronica called. "I'm trapped."

I saw that she was stuck behind a group of tall men dressed as Catholic cardinals.

"Push 'em the hell out of the way," I yelled and turned back around.

Bradley and the blonde had disappeared.

I scanned the crowd for any sign of them.

"Hey, catch," a sexy male voice shouted from a balcony above.

I looked up and a bead necklace hit me in the face.

The man who had thrown the necklace winked and raised his glass in a silent toast. A group of his friends gathered around him and smiled at me.

"Here ya go, beautiful." One of them tossed a handful of necklaces in my direction.

I stood there, surprised. I'd been to Bourbon Street several times before, once even in my pre-cellulite days, and I'd never seen that kind of action.

"Are you supposed to be Poison Ivy or Eve in The Garden of Eden?" a drunken male voice asked.

I looked away from the balcony and saw a Humpty Dumpty-shaped guy in a Court Jester outfit standing in front of me. "Huh?"

He took a sip from his long, neon green, hand grenade-shaped cup. "Those leaves on your hooters and your hoo ha."

I looked down. At some point during my fall from the trellis and the ensuing struggle with the shrub, my three-quarter-sleeve, beige knit dress had acquired leafy accessories in the nether regions. It had also gained a ten-inch plunging neckline that could only be described as Glenda-worthy. *That explains the beads.*

"Because if you're Eve," he said, "then you really should've worn a bikini instead of that big dress."

That from a Court Jester whose only exposed body parts on the chilly January night were his face and hands. "Speaking of big," I leaned in close to the egg-shaped joker, "if you don't shut your big mouth, I'm going to take your big cup and shove it up your big—"

"Franki," Veronica interrupted after she'd broken free from her Catholic-costumed captors. Then she clasped her hands to her face and stared at me. "Your dress."

"Believe me, I *know* about my dress." I glared at the Court

Jester, who took that as his cue to beat it. I bent over, collected my beads, and put them around my neck to cover my fully displayed cleavage. Then I plucked some leaves from the area below my waist. "Now let's get going. But first I need a drink."

"I think I do too."

I saw a young woman in black shorts, a bright green tube top, and white go-go boots selling Jell-O shots outside the Funky 544 club. "Perfect." I pointed to the woman. "Let's go over there."

"A Jell-O shot?" Veronica crinkled her face. "Those are so disgusting."

"I haven't eaten dinner yet, so this way I can get something in my stomach while I drink. Otherwise, you're going to have to drive home."

Veronica gave me a look. "I don't think Everclear-infused Jell-O qualifies as solid food."

I walked up to the shot seller. She shivered in the cool night air and chewed gum a mile a minute. "How much?"

She popped a gum bubble. "Three bucks for the test tubes, seven for the syringes."

"You have them in *syringes*?"

The girl smacked her gum and nodded. "You can inject 'em."

"Even better. I'll take two."

The girl handed me two syringes the size of toothpaste tubes.

"If you want, I can inject them into your mouth." She pocketed my fifteen dollars in cash and then adjusted her sagging tube top.

I looked at her hands. "Thanks, but I can handle it from here." I squirted them one by one into my mouth.

Veronica looked annoyed. "Can we go to the office now? I'd really like to get these pictures printed."

"Let's go." I said it as though I'd fully intended to go to the office after drink-eating Jell-O shots.

The mob on Bourbon seemed to grow by the minute, so it took a while to make our way back to the car. At around the halfway point, we were forced to stop behind a huge crowd that had gathered in the middle of the street to listen to a traveling jazz band that was playing "Shake It and Break It."

"Let's wait until the song ends and then forge ahead," I shouted over the music.

Veronica nodded.

We stood at the edge of the crowd, and I got the creeped-out feeling that someone was watching me. I looked over my left shoulder but didn't see anyone out of the ordinary. Then I glanced to my right.

There, down a side street, was Domenica with a group of Goth teens. The others were absorbed in conversation, but she was watching me, her face so full of loathing that I took a step backward.

I tapped Veronica on the arm. "You'll never believe who's standing down the street over there."

She turned and huffed. "Domenica? She's not drinking is she? All she needs right now is a minor-in-possession charge."

"I don't see a drink. She's just glaring at me. Maybe she thinks we're following her."

"Who knows." She turned to watch the jazz band. "But it would be best to stay away from her right now."

"Fine with me." The farther I stayed from Domenica, the better.

The song ended, and the crowd dispersed.

I looked in Domenica's direction, but she'd vanished.

Veronica and I resumed our trek to the car. My high-heeled feet moved slowly, but my mind raced.

*If Domenica was Jessica's strangler, would she be desperate enough to try to kill me or Veronica to silence us? And what about Stewart Preston? He'd already killed once. What would he do if he found out I wasn't a friend of Jessica's at all but a private investigator working her murder case?*

As I contemplated the questions, not even the warm glow of my syringe-shot buzz could eliminate the chill that had spread through my body.

## 22

I took a bite of my boudin and tossed my fork onto the plate. Even though I'd lost my appetite after seeing Bradley with the blonde bimbo the night before, I'd ordered Thibodeaux's breakfast special—Cajun-style eggs Benedict with boudin patties and home fries, a side of *pain perdu*, otherwise known as French toast, and unlimited juice refills. But I asked for carbonated water to cut calories.

"Cheer up, Franki." Veronica sat across from me with a half-eaten Creole omelet and a few remaining mini baguette slices.

I swallowed a mouthful of oozing eggs and Tasso ham Hollandaise sauce. "How, exactly, am I supposed to do that? I mean, it's bad enough that Bradley turned out to be married, but then I have to see him with a beautiful blonde on his arm."

Veronica picked up her *café au lait*. "You're an attractive woman too, you know. Have you forgotten that men were throwing beads at you left and right on Bourbon Street last night?"

I shot her a look. "Maybe that had something to do with the fact that my boobs were bursting out of my dress and my vajayjay was framed in leaves."

"That wasn't the only reason."

"Whatever. Looks aren't the issue here. His marriage certificate is the problem."

She buttered a slice of baguette. "Have you considered the possibility that he might have a logical explanation for all of this?"

"You mean, for going out with a barely dressed Mardi Gras queen instead of his wife?" I stuffed a cluster of fries into my mouth.

She rolled her eyes. "Well, that and the fact that he's married. You never really let him explain."

My look was pointed—like a dagger. "What's there to explain?"

She shrugged. "For one thing, why his wife lives in Boston while he lives here. Maybe the marriage is over."

"Or maybe they're living apart while he spends a year at a New Orleans bank." I cut into my boudin with a little too much zeal.

"Maybe. But that's the kind of thing you should find out. Because it's real obvious that you still care about Bradley."

I put down my knife and fork, in case I got the urge to stab myself. "It doesn't matter how I feel about him. I'm tired of sharing my boyfriends with other women. I want a man all to myself. So, as long as Bradley's married, he's off limits."

"That banker man got you down, sugar?" Glenda stood at our table.

She was in all her glory. Her top was nothing special by her standards, just a red spandex jog bra, heavy on the cleavage. It was her matching red spandex pants that were so spectacular. They were essentially crotchless, but it wasn't only the crotch that was missing. It was all the fabric below the waistband. So her red G-string was prominently exposed, from hip to hip and on down, so to speak. *And to think I was worried about a few lousy leaves.*

"Oh, Glenda." Veronica put a hand to her chest. "You look sensational in red."

She batted her two-inch false eyelashes. "It's scarlet."

Veronica stared expectantly at me.

I spit out the first compliment that came to mind. "Nice biceps." I chose to focus on Glenda's upper body. "Have you been going to the gym?"

"No, it's from years of swinging on poles."

"Uh-huh," I said, since my mouth was hanging open. I hoped that she would either sit or leave. Having that G-string right next to my face was killing my urge to emotional eat. Then again, maybe that was a good thing—diet by disgust.

Veronica looked up at Glenda. "Would you like to join us?"

"No, I phoned in a to-go order." She paused and shot me a guilty look. "I have a gentleman caller at the house."

I knew she was talking about Guido. For a split second I felt something akin to jealousy—certainly not of Glenda having the Jersey juicehead in her bed, but of her ability to attract men so easily. But ultimately I was happy. I needed their relationship to continue to keep my nonna off my back. "If you mean Guido, I'm totally fine with the two of you seeing each other."

"Well, if you need a man to replace that banker, sugar, I'm willing to share." Glenda gave a Vanna White-like flourish of her arm. "A body like this can't be wasted on only one gentleman, even if he is a strong man in the circus."

"A strong man?" Veronica clapped. "Tell me more."

I, on the other hand, had already heard all I wanted to hear. I picked up my phone and stared at the time. "Gosh. It's almost ten thirty. We'd better get going if we're meeting Twyla at the office at eleven."

Veronica frowned. "Duty calls." She pulled two twenties

from her wallet. "Let me get this since you're having to work on a Sunday."

"Thanks." I grabbed my purse and fled the bar.

~

"GOOD AFTERNOON, LADIES." Twyla's tone was somber as she entered the office lobby. Her vibrant pinkish-yellow sack dress made her look a lot like a giant grapefruit.

"Hi, Twyla." I scooped up the photos of Harry and the brunette that Veronica and I had been reviewing on the coffee table.

She took a seat on the couch across from us, clutching a vintage wooden decoupage purse to her chest as though it were a shield she could use to protect herself from the news she was about to receive. "I'd like to thank you girls for so kindly agreeing to meet me at your office on a Sunday." Her ruby red lips set in a thin line. "I would have dearly luuuved to invite you to tea, but Harry is at home right now playing with his train set."

*A train set?* Harry was the opposite of a catch—he was a release.

Veronica rose and sat beside Twyla. "It's not a problem. It's probably better if you look at the pictures here, anyway."

A muscle twitched in Twyla's cheek. "What did you find out, Veronica?"

"We—"

Twyla raised her right hand. "Don't tell me yet." She opened the clasp of her purse with pinkish-yellow-lacquered fingernails and took out her smelling salts. She placed the bottle on the coffee table and pulled her purse back to her bosom. "Okay. I'm ready now."

Veronica cleared her throat. "As you know, we've followed Harry for the last two nights. On Friday, he went to Pascal's

Manale restaurant in Uptown, and on Saturday he went to a private residence in the Garden District."

Twyla's eyes grew wide at the mention of a home. "Was this house on Magazine Street, by any chance?"

I shook my head. "Prytania."

She blinked.

I pushed the photos of Harry and the brunette across the table to Twyla. "He met this woman on both occasions."

She peered down at the photo on the top of the pile with one eye closed. With a sharp intake of breath she jerked her head up in alarm. "That's not Patsy."

Veronica glanced at me. "No. We haven't been able to iden-tify the woman yet. The house where Harry met her is listed in a man's name."

Twyla stiffened, her eyes rolled back in her head, and she fell back against the couch, her head hanging over the back.

She was out cold.

Veronica fanned her with a photo. "Grab her smelling salts."

I snatched the vial off the table and snapped it open. Veronica lifted Twyla's head, and I waved the vial under Twyla's nose.

She jerked. Her eyelids fluttered, and she opened her eyes. She blinked a few times. "Am I in heaven?"

I half-smiled. "No."

She raised a brow. "The ICU?"

"You're at Private Chicks," Veronica said. "You hired us to investigate your husband, Harry."

Twyla furrowed her brow as though deep in thought and went straight to despondent mode. "Haaaarry." She choked back a sob. "How could he *do* this to me? And after almost fifty years of wedded bliss."

Veronica handed her a box of tissues. "Twyla, we don't know

if Harry has done anything to you. All we know is that he met with this woman two nights in a row."

Twyla's tears shut off as quickly as water from a closed faucet. "You mean you don't actually *know* whether he's been unfaithful to me?"

I shook my head. "No."

She dabbed her tear-stained eyes with a tissue. "Well, Harry's quite fatherly, you know. Maybe that was the daughter of one of his clients, and he was just trying to be of assistance in some way?"

I looked at Veronica, and my gaze said *Unlikely*.

Twyla patted my knee. "You don't have to answer that, darling. It was just a rhetorical question."

Veronica looked concerned. "We apologize if there was any confusion about our findings."

"Not at all, dear." Twyla rose to her feet. "I want to thank you girls for all your trouble. I'll let you know if I need you to investigate this unseemly matter any further, after I've talked to Harry." She walked to the door and then turned to face us. "Whatever you girls do, don't make the tragic mistake of choosing a dashing man like my Harry to be your groom. Because if you do, you'll have to protect him from shameless trollops for your entire marriage."

～

"BAD BOY, NAPOLEON." I scolded him for the second time since carrying him into the house. I'd taken him out for a walk, and he'd pulled the leash from my hand to chase a cat through the cemetery. Nothing like a romp through a graveyard hours before a meeting with an alleged murderer to lift your spirits, so to speak.

I hung the leash on a hook by the front door and looked

around the living room. It was three o'clock, so I still had a good hour and a half before I had to leave to meet Stewart Preston at the Carousel Bar. I needed to find something to do to keep my mind occupied because I was nervous.

*Dust the furniture?*

I was never that desperate.

*Read?*

I wouldn't be able to focus on the page.

*Have a snack and watch mindless TV?*

Sounded like a plan.

After grabbing a bag of Mint Milanos and the Nutella from the pantry, I headed for my bedroom. I swung open the doors of my hot pink and black armoire and switched on the tiny TV set I'd received as a hand-me-down from my parents. I flopped onto the bed and flipped through the channels with the remote. The first movie I came across was *The Silence of the Lambs*.

*FBI trainee meets cannibalistic serial killer?*

Definitely not. I shuddered and changed the channel.

*Unsolved Mysteries?*

Not that either. There was every possibility that I would become an unsolved mystery myself.

I switched off the TV.

*Now what?* Eating the entire bag of Mint Milanos—dipped in Nutella—would while away some time. I pulled out the first cookie and heard a whimper coming from the floor.

I narrowed my eyes. "Not a chance, Napoleon, especially not after that cemetery caper."

My phone rang—a nice old-fashioned phone ring.

Talking on the phone was always a good distraction. I checked the display, and my heart thudded.

*Bradley.*

I wanted to answer with every fiber of my being and ask him what the hell he'd been doing with a bikinied bimbo when he was married. But I couldn't. Bradley's wandering ways were no concern of mine. But I *did* wish I knew what it was about me that attracted cheaters. *Was I not interesting or attractive enough to keep a guy? Or did I give off a cheat-on-me vibe?*

The ringing stopped, and I waited with to see whether he had left a voicemail. At least two minutes passed. I checked the voicemail box—nothing.

*Inconsiderate jerk.*

I had to find a way to take my mind off him. I decided to check my email. I grabbed my laptop from the bedside table and logged in. Some of the messages were spam—an ad for Viagra, news I'd won an overseas lottery, and an offer of marriage from a Russian bride. But then I saw "photo request" in the subject line of one of the messages.

It was the picture I'd requested from *The Times-Picayune* of Stewart Preston waving on the courthouse steps.

I opened the message and double-clicked the attachment. It wouldn't open. I tried two more times and discovered that the file was corrupt. I started to reply to the email but changed my mind. I was meeting Stewart in less than two hours, and I needed to know whether my hunch about his watchband was right. I checked the email for a signature and saw the name Dmitriy and a phone number. I entered the number into my phone and waited.

"Times-Picayune," a youthful male voice responded.

"Hi, could I please speak to Dmitriy?"

"You got him. How can I help you?"

"My name is Franki Amato, and I just got an email from you with a corrupt .jpg file."

"Was it the photo of Stewart Preston?"

I was surprised that he'd remembered the picture. "Yes."

"What is the *deal* with that image?" he muttered under his breath.

"Pardon?"

"Oh, I wasn't asking *you*. It's just that when I originally went to retrieve the photo, it wasn't on our server. Luckily, my friend Norm was the photographer assigned to that story, so I was able to get the picture for you from his personal archives. It's just weird that now there's a problem with the file."

My heart sped up. "So, the photo was deleted from your server?"

"Yeah, because it was used in an article, it should've been in our process file, but it wasn't there. It wasn't in our stock file either. But hey, when your staff consists of mainly unpaid interns, these things happen. Someone probably deleted the image by mistake."

I doubted that an intern would've accidentally deleted the picture from two separate files. "Are you still able to open it?"

"Yeah, it opens right up for me. It's a pretty big file, though. It could be that the picture didn't completely download from our server."

"Could you email it to me again?"

"I hit *Send* a second ago."

Holding my breath, I refreshed my inbox. The message was there. I clicked the attached file, and it opened without incident. "Got it. Thank you so much for your help, Dmitriy."

I closed the call and laid back on my bed, stunned. *Who would've deleted the file from not one but two places on the newspaper's server? Could it really have been a careless intern? Or was it someone connected to Stewart Preston?* If it was the latter, then it could mean only one thing—there was incriminating evidence in that photo that Stewart and his family didn't want anyone to see. Like I'd suspected.

I picked up my laptop and scrutinized Stewart's raised hand and wrist in the photo. The watchband protruded about a half an inch from the cuff of his suit coat. I enlarged the area click by click until it consumed the screen. On the fifth click, my body stiffened. Stewart wasn't wearing a chunky watchband.

Hidden beneath the sleeve of his suit coat, he wore a bracelet of skull beads—exactly like the one I'd found lodged underneath the scarf rack at the crime scene.

My mind flashed to the night of Jessica's murder. *Had Stewart gone to LaMarca wearing the bracelet?* If he had, then it was possible that the bracelet had been broken during a struggle. Jessica could've ripped the bracelet from Stewart's wrist and lodged one of the beads under the rack to implicate him as he strangled her.

Unfortunately, the only person who could've confirmed my theory was Jessica. There was only one thing I could do—find out whether Stewart still had the bracelet. It seemed an impossible task, but it was a matter of life and death.

Specifically, my own.

## 23

"I just can't get over it." Veronica stood at her kitchen sink wringing water from a cashmere sweater. "I've looked at that picture of Stewart a dozen times, and I never noticed anything unusual."

"That's because you don't like watches." I'd paced back and forth on Veronica's green shag carpet so many times in the past five minutes that I was wearing a path into it.

"True, but I still don't get it. What made you suspect that Stewart wasn't wearing a watch?"

"First of all, I've never seen a watchband with big bumps on it like that. Even the Gucci bamboo watch that I've been lusting over has a smooth silver link bracelet for a band. Plus, in the photo there's no buckle or clasp showing on the underside of Stewart's wrist. So I thought it might be some kind of bracelet."

"Well, I'm impressed." She placed the sweater on a drying rack near the sink.

"Thanks, but now we have to figure out what happened to that bracelet. If Stewart wore it to the murder scene, then he must've picked up the beads after it broke, except for the one that rolled under the rack."

Veronica entered the living room and took a seat on the couch next to a bowtie-adorned Hercules, who had been watching me pace with a worried gaze. "In that case, I seriously doubt he would've kept the beads. He would've gotten rid of them right away."

I stopped in my tracks. "So what do I do? I can't just say, 'Hey, Stewart, did you ever happen to own a skull bead bracelet from Marie Laveau's?'"

She stroked Hercules's fur. "Actually, you could ask him that and see what kind of a reaction you get."

"Unless his reaction is to lunge for my throat, that won't tell me anything definitive." I resumed pacing. "I'll have to think of some other way. Maybe I could work voodoo into the conversation somehow."

"Whatever you do, don't mention Odette Malveaux. I don't believe for a minute that Stewart Preston is the Hollywood movie-style voodoo worshipper that Concetta made him out to be."

"Maybe not." I pointed at her. "But he did wear a skull bead bracelet to court. That has to mean something."

"It just makes me think that he's one of the countless people in New Orleans who are superstitious enough to turn to voodoo trinkets in moments of crisis."

I threw up my hands. "I guess that makes sense. It's just so unsettling to find out about the bracelet and then the whole missing photo thing right before I meet the guy."

Veronica furrowed her brow. "Yeah, the fact that the photo disappeared from *The Times-Picayune* archives looks bad for Stewart, doesn't it?"

I put my hand on my neck. "I've had heartburn ever since I found that out."

Her face softened. "I know you're scared. To be honest, I'm worried too."

"Well *that* doesn't make me feel any better."

"Remember what you told me—you'll be meeting Stewart in a public place during the daytime. And don't forget that I'll be there to back you up."

I wrung my hands. "Ah, yes, with the pink breast cancer special."

Veronica blinked, as though offended by my jab at her girly gun. "It's a nine-millimeter handgun, Franki. Its color won't affect its performance, I assure you."

"You're right. I'm just on edge." I collapsed into the armchair. Ten minutes of pacing was an intense workout.

"Can I get you something? A nice hot cup of tea might help."

I looked at the angry island god perched on the back of my chair. "I think it would take a couple of shots of tequila."

She frowned. "This is definitely not the time for a drink."

"I know, I know." I sighed. "Let's just go back over the plan."

"Okay." Veronica leaned forward. "We're going to rent a car for you so that Stewart can't trace the license plates. Then I'll follow you from the rental lot to the Carousel Bar in my car. We'll both park at the Hotel Monteleone."

"Do they have a parking lot?"

"Yeah, it's beneath the hotel. You pull into the garage, and a valet takes your car and parks it underground for you."

"All right. After we park, I'll go to the bar and—"

She shook her head. "It rotates like an actual carousel. You know how dizzy you get on merry-go-rounds."

"True." It was a well-known fact that I'd never gotten my carousel legs. Within seconds of stepping foot on one, I was on my knees, puking.

"Besides, there's no way you'd be able to have a private conversation with Stewart at that bar. It's always crowded, and the seats are too close together. You'll have to meet him at one of the seating areas in the lounge. It's down a small flight of stairs, which is great because that way I can sit up at the bar and have a clear view of the two of you."

"So, if he's at the bar when I get there, I'll ask him to move downstairs."

"Right, and then if you leave before he does, I'll stay and keep an eye on Stewart. I'll text you when I leave. Will that work?"

I nodded.

"Okay then. Go get ready." Veronica adjusted the bow on Hercules's head. "We leave in thirty minutes."

∾

I PULLED my rented Chrysler convertible around the back of the Hotel Monteleone and encountered a line of cars waiting to get into the parking garage. I looked in my rearview mirror and was relieved to see Veronica waiting three cars back.

*So far, so good.*

As I waited to park, I leaned my head on the headrest and looked at the sky. Usually, when I put the convertible top down and let the wind blow my hair and the sun shine on my face, it was a stress reliever. But not at that moment. All I could think about was meeting a murderer. Well, someone I was fairly sure was a murderer, anyhow. And unlike my cop days, I had no uniform, no badge and, worst of all, no gun since I'd turned in my service pistol. But the Evans case had made it clear that I needed to get one—nothing pink or disease-related like Veronica, just a plain purple Ruger.

The car in front of me pulled ahead, and I inched the Chrysler forward. A flash of bright red caught my eye. It was a guy dressed like a giant crawdad—complete with red tights, torso and tail, and a headpiece with eyes and antennae—leaning against the wall smoking. He'd had to remove one of his pinchers to hold the cigarette. While I was taking in his costume, our eyes met. He narrowed his gaze as he took a drag and nodded appreciatively in my direction. I looked away. After my last experience with a crawdad, I didn't want any more trouble.

Finally, I pulled up to the valet. I was so nervous that I practically jumped from my car and jogged the few steps from the garage entrance to the hotel. As I crossed the busy lobby, I had the unshakable sensation that I was walking toward my doom. Nevertheless, I forged ahead. I was so close to solving Jessica's murder that there was no way I could turn back. I took a deep breath and entered the Carousel Bar and Lounge.

With Mardi Gras season in full swing, the place was packed and buzzing with an electric energy. I scoured the patrons for Stewart Preston and tried not to look at the brightly lit merry-go-round-style bar as it rotated beside me. I was already nauseated from fear. I didn't want to add motion sickness to my existing stomach woes.

When I didn't see him, I scanned the customers in the adjoining lounge. I spotted Stewart immediately. He sat on a couch in the middle of the room with a drink in his hand. I looked at him from the top of the steps, and he stared at me and then lowered his gaze to my breasts.

My fear turned to anger.

I balled my fists and marched down the stairs. As I approached him, I was struck by how bloated his face was. *Could that be from drug use?* I thought of Odette Malveaux's mysterious warning to "Watch out fo' dem who take magic." And I took a deep breath. "Stewart Preston?"

He took a sip of his drink and, with bloodshot eyes, gave me a slow, insolent once-over.

"I'll take that as a yes." I sat on the couch opposite him, my back to the bar.

"So, what is it that you're calling yourself?" He raised his cleft chin. "Tina, was it?"

He hadn't bought my cover. "Gina. Gina Mazzucco."

Stewart narrowed his eyes. "Why don't you drop this little charade and tell me who you really are?"

I swallowed hard. "I don't know what you're talking about."

"Lady, you and I both know that Angelica Evangelista didn't have any girlfriends. And if she did, they sure as hell wouldn't be investigating her murder."

The jig was up. I had to stop playing games. Otherwise, he might walk. I calculated my risk and went for broke. "That's not true. Immacolata Di Salvo was her friend."

Stewart showed no sign of emotion at the mention of Immacolata's name. "What would make you think I care about Immacolata Di Salvo?"

"I know you were charged with her murder."

A muscle worked in his jaw. "And I was acquitted."

"I know that too."

For some reason, he relaxed. Then he grabbed a handful of mixed nuts, leaned back against the couch, and propped his foot on the coffee table between us. "So, you're a private investigator."

I didn't respond.

"I'll take that as a yes." He sneered and popped a few nuts into his mouth.

I seized the moment to look at his jewelry. He wasn't wearing a voodoo bracelet, just a top-of-the-line gold Rolex.

He took another sip of his drink. "So what is it you want to know?"

"I want to know if you killed Angelica Evangelista."

Again, no reaction from Stewart. He turned and flagged a passing waitress. As she approached us, I glanced over my shoulder at the bar. Veronica was there with a strawberry daiquiri looking right at me.

"I'll take another Maker's Mark, darlin'. Get this lady here whatever she wants."

I turned and looked at the waitress. "Nothing for me, thanks."

She nodded and headed to the bar.

I looked Stewart in the eyes. "You haven't answered my question."

He drained the whiskey from his glass and placed it on the coffee table. "Oh yeah. I did not kill Angelica."

"Then why was your father's company putting ten thousand dollars a month into Angelica's account, under the assumed name of Jessica Evans?"

"She was working for my dad as a textile consultant."

I snorted. "I don't believe you."

He yawned. "That's not my problem."

Time to shift tactics. "Where were you the night Jessica was killed?"

"What business is it of yours?"

He was playing games with me. It was time to get real. "You can drop the act, Preston. I know you strangled Immacolata in her dorm room. Angelica knew it too, so your father paid her to keep her mouth shut and sent her packing to Milan. But she defied your daddy's orders and returned to New Orleans, so you went to LaMarca and told her to leave town. When she didn't comply, you went back to LaMarca and killed her the same way you killed Immacolata. You strangled her with a scarf."

Stewart leaned forward. "You be careful who you tell that story to, understand? Because I'll sue you for slander, and I'll win." He sat back and crossed his leg over his knee. "Do you really think I, or anyone in my family, was worried about a lousy hundred and twenty grand a year? With all the money we're worth?"

"Maybe it wasn't about the money." I was pretty sure I'd

struck a chord. "I'll bet Angelica had information that proved you killed Immacolata, and you needed to shut her up once and for all before she went to the police."

"What reason would I have had? I can't be tried for the same crime twice." He grinned. "That's what they call double jeopardy, darlin', and it's illegal."

"No, but the Di Salvos could've brought a civil suit against you, which would've put a nice dent in the family fortune."

"Nah. The only gold digger in that family was Immacolata. And she's dead, isn't she?"

A chill ran down my spine, and my courage wavered.

The waitress returned with his drink, giving me a moment to regain my composure.

Stewart took a sip from his glass. "What's the matter? Didn't you know about Immacolata's fortune-hunting ways?"

I stared at him coldly.

"I'm surprised, you being a private investigator and all."

"I don't see what her wanting to marry into money has to do with her murder."

"Oh, but it has everything to do with it. For the record, Angelica was sexy and savvy. She didn't need to blackmail anyone for money." He swirled the brown liquid in his glass. "But poor little Immacolata didn't have Angelica's business sense. The only thing she knew was men and money. And she was willing to do anything to catch her a rich husband. When she died, she was sleeping with half the men on campus. But I was the one she'd told her parents about. So when she turned up dead, I was the obvious target."

I pursed my lips. "You're saying that you had nothing to do with Immacolata's death?"

"That's right, and a jury of twelve of my peers agreed with me." He took a long drink and wiped his mouth with the back of his sleeve. "I rue the day I met her and that crazy twin of hers."

I blinked. Concetta had told Veronica and me that she didn't know Stewart. "You know Concetta?"

He burst out laughing. "Indeed I do. In the biblical sense."

My jaw practically hit the floor. "You had *sex* with her?"

"Before I knew Immacolata was better in bed."

I ignored his crude comment. "How did you meet her?"

"We met at a happy hour at the Columns Hotel. Then I met Immacolata by chance at Mardi Gras a couple of months later, and Concetta flipped out. She was jealous of her sister, big time. After I started sleeping with Immacolata, Concetta kept showing up in the middle of the night at my apartment, acting all psycho. I still can't shake her."

I was stunned. "What do you mean you can't shake her?"

"I mean that the freak stalks me to this day. She even broke into my apartment once, right after I was acquitted."

I scrutinized his face for signs that he might be lying, but it was impossible to tell. "How do you know it was her?"

"I had a security camera installed. It was definitely Concetta on that tape."

The more Stewart spoke, the more I felt that he might be telling the truth. "What did she take?"

He laughed. "That's the funny part. I have a wooden chest on my dresser that I keep my cufflinks and watches in. I guess she was trying to save me from the devil or some religious BS like that, because she took a fifteen-dollar bracelet I bought at a voodoo shop and left all of my Rolexes."

My blood ran cold. "A v-voodoo bracelet?"

He waved his hand. "Yeah, you know, one of those kitschy bead things they're always selling to tourists."

"With little skulls." I said it more to myself than to him. *But a nun couldn't have planted a skull bead at the scene of a crime just to implicate someone who'd spurned her, right?*

"Yup." He grabbed another handful of nuts. "What a friggin' whacko."

The lounge seemed to close in on me. I had to take my leave and tell Veronica. If Concetta was stalking Stewart, then she could be in the area. And that meant we could all be in danger. I shot to my feet.

Stewart cocked an eyebrow. "You leaving already?"

"Yeah, I have all the information I need."

"And this was starting to get fun." He downed his whiskey.

I turned and walked up the steps to the bar, avoiding eye contact with Veronica. I stepped into the hotel lobby and pulled my phone from my bag. As I headed for the parking garage, I sent a text to Veronica telling her that Concetta could be in the vicinity and might be dangerous.

And then Mambo Odette's warning came to me, and it finally made sense—Concetta had taken magic when she'd stolen Stewart's voodoo bracelet.

## 24

"Where are you, Veronica?" I talked to myself as I pulled into the empty Lenton's parking lot to feel less alone—and less scared.

I parked near the employee entrance and left the engine running. I looked in my rearview mirror for about the thirtieth time since I'd left the Carousel to make sure that neither Stewart nor a crazed Concetta had followed me. I grabbed my phone and called Veronica.

She answered on the first ring. "Hey. I'm almost there."

I could hear traffic in the background. "Why did you text me to meet you here? This place is deserted, and creepy."

"Ed Orlansky's secretary called me right before I left the Carousel and said that the DVD had arrived from Baton Rouge. He's waiting for us inside."

I breathed a sigh of relief. Given the circumstances, I felt like I had a giant target on my back. "So what happened when you left the bar?" I glanced out the window. "Was Stewart still there?"

"Yeah, he was putting the moves on that waitress."

"Oh, no. I wonder if she knew he was an alleged murderer."

"I made sure she did before I left."

"Good." We women had to look out for one another. "So what do you think about this business with Concetta?"

Veronica was silent. "It's a pretty far-fetched story."

"I think so too. But I'm still freaked out that Stewart brought the bracelet up like that, without me even asking him about it." I glanced at the chipped violet fingernail polish on my left hand.

"That could have been a calculated move on his part. I mean, if he knew you were a PI, he may have also known that you'd found the skull bead at the crime scene. After all, you did tell Ryan Hunter about the bead—"

"And he told his attorney who probably told the police." My heart sunk, and I sunk further into my seat.

"Right. And you know darned well that Stewart is keeping a close eye on the police investigation into Jessica's murder."

"Oh yeah, I'm sure of that."

"Anyway, I'm pulling into the parking lot right now. See you in a sec."

I hung up and scanned the area for lurkers. I no longer knew what to think about Stewart, Concetta, or anyone else connected to the case, so I had to stay on my guard.

～

ED ORLANSKY LEANED FORWARD to adjust the brightness of an old PC monitor in an armoire in his office. The combined scent of his Old Spice aftershave and the pomade he'd used to slick back his hair overwhelmed the tiny space.

He leered at Veronica—make that her breasts. "Is that better?"

"Yeah." She frowned.

Since we had the DVD of the last two scarf purchases in the bag, Veronica had dispensed with the bat-and-twirl. I scrutinized the grainy image of the teenaged girl standing in front of the sales counter. "I think we can move on to the next one."

Ed used the mouse to click and drag the video progress bar to the start of the next purchase.

The video played for thirty seconds before a young man with a Lenton's nametag approached the cash register. He held the Limoncello scarf in one hand as he scanned the price tag in the other.

I held my breath as a woman with waist-length brown hair and long bangs stepped to the register holding a billfold. She avoided eye contact with the employee. "This may be our suspect."

Veronica nodded. "It's hard to tell with the quilted down coat she's wearing, but her body type could be similar to Domenica's."

"Or Concetta's. It would help if we could tell how tall she is."

The employee asked the woman a question, and she shook her head, keeping her gaze lowered.

Veronica looked at Ed. "Too bad there's no sound on this video."

"We'll have sound soon now that corporate has finally approved our new digital system. It's got all the bells and whistles." He beamed, trying to impress her with the equipment upgrade.

I turned to Veronica. "Can you make out her face?"

"Not really. I wish she would look up."

"Then we could at least see the shape of her face and mouth. With those bangs, I can't see her eyes at all."

The woman opened her wallet and handed cash to the employee, who placed it in the register drawer. As he handed her a few bills and some coins, she raised her face.

I sat forward and turned to Ed. "Could you rewind that?"

"Sure." He spoke to Veronica instead of me. He rewound the video and paused on the woman's uplifted face.

I touched the screen. "Look at her lips. Doesn't that look like it could be either Domenica or Concetta's mouth?"

Veronica cocked her head. "I don't know. Maybe."

I slouched in my seat. "Okay, Ed, you can hit play."

"You got it." He again replied to Veronica as he clicked the button.

While the employee placed the scarf into a bag, the woman put the bills into her wallet but dropped the change. She bent to retrieve the coins and shook her hair from her eyes as she stood.

"Freeze it right there," I shouted.

Ed had been so busy gazing at Veronica's chest that he started in his seat. "What? What happened?"

Veronica rolled her eyes. "There's something we need to see. You know, on the video?"

"Oh. I knew that."

"Here, let me do it." I batted away Ed's outstretched arm. I grabbed the mouse and rewound the tape to the shot of the woman's face. I clicked pause and immediately recognized the close-set eyes.

Veronica gasped. "That's Concetta."

"Let's see what happens next." I clicked play again.

The woman put the coins into her wallet, took the bag from the employee, and walked away.

Veronica turned to me. "I think it's time we take the video and the skull bead to the police."

"Hey." Ed's eyes opened wide. "What about our dinner tonight?"

Veronica glared at him, and I stood, crossed my arms, and followed suit.

Ed's eyes darted from Veronica to me, and he licked his chapped lips. "I'll take a rain check?"

∽

I INSERTED the key into my front door lock.

Veronica sighed. "Next time, promise me you'll keep any evidence you find at the office."

"I said I was sorry." I pushed the door open. "It's just that so many people pass through there. I thought the bead would be safer here."

Veronica followed me into the dark apartment. "Napoleon doesn't come to greet you?"

"Not unless he has to tinkle." I laughed. "Nine o'clock is past his bedtime." I flipped the light switch by the front door, but the light didn't come on. "Shoot. The light bulb's burned out. Will you turn on the kitchen light?"

"Sure." She headed toward the kitchen, and I bolted the door behind us.

The light came on, and Veronica let out a bloodcurdling scream.

I ran to the kitchen doorway and stopped short.

Concetta stood in the middle of the room wearing a full habit and surgical gloves, and she held a butcher knife to Veronica's throat.

I put my hands to my mouth.

"Nice décor, Franki." She smirked. "What are you, a PI by day and a prostitute by night?"

"Let her go."

"I don't think you're in any position to call the shots." Her voice was eerily calm. "Now, why don't you come over here and sit at the kitchen table?"

I nodded and did as I was told. I knew from my police training that I needed to establish a rapport with a hostage-taker so that he or she wouldn't see me as a threat. But there was one glaring problem with that tactic. Veronica and I *were* threats to

Concetta because we were the only ones standing in the way of her freedom. I took a seat and hoped that Veronica was still armed.

Then I saw the rope on the table.

Concetta walked Veronica behind me. "Okay, take a piece of rope and start tying the big one up."

*The big one? It wasn't enough that she was going to kill me, she had to insult me too?*

"And don't try any tricks, either. If you don't tie those knots nice and tight, you're a goner."

Veronica tied my hands behind my back, and I glared at Concetta over my shoulder. "What did you do with my dog?"

She looked at me like I was an idiot. "I let him out. I'm allergic."

I prayed she was telling the truth. If she'd hurt Napoleon, I wouldn't be able to live with myself. That is, *if* I lived.

Veronica tightened the rope around my wrists. "Why don't you let us go, Concetta? You're in enough trouble, as it is."

She let out a hysterical laugh. "I'm not in any trouble. You'd think that would be pretty clear by now to you two crackerjack PIs."

I had to keep her talking in hopes that she would get distracted and slip up somehow. "We know you killed Angelica, and the police know it too. Veronica brought them the video file that shows you bought the murder weapon."

"You're bluffing. If she'd stopped to drop off the video, she wouldn't be here with you now, would she?"

She had me there.

Concetta pushed Veronica to the floor and threw a rope at her head. "Tie her feet."

Veronica threaded the rope around my ankles, and I glared at Concetta again. "We have proof that you did it."

She smiled to herself. "*You* do. But the police don't."

My stomach felt like it had been ripped from my body. That last comment didn't bode well.

"You're right, though." Concetta's tone was strangely chatty. "I did kill Angie."

Veronica tightened the rope.

"Get up," Concetta said through clenched teeth. She pulled Veronica by the hair, causing her to cry out.

I bit my lip to keep from screaming at her.

Concetta put the knife to Veronica's neck with her right hand as she checked the knots with her left. She stood and shoved her into the table. "Take a seat."

Veronica stumbled and fell into a chair, and we exchanged a frightened look across the table. If Concetta tied up Veronica, we were goners.

After selecting a length of rope, Concetta held the knife as she tied Veronica's wrists behind her back.

I worked my hands and wrists, trying to loosen the rope. Under threat of death from Concetta, Veronica had tied the knots tightly, so I could move each wrist only a fraction of an inch. To make matters worse, the rope cut into my flesh.

Concetta finished tying Veronica's hands and took a step back. "I had to do it. Angie knew Stewart had strangled Imma, but she wouldn't testify against him. She let those horrible people buy her silence so she could get herself a degree, designer clothes, and a career in the fashion industry, all courtesy of the Preston family. But that wasn't the only reason I killed her."

Veronica looked over her shoulder. "What other reason would you have?"

Concetta grabbed another piece of rope from the table and knelt to tie Veronica's feet. "You're both Italian, so you should know about the concept of vendetta. It's a question of honor."

As soon as she said vendetta, I thought of the word *vendicata* that Domenica had spray-painted on Immacolata's tombstone. "Did Domenica know you killed Angelica?"

"Of course not." She tugged at a knot. "In case you haven't noticed, my little sister's not the brightest bulb on the Christmas tree."

"Then why did she spray paint that Immacolata had been avenged on her tombstone?"

Concetta stood. "She was celebrating the fact that Angie was strangled with a scarf the same way that Stewart strangled Imma."

I continued working my wrists, but I didn't seem to be making any headway. I hoped that Veronica was making more progress. "Angelica hated cheap scarves and the color yellow. Is that why you chose the yellow-bordered polyester scarf?"

Concetta smirked. "I wanted her to see yellow and feel cheap fabric on her skin as she was dying. I had to make sure that the last thought she ever had in her wretched life was that she was nothing but a two-bit coward, like her dad."

Veronica looked up. "What do you mean?"

Concetta's eyes opened wide. "Isn't it obvious? Angie ran out on her best friend for money. Instead of paying her own way through school and trying to work her way up from the bottom, she did it all the easy way. She kept her mouth shut at the trial so she could get her education and her career bought and paid for."

I met her gaze. "And to get even with Stewart, you planted the bead from his bracelet at the scene of the crime."

Her eyes twinkled. "Yeah, and by the way, he was telling you the truth tonight when he said I'd stolen that bracelet from his apartment."

Veronica gasped. "You were at the Carousel Bar? But we would've seen you in your habit."

I stared at Concetta, openmouthed. So Stewart had been telling the truth about the stalking too.

She gave Veronica a mock sad look, as though she were nothing but a pathetic fool. "I've been following the two of you since you took the case, genius. And I definitely know how to dress for the occasion. I was sitting on the couch behind Stewart, with my back to him, and not a one of you was astute enough to see me."

So she *had* been following me the day I saw her at CC's Community Coffee, and who knew where else. "But I don't understand why you'd frame Stewart. Why didn't you kill him like you killed Angelica?"

She rolled her eyes. "Because Stewart is different than Angie. For him, there's a fate worse than death—rotting day after day, year after year in prison, cut off from his money and privilege and, most importantly, from women and partying. And since those imbeciles on the jury acquitted him of Imma's murder, I had to make sure there was another murder he'd be found guilty of."

Veronica shook her head. "How could you, an ordained nun, take another human life?"

Concetta curled her lips at Veronica. "You have no idea what it's like to lose a twin. After Imma was gone I felt lost without her, empty. At first I thought the Lord would fill me up. But one day I realized that I couldn't serve a god who'd allowed my sister to be murdered by a lowlife like Stewart Preston."

Any shred of hope I'd had that she might spare Veronica and me was lost with that statement.

"Plus, if you'd known Angie, you probably would've killed her too. She was something else, that one. Take the night I strangled her. When I showed up at LaMarca with that scarf, I presented it to her as a gift. Being the bitch that she was, she ripped open the package, took one look at the scarf, and said it was ugly and tacky, just like me."

Concetta stared at the floor and chuckled. "If you could have seen the horrified look on her face when she realized that I'd come there to strangle her with that scarf." The chuckle turned cackle, and tears streamed from her eyes. "Priceless."

I couldn't bear to listen to her laugh about the last moments of Jessica's life, particularly while Veronica and I faced the last moments of our own. "So what are you going to do to us?"

"Well, the first thing I'm going to do is search your cars for the video you got at Lenton's." She looked at me. "Yes, Franki, I followed you there too. Then I'll dispose of the disc and the skull bead, which I found in your nightstand. And tsk tsk." She waved the knife. "Such an obvious hiding place.

I shot her a go-to-hell look.

"After that, I'm going to go call the police and say that when I was driving through the area, I saw a masked intruder leaving your apartment. In theory, he would've exited through your bedroom window, Franki. The same one I broke to get in to your little bordello here."

Veronica glared at her. "What excuse are you going to give them for being in the neighborhood?"

"I'll tell them I was coming to talk to the two of you since you were investigating the murder of my twin and her best friend." She gave a wicked grin. "And I can tell you this. The New Orleans PD doesn't usually question the motives of a nun. And if they did, thanks to my gloves here and this handy coif on my head, they certainly won't find my fingerprints or DNA in this whorehouse."

Her gloating made me so angry and so frustrated that I alternated between wanting to cry and wanting to scream bloody murder. And it was more apparent by the second that I was powerless to stop her. My hands were numb, and I was no closer to freeing them. And judging from the sick look on Veronica's face, she wasn't faring any better. The situation looked grim, so I had to buy more time. "You still haven't said what you're going to do with us."

"Oh, that's because I like drama." She giggled.

I held my breath.

Concetta put her finger to her cheek. "One night I asked myself, 'What would be a fitting end for two busybody PIs who kept sticking their necks out to help that awful Ryan Hunter and that scumbag Stewart Preston?' Of course, whatever it was had to be symbolic." She gave a dry laugh. "I mean, once a Catholic, always a Catholic, right?"

Veronica snorted.

The smile faded from Concetta's face, and she studied Veronica. "The answer actually came to me in prayer." She placed the butcher knife on the counter, reached into the pocket of her habit and pulled out a dark red scarf. "Strangulation."

## 25

Concetta wound the red scarf around each of her gloved hands and walked toward Veronica. A devilish smile spread across her face. "You first, Miss Private Chicks, Incorporated."

"Wait," I shouted, desperate to stall. "Don't you want to tell us what the red scarf means? Otherwise, the symbolism will be lost on us."

Her eyes rolled to the heavens. "Well, if you read the bible, Franki, you'd know what it meant. But judging from this den of iniquity, it's pretty clear that you don't spend your leisure time perusing the word of the Lord."

"I just haven't unpacked my bible yet." I made a quick promise to God that I'd redecorate if he let me live.

"Red is the color of Christ's blood." Concetta's tone was patronizing. "It symbolizes atonement for one's sins, so as you can see—"

"How have *we* sinned?" Veronica's eyes blazed with anger.

"Oh, don't act so innocent. You've been aiding a murderer. Last time I checked, honey, that qualified as a sin."

From the corner of my eye, I saw movement in the kitchen

doorway. To my astonishment, there stood Glenda. Although her thin, lined face was red with rage, and she was wearing an S&M outfit replete with a silver boa, she looked nothing short of a saving angel.

I turned and saw to my horror that Concetta had wrapped the scarf around Veronica's neck, and my best friend thrashed in her chair.

With the stealth of a ninja, Glenda snuck up behind Concetta and clubbed her with the tallest stripper shoe I'd ever seen.

A dull thud echoed, and Concetta collapsed to the floor in a pool of black fabric like the Wicked Witch of the West.

"Glenda?" Veronica croaked wide-eyed, no doubt from the lack of oxygen. "Is it really you?"

Despite the fact that she'd just knocked out a homicidal maniac with the shoe in her hand, Glenda nevertheless held her signature cigarette holder in the other. "In the flesh, sugar."

Judging from her S&M outfit, I assumed she'd meant that literally.

Glenda slipped the shoe back on her foot and turned to me. "I called the cops right before I let myself in. You girls all right?"

"I think so. Thank God you're here."

"You can say that again, Miss Franki. Now give me a minute while I take care of some unpleasant landlady business."

I watched in a mixture of awe and amazement as Glenda made quick work of Concetta. She put her cigarette holder in her mouth and removed her black leather garter belt, which was attached to partial black leather pant legs. First she detached the pant legs, and then she used the belt to tie Concetta's hands behind her back. Next, she used the garter straps to bind her feet to her hands. When she was done, Concetta looked like she was doing the yoga bow pose.

Glenda stood up, adjusted her short, zippered black leather

vest, and took a long drag from her cigarette. Then she put her cigarette holder on the counter and picked up the butcher knife. She walked over to Veronica and began cutting the ropes binding her hands.

I was still in shock. "How did you know we were in trouble?"

"Well, I was entertaining Guido, and he happened to glance out the window and see a nun pass by. Naturally, I got suspicious."

"Makes sense to me." With a Visitor Policy that allowed women to have two men stay the night, the fourplex was no convent.

"I would've come to check on you two sooner, but Guido was all in a panic. He started crossing himself and saying Hail Marys and Our Fathers like he was possessed."

I stared at her, speechless.

Veronica rubbed her wrists as Glenda freed her feet.

When Glenda was done, she walked over to the counter and took another drag off her cigarette. "And then Guido started going on about how what we were doing was a sin." She exhaled a frustrated puff of smoke. "So, I had to kick him out." She walked over to cut my binding and gave Veronica and me a knowing look. "I don't think I need to tell either of you ladies that a man who doesn't sin isn't sexy."

Veronica shook her head. "Of course not."

"Around that time I heard a scream, and that's when I knew the nosy nun was up to no good. So I came downstairs and found Napoleon outside—"

"Is he all right?" I interrupted.

"He's fine, sugar." She freed my hands. "He's in the pleasure palace."

I had no idea what she meant, but I hoped she was talking about her apartment.

As she knelt and cut the rope from my ankles, I looked at

Concetta and saw that her head moved from side to side. "She's coming to."

Concetta raised her head and swore. "What the—?" She rocked back and forth on her belly trying to break free. "Who did this to me?"

Glenda sighed and put down the knife. Her eyes narrowed to slits and, in a move that undoubtedly came from one of her stripteases, she crawled to Concetta and leaned low so she could look her in the eyes. "I did. Now, until the cops come and haul your unholy heinie away, you keep your trap shut, sister, or I'll be forced to club you again. And while you're lying there all nice and quiet, you'd best pray you didn't scratch my Ginsu knife."

She sat up, removed her boa, and stuffed one end into Concetta's mouth.

Concetta's eye twitched, and she went limp.

Because Glenda prided herself on her stripper clothes, I decided to pay her a costume compliment. "You and your S&M outfit saved our lives."

"Miss Franki, this is my biker stripper costume. I don't dress S&M. That's not ladylike."

I heard the wail of police sirens in the distance.

Glenda rose. "Well it's about damn time the cops got here. I've got a reputation to protect, and I sure as hell don't want people to think I'm running a home for wayward nuns."

～

I TOOK a sip of my double soy latte and leaned back in my desk chair, relishing the early morning silence of the empty office. I hadn't slept a wink after the events of the previous night. All I could think about was my family and how they were going to react to the news that I'd solved my first murder case. I half expected my parents to insist that I come home and fulfill my pre-ordained destiny to work in the deli. Of course, my nonna was going to tell me that I needed to use my newly honed investigative skills to get serious about finding a husband. I wondered what she would say if she knew that I'd actually found a husband—one who belonged to someone else.

The lobby bell sounded.

I stood and peered out my doorway.

Veronica walked up the hallway.

"Good morning." My words sounded strange after everything that had happened.

"How do you feel today?" Veronica asked as I followed her into her office.

I took a seat in front of her desk and noticed that she looked as tired as I did. "Other than rope burn on my wrists, I'm fine. How about you?"

"Same. It kind of seems like it was all just a crazy, bad dream."

"I wish it were."

She toyed with a pen on her desk. "You know, I wouldn't blame you if you wanted to resign after almost getting killed."

I looked her straight in the eyes. "I'm not going anywhere. I knew that being a PI could be every bit as dangerous as being a cop. Besides, I've learned more after two weeks of working for you than I did the whole time I was on the force, and I've figured out something really important about myself too."

"Oh?"

I shifted in my seat. "This may sound kind of weird, but it has to do with what Concetta said when the police were taking her away."

"You mean, when she kept screaming, 'What did I do to deserve losing my twin?'"

"Exactly. Last night I was thinking about how she was looking at Immacolata's death from the wrong perspective. She thought she'd done something to bring about Immacolata's death, when it's so obvious that it had nothing to do with her. I mean, she's not responsible for Stewart Preston's actions."

Veronica raised her brow. "And so?"

"It just got me thinking about myself and how I've been taking it for granted that the way men have treated me was my fault."

She stared at me, expressionless. "I'm not following."

I straightened. "The cheating. I've been driving myself crazy trying to figure out what it is about me that leads my boyfriends to cheat. But, like Concetta, I had it all wrong. It's not about me. It's about them and their own weaknesses. And you know something else?"

"What?"

"I'm done taking responsibility for other people's bad decisions."

Veronica leaned back, crossed her arms, and smiled. "I'm so lucky to have you working for me."

"Why do you say that?"

"Because you're one smart cookie. And you're resilient too."

I laughed off the compliment, but inside I was glowing. "Just the same, after last night I'm hoping we get nothing but a steady stream of insurance fraud and cheating spouse cases. That reminds me, did we ever hear back from Twyla Upton?"

"Not a word. But I did talk to Ryan Hunter. He was very grateful, and he apologized when he heard we were almost killed."

"That's nice of him and everything, but I'm glad to be done with that guy and with the whole Evans case."

"I know. I just feel so bad for the Di Salvo family, especially Maria."

I wrinkled my lips and looked at the floor. "Me too. Can you even imagine what she's going through? First Imma, then her husband, and now Concetta, the one who was supposed to be so good."

"It's just awful."

"And all she has left now is Domenica. You can bet that one is going to give her more trouble."

Veronica sighed. "I really hope not."

The front office door slammed.

I grinned. "David's here."

He rushed into the room. "Are you guys—uh, ladies—okay?"

I smiled. "I guess you heard what happened?"

"Did I? Private Chicks is all over the morning news."

Veronica's face lit up. "Franki, turn on the TV."

I stood and switched on a small television set on top of a file cabinet. The first image I saw was Glenda sidling up way too close to a local news reporter.

Veronica gasped. "What in the world is she doing?"

David rubbed his nose. "A lot of interviews. I can't believe you didn't know. Everyone's talking about how a gutsy stripper saved two PIs from an evil nun."

She groaned and put her face in her hands. "Turn the sound down. I don't want to hear it."

I did as she asked. "Come on, Veronica, it's not as bad as all that. You know the old saying, 'There's no such thing as bad publicity.' Plus," I glanced at the TV, "at least Glenda's dressed somewhat chastely for her interviews." And she was because the TV station had blurred out her royal blue velvet Prince pants, the ones with holes that fully exposed the butt cheeks. There was also the little matter of a three-inch rhinestone choker around her neck that spelled VIXEN.

"Uh..." David nudged me. "Is that your phone?"

"Oh, yeah, thanks." I'd been so absorbed in the details of Glenda's outfit that I hadn't heard it ringing. I walked into the hallway to take the call.

"Hello?"

"Francesca?" My mother's voice was crazy shrill, even for her. "This is your mother, dear."

"Yeah, hi, Mom." The familiar tension rose in my chest.

"Your nonna called your father and me at the deli and said that you and a stripper had a nun arrested. I know you haven't been comfortable with your Catholicism, but this is taking things too far, don't you think?"

I sighed. "Mom, that nun almost strangled Veronica and me. She was the one who murdered Jessica Evans."

"What?" Her shrill had turned shriek. "Almost getting killed by a nun is big news, Francesca. Why didn't you call us?"

"I wasn't exactly in the mood to chat after it happened. And I had no idea it would be on the news, especially in Texas. I was going to call you guys tonight to tell you about it. But how come nonna called you and not me?"

"She wanted to let us know that she was going straight to Saint Mary's."

"Why did she go to church?"

"To pray for your salvation, dear. She says it's a very serious sin to have a nun sent to jail."

*Naturally. Wait until she hears that I've broken up with Guido.* "Listen, I'm at work, so I'll call you tonight, okay?"

"Wait a second. Your father has something he wants to say to you."

A knot the size of the ones in Concetta's rope formed in my stomach.

"Franki," he sounded surprised, "Mr. Giangiulio told me you solved that murder case."

"I had some help from Veronica and David."

"Well, I'm glad that you're okay."

I held my breath and waited for the *but*.

"And I wanted you to know that I'm proud of you," he said in a soft, almost embarrassed tone. "Real proud."

My eyes opened wide, and a rush of warmth filled my chest. "Thanks, Dad," I breathed. "That means a lot."

"Now you be careful out there." He'd switched to his usual gruff tone. "And come home for a visit soon."

I smiled. "I will, Dad. I promise."

I closed the call and returned to Veronica's office.

She looked up from her notepad. "Is everything okay?"

"My Dad just told me he's proud of me."

"Do you think he's starting to see the light?"

I flashed a sardonic smile. "I wouldn't go *that* far. But it's a start."

The office phone rang.

"Private Chicks, Incorporated," Veronica answered in her professional voice. "If you give us the time, we'll solve your crime. What can I help you with?"

I watched as she scribbled some notes on a scrap of paper.

"We can definitely handle that. How did you hear about us? On TV this morning." She glanced at me. "How about today at two o'clock? Perfect." She hung up.

"I hate to say I told you so..."

She smirked. "No you don't."

The office phone rang again at the same time the bell in the lobby sounded. Veronica and I exchanged a look.

"It looks like Private Chicks, Inc. is on the map." I rose and went into the lobby.

Twyla Upton, staying faithful to the citrus family, stood by the door in a lime-green sack dress. "Oh, Franki." She clasped her hands in front of her face. "The case is solved."

"Wait, you're not talking about the Evans case, are you?"

She gasped and put lime green-lacquered fingers to her

orange-painted mouth. "Did poor Mrs. Evans think her husband was cheating too?"

I smiled. "No, Twyla. I was just confused."

"Oh good." She was visibly relieved. "I just came to tell you that my Harry wasn't betraying my honor with that delightful woman in your pictures."

I would have bet all the toupees in Hollywood that Harry had been unfaithful. "Really?"

"Ye-es," she said in two distinct syllables. "That woman is one of the best interior designers in all of Louisiana, and she's been helping Harry with the plans to redecorate a *charming* little mansion he's bought me for our upcoming anniversary."

"Well, that's terrific news."

"So, I came to invite you all to Brennan's for a celebratory brunch. The head chef has agreed to open the restaurant early today just for us."

I imagined a meal of bananas foster and more bananas foster. "We would love to, Twyla. Let me go and get Veronica off the phone."

"You take your time. I'll meet you all there when you're ready. Toodles." She waved and slipped out the door.

I entered Veronica's office.

She hung up the phone. "That was another client. We have three new cases."

I leaned against the doorjamb. "All thanks to TV?"

"Yes, every one of them mentioned Glenda."

"Then maybe you should hire her," I joked. "Apparently, she's a natural-born marketer, and she's got some mean self-defense skills. While you're at it, you might want to put Mambo Odette on the payroll. I mean, she had the answers to the Evans case all along."

Veronica smirked. "I wouldn't go that far. Who was in the lobby?"

"Twyla. She's taking us all to brunch."

"What? I can't leave now. I might miss a call from a new client."

"Whoever calls will leave a message. I mean, who would hire a regular PI when they could hire two PIs who were saved from a nun by a stripper?"

Veronica shot me a look. "What's the occasion for the brunch?"

"Turns out we were wrong about Harry. He wasn't cheating with the brunette, after all."

"Well, that's good news."

"It is. And Twyla's waiting for us, so we've got to get going."

Her brows furrowed.

"Don't worry, we're going to have plenty of business after this case."

Veronica looked at me, a smile spreading across her face. "We are, aren't we?"

"Um, *yeah*. So let's take the time to celebrate the end of our first big case before we dive into all these new ones."

"Great idea." She smiled and rose to her feet.

Veronica and I entered the lobby, and I looked at David. "Come on. You're going to that brunch too."

He spun in his desk chair. "Aaaawwwesome."

My phone rang, and I whispered a prayer that it wasn't my nonna before looking at the display. "It's Bradley." I bit my lower lip. "Hang on, I'm going to take this in my office." I hurried down the hall. "Hello?"

"Franki, this is Bradley."

"I know." I used my telemarketer tone.

"I'm calling on business. Do you have a minute?"

"Business?" I repeated, taken aback. "Did you see us on TV this morning?"

"You were on TV?"

"In a way," I hedged. "So what's this about?"

"I need to hire you to investigate an important case. It's about a woman I met."

I recoiled, outraged. "If this is about that scantily dressed Mardi Gras queen I saw you with on Bourbon Street, then you can take your business somewhere else."

"You mean, Sheilah."

"*That* was Sheilah?" I disliked her even more.

"Yes." He sighed. "She came by the bank after hours. Because it was dark out, I offered to walk her to a party she was attending that evening."

My stomach clenched, annoyed. "What does this have to do with me?"

He paused. "You have the wrong impression of me."

"I doubt that," I muttered, remembering my earlier revelation about cheating.

"Look, it's true that Sheilah and I are married—"

"No kidding."

"—and will be for about three more weeks."

I blinked. "Come again?"

"That's how long it'll take the divorce papers Sheila signed at the bank the other night to go through the courts."

"Oh." My jaw shut with an audible click. The word *divorce* had never sounded so sweet.

"I swear I wanted to tell you, but I was under a gag order until now. Sheilah and I got married too young, mainly because our families were close. We wanted to end it almost immediately, but her mother got sick, and after that her father's business fell apart. So, we waited. In the meantime, I left Boston to kickstart my career, so the divorce delays weren't a huge issue. All of that changed, though, when I met the woman I mentioned."

I pulled up a chair. The case was starting to pique my interest. "This woman...what can you tell me about her?"

"She's a knockout private investigator with a mean right hook. I'm crazy about her, but she's not talking to me. I need you to do some investigating to find out whether I still have a chance with her."

My smile was as big as Julia Roberts' in *Pretty Woman*. "Sounds like an exciting assignment. Too bad Veronica and I are booked for the next month."

"The whole month, huh?"

"Yeah, but since the situation is obviously urgent, I suppose I could have you over for dinner tonight at, say, sevenish to discuss the details?"

"I'll be there." The playfulness had left his tone.

"I look forward to it," I said. And boy did I.

# FREE MINI MYSTERIES OFFER

Want to know what happens to Franki after *Limoncello Yellow*? Sign up for my newsletter to receive a free copy of the *Franki Amato Mini Mysteries*, a hilarious collection that contains "Prugnolino Purple" (Franki #1.5) and five other fun short mysteries. You'll also be the first to know about my new releases, deals, and giveaways.

Here's the blurb for "Prugnolino Purple:"

It's springtime in New Orleans, and Franki Amato's BFF and boss, Veronica Maggio, has dragged her to an art auction at one of the city's historic house museums. Up for sale, a provocative, not to mention peculiar, painting of their sixty-something ex-stripper landlady that is anything but priceless. Franki thinks the only crime at play is the image on the canvas until a cocktail waitress is found unconscious in front of an empty easel. After Franki finds a purple splotch on the presumed weapon, she and Veronica spring into action to ID the attacking art thief and locate the missing painting. But Franki's biggest surprise isn't the culprit—it's the "blooming idiot" who bought the portrait before the auction started.

And don't forget to follow me!

BookBub
https://www.bookbub.com/authors/traci-andrighetti

Goodreads
https://www.goodreads.com/author/show/
7383577.Traci_Andrighetti

Facebook
https://www.facebook.com/traciandrighettiauthor

# BOOK BACKSTORY

*Limoncello Yellow* came to be because of five random events in my life:

1) A car trip from Texas to New Orleans that I took with my parents in the early nineties so that my father could stock up on Italian deli meat at Central Grocery (Italians will go to great lengths for their food);

2) An accidental encounter on Bourbon Street in my twenties with half-dressed day-shift strippers and a bucket of Popeye's fried chicken;

3) An unexpected introduction to limoncello on my honeymoon thanks to Serbian waiters in Rome;

4) A superb and inspiring online writing class I took from Internationally Bestselling Author Kristin Harmel;

5) The amazing "Femme Fatale" contest I entered on *New York Times* Bestselling Author Gemma Halliday's website (the grand prize was a Kindle and month of mentoring, and yet I ended up with a two-book deal!).

If I could go back and thank each and every one of the above individuals—especially the strippers and the bouncer that let me into Big Daddy's when it was closed for an emergency bathroom stop—I totally would. It's funny how random events can all add up to a big, life-changing thing like writing a book.

While I'm thanking people, there is no way I could have finished this book without the help of my husband, my parents, and my parents-in-law. My guilt for taking precious time away from my young son, was lessened by the knowledge that he was in their loving hands. I owe them a huge debt of gratitude that I will never be able to repay (and no, Dad, I'm not giving you any of the royalties).

Speaking of my son, I'd like to thank him for putting up with all the writing. D, you will always be my boy.

I would also like to thank the fabulous Barbara Marking Steiner (ex-cop-turned-elementary-school-principal who owns a pink handgun, y'all!) for being available on a moment's notice to advise me on police matters.

Words cannot express how grateful I am to Linda O'Krent for pushing me (forcefully) down the writing path and to Chelsea Drescher for telling me that I didn't want to write academic texts anymore. I should have known that I didn't want to be a professor when I chose Italian mystery writer Andrea Camilleri as the subject of my dissertation. (Incidentally, *giallo*, the Italian word for "yellow," also means "mystery novel" because the covers of the first mysteries published in Italy were yellow. Of course, this is why the color yellow simply *had* to be in the title of the first book in the Franki Amato Mystery series.)

On the subject of symbolism, I need to say *grazie mille* to Matthew Amato, Marissa Maggio, Benji Orlansky, Mike Reiff, and Bill Savoie for letting me use their last names, which are every bit as vibrant as they are, and to Brady Harris for unknowingly lending me his appropriately individualistic first name. It bears noting that I chose the Italian surname "Amato" for Franki because it sounds tough but means "loved" and because Matthew Amato, who was one of my Italian students at the

University of Texas, is one of the finest young men I know. I selected the name "Francesca," a.k.a. "Franki," in memory of my parents' cairn terrier—one of the most inquisitive, determined and flat out adorable dogs who ever lived.

Last but not least, I would like to extend my appreciation to The Flight Path Coffee House in Austin, Texas, for being my local source of inspiration and to the city of New Orleans for being the weird, wild, and wonderful place that it is. My plan was to write a mystery with a colorful title and colorful characters, and from the moment I came up with that goal, I knew that The Big Easy was the *only* possible setting for *Limoncello Yellow*.

*Cin cin* (Cheers)!

Traci

# COCKTAILS

Franki Amato appreciates a good cocktail every so often—okay, maybe more often than not. After all, it's hard work fighting crime in New Orleans. In general, her motto is "When life gives you lemons, make Limoncello." But in extreme cases she revises it to "When life gives you lemons, skip the 'making Limoncello' part and go straight to drinking it."

LIMONCELLO

Here is Franki's recipe for three bottles of pure lemon heaven.

*Ingredients*
    10 medium (or 15 small) Meyer lemons
    1 quart Everclear (a brand of grain alcohol)
    1 and 1/2 quarts water
    2 and 3/4 pounds of sugar

Wash and peel the lemons. Soak the lemon peels in three quarters of the Everclear for one-to-two months, storing the mixture in an airtight container in a cool, dark place.

When the peels are infused with the Everclear, boil the sugar and water until it makes syrup (about five minutes). After the syrup has cooled, pour it into the lemon-peel mixture along with the remaining Everclear.

Store the Limoncello mixture in a cool, dark place for forty days. Then strain it with cheesecloth to remove the lemon peels before bottling the Limoncello. Serve chilled. *Cin cin!*

## LIMONCELLO MARGARITA

Because Franki is originally from Texas, she occasionally enjoys her Limoncello with a Tex-Mex twist.

*Ingredients*
    2 ounces tequila
    1 ounce Grand Marnier
    1 ounce Limoncello
    1/2 ounce fresh lemon juice
    1/2 ounce fresh lime juice
    1/2 teaspoon sugarsalt for the glass rim

# ABOUT THE AUTHOR

Traci Andrighetti is the *USA TODAY* bestselling author of the Franki Amato Mysteries and the Danger Cove Hair Salon Mysteries. In her previous life, she was an award-winning literary translator and a Lecturer of Italian at the University of Texas at Austin, where she earned a PhD in Applied Linguistics. But then she got wise and ditched that academic stuff for a life of crime—writing, that is. Her latest capers are teaching mystery for Savvy Authors and taking authors on writing retreats to Italy with LemonLit.

To learn more about Traci, check out her websites: www. traciandrighetti.com
www.lemonlit.com

# ALSO BY TRACI ANDRIGHETTI

*FRANKI AMATO MYSTERIES*

*Books*
Limoncello Yellow
Prosecco Pink
Amaretto Amber
Campari Crimson
Galliano Gold
Marsala Maroon
Valpolicella Violet
Tuaca Tan (forthcoming in 2022)

*Box Set*
Franki Amato Mysteries Box Set (Books 1–3)
Franki Amato Mysteries Box Set (Books 4–6)

*Short Stories*
Franki Amato Mini Mysteries
(short mysteries free to newsletter subscribers only)

## *DANGER COVE HAIR SALON MYSTERIES*

Deadly Dye and a Soy Chai
A Poison Manicure and Peach Liqueur
Killer Eyeshadow and a Cold Espresso

# SNEAK PEEK

If you liked this Franki Amato mystery, read the first chapter of:

PROSECCO PINK
Franki Amato Mysteries Book 2

**2015 Mystery & Mayhem Award Finalist**

by
Traci Andrighetti

## CHAPTER 1

"Who takes their secretary to a working dinner at a freaking bed and breakfast?" I asked aloud as I sped down Great Mississippi River Road in Louisiana plantation country. I didn't usually talk to myself, but the stress of the situation more than justified it.

"I mean, what's wrong with a restaurant in the French Quarter? People travel from all over the world to eat there."

I steered my 1965 cherry-red Mustang convertible out from behind the 18-wheeler to make sure the black BMW was still up ahead. As soon as I'd spotted it, I dropped back behind the hulking truck. I couldn't let Bradley know I was following him.

Bradley Hartmann was the president of Ponchartrain Bank on Canal Street in New Orleans. With his shocking blue eyes, full lips, and chiseled jaw, he was without a doubt the sexiest bank executive this side of the Mason-Dixon line. And he was mine. We'd been seeing each other for the past three months, ever since his divorce was finalized. Okay, maybe we started seeing each other a bit before then, but that was an accident. I promise.

The problem was, now that his ex-wife was out of the way, his sexy new Chinese-French secretary was in the way. All six feet of her. And at five feet ten inches myself, I wasn't used to looking up to a woman, especially not one as lowdown as Pauline Violette. She did everything she could to keep me away from Bradley—including scheduling these weekend working dinners at bed and breakfasts outside of town. And judging from the way she batted her violet, almond-shaped eyes at him, it was clear why.

"How is it even possible that her eye color matches her last name?" I asked as I hit the gas. "Her boobs are clearly manmade, so those eyes have to be too."

I glanced out the passenger window to try to catch another glimpse of Bradley's BMW, and a flash of pink caught my eye. But it wasn't the coral-pink hue of the thousands of oleanders that framed a stunning, three-story, columned plantation home. It was the pink crinoline skirt of the woman standing on the balcony. It was a hauntingly beautiful image, like something you'd see in an old oil painting.

Unfortunately, the road started to curve sharply, but I was too busy staring at the Southern belle to notice. My tires hit the soft shoulder, and I jerked the steering wheel hard to the left. But it was too late. My car slid sideways right into a swamp.

"*Mamma mia!*" I exclaimed as I realized what had happened. And I did want my mother. Because when I restarted the engine and tried to drive to land, I discovered that I was stuck in the filthy swamp mud.

I threw open my car door, mentally whispered a farewell to my new boots, and stepped into the black swamp water. I trudged around to the back of the car and saw that the rear passenger tire was the problem. I needed to find some wood or stones to put beneath it to try to gain traction. Just as I was about to turn around and head for shore, I made a horrifying discovery. The water was moving.

That's when a bumpy black reptile lifted its moss-covered head above the surface of the murky swamp water, and I came face-to-face with an alligator.

The unsightly beast opened its toothy, cavernous mouth and made a loud hissing sound.

Make that an angry alligator.

"G-good gator," I stammered, frozen with fear.

The alligator lowered its head back into the water and began swimming in a circle, its large cat-like eyes trained on me like the sight of a gun.

"Nice b-boy, Al," I said as I began inching backward through the watery, foul-smelling mud. In case the alligator decided to charge at me, I needed to make it to the driver's side taillight to have a clear shot at the open car door. "Or, maybe you're an Alli?"

As though confirming my suspicion, she slapped her tail hard against the surface of the water.

I estimated her to be around six feet in length—precisely Pauline's height. Then I promptly reminded myself that during my rookie cop days in Austin, Texas, I'd once tackled a male ostrich that was getting frisky with some mothers at a petting zoo. Plus, I'd seen the Gator Boys *and* the Swamp Men wrestle alligators on TV, so I figured that I could take her if push came to shove, er, thrust came to lunge.

Alli stopped near the stump of a bald cypress tree and opened her mouth, revealing eighty or so two-inch-long yellow teeth.

Okay, maybe not.

I took another step backward, and she resumed circling.

"That's right, girl. Just keep swimming," I whispered, advancing another inch or two. "It's good for your waistline." I took another step, and my right foot sunk into what felt like a muddy mass of tree roots. I tried to pull it out, but it was stuck solid. Just like the rear tire of my Mustang.

I felt a fresh wave of fear wash over me, but I knew I had to keep calm. I took a deep breath of the putrid swamp air and tried again to free my foot.

"Franki?" a male voice called.

"Bradley," I breathed. "Oh thank God." My relief quickly gave way to dismay, however, when I realized that he must have seen me following him and Pauline before I ran my car off the road. But surely he would overlook that minor detail now that I was standing in filthy, mosquito-infested swamp water *and* being stalked by an alligator.

"Don't move," he said in a calm, even tone. "You don't want to startle him."

*No, I most certainly don't,* I thought.

"As soon as he turns to swim away, make a dash for the other side of the car."

"Don't you think I would've done that by now if I could?" I asked, trying to control my increasing hysteria.

"Why can't you? What's wrong?"

"Let me see... Where should I start?"

"Franki," he began, a note of tension creeping into his voice, "why can't you get to the car door?"

"My shoe is caught on something." Should I add that my new boots were the knee-high lace-up kind—with triple buckles?

"Okay, then slip your foot out of your shoe," he said through clenched teeth.

No, now was clearly not the time to tell him. "Um, it's not exactly the slip-your-foot-out-of-your-shoe kind of shoe."

There was a heavy silence.

"Then we're going to have to wait him out," he said.

I gasped. Was he seriously not going to come into the water and pull me out? I mean, saving me from an alligator was the least he could do after planning to take his secretary to a B&B, right?

"If I move, he could attack," Bradley explained. "And you're his closest target."

Before I could protest, I heard an ear-splitting bellow behind me. I jerked my head to the left and saw the largest alligator I'd ever seen. At roughly fifteen feet in length, he was practically a dinosaur.

Terror shot through my body like a white-hot flash of lightening. But I fought to keep my wits about me because the gargantuan gator was standing near Bradley. And as mad as I was about Pauline and the whole leaving-me-to-the-gator thing, I could hardly let Bradley be eaten by a Tyrannosaurus alligator on my account. I had to do something. And fast.

I started jerking my trapped foot as hard as I could. But each time I did, I sunk deeper and deeper into the gooey swamp bottom. The water level was now above my knees, and my panic level was considerably higher.

"You've got to stay still," Bradley warned. "He's extremely dangerous."

"No kidding."

"April is mating season. I think he's looking for a mate."

"Well, tell him Alli isn't interested. And neither am I," I added, just in case.

The big gator bellowed again, causing the hair to stand up on my arms.

*Had my refusal offended him or something?*

"He's headed toward the water now," Bradley said. "Stay calm."

"Easy for you to say," I muttered under my breath.

I heard a splash as the alligator entered the swamp. At that same moment, Alli dipped beneath the surface of the water. Now there were two of them. Lurking.

*Oh God, oh God, oh God. I promise I'll never lust after an alligator handbag or shoes again for as long as I live if you let me survive this,* I thought. Then I held my breath and waited.

The swamp was deadly silent, except for the croaking of some green tree frogs.

I started when I heard the sound of a car door opening.

"Bradley, get back in the car!" Pauline called. "It's not safe."

*No need to worry about me, Pauline,* I thought. Not only was the sultry secretary trying to steal my boyfriend, now she was also trying to convince him to leave me for gator food.

"I need you to stay in the car, Pauline," he replied. "I can't have anything happen to you."

*Wait a minute. He can't have anything happen to* her? *What about* me? I felt a sudden surge of anger-induced adrenaline course through my body. With a steely calm, I crouched down, unbuckled and unlaced my boot and pulled my foot free. Then I yanked the boot out of the tangled roots and rushed around to the driver's seat. I'd paid three hundred bucks for those boots, so there was no way I was leaving one of them in the swamp— gators or no gators.

The second I got into the car, I pulled my 9mm purple Ruger from the glove compartment box. I looked out my driver's side window and saw Bradley kneel down to examine my rear tire.

"Start the engine and press the accelerator," he called.

I did as I was told and watched through the rearview mirror as mud flew from the spinning tire.

He motioned for me to stop. "Let me find something to put under the tire, and then I'll have you try again."

"Be careful," I said.

With my gun in hand, I surveyed the area for hungry—or horny—alligators while Bradley gathered a few small cypress branches.

He arranged the branches beneath my tire and stood up, wiping his hands. "Okay, now."

I hit the gas full throttle and felt my tire gain traction. The car started forward and then spun out to the right, just as something struck the side of my car. I had a terrifying thought. *One of the alligators had lunged for Bradley and hit my car instead!* I threw the car into park and leapt out with my gun drawn.

"Are you crazy?" Pauline screamed. "You could kill him!"

*Oh, so now she was worried about the alligator too?* Ignoring her protests, I scoured the scene for the offending creature, and that's when I saw him. Bradley, that is. Covered in mud and propped up on his elbows in three-inch-deep swamp water. That was no gator I'd hit, it was my boyfriend. At least, I really, really hoped he was still my boyfriend.

I rushed into the water and knelt at his side. "Are you okay?"

He spit something brown and slimy into the water. "Fine," he replied, a tad tersely.

"Let me help you."

"Now there's an offer you can refuse," Pauline said.

I shot her a look. Was that a Mafia jab?

Bradley stood up in silence and did a quick body check before walking to the shore.

"Let me see if I have a towel or something in the car," I said. I ran to the Mustang, but all I could find was a travel-sized package of Kleenex.

I hurried back to Bradley and began dabbing at the mud on his shirt with a tissue. "I'm so sorry about your suit."

He pulled away.

I blinked, surprised. "I said I was sorry."

"It's not about my damned suit, Franki."

"Oh?" I asked, doing my darnedest to feign innocence. But I knew exactly what this was about.

"What were you doing out here on River Road, miles from New Orleans?" he demanded.

Pauline sauntered over and folded her arms across her chest. "Yes, what *were* you doing? Shopping for a plantation home?"

I met her arrogant gaze straight on but avoided her question. "Nice of you to finally get out of the car."

Bradley looked from Pauline to me and sighed. "Never mind, Franki. We'll talk about this later."

Pauline glanced at her smartphone and turned to Bradley, instantly dismissing me. "We still have twenty minutes before your meeting with Mr. Stafford, and according to Google we're only about twenty-five miles from the bed and breakfast. We can still make it if we hurry."

Bradley looked down at his wet, mud-stained clothes. "I can't go looking like this."

"Well, you have that extra shirt and your suit coat in the car, and I have a bottle of Perrier in my purse. If you slip off your pants, I can have some of the more visible stains out before we get there."

Bradley nodded and started for his car.

I gasped. "You're not actually going to take your pants off for her, are you?"

He turned to look at me. "Franki, it's business. This meeting is critical to the future of the bank, and it's my job to do whatever I can to make sure it's a success. I've got to go."

As Bradley climbed into his car, Pauline spun around to face me. She was standing so close that her long, black hair lashed across my face like a silken whip, and her heavy perfume stung my nostrils. "Well, I hope you're satisfied," she said. "Thanks to your little spy game, you've not only ruined Bradley's thousand-dollar suit, you've also potentially cost him a multi-million dollar business deal."

I stared at her open-mouthed. When Bradley told me that he couldn't come over because he and Pauline were having a working dinner at a B&B outside of town, I'd assumed it was just the two of them. I had no idea that they were meeting a client there, not to mention such an important one.

"Now close your mouth and go get cleaned up," Pauline continued. She narrowed her undoubtedly fake violet eyes and looked me up and down. "You're a hot mess."

She did a runway-model turn and strutted to the car.

Oh, I was hot all right. With shame and blinding rage.

~

Still smarting from Pauline's smackdown an hour later, I kicked open my front door and threw my mud-caked boots onto the floor.

"Well, look what the cat dragged in," my landlady, Glenda O'Brien, said from a backbend position on the bearskin rug on my living room floor. For a sixty-something-year-old woman, she was startlingly flexible, no doubt due to her forty-something-year career as a stripper.

My best friend and employer, Veronica Maggio, was on the floor beside Glenda, looking exactly as she had when I first met her in our freshman dorm at The University of Texas at Austin.

She had her tongue sticking out one side of her mouth as she put the final strokes of Raspberry Fields Forever nail polish on her pinky toe. When she finished, she gave me the once-over. "What happened to *you*?"

I sighed and tossed my purse onto the velvet zebra print rococo chaise lounge. I'd forgotten that Sunday was movie night, or "ladies' night" as Glenda had christened it, and that it was my turn to host. "Oh, not much. I spied on Bradley and Pauline, I nearly got us all killed by a couple of alligators in heat, and then I hit Bradley with my car and pulled a gun on him."

"Oh, sugar," Glenda said, kicking her skinny, veined legs forward out of her backbend and coming to a standing position. "That sounds sexy."

I rolled my eyes. "I'm dead serious."

A coy smile formed at the corners of her mouth, and then she took a long, sensuous drag off her signature Mae West-style cigarette holder. "So am I, child. So. Am. I."

I didn't bother asking her not to smoke since she owned the fourplex that all of us lived in as well as the rather unique bordello-style furnishings in my not-so-humble abode. But I did make a mental note to ask her to stop letting herself in to my apartment.

"Why would you spy on Bradley?" Veronica asked, her brow furrowed. "You said you trusted him."

She never ceased to amaze me. "So, the trust thing is what you're worried about? Not the part about the gator or the gun?"

Veronica screwed the cap on the bottle of nail polish. "Well, you're in one piece, and you're not in jail, so I assumed that those other things got worked out somehow."

"Well, you could at least *act* concerned, you know."

"I'm sorry," she said, fidgeting with the ribbon on her pink baby doll pajamas. "It's just that I thought you were finally over your trust issue with men. That's all."

"I was. I mean, I am," I hurried to add. "I trust Bradley, but I don't trust Pauline around Bradley."

Veronica cocked her head to one side. "Well, isn't that the same thing?"

"No, it isn't. You have no idea how manipulative she is. Plus, she's always so perfect and prepared. I mean, the woman carries a bottle of Perrier water around with her just in case she needs to remove a stain."

"Perrier?" Glenda asked, wrinkling her mouth. "I don't get women who drink bubbly water when they could be drinking champagne. This Pauline sounds suspect, if you ask me."

I cast Veronica a triumphant look. "See? Glenda doesn't trust her either."

Veronica shook her head. "Trusting Pauline isn't the issue. The problem is that you're underestimating Bradley, and it's not like he's stupid."

"No, but he's a man, and she's drop-dead gorgeous. She's built like a model, and she looks like Lucy Liu. To top it all off, she has violet eyes, just like Elizabeth Taylor. And you know how good Liz was at stealing other women's men."

Glenda batted her inch-long, blue false eyelashes. "You know, Ronnie, I think Miss Franki's right. If there's one thing I learned while I was stripping, it's that even the smartest man is no match for a cunning woman."

I nodded, vindicated, although I wasn't entirely sure that you could compare my Harvard-educated, bank president boyfriend to the average strip club patron. But then again, maybe you could.

"You know what I think, sugar?" Glenda continued after taking a long, thoughtful drag off her cigarette.

"What?" I asked, eager to hear her opinion. Glenda was a little rough around the edges, but she often had sage advice.

"You need to make sure that she doesn't put nothin' over on

you," she replied, exhaling a cloud of smoke. "So you're gonna have to stick to this Pauline like a pastie on a titty."

Veronica cleared her throat. "Franki, will you let the dogs in? My toes are still wet."

"I'll do it," Glenda said, hopping to her five-inch-high-heeled, slipper-clad feet. "I need to freshen up my glass of champagne, anyway."

As Glenda paraded past me to the kitchen, I noticed that she too was wearing baby doll pajamas—in tight black fishnet with large holes cut from beneath her armpits all the way down to below the hip. It was quite possibly the most clothing I'd ever seen her wear.

Glenda opened the back door, and my brindle cairn terrier, Napoleon, bounded over to me, his tail wagging.

"There's my good boy," I said, bending over to greet him.

Napoleon skidded to an abrupt stop, gave a quick sniff of my feet, and took a giant leap backward.

"So much for the unconditional love of pets," I said. "I guess I'll take that as my cue to go shower the swamp off me."

Veronica adjusted the bowtie on her cream Pomeranian, Hercules. "Hurry up so we can start the movie."

"What did you get?" I asked, even though it really didn't matter what the movie was. The only thing I'd be watching were the images of Bradley's hurt face and Pauline's haughty one that kept replaying in my head.

"*Zombie Strippers*," Glenda called from the kitchen.

*Obviously her turn to pick the movie*, I thought.

"By the way," Veronica began, "I made sugar cookies, and Glenda brought an extra bottle of champagne. Isn't this going to be fun?"

I gave her a blank stare. "Yeah. Tons."

Veronica placed a reassuring hand on my arm. "I know

you're worried about Bradley, but try to relax and enjoy the evening."

"I can't. On top of everything else, I might have cost him an important business deal. Do you think I should call and ask how it went?"

"No," she replied. "Let him have tonight to cool off. Then tomorrow you can apologize and explain how you feel about Pauline. I'm sure he'll understand."

I nodded, but I wasn't so sure about the understanding part, especially after my jealousy had almost gotten him killed—first by the alligators and then by me. I set off for the shower thinking that it was going to take a lot more than champagne, sugar cookies, and strippers to get me through the night.

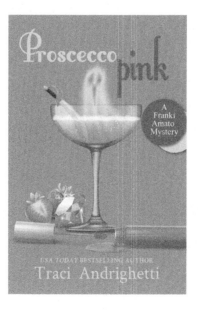